Mirror Image

Erika Crosse

ISBN: 9798639940026

Front cover attributions: Images from Susan Cipriano and Gordon Johnson
from Pixabay

Other titles by the author:

A View from the Window
The Girl Who Wanted a Broken Heart
Faith
A Knight's Challenge

For Naomi

1

Sophie

Sophie ground to a halt and stepped out of the freshly polished azure blue car. Her mouth hung open as loosened strands of hair blew wildly about her face.

"Sophie, darling!"

The colossal six-panelled front door forced itself steadily open and from behind it came a slender middle-aged lady, whose air conveyed a tone of complete confidence. She strode down the single step onto the gravel which crunched softly underneath her heels.

"Where have you been, we expected you hours ago?"

Sophie tore her eyes away from the mesmerising building before her, which hosted an uncountable number of windows. "The traffic was busy in London, you know what it's like, or have you forgotten?"

The lady, dressed in a tight scarlet jumper and flared black trousers, kissed both her daughter's cheeks lightly, almost making no contact with her skin at all.

"Well… this is different." Sophie's gaze was drawn directly back to the magnificent structure standing behind her mother. "I'm surprised your butler hasn't greeted me."

"Don't be smart Sophie," Elizabeth Hastings scolded in response to her daughter's broad smirk. "You know we didn't have a choice in the matter."

"I'm sure it's a great hardship." Sophie turned away, focusing on the imposing turrets which rose high into the sky and the flag which fluttered gently on top of the central tower. Her mother's new position was no hardship at all, but from the corner of her eye she noted her mother's warning glare. "Sorry," she mumbled in apology.

"I told your father this would happen, but he didn't listen."

"Mum, please don't start this again." It's all she'd heard for the past three years.

"If you'd been educated like *I* wanted, you would speak to your mother with more respect."

Sophie took a deep, steadying breath to contain her rising irritation. A tactic which had become customary when dealing with her mother. "I do respect you."

"It wouldn't hurt to show it once in a while," Elizabeth stuck her nose snootily in the air. "It's bad enough I've been entertaining your guests all afternoon." Without further explanation, Elizabeth abruptly proceeded back towards the front door which was peeling shards of green paint.

"Hang on a minute…" Sophie chased after her. "My guests?"

"You should have been home hours ago, Sophie."

"You didn't tell me what time to arrive, I thought I was on my own schedule."

This was just like her mother. How was she supposed to meet her high expectations if she wasn't told the details? It was impossible, like playing a game she was doomed to lose from the beginning.

Momentarily the immense size of the hallway distracted Sophie from their conversation, a great ceiling looming metres above her head. It was the first time she had seen the manor.

"What guests, mum?" she asked drawing her attention back.

"The Donaldsons - of course."

"The Donaldsons!" What on earth was her mother thinking? "Mum, I've just got home after travelling for hours in a swelteringly hot car." This visit was completely unnecessary, surely even she could see that.

"What's your point, Sophie?" Elizabeth placed both hands on her hips and pouted out her lips.

The skin on Sophie's back began to prickle. On the drive home, she'd almost convinced herself they could get through the first twenty-four hours of living under the same roof without any confrontations - how stupid was she to think this. However, now it had started argument was fruitless because Sophie's track record was always one of defeat. Lowering her shoulders, she noticed for the first time how badly cracked the contrasting black and white tiles were beneath her feet. "Can you at least give me ten minutes to freshen up?"

Elizabeth didn't answer straight away, but instead studied her daughter's appearance, fixing her eyes critically on her jeans ripped at the knee and her flimsy flip-flops. A look of disgust spread across her face. "I think you need to freshen up, you certainly aren't dressed appropriately for guests."

"I wasn't expecting any."

"They are *your* guests, Sophie."

"Guests *you* invited and didn't tell me about." She clenched her fists, trying to contain the rapidly rising frustration, turning the knuckles white as she did so. "The Donaldson's are your friends, not mine."

"Rupert is not *my* friend."

"Maybe you shouldn't have invited him if he's not your friend."

"I invited him on your behalf."

"Well, it wasn't necessary."

"I beg your pardon, Sophie Hastings!" Elizabeth's voice echoed around the room, bouncing off the high vaulted ceiling. "I hope you will not speak to the Donaldsons in the same disrespectful tone you have just used with your own mother. They have been invited - end of discussion."

Spinning on her heel Elizabeth began to exit the hall, but stopped by a bust raised high onto a pillar, whose marble face was missing many features. Slowly tracing the uneven stone jutting out where a nose had once resided, she changed her tone to one of melancholy. "Not that this house is in any fit state to receive visitors." For an instant her chin hung crestfallen upon her chest, before she slowly arched her face round to focus on her daughter. "We will have you working this year, Sophie, none of this lazing around the house like you normally do."

This comment wasn't worth responding to. Sophie knew it wasn't true. Every year when she returned home from university, she had purposefully found a summer job, which allowed her to escape the insanity of being at home with her mother. This year was going to be no different, except that Sophie looked upon the opportunity with even greater joy than usual. With a completed degree in her hand, whatever employment she found would be the start of a brand-new career, signalling the end of her mother's dominance since there would no longer be a need to rely on her for anything.

"Why have you invited the Donaldsons if the house is not ready?" asked Sophie eyeing the speckled damp spots climbing up the crumbling sand coloured walls.

"When needs must." Elizabeth touched the back of her hand to her forehead and pressed her lips tightly together in an attempt to contain her emotion.

Sophie had to make every effort to keep her mouth clamped shut, she found her mother incredibly infuriating. *When needs must* - she laughed inside her head. There was no need. The Donaldsons didn't need to be here. All her mother wanted to do was meddle in an area that didn't concern her.

"Can't we just eat out?" Sophie suggested thinking a less intimate setting might be more bearable.

"Eat out?" Elizabeth wrinkled her nose in disapproval. "Eat out?"

"People do eat out."

"Not when you have a house like this," flinging her arms dramatically around, Elizabeth tried to find some great masterpiece to prove her point.

Sophie failed to see her argument. The grand manor house had certainly seen better days and Sophie looked uncertainly at the peeling fresco above her head. "It's falling down, why don't you and dad live somewhere else while you renovate?"

12

"Do you think I've money to waste? Anyone would think I'm a millionaire the way you're talking. I'm not going to throw everything away eating out in posh restaurants and living in fancy hotels."

Sophie heaved a sigh. This was not what she had meant... and when was the last time her mother had been so concerned about money? As far as she knew, Elizabeth was still the same person who threw out all her clothes when the season ended, dined at the most prestigious restaurants in town and travelled only in first class. Considering she didn't lift a finger to produce any income, her mother never thought twice about spending it.

"Aunt Patricia only lives ten miles away; you could stay with her."

"I'm not going to be someone's house guest for months on end."

"You don't have to stay there forever, just until you've finished enough rooms to live comfortably."

"You seem to have forgotten about the will, which said we have to live here."

"If it's uninhabitable, surely you can have a temporary residence."

"Have you studied law?" Elizabeth spat out viciously.

"No, but..."

"Then don't try and solve something you don't understand." Elizabeth haughtily paced away.

Sophie let her leave. No matter how good her arguments were, when her mother didn't want to listen, you might as well be banging your head against a brick wall. Already a headache was starting to form, the kind she only got when around Elizabeth. She closed her eyes and took another large steadying breath. This was going to be a long summer.

****

Four months earlier Sophie had been running late for a lecture. She was dashing around the student house stuffing whatever she could find into a plum-coloured rucksack. Her phone began to ring and without looking at the caller ID, she answered it. "Hello?"

"Hi pumpkin."

It was her dad. Questions immediately swirled around Sophie's head. He never rang during the day; shouldn't he be at work?

"Is everything okay?" She grabbed some keys from the shelf and rushed out of the first-floor bedroom.

"Don't worry, everything is fine."

His tone had convinced her.

"What can I do for you, dad?" she fumbled with the key, trying to lock the door too quickly in her rush to be out the house. With the mobile caught between her shoulder and ear, both hands were free to re-slam the jammed door, and she turned the latch again.

"Have you got time? You sound busy!"

Sophie pushed her arms into both straps and shoved the rucksack onto her back. "I'm a little late for a lecture, but I've ten minutes as I walk."

"I can ring back, pumpkin."

Wishing she'd grabbed a coat in her haste, Sophie zipped up her hooded jacket finding the spring air chiller than expected. "No, dad, it's fine. I can talk."

"Great," he paused. His heavy breathing could be heard down the phone. "I'm ringing to tell you something has happened."

"What do you mean?" asked Sophie, worry creeping in again. "You said everything was all right?"

"It is… in a manner of speaking. I got a call this morning."

"From who?"

"A solicitor."

"Why is a solicitor calling you?"

"That's what I thought too. It turns out your Great Uncle Albert has passed away."

"I'm sorry to hear that, dad."

Who on earth was Great Uncle Albert? Sophie quickly set her brain into gear, trying to decide if she knew who the man was. Eventually it became clear that she didn't. "I don't think I ever met him, were you close?"

"Not really."

Sophie scrunched up her face until it filled with wrinkles, she couldn't understand why he was telling her this. It didn't make sense. "Okay… thanks for letting me know."

"No, Sophie." George Hastings recognised his daughter did not understand. "I'm not ringing to tell you he's died."

"Oh, then why are you ringing?"

"I'm ringing to tell you about the consequences of his death."

"Consequences?"

"Yes, there are big consequences."

"Really? I don't see how if you didn't know him."

"Sophie, think about it."

"Think about what?"

"Who was Great Uncle Albert?"

"I don't know dad," she was trying to be patient, but he wasn't making it very easy.

Upon reaching the traffic lights she pressed the button and waited to cross the busy road with four lanes of traffic.

"I'm nearly at uni, can't you tell me rather than have me guess."

The lights beeped and she started walking to the other side.

"Great Uncle *Bertie,*" George said with emphasis.

Stopping half-way across the road, Sophie gasped in realisation, until a car hooted its horn and she came back to reality. Raising a hand in apology at the irritated driver, she raced across to the other side of the road.

"Oh, my goodness. Great Uncle Bertie!"

"Exactly," said George knowing his daughter now fully understood the situation.

"You are Lord of the Manor."

15

"Indeed, I am," he said with little enthusiasm.

"What does this mean for us now?"

"It means I'm Lord of the Manor, Sophie."

"But you don't want to be," she said becoming defensive.

"Try telling your mother."

"She must know it's detrimental to your health."

"She won't hear any of it. I've tried to tell her it's not in our best interests, that we could easily sell the manor and its estates, except you know what she's like."

Sophie grunted. "I can imagine."

"The will states whoever is Lord of the Manor must live in the manor house otherwise it will be passed to the next true and rightful heir."

"No dad." Sophie was visibly upset by the news. "You can't move." She immediately thought of her childhood home. The purple clematis growing up the side of the garage. The bedraggled basketball hoop still hanging there, neglected since her and Dylan had moved away. The beautiful kitchen-diner leading into the bright south-facing garden-room. Her bedroom. The secret floorboard, that when loosened, stored a secret stash of chocolate hidden away from the eyes of her mother.

"Your mother is determined, pumpkin."

"I'm so sorry, dad."

She knew what this meant for him. The end of his retirement plan and everything he had been working so hard for, running the estate would now be his job for life.

"Don't pity me, Sophie. It's called life, you can't tell what's waiting for you around the corner. At least I had an idea what was coming, I just didn't know when."

Sophie entered a building and climbed the steps two at a time, stopping at the top outside a lecture room.

"I need to go, dad," she said cautiously peeping through a small square window in the door. "I think my lecture has started."

"Of course, pumpkin. I'll call you later."

Sophie hung up. Her professor hated late arrivals, however, sneaking in the back row was now the least of her worries.

****

Sophie loitered in the hall after her mother's exit. Central to the room a grand staircase drew her eye upstairs, where a pillared arch stood magnificently at the top. Following the upper balconies round, Sophie moved slowly clockwise, until her foot became tangled. Looking down, she released her shoe from the threads of a tatty, moth-eaten rug. The initial impressive dimensions of the room began to fade away as she caught sight of ancient portraits thick with dirt and fractured antique pots covered in cobwebs. This was the reality of her father's inheritance.

"Hi pumpkin," the familiar voice coming from the front door instantly filled Sophie with warmth and made her feel more at home.

George Hastings opened his arms wide and planted a kiss on top of his daughter's head. "You're late," he smirked.

"I didn't realise I was being timed. You could have given me a heads up."

"I had no idea the Donaldsons had been invited until they turned up." George shut the tall panelled door behind him. "Journey okay?"

"Busy." Sophie looked around the disintegrating hallway. "Well, this is… interesting."

"That's a polite way of putting it."

"Is every room like this?"

"Yes, or worse."

"Oh…" She searched for a positive, but it was impossible to find one. "Great Uncle Albert wasn't house proud then?"

"Seemingly not. Have you unpacked yet? I'll fetch your cases in for you?"

"Everything's in the car boot. Erm… dad." She stopped him as he twisted the golden door handle. "How are things…really?"

17

"Practically unbearable," he said with a wan smile. "But I'll cope."

"You look tired. Have you been sleeping?"

"I'm fine, Sophie…really."

His daughter continued her scrutiny. There were more silvery threads in his hair then the last time she had visited and his eyes were framed by red circles, suggesting to her that he hadn't really been sleeping well at all.

"Why don't you sell the place. If every room is like this, or worse, how on earth are you supposed to have the funds to restore?"

"I would sell if I could, Sophie," he lowered his voice. "But do you think I'd ever hear the end of it from your mother?"

"You could try talking to her about it."

"She's not an easy woman to talk to."

"I know, we fell out the moment I stepped in through the front door."

"She'll get over it." He opened the aged door. "You'd better go on up, after all, your guests are waiting." He grinned and for a moment Sophie saw his face light up. "I'll bring your things inside."

2

Georgiana

The dining room at Denholm Park buzzed with chatter and laughter. Lady Davenport sat on a beautifully carved mahogany chair and cast her eyes around the room to survey her guests. A half-smile of pleasure spread arrogantly across her face as she congratulated herself on her own success. Her daughter had just married the most eligible bachelor in the county.

Across the long elaborately dressed table sat Georgiana. She could feel her mother's overbearing presence and uneasily sipped her wine. Convinced she was being watched, Georgiana gingerly raised her gaze towards the upper-end of the table and immediately caught sight of her mother. Their eyes locked together and fear paralysed the young girl as Lady Davenport promptly wiped away her conceited expression and exchanged it for a pair of foreboding eyes.

"Try this bread, Georgiana. It's delicious."

Blinking, Georgiana forced her focus back onto her friend, who was seated to the left. "Pardon?"

"The bread, it's delicious. Is it from Freddie?"

Georgiana warily glanced back towards the end of the table, where her mother was now happily in conversation with the lady sat next to her. "Erm… no. Mama sent a boy to Upper Cranley early this morning. Edward swears by the baker there."

"I thought Freddie was a master of his profession, but this is something else," Annabelle Hastings sat munching a piece of heavily buttered roll. "Your mother seems pleased with herself."

"She should be - one daughter married higher than her station and a son about to enter the regiment, what is better than that? I'm the only blot in her life that remains."

"Don't talk like that. Whatever your parents think, it's not true."

Georgiana gulped down the last mouthful of wine from the sparkling crystal glass cradled snuggly in the palm of her hand. "What else am I supposed to believe? We are currently sitting at my sister's wedding breakfast and who does mama choose to scowl at? Me. I've done nothing but breathe, but apparently, I've still managed to offend her in some way. Pass me the bread, please."

Annabelle handed her good friend the plate. "You're only assuming she's offended. You don't know for certain. Do you want the plate of cold meats too?"

Georgiana nodded and swapped the bread platter for one laden with thick slices of beef and pork.

"More wine, Miss Davenport?" asked a footman behind her.

"Yes, please. Thank you." Georgiana smiled politely and waited until he had removed himself to continue their conversation. "Last night she warned me again of her expectations and was cross because things haven't materialised yet."

"He hasn't asked you though, has he?" Annabelle stopped eating and placed her roll down, anxious eyes flickering across her face.

"No, of course not. I would have told you. I really don't know how much longer he can resist conforming to our parents' desires. He's not one for rebellion."

"It wouldn't do to have the younger sister married before the older one anyway," commented Annabelle, her fears slowly receding.

"True, however, Emma is married now and therefore I am next."

The sound of a clinking wine glass stopped Georgiana from further speech and distracted the girls from their conversation. In unison, the guests all swung their heads to seek out the individual who had attracted their attention.

Edward Davenport stood by the door and held a raised glass steadily in the air above his head.

"Ladies and gentlemen," his voice boomed, reaching every ear in the room. "Let us make our way to the long gallery where I believe some dancing is in order." He grinned enthusiastically as one by one his parents' guests left their places and swept out of the dining room to the sound of a pianoforte playing in the room adjacent to the hall.

Trapped amongst the enthusiastic and animated crowd Edward saw his sister. He hurried against the flow, trying to reach Georgiana before she disappeared from sight. Springing forward he gently clasped her arm.

"Can I reserve the first dance, my dear sister?" Edward asked slightly out of breath from his exertion against the throng of people. "If I may have the honour, I do declare I shall find your smile, it seems to be hidden on this merry day."

"Of course, Edward," Georgiana fixed her speckled copper brown eyes upon her brother which instantly affected his disposition. "Although you cannot dance with me all night and we all know who will follow after."

An elderly gentleman bumped into the pair as the guests continued to push past them, eager to participate in the festivities taking place in the other room. They stepped out of the gentleman's way.

"Has he asked yet?" asked Edward furrowing his eyebrows in concern.

"No… although I'm certain he will."

Edward took his sister's hand and squeezed it softy. "I'm so sorry, Georgiana."

"Don't be." Attempting to soothe her brother's guilt, she flippantly shrugged her shoulders and wriggled free from his touch.

"Georgiana, I won't go - I will stay."

"Don't be silly, Edward."

A lady pushing past, wearing a horrendously out-dated wig, stole Georgiana's attention. She was grateful for the distraction, since the pain frozen into her brother's expression felt like a dagger in her heart. The thought of Edward leaving Denholm Park upset Georgiana greatly, but she mustn't cling to him, or even beg him to stay, because she knew his departure from her was inevitable.

Edward drew back her gaze, placing a warm hand on her cheek. He studied his sister's face. "Will you manage without me?"

"I should be old enough to protect myself."

Edward pressed his lips together. He was not convinced. This conversation had started four months ago and had been repeated ever since, never producing a conclusion which convinced Edward of his sister's happiness.

They stood silently for a few seconds, until a new wave of guests forced him to let go and watch his sister sail helplessly out of the dining room.

The long gallery was full of the festivities a wedding occasioned. Dancing had commenced in the centre, whilst admirers and spectators stood to the sides. Georgiana took sanctuary behind a group of ladies.

"Ah, my dearest Miss Davenport," a deep jovial voice addressed her from behind.

"Good day, Sir Gillingham." Georgiana curtsied gracefully in acknowledgement of one of the Davenports' oldest friends.

Sir Gillingham was a jolly, rotund man, boasting rosy cheeks and a pair of overlarge grey sideburns. "This is such a happy occasion for you all. Your parents are to be congratulated on such a prosperous connection."

"Thank you, sir. It is a good match."

"Your sister will be missed," he said, referring to Emma Davenport's removal with her new husband to the north. "But she will be well looked after by the Favershams; they are a highly esteemed family," he nodded in the direction of the bride.

Georgiana followed his gaze and saw Emma leaning elegantly against the mantlepiece, her wedding guests gathered around her, mesmerised by her radiant beauty. It always seemed so easy for Emma. The pressure to perform socially never appeared to daunt her, she had the natural ability to master music, art and needlecraft effortlessly and, on top of all that, she possessed the highly desired capability of pleasing their parents time after time. Georgiana often puzzled over what she did differently to her sister. She carefully

22

evaluated each social situation for potential pitfalls, she practised and studied day and night and aimed to delight her parents continually, just as Emma did. The only difference Georgiana could see was the result. Emma was always praised, whilst she was always criticized.

"You will be dancing, Miss Davenport?" asked Sir Gillingham breaking into Georgiana's thoughts.

"Yes, of course," she answered politely. "I will dance the next round with my brother."

"Very good, very good," said Sir Gillingham with delight. "I am pleased to hear it. A beautiful young woman such as yourself should not be sitting idle at her sister's wedding."

The minuet eventually ended giving the couples an opportunity to change partners and allowing others to join them for the next dance.

Edward appeared by his sister's side. "Can I claim my dance, Georgiana?"

"Would you excuse me, Sir Gillingham."

"Of course, of course," he stepped away so Edward could come forward to take his sister away by the hand.

Edward and Georgiana stood opposite each other to begin their journey down the line when the music began. At first, they danced in silence, spinning in opposites circles and following the lead of the dancers around them.

"I can change my departure date," Edward suddenly spurted out.

"There is no need," said Georgiana as they clapped couplets in time to the beat. "Listen to me. You will join your regiment and I will be fine. Do not worry about me."

Edward pulled his eyebrows together as they performed a chasse step around each other. Perhaps his sister was right - maybe she would be okay.

"You know I would stay if I could. I really don't understand why they are sending me away." Edward almost stopped dancing in his agitation, until his sister prompted him to look up and consequently reminded him of his duty.

Four months previously, Edward had been summoned before his father and was surprised to learn he had been bought an officer's commission. His new regiment was based in Portsmouth and he was to join them there the day after his sister's wedding. The news perplexed the young man immensely. It had never been his intention to find a career, much less to wear a red uniform. This was not because Edward was indolent, in fact, he was considerably the opposite. Being his father's only son, he was sole heir to the Denholm estate and consequently, he would spend his days liaising with tenants and considering how best to invest his income in preparation for the inheritance that would one day come his way. As the firstborn son there should be absolutely no need for him to leave Denholm Park and so Edward found this sudden change of direction a little strange. A career in the army had never been discussed with his father before and when he asked why he had to leave the answer was unclear.

Edward gravely watched his sister dance lightly down the centre, arms linked with a broad-shouldered gentleman before she exchanged partners with another. Being six years older than Georgiana, he had always seen it as his role to protect her, as any older brother should. This desire began early on in childhood. As a boy, he noticed Georgiana was treated differently to Emma. For some reason, one that Edward had never solved, his younger sister had always failed to achieve the high standards of their parents. Georgiana was a sweet girl with a handsome face, she had the ability to hold delightful conversations, was well accomplished in many pursuits and continuously upheld the family honour by being as genteel and polite as she possibly could. Not once had he ever comprehended why his mother was constantly harassing her and proclaiming her a disgrace.

Lord and Lady Davenport ran a strict household and their children all knew their rightful place. Even though Emma had a strong relationship with her mother, Edward was blessed and favoured more than his sisters. From a young age he had discovered in himself an ability to calm escalating situations quickly, if he chose his words wisely. When Georgiana was in the firing line he would intervene, bringing a new perspective to manage his mother's quick anger. Leaving Denholm Park filled Edward with great anxiety, for who would protect his younger sister in his absence?

All of Edward's contemporaries had parents exactly the same. Every aristocratic family spent their days protecting their social status and desiring to further increase their level of influence in society, such aspirations were not unusual and each member of the gentry shared this joint goal. Fathers wanted to secure the best education and commissions for their sons, mothers wanted their daughters to be accomplished at every possible pastime and marry a gentleman higher than their own social rank, these ambitions were normal. Lord and Lady Davenport supported all of these ideals, however there was a distinct difference because they chased after all of these things without a hint of love or consideration for the feelings of their children. They had become obsessed with defending their position and honour and they made it their duty to ensure their children did the same at all costs.

The music ended. Edward bowed deeply before Georgiana and slowly lifted his eyes to see a loitering figure. "If you took the option presented to you, my dear sister, you would find an escape from Denholm Park and I would know you are being looked after."

"You know I cannot, Edward. We have discussed this before."

"Consider it, Georgiana…please."

Edward's compassionate request was so intense Georgiana had to turn her face away for fear she would concede to his wishes. "I have considered it, Edward… a lot, and each time I come to the same conclusion."

Before further conversation could be had, Thomas Compton stepped forward. Edward gave a single nod towards the overly tall, gangly young man and handed across his sister's hand, before departing the dance floor.

"M-may I have the honour of the next dance, Georgiana?"

Smiling politely in acceptance, for she dared not decline the gentleman, Georgiana got into line amongst the dancers again.

"W-well," Thomas said timidly, he always stuttered more when he was nervous. "Emma is married. You shall m-miss her."

Georgiana wished people would stop assuming she would pine for her sister, because the reality was, there no friendship between them at all. Emma's manner toward her was cold, bordering on being uncivil and she permanently lived in her shadow. Being similar in character, Emma and their mother formed a natural bond, they were a force to be reckoned with and left the younger sister excluded time after time.

"Yes, Emma will be missed by many," Georgiana said diplomatically as she left the grip of Thomas' hand and made her way down the line. Skipping in and out of the other ladies, she caught a glimpse of her mother's eyes upon her again as she arrived back into the awkward arms of Thomas. "You didn't need to dance with me."

"I know I didn't. B-but..."

"*She* told you to."

"Y-yes," he stammered. "I am not one to disobey, Georgiana - and neither are you. When was the last time you stood up to your mother?"

Georgiana reddened and looked away. "Never."

"That's exactly my point. Look - she's watching at us now. It's going to happen sooner or later, why not accept it?"

"Because it's not right, Thomas."

Georgiana left his side with great frustration and circled around the lady dancing next to her. It took everything within her not to leave the dance floor. She felt trapped. The sound of guests chatting merrily boomed in her ears, the watchful glances of her mother suddenly appeared from all angles and every beat of her heart felt like a hammer hitting against her chest. The lady took her hand and spun Georgiana round, bringing her back to her senses. In reverse they circled again and a sudden glimpse of Edward helped soothe her elevated anxiety before she was handed back to Thomas.

"It might not sit right with us," continued Thomas. "However, you cannot deny we are the perfect m-match."

"A perfect match in regard to money and standing, I agree… but nothing else."

"It would be a marriage of friendship, Georgiana. Unions like these are not uncommon."

"I have no problem with such an arrangement, believe me when I say I would not willingly upset the wishes of my parents."

The music led her away again, giving a welcome opportunity to compose herself. She danced momentarily with another gentleman and swung back round to Thomas.

"You would rather displease your parents than marry me?" he asked in a whisper barely audible above the music.

"Don't worry, Thomas. I am used to displeasing them."

Thomas shook his head in disagreement as the music finally ended. Georgiana curtsied to her partner and hurried away before he could ask her for a second dance. It was not wise to be ensnared by Thomas Compton all evening, it would add further gossip for wagging tongues and make the absence of a proposal even more shocking.

"Where are you going, Georgiana?" snapped Lady Davenport blocking her daughter's path amongst the crowd of older ladies congregated around the edge of the room.

"I am feeling a little tired, mama." Georgiana tried not to catch a glimpse of her mother's terrifying features. It was a pathetic excuse, and she knew it, but it was all she could think of to escape public judgement.

"You will dance with Mr Compton again," her mother demanded. "One dance is not enough." Lady Davenport looked out towards the middle of the room and snorted reproachfully. "For goodness sake, he is dancing with Miss Hastings now. You have lost your chance, stupid child."

Georgiana flinched as her mother abruptly stepped back in the attempt to gain control of her rapidly rising anger.

Lady Davenport knew she must compose herself; she could not afford to let her guests witness this display of emotional behaviour. "Your sister," she continued through gritted teeth, "was so easy and obliging." She pulled intimidatingly closer, so her mouth almost tickled her daughter's ear with the warmth from her breath. "*She* knew how to get a husband. Can I suggest it is not in your best interest to bring ruin upon us, Georgiana, I would not recommend it; the consequences will be too much for you to bear."

Lady Davenport stepped back and looked contemptuously away from her youngest daughter. "Sit down, child, if you must, but make sure it is the final time this evening."

3

Sophie

"Your plumber is ignoring my calls; I don't know how many times I've rung. I don't think much to him Dorothy and I can't understand why you recommended him."

Sophie stood outside the room where her mother's guests were being entertained. The words she had just heard spoken brought her to a stand-still with a hand poised over the handle. How many times had her mother in stubborn persistence pestered this poor plumber? She shook her head, embarrassed by Elizabeth's obnoxious speech.

Much to Sophie's regret, the door groaned when she finally decided to twist the handle and enter the room. She had hoped to enter without the eyes of the entire party turning in her direction, unfortunately the unoiled hinges made this impossible to achieve.

"Sophie, there you are! You are looking absolutely gorgeous." A plump lady raced across and implanted bright red lips onto Sophie's cheek.

"Nice to see you again, Mrs Donaldson," said Sophie attempting to break away without further kisses, however the firm grip of the kisser pulled her back to complete the greeting and planted one on the other side.

Dorothy Donaldson's personality was reflected in her outfit. Bright colourful roses ornamented a shoulder padded jacket with pink straight cut trousers to match.

"Look who we brought with us..." The lady beamed with pleasure as she stood back, excitedly pushing forward a young man, dressed in a dinner jacket with rolled up sleeves, grey chino trousers and canvas shoes.

"Hey Soph," the young man said with a mild hint of pink shading his dimpled cheeks.

Sophie mirrored his awkwardness knowing everyone was watching their reunion.

"Hi, Rupert." In an attempt to act as casually as possible, she immediately turned her attention to the older gentleman standing behind. "It's a pleasure to see you too, Mr. Donaldson."

"It would be more of a pleasure if the environment was more hospitable." Roger Donaldson grumbled with his American twang. "What do you think to the dump your parents have been landed with?"

"Oh, well… I haven't seen it all yet. I couldn't possibly comment," she responded diplomatically, sensing her mother's radar eyes upon her.

"Don't look at the negative, Roger," said Dorothy lightly tapping her husband's shoulder, endeavouring to scold him whilst continuing to smile broadly. "Imagine the balls that would have happened in this place all those years ago. The ladies giving out their dancing cards and using their fans to flirt with the men," she lifted her hands to her face in girlish glee.

"I wouldn't have guests in a place like this," Mr Donaldson continued to mutter. "Unsanitary."

Elizabeth could hold her tongue no longer. "I can assure you everything is completely sanitary, Roger. Otherwise I would not have allowed our little gathering today."

Mr Donaldson grunted something inaudible before removing himself from the conversation to stand by the tall sash window at the other side of the room.

"Ignore him, Lizzie." Dorothy pottered across to her friend and put a comforting arm around her. "I think it's wonderful and you'll restore it all beautifully over time."

"Of course I will, Dorothy," Elizabeth shrugged her friend's arm away. "With no help of yours may I add." Dorothy looked puzzled and her smile momentarily left her face. "Your plumber," Elizabeth reminded her.

"Oh, Darren is normally very good. Shall I ring him for you?"

"Very good isn't good enough. So no, I do not need you to ring him. Excellent workmen start by having the common courtesy to answer the phone. I would actually like a bath that isn't lukewarm, or is that too much to ask?"

"You are living in a house last renovated in the 1950s, not to mention that it was built in the eighteenth century," commented Sophie.

Elizabeth disregarded her daughter's remark. There should be no excuses in her opinion, for four months she had been living in Middleton Manor and the place still looked like it was about to collapse.

"Thank you for your help, Dorothy, but I won't be requiring any more names of so-called reliable tradesmen. My home is worthy of excellent craftsmen, not merely satisfactory ones."

"Dinner is served, madam."

Sophie was surprised to see a man dressed in a full black suit with tails and a bow tie enter the room. She raised her eyebrows questioningly, had her mother really hired a butler for the occasion?

"Thank you, Pritchard. Shall we?" Elizabeth gestured towards the open door.

Rupert ushered his parents forward, allowing him the opportunity to pause as he walked by Sophie. "Sorry about the old man, Soph," he whispered. "Must have got out of bed the wrong side this morning."

"Don't worry about it, I remember what he's like."

How could she forget? When Sophie was three years old the Donaldsons moved next door to their home in one of the many busy London suburbs. For some reason, the two mothers hit it off immediately, although contrasting exceedingly in character. Elizabeth Hastings was quick to judge, headstrong and austere, whereas Dorothy Donaldson was high-spirited, wore a constant smile on her face and had the incredible ability to find the good in absolutely anything. The two younger children followed suit in friendship. Sophie's older brother, Dylan, being five years older, was nonplussed about the new boy next door, he already had his own friends. But Sophie and Rupert, who was an only child, became inseparable. They acted like twins finishing off each other's sentences, knowing instinctively what the other was thinking and grieving during times when they were forced to be apart. In fact, they never seemed to tire of each other's company.

When Sophie and Rupert were twelve the Donaldsons decided to move to the Peak District. The two children wrote to each other during term time and spent the school holidays together, however new friendships formed naturally on both sides. By the time university arrived communication was virtually non-existent and so the last three years had seen barely any contact at all between the two friends, since Sophie had chosen to study in London, whilst Rupert had headed off to Edinburgh.

Sophie had always remembered Mr Donaldson being a glass half-empty kind of man. His company had forced him to move across the Atlantic thirty years ago and he was probably the only American on earth not to adore English customs and heritage. In fact, Roger Donaldson was the sort of man who seemed to complain every other second and never had anything nice to say.

Dinner had been eaten and the two families were relaxing in the drawing room. The two fathers were conversing quietly in the corner, trying to keep as invisible as possible for fear their wives might require something from them. The rest of the party were gathered on faded pink sofas which surrounded the huge fireplace, sipping tea out of delicate porcelain cups.

"What an achievement, Sophie, to have finished your degree with a first class," said Dorothy. "We were so proud of our Rupert as he stood on the stage and collected his diploma." She squeezed her son's cheek as if he was still a little boy.

"Ma!" Rupert protested and moved her hand away, rubbing the pinch marks on his face.

"So..." continued Dorothy ignoring her son's objections. "What are your plans now?"

Sophie opened her mouth to answer, although no sound was allowed to escape because her mother spoke first.

"She will work here, of course," Elizabeth commented, talking about her daughter as if she were not in the room. "Do you not listen to our conversations at all, Dorothy?"

"Oh yes, I do Lizzie. I didn't realise they were definite plans."

Elizabeth tutted, sometimes she wondered at her friend's intellect. "She will live and work here on the estate."

"That does make sense." Dorothy tried to correct her error by smiling and nodding with great emphasis at everyone around her.

"Actually," began Sophie.

Elizabeth twisted her body to face her daughter, arching her perfectly plucked eyebrow in disapproval. Sophie instantly recognised the signs. Her mother was preparing to fight her ground, which meant whatever viewpoint she was about to express would undoubtedly be met with hostility. Now Sophie had to choose, should she instinctively retreat because past experience told her she would be the wounded party, or should she engage in a bitter battle, locking heads together until her inevitable withdrawal would end the conflict?

As she had been driving home earlier that day Sophie had decided on her plan, it was the only way forward. At the first utterance from her mother of predestined ideas it was imperative she laid out her intentions so as to make it clear there was no way she was becoming trapped in her father's inherited estate. Failure to do this would diminish her chance of escape dramatically.

"Actually," Sophie repeated again. "I've a few options to consider before making a final decision."

"Options?" questioned Elizabeth. "What options are those, darling?" she smiled, but you could tell it was forced.

"There are lots of other jobs I could do, other places I could go, maybe even do a master's."

Elizabeth laughed. "Don't be silly, Sophie."

"I'm not being silly, mum."

"Didn't I tell you this would happen Dorothy." Elizabeth turned back to her friend, who nodded in agreement and lifted a teacup to her mouth, trying to avoid being pulled into the brewing argument.

"What are you talking about?" asked Sophie.

"I allowed you to choose the university you wanted to attend and now you think you can diverge away from the plan," Elizabeth continued to laugh lightly, looking towards Dorothy for support.

"It's not my plan," Sophie knitted her eyebrows together in determination, her mother could not do this to her.

"You are needed here."

"You've managed okay without me these last four months."

Rupert hastily rose from the sofa. "Let's go and explore, Soph," he burst out in his agitation to break the tension. "I'd love to see the old place properly, that's if…" he respectfully looked over to Elizabeth. "If your mother doesn't mind?"

"No Rupert, you are not to look in the house, it's all in such a state," she flapped away the suggestion with a hand.

"Aww, let them look, Lizzie," encouraged Dorothy, who was just as eager to distract the two Hastings women from their dispute. "We know you are not choosing to keep the house like this forever."

"That is not the point," Elizabeth said and crossed her arms irritably.

"You are too house-proud," cried her friend. "We are good friends and don't think any less of you for the mess. You've only been here four months and it wasn't exactly maintained to a high standard by the previous owner."

Dorothy paused and tilted her head towards Sophie and Rupert. Her action was supposed to be nonchalant, but her repeated nodding as she looked towards the pair distorted her face, and if the atmosphere hadn't been so tense, could easily have caused much amusement.

"Let them look around, Lizzie," she finished the act with a wink that was so conspicuous anyone looking in her direction could have clearly seen.

Catching her friend's obvious meaning, Elizabeth huffed. "Fine. If you insist Rupert, I will allow you to explore the grounds. I suppose overgrown weeds aren't as bad as dust and debris."

"Thank you kindly, Mrs Hastings," gushed Rupert.

As Sophie got to her feet, she could feel the eyes of the two mothers upon them. Her cheeks turned a rose-like colour and the two of them left the room, which she knew would be misinterpreted.

The old friends stepped out onto the large gravelled drive. The air was still warm and the sun was only beginning to drop in the sky, transforming the few wispy clouds into a pale pink colour.

"Thank you for rescuing me from mum," said Sophie, as they walked side by side into the garden that was a tangle of overgrown weeds.

"You are welcome," Rupert slightly bowed his head as he accepted her thanks.

"I don't care how much she stamps her feet; I can't stay here - I just can't."

"No one's making you stay, Soph."

"You saw how quickly she jumped on me when I had the audacity to mention I might have other plans."

Rupert shook his head and snorted.

"What's so funny?" demanded Sophie as they wandered under an archway being strangled to death by ivy.

"Everything's exactly the same, nothing's changed since we last met. You complaining about her and me coming to the rescue."

"I'm glad my relationship with mum amuses you so much," said Sophie standing still. The smirk on her friend's face suggested the next point needed more emphasis. "Tonight's dinner was for us, you know?"

"For us?" Rupert's merriment vanished.

"Yes, didn't you realise?"

"No, I had no idea."

"Do you really think mum would hold a dinner party inside a house looking like a demolition site for any other reason? I know she wants to show off, but normally her sense of dignity and propriety would curl in horror at such a notion… think about it, you were even here before I arrived home."

"Late… may I add," he exchanged his fleeting seriousness for a toothy grin.

"Me being late was part of her sneaky little plan. I didn't know you were coming therefore I couldn't voice my objection."

"That's hurtful, Soph." Rupert jokingly put a hand to his heart and lowered his bottom lip.

"I don't mean it like that, of course it's good to see you." She tucked an arm through his and they continued walking.

Rupert sniggered. "You take life too seriously."

"You have to with a mum like mine. If you don't keep up, she'll attack you when you least expect it."

This time it was Rupert's turn to halt their progress and the scent of lavender amongst the weeds wafted up into their faces. "Listen, our mothers are not plotting against you. You don't need to be paranoid on that front because their plan shouldn't be in existence anymore."

"Believe me, it is."

"It's not," he scanned her face to assess if she believed him.

"How can you be so certain?" she asked.

Rupert stepped back. "I have a girlfriend now."

"I wouldn't be so certain your mother got the memo."

Sophie moved on towards a border that had once been filled with colourful chrysanthemums, though now, the few which remained had been covered in a powdery white mildew leaving the flower heads looking incredibly bedraggled.

"Are you coming?" She turned back to Rupert, who was still planted to the spot where she had left him and he jogged the distance between them to catch up.

"Why don't you think my mother knows?" he asked.

"Did you not see her gigantic wink as we left the room?"

"I don't understand," he brushed a hand through his curly brown hair. "I told her it wasn't going to happen and to forget about it."

"Am I that unmarriable?" Sophie jested.

"Soph, no - I didn't mean…"

"I'm kidding, Rupert," she momentarily placed a hand on his shoulder. "You just told me to take life less seriously."

"So I did." Rupert smiled and the pair strolled on, exiting the more formal gardens through a rusted rickety fence, attached only by a single hinge to the crumbling brick wall.

"What's she like then?" asked Sophie.

"Who?"

"Your girlfriend."

"Oh…" he paused to consider his answer. "Actually, I would say she's a lot like you. Maisie is kind hearted and adventurous, she even laughs at my jokes."

Despite the fading sunlight, Sophie could tell his cheeks had changed to a brighter hue of pink than usual.

"The only difference is her eyes are emerald green…" He gazed off longingly into the distance, caught up his own dream.

"I'm really pleased for you, Rupert," said Sophie, satisfied to see her old friend so happy, although she knew full well her mother would not be so delighted.

For a reason unknown to Sophie, the two mothers had paired herself and Rupert up for life. She had noticed plans for the predestined marriage beginning to form after Rupert moved away at the age of twelve.

At first it didn't bother Sophie. She assumed the novelty of matchmaking would fade away - but it didn't. When she told Rupert, he just laughed, "Sounds like my mother," he had said. Subtle hints reminding her to correspond with Rupert and the inevitable prolonged visit every school holiday began to irritate Sophie. It was just another way for her mother to control her life. Then at last university arrived and the pressure eased away.

George Hastings had been the next heir to the Georgian mansion of Middleton Manor for the last eleven years. Sophie was well aware of the inheritance and what it would mean for the family. However, what she hadn't realised was that it was located a mere two miles away from the Donaldsons country home in the Peak District. No matter how far apart Sophie and Rupert lived, the mothers could always be confident their children would eventually come together. For as long as she lived with her parents, Rupert Donaldson would be her neighbour once again.

It wasn't that Rupert was unattractive. In fact, he was the complete opposite, with mousy brown hair that curled to the top of his ears and sparkling cobalt blue eyes the colour of a tropical sea. He had the manners of a gentleman and knew how to please. One glance could melt any girl's heart. But Sophie knew him best and no amount of swooning and perfect curls could overcome this. She knew him to be carefree and high-spirited, someone who got bored quickly and seemed to be allergic to hard work.

"Your parents aren't really going to keep this place, are they?" Rupert looked up at the imposing manor as they made their way back along the gravelled drive.

"I think they will."

"But why, they should sell it and have the money?"

"I'm sure my dad would in a heartbeat," said Sophie, knowing this to be true. There were no family loyalties to the place, no one had spent summers there as a child, or had heard heart-warming stories about the people who had lived there long ago. It meant nothing.

"You know what mum's like though, she's been waiting years for this."

Elizabeth Hastings had been counting off each passing year since her marriage twenty-five years ago, mentally ticking off each family member who lay in her way, until finally it was her turn. For some reason her self-worth and identity had become wrapped up in becoming Lady of the Manor at Middleton Manor and no one was going to take it away from her.

"Surely your dad will stand up to her and make her see sense? They can't have enough money to run this place, it's financial suicide."

Sophie felt her insides tighten: she'd been worried about the same thing.

Reaching the six-panelled door, Sophie lifted her foot onto the step and stretched to turn the handle, but Rupert stopped her, laying his hand on top of hers before she could go inside.

"Out of curiosity," he said. "What are your plans? Clearly not what your mother desires?"

Sophie released the handle and stepped back onto the gravel. "Plan A is to escape as quickly as possible."

"And plan B...?"

"Plan B will come into force if mum gets her way. I will be used as free labour in the race to restore the manor and its estate to its former glory."

"Who's going to win, do you think?"

"Who do *you* think?" she turned the question back at him with a meaningfully raised eyebrow.

Rupert looked knowingly at his friend; it was unlikely Sophie would win the battle because to his knowledge she had seldom won before.

Sophie's greatest triumph was receiving permission to choose her own university, but even this was a half victory. Elizabeth wanted her daughter to go to Oxford or Cambridge, but Sophie knew she wouldn't get the grades to qualify. A compromise was finally made and Sophie could choose where she studied as long as Elizabeth vetted it first.

"Well, I for one will be pleased to have the heiress to the throne stay around for a while," said Rupert smiling in commiseration.

"Heiress to the throne." Sophie snorted. "Dylan is before me."

"True, but you're still second in line - quite a catch really."

"Shame your mother's missing out then."

"Yes," agreed Rupert reaching for the handle and twisting it open. "Yes, it is."

4

Georgiana

Georgiana pulled a piece of thread slowly through the fabric, it was so quiet you could hear the sound of the fibres passing through the muslin. She tugged it tight and pierced the needle through again.

"Emma looked incredibly handsome yesterday," commented Lady Davenport as she flicked over the page in her book. "Then again she should do, after the prestigious marriage she had just made."

Georgiana knew this was not some amiable pleasantry. There was without doubt a concealed motive behind this innocent sounding observation.

It was early afternoon and the two women had been forced together since a light drizzle had prevented them from being elsewhere. Georgiana glanced up from her work, alert and ready to make conversation. Lady Davenport's eyes lingered on the book in her hand and Georgiana shifted uneasily in her chair, with the repetitive tick of the mantle clock pulsing innocently in her ears. Each passing second heightened her distress as her mother's excessive silence dominated the room.

At last Lady Davenport spoke. "You did not dance many dances yesterday."

Uncertain whether she preferred the silence to her mother's accusing tone, Georgiana answered. "I was not asked, mama."

"What nonsense, child," scoffed the older lady.

Georgiana decided to make no comment, one word spoken out of place would be enough to start a fire.

"I expected you to dance more with Mr. Compton."

She should have seen this coming. In fact, Georgiana was surprised the reprimand hadn't arrived sooner. Once again, she let the mantel clock fill in the space. There was nothing she could say that could possibly divert her mother's frustration away from her. It was true, she had barely danced with Thomas all night.

"Speak child!" Lady Davenport slammed her book shut.

"I danced three times with Mr Compton," said Georgiana in a hurry, twisting a cotton thread round her finger.

"Five or six would have been more advantageous to your cause. You also danced too many times with your brother."

Speaking directly to her lap, Georgiana feebly attempted to defend her actions. "Edward offered me his hand," she muttered. "I was not going to object."

"You must indicate your availability, Georgiana."

"I would not want to bring disrespect upon our family by acting too eagerly." She dared not lift her head to see the heart-stopping eyes of her mother, it would only make her tremble more.

"Excuses," pronounced Lady Davenport. "You will not rise to the station of your sister if you decline every man put in front of you."

"I have declined no one, mama. So far nobody has proposed marriage to me."

"Whose fault is that? It certainly isn't mine - all the better when Edward has gone to his regiment," she calmly opened her book again and smoothed out the crinkled pages. "He protects you too much."

Silence reigned again. With the conversation seemingly over, Georgiana forcefully threaded her needle through the cloth, knotting the thread as she did so. Her work always bore the brunt of her frustrations, for certainly she could not display them openly. Over the last few months she had considered the reasons for Edward's removal. Time and time again her thoughts were pulled back to the same notion. Without Edward, her parents could finally rid Denholm Park of her unwanted presence and her mother's words now confirmed it.

The parlour door opened sending a beam of sunshine across the well-polished floor and indicating the rain had come to an end.

"I am about to take my leave, mama." It was Edward, wearing a navy multi-caped overcoat.

Lady Davenport placed the mistreated book to one side and stood up, her bad temper quickly evaporating in the presence of her beloved son.

"My dearest Edward." She left her chair and strode across to Edward, who stooped to receive a kiss on the cheek. "I do wish you well in your new career. Have you seen your father?"

"I have," Edward affirmed, glancing at his sister whose flushed cheeks indicated she had just had an altercation with their mother. "Will you walk out with me, Georgiana?"

Bravely raising her eyes, Georgiana naturally looked across to Lady Davenport, who silently nodded and allowed her daughter to leave the room with her brother.

Edward took his sister's hand and held it tightly in his as they reached the carriage waiting outside. "I will visit you soon…I promise."

"I am unlikely to be at Denholm when you return." She had told him this many times, but he had always refused to believe it.

"Why, are you off on your travels?" he chuckled, however his attempt to lighten the farewell failed and Georgiana's face remained emotionless.

"She will have me married, Edward - to the next stranger who passes this way, if it is not Thomas. Mama is desperate to have me gone now Emma is wed. You were the only thing standing in her way and now you are to be removed. I am at her will and no one is able to stop her."

"At least you can be assured your husband will be a gentleman of good connection, mama won't fail you there." His lips curled up at the corners again.

"It is not funny," scolded Georgiana who wished her brother would take things more seriously. His departure would inevitably bring sorrow and no amount of humour could change that. "Emma has been fortunate to fall in love with one of the most eligible suitors in the county. And me? Mama couldn't care less whether I am content or miserable… in fact, she would probably prefer me to be miserable."

"My dear Georgiana, don't paint such a bleak picture for yourself."

"It is my reality."

Edward sighed. The guilt of leaving his sister, which he had been striving to ignore, rested heavily upon his chest. No words could express his anguish and so he promised to return again as soon as he was granted leave, kissed her hand and stepped into the carriage.

The instant Edward's carriage left the grounds another chaise entered and Georgiana waited dutifully to greet whoever was inside. Nobody was expected and she watched curiously as the horses came to a halt. The coachman jumped down and opened the door widely for its owner to alight.

"Thomas," she cried in surprise when her friend stepped out of the chaise. "I was not expecting you today."

"Your mother has invited me for t-tea." He brushed the creases out of his coat as he spoke. "Are my tails neat enough? It's p-practically impossible to remain pristine sitting in a chaise." He strained his neck to check the back of his tail coat for blemishes.

"You look fine, Thomas," Georgiana said looking distractedly back towards the house, her suspicions being aroused.

Thomas Compton had been Georgiana's friend for many years. His family lived in the next village and they often met at dinner parties and balls. He was a gentle soul, lived a quiet life and had accomplished everything expected of him. Thomas was one of the few unmarried bachelors left in the neighbourhood. His good income made him highly sought after, but everyone knew Lady Davenport had claimed the young man for her own daughter. The imposing influence possessed by both Lord and Lady Davenport caused nobody else in the neighbourhood to challenge their authority and they kept their single daughters on the side, waiting to pounce if the opportunity arose.

Georgiana's suspicions were raised further when Lady Davenport welcomed the young pair into the parlour with a smile, a facial feature her daughter rarely saw, never mind being on the receiving end.

"Mr Compton, how lovely to see you again so soon," the older lady purred.

"Al-w-ways a p-pleasure, Lady D-Davenport." Thomas bowed, his slight stammer intensifying, alerting Georgiana to his rising nervousness. "I-I hope you are not too t-tired after yesterday's festivities?"

"How very kind of you to enquire. I am quite well, thank you," Lady Davenport straightened out her dress and sat upright on her chair. The bell was rung and within minutes a girl carrying a tray of tea things entered discreetly through the door. "Thank you, Lottie. That will be all." The girl curtsied and left as quickly as she came.

"Are your parents well, Mr. Compton?" Lady Davenport asked pouring the tea.

"V-very well, thank you," said Thomas.

"I heard your father has recently purchased a new property in Kent."

"Y-yes, you heard correctly. He w-wanted to be closer to London and also away from the crowds. It suits his n-need perfectly."

"Very impressive."

She handed out the porcelain cups, her presence demanding complete silence unless spoken to.

"It is my delight that Emma will now participate in such grandeur herself. Mr Faversham has a place in the capital and has also recently acquired a country estate, an incredible achievement for a man of such a young age. I am immensely proud to call him my son-in-law."

"A-a-absolutely."

Thomas sipped his tea. Georgiana looked curiously at him from the corner of her eye, she couldn't help notice his hand shook a little as he lifted the cup to his lips. This visit was no coincidence, he had come for a purpose.

"This tea is de-d-delicious, Lady Davenport."

"Thank you, Mr. Compton. I have a new supplier who gets me higher quality leaves," Lady Davenport placed her teacup and saucer gently back on the tray. "Would you please excuse me; I have something I must see to in another room."

With great elegance she stood up, straightening out her posture as far as she could stretch to display the importance of her position and warn against any insubordination. Purposefully she glided by Georgiana on her passage out of the room and subtly trod upon her foot.

"Ouch."

"My apologies, Georgiana." She spoke without feeling as her daughter rubbed her foot in discomfort. "You should keep your feet tucked away or accidents like that are bound to happen." The words sounded pleasant, however the penetrating glare suggested otherwise. Lady Davenport had not stood on her daughter's toes by accident and Georgiana knew this full well, the time had arrived and there were certain expectations that must now be followed.

A quietness descended after Lady Davenport had left the room and only the reliable ticking of the mantel clock could be heard.

Thomas coughed. "It really is n-nice tea," he sipped again, trying to calm his nerves. "W-we have known each other for a l-long time, haven't we?"

"Thomas, please don't," said Georgiana casting pleading eyes upon her friend.

"Listen to me, Georgiana…p-please," he looked away from her and focused on the floor. "We have known each other a long time. We are f-f-friends. Good friends." He stopped, having to breathe deeply to steady his nerves.

"No, Thomas. It's not right."

He lifted his eyes to meet hers. "I am better for you than a complete stranger, Georgiana," he said, his frustration momentarily stopping him from stuttering.

"Yes, I know, but…" she trailed off. There was no plausible excuse to give for declining a proposal.

"Your mother has arranged this moment, I c-cannot leave without your hand."

"Then you will be staying a long time," as she spoke the rejection in his face became obvious and she had to look away.

"Georgiana, we both know this must happen. Do you want to endure the wrath of your m-mother if you do not agree?"

Georgiana closed her eyes to escape the reality of the situation before her. She had known for many months Thomas Compton was the man her parents had chosen. His parents owned the biggest estate in the county and Thomas himself earned ten thousand a year. The match was perfect, even though there was absence of love on both sides. Georgiana would have happily agreed to the arrangement, for she greatly respected Thomas as a friend and she knew he would look after her well. Yet, there was one thing that stood in her way.

"No," Thomas scrunched his eyebrows into a frown. "I must do this…" He clumsily took Georgiana's hand and she immediately felt his warm clammy skin encircle hers. "W-will you make me a happy man and become my w-wife?"

"I cannot."

Thomas looked her square in the face. "You cannot mean this?"

"You do not love me," she slipped her hand away.

"It isn't about love, Georgiana. We've discussed this before," he was irritated and had good reason to be. Her rejection would fuel rumours neither family would want to experience. Thomas' reputation would recover in time. Hers would be a different story.

"You will be miserable."

"Don't you think this refusal will bring me misery too? Our parents have designed the path we must take, it is called life, Georgiana, the sooner you accept it the better."

"You will suffer much longer if I *do* accept. I do not think your distress will last long, Thomas, please accept my refusal." She leaned forward in earnest, turning large pleading eyes upon him. "Your parents may be upset for a time, though I'm sure they will soon get over it, especially when you have other options." Leaning back, she blew out a deep breath. "Besides, you have played your part, you have proposed, it is I who have declined to comply."

"Your parents will not be as understanding as mine."

Georgiana smiled, through the tears that threatened to fall. Thomas was such a kind, sensitive man, more concerned about her welfare than for his own. Was she being a fool rejecting him?

"Do not worry about me," she sniffed and Thomas passed across a handkerchief which she dabbed onto her cheek.

"I do worry about you, Georgiana. We have been dear friends since childhood."

"I would rather see you happy."

For a moment he looked at her, mouth pressed together in contemplation. "You are adamant in declining my offer?"

"Y-yes," Georgiana said, stuttering in her turn, as she made her final decision. It was the most courageous thing she had ever done in her life.

Thomas stood up. "I-I will take my leave, Georgiana." His friend had made her decision and it wasn't worth continuing the discussion any longer. "I wish you all the best."

The two friends locked eyes before he bowed respectfully and left the room.

5

Sophie

"Goodness me, dad. It's like a mountain."

George Hastings nodded defeatedly as they stood in the estate office connected to the back of the manor.

"Is this everything that needs dealing with?" asked Sophie fingering a tall, unstable pile of folders.

"I wish," George groaned. "That pile needs dealing with soon, although it can wait because…" he pivoted and pointed toward to his desk which was overloaded with papers flowing onto the floor, "… this lot needs dealing with immediately, except I can't begin work on these because…" This time he walked over to the window seat where there was yet another mound of papers: "These should have been dealt with months, if not years ago."

"How…how?" Sophie was flummoxed. "I don't even have the words."

"The estate is in a mess," he sighed. "I don't know what your great uncle was doing, but it certainly wasn't paperwork."

"Where are you going to start?"

"No idea. I come in here every day and just sit, overwhelmed by the amount of work there is to be done."

An envelope which was balanced precariously on top of the unstable pile of papers near the window, slipped, causing an avalanche to follow after it. George winced and watched helplessly, not even making an effort to stop the documents and letters as they became one enormous mess on the floor.

"At least you've made a start on it," Sophie said endeavouring to find the positive. "Look, you have three piles…" she glanced at the freshly made heap in front of them. "Okay, you *did* have three piles… but a bit of mess is easy to solve."

George didn't respond and his glassy eyed stare began to unsettle her.

"Come on dad, you're a bank manager - you can do this."

"But the question is, do I want to do this?"

"You told me you have no choice. You said mum wouldn't hear otherwise."

"Maybe I'm beginning to change my mind."

The sudden change in her father's emotions disturbed Sophie further. Yesterday, George was willing to convince her everything was fine and had promised he was okay. Today, he wanted to throw in the towel and was ready to concede defeat. What had happened overnight to cause such an abrupt change?

"Sophie, I'm not sleeping well," he admitted running a hand over his face and into his silver speckled hair. "You could see that yesterday and I tried to convince you everything was fine. I'm an old man, I don't want this responsibility."

"Dad, you're fifty-six, that's not old."

"Well, I feel like an old man." George slumped miserably onto the chair behind the desk. "I was slowing down, Sophie. Retirement was imminent."

"You could get an estate manager," Sophie suggested in desperation to find a solution. "You would only need to supervise then and let someone else do all the hard work."

"Can't afford it," George said bluntly. "All our savings will be spent in a matter of months on the house alone… especially at the rate your mother is calling in every builder, electrician and plumber. If the estate is inefficient it will produce no income. I imagine I will be bankrupt by the end of the year - my entire life savings wiped out."

Sophie felt her stomach tighten, she hated hearing her dad talk like this. "There'll be ways of raising income, I'm sure of it."

"Let's not deny the inevitable, Sophie." He leaned forward and rubbed the bridge of his nose as he often did in moments of great stress.

The conversation lulled, causing Sophie to begin an inner battle. Her dad couldn't be left in this state, but what else could she do? In theory the solution was simple, but Sophie didn't like it. She frantically searched the depths of her mind; however, she could find no alternative.

In hesitation, her mouth hung open in suspense. Could she lay down her own plans? "I'll stay and help you," she said, eventually allowing the words to pass through her mouth. "It's what mum wants anyway."

"No, Sophie, you're not wasting your life away here."

It was what Sophie wanted to hear, but she'd never leave him, she'd feel too guilty if she did.

"Help me by all means whilst you're here," George continued. "But I need you to keep looking for a job as well - I'll deal with your mother when the time comes for you to leave." As he finished talking, he let his head fall into his hands in an attempt to shut out the world around him.

Sophie shuffled uneasily. Where should she go from here? Her glanced ranged between the slumped figure of her dad and the letters and documents scattered all over the floor. Pressing her lips together in determination she pottered over to the tower of papers leaning delicately against the filling cabinet.

"Let's start trying to answer some of these letters," she said, her tone trying to imitate an optimism she didn't feel herself. She picked up the top letter and the envelope crinkled as she pulled out a single sheet of paper.

"Mr. Morgan…" she read. "From Morgan's farm. He has concerns relating to his land and wishes an immediate meeting." Sophie looked to the top left of the letter. "This was six months ago. Let's start with him." She beamed an overly enthusiastic smile at her dad who lifted his head as if in pain. "You've got to make the effort, dad. Mum won't discuss any idea of opting out if you haven't tried."

"I guess you're right, pumpkin." George heaved himself out of the chair. "Okay, where is this Morgan's farm?"

****

Mr Morgan stretched his hands behind his back and straightened up after placing four mechanical teats underneath the final cow.

"Our livestock is in excellent health thank you, Miss...Miss... I'm sorry, we didn't have much to do with the previous Lord of the Manor. Are you a relative?"

"It's Miss Hastings, but please, call me Sophie." She smiled kindly at the farmer. "The previous Lord of the Manor was my father's late uncle." Sophie turned to George who was standing beside her, trying to include him in the conversation, though it wouldn't have mattered if she'd paid him no attention at all, since he remained silent anyway.

Mr Morgan cleared his throat and patted a cow on its rump, unsettling a fly that had been resting on the animal. He looked up at the small holes in the roof which allowed the bright morning sun to break into the cowshed.

"As I was saying Miss Hastings, our livestock is in good health, however, as you can see, some repairs are needed."

Sophie scanned the letter she held in her hands, which she had brought with her for reference.

"No, no," said Jack Morgan waving his hand upon seeing her confusion. "This wasn't the reason I wrote to your predecessor. Please, if you would follow me." The farmer ushered Sophie and her father out of the shed and into the yard.

"I didn't realise you had so much land, Mr Morgan," commented Sophie after they had been walking continuously for five minutes and had still not reached their destination.

"We do have a fair bit," agreed Jack walking at quite a pace and leaving Sophie slightly breathless. "Not nearly enough for our organic produce, which is why I wrote to you."

"Organic produce… I thought you were a dairy farmer?"

"I see you've been doing your homework." Mr Morgan grinned; he was already impressed by this girl. "You are right, I am a dairy farmer. It's Charlie's produce that's outgrowing us."

"Charlie?" enquired Sophie.

"My son," Jack explained. "He began growing organic fruit and veg for the local market about a year ago. It has been met with such high demand he now needs to expand."

"That's good to hear." Sophie turned to her dad hoping he would be encouraged and realise not everything about this estate was going to be a failure. However, if he had heard the words of the farmer, it didn't show on his expressionless face.

Jack Morgan stopped.

"Over here…" he pointed over a drystone wall separating the field where they were standing from the one beyond. "This is our problem."

Sophie halted by the wall and peered over, failing to understand what the farmer was talking about.

Jack quickly enlightened her. "This is the only area we have left to expand."

They looked out across the field, which was covered with a long grass, the odd yellow leafed clover and a couple of animal troughs.

Looking puzzled, Sophie spun back to Mr Morgan. "I'm sorry - I don't understand. Isn't this your land?"

"Have you met Mr Jones?"

"No, I don't think so."

"Then you haven't, you would know if you've met him. The problem is he claims to own this land."

"Oh, there is a land dispute?"

"He grazes his sheep here. It's been a long-standing agreement for the last three generations. My grandfather and father allowed the Jones' to use this field until a time came for Morgan's farm to expand. Except now the time has come and he won't budge. He's even claiming it as his own. I have the original deeds, Miss Hastings. I can easily prove he's in the wrong. I wouldn't be making all this fuss if it wasn't for the good of the farm and the estate."

"I see – and this is Mr Jones' farm?" Sophie shaded her eyes from the glaring sun and pointed across to a tiny farmhouse that looked like a pin prick in the distance.

"Yes, that's why the borders have become so confused. Our boundaries naturally run next to each other."

Sophie's first thought was to include her father, this was his job and he needed to be part of the discussions. "What do you think, dad?"

"Mm...?" George Hastings had been in a daydream again. Sophie knew straight away he hadn't been concentrating and would not have the vaguest idea what Mr Morgan had said. She didn't wait for a further response and immediately fixed her attention onto the farmer. If the estate was going to thrive, it was vital to appear professional and her dad wasn't helping.

"I think the best thing is to have a word with Mr Jones. If we can solve this quietly it will be best for both sides." She got out a notebook and pencil and began scribbling a note to herself. "We've a lot of things to see to at the moment, I will put the matter on our list and get to it as soon as we can." Flipping the pad closed she smiled at the farmer.

"Thank you very much, Miss Hastings. That's very kind of you. I appreciate you coming down here to see me."

"You're welcome. Is there anything else we can help you with whilst we are here?"

"I've a list as long as my arm, but that will do for today."

Sophie dropped her father back at the manor house. She had no desire to spend the remainder of the day with her mother and she fancied exploring the estate village. She had been pleased with the way their first visit had gone and had said so to her father as they drove home along the country lanes. However, conversation had been limited, with the majority of the talking depending heavily upon Sophie, with only a few grunts and acknowledgements from the passenger beside her.

Middleton high street was bustling with a surprising number of shoppers considering the size of the place. After parking her car and crossing over an ancient bridge, she passed by numerous little shops all situated down one long, winding road. Multi-coloured bunting from a recent festival fluttered from side to side and the scent of fresh coffee floated into Sophie's nose, causing her to search eagerly for a cosy little café, which she found situated across the road. She smiled at the sight, knowing a sanctuary was not far away.

Transfixed by the thought of something sweet and warm, Sophie headed cautiously across the road towards the little café. Seconds before her feet reached the doorway, something caught her eye, making her change direction.

A sign on the building a few shops down had been the cause of her distraction. A little bell tingled above the door and a friendly lady behind a desk lifted her head as Sophie entered.

"Hello. Can I help you?"

"Erm… I don't know actually." Sophie looked back towards the door where the little bell was still jiggling from side to side.

"What is it you are looking for?" The lady, whose overly conditioned fringe bounced in a straight line across her forehead, smiled patiently.

"The sign says you are a recruitment agency."

"That's right."

"I might be looking for a job," she chose her words wisely, not convinced it was the right thing to do. "Do you only place people locally?"

"Oh no," the lady corrected her. "I place people all over the country."

"I wasn't expecting to find anything like this in such a tiny village."

"A lot of people are surprised. I moved from London five years ago and set up business here. I have a lot of credible contacts. So," she smiled again. "How can I help you?"

An image of her father flashed before her eyes. She wasn't letting him down by enquiring, it didn't mean she was leaving him alone just yet.

"I've recently finished my degree and I'm looking to start a career."

"Congratulations. What did you study?"

"Land management."

"Okay," the lady leapt into action, tapping away on her keyboard. "Do you have a specialism?"

"Not really."

"That's fine."

Sophie stood there, gnawing her bottom lip and keeping a watchful eye on the window. If her mother saw her, she didn't like to think what might happen.

The lady scanned the computer screen in front of her. "What location are you thinking about?"

"Anywhere," Sophie spurted out a little too keenly and immediately felt guilty.

The lady laughed. "Most of our young folks want to escape Middleton, not much happening around these parts to keep them. Have you a CV?"

"I have been working on one."

"Excellent. If you could write down your details here," the lady passed across a form fastened onto a clipboard. "Then I can create a new profile for you."

Sophie sat down in front of the desk and began filling out her details. The lady looked over her shoulder as she was writing. "Well then Sophie, email me your CV as soon as you can and I will begin sending your profile to potential employers." She handed over her business card. "My name is Marie."

"Thanks." Sophie took the card and handed back the clipboard. "I'll be in touch."

Sophie emerged out of the agency to find she had momentarily lost her bearings. Which way was the café, she never did have a good sense of direction? The midday summer sun was so bright it forced Sophie to shield her eyes as she looked up and down the high street. Taking a step backwards into the shade, a sudden shout and crash made her spin sharply round.

"Oh, my goodness! I'm so sorry... are you okay?" Not waiting for an answer, Sophie hurried after a pile of green granny smiths rolling down the sloped street. Scooping them up in her arms, she collected them all and walked back to the scene of the accident, where a young man was picking himself up off the floor and dusting down his trousers.

"I'm ever so sorry," she said again apologetically. "Are you alright?"

"Only injured pride," he smiled a little embarrassed and pointed to one of four crates now scattered all over the pavement. "You can put those apples back in the wooden crate."

Sophie dropped the apples carefully inside the crate, her own embarrassment causing her to explain further. "I didn't see you; the sun was too bright."

"I kind of figured that," the young man chuckled and bent down to retrieve some escaped carrots. "I couldn't see you very well either, my dad tells me off all the time for carrying too many crates in one go, he says it obstructs my view, I guess he has a point... but don't tell him I said that," his bright blue eyes lit up in amusement.

Sophie watched him pile the crates on top of each other again, all four together... he clearly hadn't learnt his lesson.

"Don't worry," the young man added as he saw Sophie looking concerned. "Just be glad it wasn't the eggs." He grinned and heaved the boxes into his arms, which were piled so high Sophie couldn't see his face until he walked past her.

"It was nice bumping into you," he called making his way down the high street.

6

Georgiana

Outside a new day dawned. Bright rays of sunlight had begun to cast themselves across the front lawn, causing droplets of dew to sparkle like scattered jewels. A multitude of sparrows sang morning songs and their notes danced melodiously along the cool gentle breeze into the ears of any one listening.

Whilst the morning hinted at new life and restored hope, inside Denholm Park Georgiana was finding it much more difficult to generate a similar feeling of renewed freshness and optimism. Puffing out an elongated sigh through her lips, the girl gazed out of the bedroom window, resting a hand upon her chin. Yesterday she had endured the worst chastisement in her memory.

Lady Davenport had shouted and scolded and even shaken in her anger. At the peak of her wrath she promised to disown her daughter several times and cast her out of the family for good. Even in her more restrained moments, she threatened to personally escort Thomas back to Denholm and force Georgiana to accept his proposal. Her mother lectured about the value of good family connections and the importance of honouring parental decisions at all times. She reminded her daughter that under no circumstances did she ever get to have an opinion, make her own decisions or believe she knew better than her elders… because she didn't and never would.

Lord Davenport had stood there mutely. It was not unusual for his anger to turn into a deep silence. In fact, his looming and intimidating figure complemented his wife's quick tongue perfectly. In the midst of her father's terrifying presence and her mother's cutting remarks, Georgiana lowered her eyes to the ground, her spirit greatly wounded and waited for it all to end.

Finally, and unexpectedly, her father's voice boomed out, "Go to your room."

Georgiana now sat motionless. She had cried all night, in between moments of restless sleep and had no tears left to give. When she had slept, her dreams had been filled with Edward. In desperation he raced towards her, urged on by his sister's wretched face. She screamed and he ran faster. When he had nearly reached her, their hands almost touching, a cruel and overwhelming darkness swept over him... leaving Georgiana instantly alone.

After her fourth nightmare she awoke in a sweat. Chest rising quickly in panic, she shot out of bed and thrust open the shutters, heaving up the sash to gasp frantically at the cool air flowing into her face. There she had stayed by the window, grieving for Edward and watching the sun rise, heralding the start of a brand-new day.

The sound of a maid scurrying along the landing snapped Georgiana out of her reverie. She looked out of the window again and a sudden desire to be outside surfaced out of her suffering.

Georgiana's feet pattered across the cold wooden floorboards and she opened the door with a creak. Flashing her eyes up and down the landing she could see the coast was clear. Re-entering the room, she hastily changed out of her long cream nightgown, dressing in a blue pinstriped cotton dress and securing her hair in a neat plait which she coiled neatly into a bun, allowing two curly ringlets to hang lose at either side.

The bird's morning song met Georgiana's ears as she stood on the front door step. Taking a deep breath, she shut her eyes and allowed the gentle breeze to revive her spirit and soothe her tear-stained face. The loneliness that had descended upon her in the early hours began to lift and she lightly ran down the remaining steps, heading instinctively towards the river that lay besides Denholm Park in the surrounding woodland.

The river held many happy memories for Georgiana. Over the years it had become a sanctuary away from her parents, hidden beneath the tall oak trees. It was here Edward had taught her how to swim. They would often come to the river to paddle and bathe when

Georgiana's governess gave time off from her studies. It symbolised a place of freedom. No parental supervision, no need for social politeness… just she and Edward. Emma never came with them. She had no desire for childish pastimes and would stay inside to practise the pianoforte or focus on whichever pursuit needed the most correction.

Georgiana reached the bridge that had been built over the water many years ago. It connected the only road running through the woods, not many people used it and only occasionally would a carriage be seen passing through. The river was flowing fast today and was particularly deep in this part of the woods. She stood in the middle of the bridge, watching the current surge along and allowing her mind to be caught up in memories, both good and bad. It wasn't long before her thoughts became trapped by one specific recollection… the day Emma had betrayed their confidence.

From the first time Georgiana had returned to the house wet from head to foot after her first swimming lesson, Emma had threatened to tell their mother. Both girls knew Lady Davenport would not approve of such an activity, even though her youngest daughter was only eight years old at the time, it was not a proper pastime for emerging young ladies of society. Edward spoke to Emma and made her promise not to inform their mother, it was a harmless occupation and Georgiana deserved to have some enjoyment in her life. For whatever reason, Emma agreed to keep her mouth shut.

Four years passed and Emma kept her promise. However, as Georgiana grew in knowledge and her accomplishments began to outshine the elder girl's efforts, jealousy began to take hold. Emma's secrecy had ended the day Georgiana successfully completed a piece of music before she did. In a rage full of pent up frustration, the older sister marched straight to their mother and told all.

From that day Georgiana was forbidden to ever set foot in the river again. Even Edward was scolded for leading his sister astray, after all he should know better. Lady Davenport repeatedly lectured her two children, whilst Emma stood smugly in the corner, on how swimming was not a genteel pastime for young ladies and, if anyone caught Georgiana, shame and disgrace would come upon the whole family.

Georgiana leant on the bridge with her chin resting on her hands. She wondered how Edward's journey to Portsmouth was going and if he missed her as much as she missed him. The sound of the whistling birds was momentarily blocked out of her hearing as her feelings intensified. A tear trickled down her face. All she could think about was Edward and her loneliness descended again.

A noise broke into her thoughts. She screwed up her eyes and shook her head, struggling to bring her focus back to reality. A swirl of noises caused her to whirl round in panic - horses' hooves - a chaise – the sound of a man shouting - but it was too late for her to react. Letting out a scream, she backed forcefully into the bridge's deteriorating wooden posts, which cracked and gave way underneath her weight. In desperation, Georgiana flung her arms wildly about, frantically searching for safety as the bridge fell further away from her. Before she knew it, her back smacked into water and down she sank, deep into the river.

A hand reached out in front of Georgiana as she scrambled up the river bank. She gratefully grasped it and was pulled onto solid ground. Plucking a piece of green weed out of her hair, she slowly raised herself to standing and squeezed the water out of her blue pinstriped dress.

"Good gracious! Are you all right?" A gentleman, dressed in a dark green tail coat and top hat looked at her full of concern.

"I'm fine, thank you sir," she said thumbing the plait now tumbling over her shoulders.

"You must get home without delay," said the gentleman. "You are wet through. Can I offer you a ride home?" He gestured to the carriage where four horses stood obediently waiting.

"I am not far away from home, I'm happy to walk," she said shivering.

The gentleman looked agitated. "I cannot leave you in this state. Please, allow me to escort you home?"

"Don't worry sir, you need not feel obliged."

"I insist."

Georgiana saw she wouldn't be able to shake the gentleman away very easily. But if he returned with her to Denholm Park the consequences would be severe. Out with an unknown gentleman, without a chaperone, swimming in the river, leaving her bedroom without permission…her sins were stacking up. With her mind racing, she stood with chattering teeth, casting her eyes down the lane leading towards home.

"Is everything all right?" asked the gentleman watching Georgiana shudder before him in the silence.

"Y-yes… yes," she said failing to control her shaking body.

"Come, we must start moving," he cupped his arm around her back. "Which way is home?"

Georgiana could think of no polite reason to leave the man behind. With no time to hesitate, she marched on with the hope he could be left behind at the gate and his existence never known.

"I am ever so sorry," said the gentleman as they quickly strode through the woodland together. "The coachman didn't see you until it was too late."

"Do not worry, sir. I should have been more observant and moved out of your way. I didn't expect a carriage so early in the morning. It is normally a very quiet road."

"We were trying a short cut, having travelled through the night we were desirous of reaching our destination without further delay."

He paused suddenly with alarm. "Please forgive me, I haven't introduced myself. What must you think of me?"

"I think formal introductions aren't necessary under such a circumstance," said Georgiana instantly putting him at ease and he smiled gratefully; thankful he hadn't brought offence.

"It is very kind of you to excuse such a lack of courtesy. Please allow me to introduce myself now," he stopped Georgiana in her stride to make his introduction. "My name is Mr Kirkby," he tilted his head quickly before rushing Georgiana briskly through the wood once more.

"It's a pleasure to meet you, sir. I don't think I thanked you for helping me. I am very much in your debt."

"I don't think you needed much assistance, you mostly helped yourself. You would have been fine without me. How did you learn to swim so well?"

"My brother taught me. I haven't been in the water for a very long time because my mother no longer allows it, although apparently one does not forget."

"It is a skill for life, I believe." Kirkby glanced at his companion. "May I enquire after your name?"

"I beg your pardon, I am Miss Davenport," she said with another shudder, the morning breeze which had revived her earlier now felt excessively chilly.

"Here, wear this…" Kirkby stopped again and pulled off his tail coat. He handed it to Georgiana.

"Oh, I cannot take this. I will get it soaking wet," cried Georgiana in alarm.

"Please, it's the least I can do. After all it was my carriage which forced you into the river." The gentleman was insistent and she took it gladly.

As they got closer to the house Georgiana's conversation waned. The corner of Denholm Park could be seen through the gaps in the trees. Anyone looking through an upper floor window could easily see them progressing towards the tall brick wall surrounding the property.

"What's the matter?" asked Kirkby noticing his companion's sudden change in liveliness.

"I… I think it might be best if we part here. This is the entrance," she nodded down the lane and handed back his coat before he had a chance to argue. "Sorry it's a little damp."

"I have a spare, do not worry."

Kirkby unwillingly stepped away, but after hesitating, he came straight back. "Are you sure you will suffer no ill effects? I can escort you to your front door."

Georgiana replied that she would be fine.

"In that case, it has been a pleasure to meet you, Miss Davenport." Kirkby tipped his hat and followed the path back to his coachman and horses.

Georgiana hurried down the drive, not daring to look up in case she was being watched. Dripping continuously, she slipped in through the front door. A stern stiff voice called her from the morning room and the colour instantly drained from her face. She had been caught. Direct obedience was now of the essence.

Terrified, Georgiana entered the room. Her mother was facing the sash window so her back was turned toward her daughter as she entered.

"Please tell me," Lady Davenport began with a forced calmness. "You have not been outside in your current appearance."

There was no point lying. She had clearly been seen running down the drive, the morning room they were currently in looked directly onto the front lawn. No grand excuses could save her now.

Lady Davenport turned, her narrow eyes first examined the grass stained dress, then they fixed upon the drips which were forming puddles on the floor, next her eyes moved upwards to Georgiana's hair, which flowed messily down her back.

"Tell me no one saw you," she fumed through gritted teeth, her chest heaving up and down, ready to explode at any moment.

Georgiana remained silent, fear making her mute.

"Tell me!" Lady Davenport shrieked, releasing her fury like a wild animal.

"No, mama," she lied; her voice barely audible.

"Speak up, child!"

"I saw no one," she repeated a little louder. It hadn't been her intention to lie, but how could she escape this room alive if she told the truth?

"Are you set on bringing disgrace upon this family?"

"Please mama, it was an accident."

"Do not answer me back," Lady Davenport barked. "You are trying to bring ruin upon us, first by rejecting a prosperous and most advantageous marriage and now this."

"I-I fell."

Georgiana had no Edward to fight her corner now, no one was coming to her rescue.

"Fell... how... where?"

"I fell from the bridge. Please, I beg you to accept my apology."

"Apologies are no good to me, Georgiana. If Mr Compton saw you now, he would be unlikely to repeat last night's sentiment. I take it, since you left your room without permission, you have reconsidered your answer to that young gentleman?"

Georgiana stared down at her sodden shoes. "Y-yes, mama."

A second lie. She stood shaking, not knowing if this was from fear or the chill slowing claiming her body.

"Good," Lady Davenport retreated back to the window, her fury slowly evaporating. "Please note, I will be telling your father about your exploits. However, since it seems no damage has been done, so we will say no more. Do not let it happen again. Be off with you child, I no longer wish to see you."

Georgiana didn't wait for another invitation. She scurried away and rang for Lottie to provide her with some boiling water so she could warm through in the tub.

7

Sophie

"Excuse me. It is not *my* responsibility," Elizabeth Hastings shouted down the phone. "I don't care if you've always had it here. This is *my* land and it's private."

"Nothing will change my mind. Good day, sir," without waiting for a reply, Elizabeth hung up.

"Liberties, Sophie," she huffed when she saw her daughter coming into the room and closing the lounge door behind her. "That's what I call it - taking liberties. It would be at my cost too, no doubt - the cheek."

"What's the matter?" Sophie asked reluctantly seeing another one of her mother's brawls brewing. She had just arrived back from Middleton and being sucked into a dispute wasn't on her list of things to do that afternoon.

"The vicar wants the village fete to be held here, on *my* grounds," she lifted her nose snootily into the air as if it was some great infringement on her rights.

If it wasn't for the survival of the estate, Sophie would have agreed instantly, not being in the mood to provoke her hot-headed mother. But how could Elizabeth not see a simple fete could go a long way in helping to heal the wounds of an injured community and restore a relationship of trust that was badly needed? The difficulty for Sophie was voicing her objections without openly accusing her mother of being wrong. Subtlety was key if she was to get out of this unscathed.

"That sounds like a lovely idea," Sophie's voice was bright and airy, despite the tension creeping up inside. She didn't dare make eye contact and casually grabbed the nearest magazine.

"A lovely idea?" Elizabeth recoiled. "Really Sophie, don't be ridiculous."

"I think it would be good for us to meet the community. There is a lot of anger at the estate's lack of involvement over the years. Great Uncle Bertie didn't exactly please the people."

"That's not my fault. He probably had the right idea, kept himself away from those trying to take advantage."

"The vicar isn't taking advantage. It's only respectful to keep traditions going, they've probably always held it here. Middleton Manor is the centre of the estate, it's only natural the community will be drawn here every so often."

"Well, *I* have never held a village fete here and *I* never will. You give in to one expectation and you have to give in to them all."

"You wouldn't have to do anything, just be the host."

"And pay for it all."

"That's your assumption, no one said you would have to pay for anything."

"It's not going to happen." Elizabeth folded her arms obstinately.

"I think you need to consider it." As much as Sophie tried to be sensitive and avoid all aggression, her words spoke loudly of her opposition.

"What do you know about it?" her mother snapped.

"You did hand pick my degree ready for such a time as this, if you remember... land management with a specific focus on country estates."

This silenced Elizabeth.

"A good relationship with the community is vital if this estate is going to flourish. I don't think you understand."

"*I* don't understand? I'm not stupid, Sophie. You might have a bit of cream-coloured paper in your hand, but it doesn't mean you know everything about managing an estate. I know all about it thank you very much and it's not going to happen. This is the end of our conversation. You can go and make yourself useful somewhere else now." Her hand fluttered in Sophie's direction to shoo her away.

"The green room needs a good clean, I need an extra guest room now you are home– go make yourself useful."

Sophie's nostrils flared, had she really believed in getting away unscathed… what was she thinking? There wasn't a time in her memory when a conversation with this woman hadn't led into an argument.

"Fine," Sophie stood up to leave. "What I don't understand is why you haven't summoned Dylan down to help too. You did send him off to study heritage and restoration six years ago, didn't you? You've lined us all up for your grand master plan and now you're not even using our expertise, we're not good enough for you."

Sophie flicked her wavy chestnut hair out of her face as she moved towards the exit. "I should have stood my ground and studied what *I* wanted," she mumbled under her breath.

"I beg your pardon?" protested Elizabeth only catching half the sentence.

"I should have studied what I wanted, at least then it wouldn't have been a waste of time," Sophie shouted… if her mother wanted a fight then she was going to get one.

"And educational psychology is going to do me a lot of good."

"It's not supposed to help *you*, it's supposed to help the children."

"Enough, Sophie. How dare you speak to me like that?"

"Why, is the truth offensive to you now?"

"Leave this room immediately, I do not wish to see you."

Elizabeth twisted herself away from her daughter and Sophie left the room with anger raging through her. She was angry partly with herself, having promised the last time the subject was brought up not to mention it again. It was too painful.

For three years she had suffered through mind-numbingly boring lectures about economic trends, environmental policies and property markets. She had completed six months of work experience consulting with difficult clients, devising land schemes for farmers and preserving conservation areas, all for a job she couldn't care less about. Yes, she understood about transferable skills, that what she had learnt could help her with any career. But what good was this to her when Elizabeth had already decided she would be the assistant estate manager for the family's inherited estate?

The engine of the azure blue Corsa revved into action. Declining the invitation to clean the green room, Sophie zoomed down the drive pushing the little car to the max, carrying years of built up resentment with her. She hurtled down the country lanes accelerating hard and braking abruptly, until a loud horn brought her swiftly back to reality. Instinctively, she jerked the wheel away from the moving obstacle, pulled onto the side and yanked up the handbrake. Her heart was beating rapidly as she rushed out of the car.

"Gosh Soph... you can't drive like that in the countryside, it's not safe."

Rupert emerged out of the apple red Lamborghini which had forced Sophie off the road. Immediately striding across to the little blue car, he fiddled with the swinging wing mirror hanging on by a thread.

"I'm so sorry... I didn't see you." She looked across to the built-up hedges which had obscured her vision and the hammering in her chest eased a little. "I know it's no excuse, but I've just had a run in with mum and..."

Rupert held up a hand, preventing his friend from giving further explanation. "Say no more, Soph. You know I understand completely, however next time, may I suggest you purchase a stress ball instead of taking your problems out on innocent country drivers. What would we do without you if something happened?"

"An awful lot according to a certain person."

Sophie flopped against her car and thrust both hands inside her jacket pockets. Living with Elizabeth had never been easy, but she had hoped living in a house the size of the manor might have given a better chance of avoiding her... unfortunately, so far this theory hadn't become reality.

"What a load of rubbish, Soph. Why are you listening to her?" Rupert frowned as a ringlet of hair flopped onto his face.

"The same reason as always, I suppose."

The wing mirror clanked against the car as a strong gust of wind blew against it.

"Follow me back to my house," said Rupert fingering the mirror again. "I'll have this fixed in no time."

"I'm sure I can find a local garage; I wouldn't want to bother you."

Reaching into her pocket she pulled out her mobile and began searching for mechanics, but almost immediately Rupert pushed the phone away.

"No - I insist, and afterwards I'll come back to help you with some jobs at the manor, I'm sure there's a lot to do. What are you working on this afternoon?"

"I've been summoned to the green room," she sighed. "I suppose I'd better do what I'm told, I wouldn't hear the end of it if I didn't."

Weakening to her mother's demand already, it was not a good start and she kicked a pebble across the lane with her foot.

"The frustrating thing is I'm better off helping dad. I'm worried about him, he's not himself." The sun shone into her eyes causing them to squint as she looked enquiringly towards Rupert, willing him to say something that might settle her anxiety.

"He's only adjusting," said Rupert who had wandered over to his pristine sports car and was licking a finger to wipe off a mark he had spied.

"They moved four months ago; shouldn't he have adjusted by now?"

"Maybe." Her friend shrugged and hopped into his car without much more thought and stuck his head through the open window. "Follow me," he called roaring the engine.

The wing mirror was easily fixed and it wasn't long before the two friends had made their way back to the manor. Carrying a woven basket, Elizabeth emerged from the panelled front door as the two cars pulled up on the driveway.

"Hello Rupert, what a lovely surprise."

The smile on her mother's face irritated Sophie as she watched the older lady receive a kiss on the cheek from Rupert. It was all a cover; this amiable person was unrecognisable to her.

"It's always a pleasure Mrs Hastings," crooned Rupert spying the basket. "You look busy."

"I'm going to cut some wild flowers before the gardener takes them all away. I'm at least attempting to brighten up the place, even if no one else is bothered."

Elizabeth didn't look at her daughter, but Sophie knew this comment was meant for her ears and she tutted under her breath.

Rupert subtly tapped Sophie on the arm to restrain her from responding to this cutting remark.

"Sounds like a pleasant activity, I hope you enjoy yourself." He grinned charmingly as Elizabeth clopped away in her designer heels.

"Typical," spat out Sophie as they headed inside. "Absolutely typical. Here's dad up to his head in a failing estate and there's my mother going to pick wild flowers, it's unbelievable."

Rupert observed his friend thoughtfully. It may have been a few years since they had spent a significant amount of time together, but he hadn't missed the cue: he could see today's altercation had really ruffled her. It was only in times of great distress that Sophie ever referred to Elizabeth as her *mother*. "Soph, you are too hard on her."

"You don't need to suck up now, she can't hear you Rupert."

He lifted both hands in innocence. "Don't take it out on me."

"She's not your mother, you don't need to convince her to like you."

"Don't be daft, she likes you."

Sophie cast him a reproachful look and they climbed the grand staircase in silence.

Suddenly Rupert started dancing the waltz around her, elegantly moving up and down the steps and miraculously not falling down them. "Ahh, don't you just want to whoosh down the stairs in a grand ball dress like in the olden days."

"It's not really crossed my mind and to be honest, I'm a bit worried it's entered yours."

Rupert laughed. "I'm trying to lighten the mood, Soph. Come on, you know your mother means well, you just misunderstand her sometimes."

"Sometimes…try all the time."

She poked her head into the first room along the balconied landing. "Which one do you think is the green room?"

"The one that's green presumably," smirked Rupert, but one glance from his friend told him she didn't appreciate the humour and he said no more as they continued wandering along peering inside the vacant rooms.

Sophie pushed the fourth door, bouncing backwards and unsettling the dust as it jammed half-way open. Peeking through the gap, cardboard boxes filled the floor all the way to the door. "This must be it… the walls are green."

After a bit of bashing Sophie managed to make the gap wide enough for her slim figure to slip through. Rupert followed and found his friend standing with a mouth fully ajar, staring at the appalling state of the room. The majority of cardboard boxes were covered in dust sheets, whilst the other half were sodden and damp; the painted frescos on the wall were either peeling paint or had mould creeping up them; the curtains, which were hanging onto the wall for dear life, were stained a murky brown colour; and the once beautifully crafted fireplace was hidden beneath layers of dirt that had built up over many years of neglect.

"Are you sure the walls are green?" Rupert ran a finger over the discoloured wallpaper, leaving the tip of his finger black with dirt.

Sophie decisively rolled up her sleeves. "Let's clear the boxes first… I'm not even going to touch the fireplace without talking to Dylan, I presume it can be restored. We'll need to get someone out to look at the damp, it's across the whole house."

She fought her way through the boxes and examined the mantlepiece. "It's cast iron, I think, and the frescos… I don't even know if they can be saved."

"Or…" began Rupert looking reluctantly at the boxes all around him. "We could grab a lemonade," he lifted a cardboard flap between his thumb and finger and wrinkled his nose in displeasure.

"Rupert, how can you suggest such a thing when we haven't started yet?"

"It's hot today and we want to start well hydrated."

Sophie rolled her eyes and continued scrutinising the room, purposefully ignoring his comment - he wasn't going to wriggle out of work that easily.

"Let's start here," she said busying herself by moving some boxes around. "Anything that looks half decent we'll try and restore, everything else can be thrown out."

Rupert groaned like a teenage boy.

"You said you wanted to help," said Sophie.

"I didn't think it was this bad."

"What did you expect? Great Uncle Bertie lived in one room for the last ten years of his life, carers came in with his meals and the rest of the house was left."

"He could have paid for a cleaner."

"With what money? He owned an estate hardly breaking even!" Sophie eyed Rupert, she wasn't messing around, either he helped wholeheartedly or he didn't help at all. "So… are you staying or not?"

Rupert peered begrudgingly at the clutter and found the smallest box he could see. "I'll start with this one," he mumbled.

Sneezing intermittently from the dust they made good progress. Rupert wiped his sweaty brow, stretched and rested both hands on his lower back. "I'll make a trip to the charity shop, Soph...Soph?"

Realising his words had fallen on deaf ears, he skipped over two cardboard boxes and tapped her on the shoulder. "Hello, Soph?"

Sophie swung round. "Oh, I'm sorry Rupert, what did you say?" She was surrounded by open boxes and an assortment of old musty books were piled on her lap.

"I said I'm going to the charity shop."

"What...now? We've only been working for half an hour."

"I've got a load waiting to go...see."

Sophie looked across at the pathetic pile he was pointing to, which consisted of a couple of old elaborately decorated biscuit tins, three scratched records, an unpolished silver frame and not much else.

"Oh Rupert, just go if you don't want to help."

"Soph, it's not that I don't want to help..." he bent down and tucked his friend's loosened strands of messy hair behind an ear. "I really want to help - I do, it's just... I forgot about an errand I need to do in the village."

Sophie knew he was lying. This is what Rupert always did when he tried to weasel his way out of something. The 'hair-tuck charm' is what she called it. The first few times he had performed the act Sophie had fallen for it... until she grew wise to the trick.

"I'll take these as well, shall I?" he tried to grab the bundle of books sitting in her lap.

"No!" Sophie tightened her grip around them and looked up to see Rupert looking at her strangely. "Erm, actually..." she loosened her grasp. "I think I'll keep these."

"Relax Soph, I was only asking." Rupert backed off and walked toward his heap of objects, trying to find a clean box to place them in. "What are they anyway?"

"It looks like a collection of diaries."

"Don't just hoard rubbish, Soph."

"Says the king of clearing out," she nodded accusingly at his tiny charity shop pile. "I just want to read them, they look interesting."

"Fine," he dusted his hands down and skipped across the cardboard boxes near the door. "I'll see you later."

"Bye Rupert," she said distractedly as her eyes focused straight back to on diary open on her knee.

Mama is heartless sometimes. I know I shouldn't be writing this and I know I should be respectful to her, but… sometimes I think she forgets I'm a person and not just a pawn in a game where I always seem to lose.

Sophie blinked and reread the words before her. These words could have been written by herself… about her own mother. The handwriting on the page was tall and curly, each letter neatly joined to the next. She scanned down to the end of the entry… Georgiana Davenport - what a pretty name. She looked up to the date… 1819. Sophie gently touched the stained brown paper, amazed by the notion of holding something so old in her hands.

Now Edward has gone away, who else can I vent my misery to but the empty pages of this book? He had barely left the grounds before Thomas came with his proposal - Mama had undeniably planned it all, it was obvious.

I had to decline it. I had no other choice. If I'd said yes, I would have regretted it forever. Of course Mama did not understand, not that I explained my position to her, but she wouldn't have listened, on no occasion has she before, so why should she now? My opinion doesn't matter, that's what I've learned, I have no significance or value at all…

Sophie glanced into the box beside her and then at the books laid out on the floor. There was an abundance of them, all discoloured and blemished with age. Flicking through one by one, Sophie discovered they were all diaries from the same girl.

A sudden noise caused her to jump as Rupert came trundling back into the dust-filled room. "Forgot my box," he explained grinning at her. "Do you want that lemonade now?"

"I thought you were running an errand in town?"

"I am, but I can bring you a lemonade on my way back - Nothing is too much for you Soph."

"Stop being so charming, Rupert. You forget I know all your hidden secrets."

"I've got nothing to hide, Soph, what you see is what you get." He paused, watching his friend sitting cross-legged on the floor, a giant black smudge streaked right across her cheek. "Why don't you come with me, escape from the madness?"

"I'm busy Rupert and so were you before your allergy to hard work made an appearance."

"How rude!" Rupert cried in mock offence. "I'll show you hard work, Sophie Hastings."

"Here's your next job then." She shoved a heavy cardboard box along the floor in his direction, knowing full well he wouldn't take up the offer.

"No, that's not what I meant."

"What did you mean then?" Sophie was interested to hear his explanation; Rupert Donaldson wouldn't know hard work if it hit him in the face.

"Meet me at the polo club on Friday," he said with a cunning look.

"Why?" Sophie narrowed her eyes: he was up to something.

"Don't worry, you'll find out."

"Okay," she said slowly intrigued by his secrecy. "Text me the directions and I will."

"Great. Prepare yourself to be amazed, Soph." He flashed his teeth in a gleaming grin again and left the room, tucking the box for the charity shop, which he had forgotten the first time, under his arm.

Sophie laughed quietly to herself, there was a strange comfort in her friend's lack of stickability.

Carefully, Sophie lifted a few more diaries out of the box and skimmed through them. Davenport? She wondered if her dad knew anything about the name. It was strange to have a box full of diaries in the house belonging to an unfamiliar family, since the manor had been owned by the Middleton family for generations.

One by one she gathered all but one of the diaries into a box and tucked them safely away under the bed in her own room. Holding one precious book in her hand, Sophie went in search of her father. Eventually she found him tucked away in the estate office, hidden out of sight.

"There you are dad, I'm glad I found you. Does the name...?"

The second she laid an eye on him it was obvious something was wrong. George had been completely oblivious of his daughter's entrance and was sat gazing out into open space, caught in a trance-like state.

"What's wrong... Dad?" Sophie crouched low to be level with his face.

"Phone call after phone call," he started quietly, still staring intensely ahead. "That's all I've had today. Complaints about one thing and demands for another. I don't want this, Sophie," he turned to face her. "I agreed to the inheritance because I assumed the estate had been looked after, that it would manage itself, pay for itself even."

Sophie put the diary to one side and took hold of his shaking hand, squeezing it tightly, for her own reassurance as well as his. "I know it looks bad now, but if we start chipping away at it, then piece by piece we'll get it organised and working efficiently again."

George didn't answer, giving Sophie chance to observe how red and drawn his eyes really looked.

"You aren't sleeping, are you?"

"Not much." This time he didn't try to deny it, openly admitting defeat.

"You should tell mum."

She heard the words as they came out of her mouth, even if he did speak to her it wouldn't make a difference. So, when George laughed heartily, as if his daughter had said some kind of joke, she wasn't surprised.

"This is *your* mother you are talking about," he said.

"She is human sometimes, rarely I know, but it does happen."

Momentarily she tried to think of an example, some kind of compassionate act stored in her memory bank, to back up her argument, but there wasn't any.

"She's much too busy sending off for swatches to be concerned about me."

"But this is about your health."

"I can't take the manor away from her, she's been waiting a long time for this. No," he said making an inward decision. "There's only one person who can take it away and that's herself."

"What do you mean?"

"It doesn't matter, pumpkin," he tried to stand up and immediately went dizzy.

"Are you okay?" Sophie rushed to steady him.

"Just a little light-headed," he fumbled to find the chair, holding a hand to his head.

Sophie watched him with worry. "You should go and rest, I'll man the phones for a while. There's a call I need to make anyway."

"Are you sure?" George hesitated.

"Of course. Just make sure you rest out of mum's sight."

"Don't worry, I will."

Sophie watched him leave and for a second she fought back a tickling sensation in her nose. The signs were clear and she feared her concern was now based on something concrete.

Pulling herself together, Sophie began rummaging around the drawers for the phonebook. Eventually she found it and scanned through the pages until she found the number she wanted.

"Hello?" came a voice at the end of the line.

"Ah, hello there. My name is Sophie Hastings, I'm the daughter of Elizabeth and George up at the manor."

79

"Oh." The man didn't sound very thrilled to be talking with her, however Sophie continued anyway.

"I'm ringing because I believe my mother…"

"Was rude, indignant and selfish?"

"Erm, well…yes," Sophie agreed, he'd summed her up beautifully. "She probably was all those things, Reverend James. However, I'd like to make arrangements for the village fete, if I may?"

"I was told it wouldn't happen," he said coldly.

"I know, but I think it's an amazing opportunity to introduce ourselves to the community and I'm sure the fete is wrapped up in our heritage."

"It's been held at the manor for one hundred and two years, Miss Hastings, even when your late great uncle was Lord of the Manor."

Sophie flinched, sensing how much Elizabeth had offended this man. "I understand, Reverend James. I will talk to my mother into it, or bear the consequences, whichever one comes first. I promise you; the village fete will be held at Middleton Manor this year. Can you email the office with further information when you have it?"

"I don't believe your office has an email address, Miss Hastings," the reverend said correcting her.

"Oh, really?" Sophie tried to sound positive, was the estate really that archaic? "In that case, could you ring the office and if no one answers, leave a message on the answer phone. I will be personally responsible the fete will take place."

"Very well," the reverend still sounded a little put out. "I will be in touch, Miss Hastings." He hung up the phone.

Sophie stared out of the small window looking over an unkempt lawn. What she had done would feel like treason in the eyes of her mother and now she must wait for the impact.

8

Georgiana

"Georgiana, come look… it's still here." Annabelle Hastings dragged her friend across the road, dodging a horse and cart clopping its way over the dusty ground. "Isn't it beautiful," she said gazing dreamily through a shop window.

The two friends had taken advantage of the dry weather and walked into Middleton village together. It was a prosperous little centre and gave satisfaction to the girls on seeing what new wares the shopkeepers had procured since their last visit.

"The colour will suit you," Georgiana eyed the dark green material of the bonnet which would undoubtedly contrast perfectly with Annabelle's buttery yellow hair. "Are you allowed to buy it, you only bought silk for a dress last week?"

"Papa would not be pleased; he says I have too many bonnets." Annabelle pulled a face. It was true her father was strict with her allowances and he did not take kindly to frivolous spending.

Georgiana laughed as she watched her friend's nose pressed up against the glass. "That's because you *do* have too many bonnets."

"I don't have one like this."

"Dreaming over bonnets again Annabelle, your father would not approve of your reckless spending." The girls turned to see Thomas Compton sauntering up behind them.

Georgiana reddened. It was the first time she had seen her friend since the proposal. A guilty feeling struck her stomach as she loitered behind Annabelle who was delightedly showing Thomas the bonnet through the shop window.

"Green s-suits you. You should buy it," Thomas told Annabelle with only a hint of his stutter making an appearance.

"Don't tempt me," cried Annabelle, her face lit up in pleasure.

Georgiana knew her friend well, it would not take much more persuading before a new bonnet would be settled firmly on top of her fair head.

"I shall buy it for you, your father would not disapprove of a gift."

"Should I, Georgiana?" Annabelle turned to her friend with eager eyes.

"You are never one to turn down a gift." Georgiana smiled at Annabelle's animated face and she entered the shop excitedly with Thomas in tow.

Being left outside gave Georgiana ample time to compose her thoughts. It seemed Thomas was ignoring the event from the day before and Annabelle was still living in ignorance. Maybe the whole event would blow over without any further mention of the subject?

"Miss Davenport?"

"Yes?" Georgiana pulled her eyes away from the silk gloves she had been pretending to admire whilst a thousand thoughts raced through her mind. She was surprised to see Kirkby standing beside her and dipped a knee politely. "Mr Kirkby, I did not expect to see you again."

"I am visiting my cousin; he lives five miles away from Middleton. Actually, I believe you know him… his name is Sir Gillingham."

This explained the shortcut over the river since the Gillingham's residence lay not far beyond the woodland. He stepped forward expectantly waiting for an answer.

"Yes, Sir Gillingham is an old family friend," replied Georgiana. "I did not know you were cousins, are you staying in the neighbourhood long?"

"A few weeks probably," he paused as if contemplating his next words. "I am very glad I bumped into you, Miss Davenport, I … I wanted to check on your wellbeing."

"I am fine, thank you," she smiled kindly as she saw the colour in his cheeks brighten a little.

"After falling in the river, I mean… no chills or fevers?" He intensely studied her face, checking for signs of ill health.

"No, none at all."

"Thank goodness." He let out a great breath of air and looked extremely relieved. "I was concerned about you and have regretted not personally handing you over into your parent's care."

This anxiety over her welfare shocked Georgiana immensely, not many people of her acquaintance would show such concern for her. "You do not need to be concerned; my parents were not worried about me."

"They weren't?" his eyebrows rose in astonishment.

"At least, they weren't worried about my physical health, they were more troubled about the state of my social condition."

"I see," he seemed to understand. "My mother would have nursed me back to full health."

"Georgiana!"

A new voice brought the conversation instantly to a standstill and Georgiana stiffened to the core.

"Papa," she spun guiltily around to see her father marching purposefully in her direction.

"Who is this?" Lord Davenport pointed his black cane rudely at the stranger violating his rules. It was completely forbidden for his daughter to have any acquaintance not previously vetted by her parents.

Georgiana stepped back and focused on the dusty ground, not daring to lift her head. "Papa, this is Mr Kirkby," she muttered.

Her name was already in disrepute, as she had spent so many months in close proximity to Thomas Compton and yet come away without an engagement. Her father would not welcome more violations of society's unwritten code of politeness and she begged inwardly that the river incident would not come up in conversation.

Lord Davenport nodded towards the gentleman. "I do not believe we have met; how do you know my daughter?"

Panic swept across Georgiana's face and quickly she pulled her eyes up to see Kirkby, seemingly untroubled by her menacing father, open his mouth calmly to answer.

"He is Sir Gillingham's cousin, papa," she squeaked before a single syllable could be produced from her new acquaintance's lips.

Kirkby eyed her with interest, this time causing her own cheeks to turn a shade of pink.

"You know Charles?" Lord Davenport's fierce gaze began to lift, though you could tell his distrust still remained. "I did not realise his cousin was visiting. Georgiana, we have not been to the Gillingham's for several weeks, I do not understand how you have met his cousin before myself?"

"That would be my fault Mr Davenport."

Georgiana's eyes widened in horror; it was crucial her father did not know about how they met.

"It's Lord Davenport," the glare of the elder man returned as his bushy grey eyebrows drew together.

"I beg your pardon, Lord Davenport." Correcting his mistake, Kirkby tilted his head low in apology. "Please accept my sincerest apologies sir, I wanted to come and see you when it happened."

"When what happened?" asked Lord Davenport suspiciously.

Georgiana stood helplessly by her father's side, inwardly begging for Kirkby's voice to become suddenly mute, or for a carriage to lose a wheel and cause some sort of commotion... unfortunately no such events happened.

"The carriage I was riding pushed your daughter into the river," Kirkby's forehead wrinkled in confusion. "Did you not know?"

Lord Davenport looked sternly at Georgiana. "I had heard of the incident, just not who was concerned in the matter." He glanced back towards the gentleman. "My daughter neglected to tell me of your role, Mr Kirkby."

The heat in Georgiana's cheeks heightened and her pink hue changed to a bright tomato red, spreading all the way to her ears. The dusty ground started swirling below her feet and she longed to be anywhere in the world but standing in the middle of Middleton high street with her father fuming by her side.

"Look Georgiana!" Annabelle flowed out of the shop wearing her new purchase with Thomas following in pursuit. However, the threatening figure of Lord Davenport soon stopped the merry newcomers in their tracks. Annabelle curtsied and came no further, loitering self-consciously by the edge of the group.

"G-good day, Lord Davenport," Thomas mumbled formally, quickly wiping the smile off his face.

"Good morning Mr Compton," Lord Davenport eyed his daughter and closed his mouth tightly. He was not willing to disclose any information that might prevent a second proposal. After learning his daughter had been found in a compromising situation with this unknown gentleman, he knew any word spoken out of place could prove disastrous.

"I-I do not believe we have met," said Thomas to the stranger standing next to Lord Davenport.

"I am Sir Gillingham's cousin," responded Kirkby politely tipping his hat.

Annabelle opened her eyes wide in dismay, recollecting the conversation she had had with Georgiana on their way into Middleton that morning about the gentleman she had met by the river. Immediately she understood the devastating consequences that would now befall her friend.

The tension rose as no one spoke until finally Kirkby cleared his throat. "I must be on my way." He shuffled awkwardly. "It was a pleasure to see you again Miss Davenport," he bowed and she blushed once more as he made his exit.

Lord Davenport bellowed for his daughter to follow as he marched hastily away, expecting his command to be instantly obeyed. Georgiana looked longingly towards her friends before trailing swiftly behind him – they could not save her now.

****

"My dear Georgiana," cried Annabelle when she caught a glimpse of her friend later that afternoon. "How are you?" She ran down the lane and grabbed her friend's hands in earnest.

Georgiana smiled as best she could, but her mind was a flutter of emotions. It had not been an easy encounter with Lord and Lady Davenport and a large number of the cruel and uncaring words spoken by her mother still remained fresh in her memory. But in addition to this, there was the sinking feeling of guilt she felt every time she thought of Annabelle, still oblivious to the affair with Thomas the day before.

"Was it very bad?" continued Annabelle full of concern. "I felt so helpless watching you leave with your father; I have worried all afternoon."

"Edward isn't here – therefore presume it was bad."

"Oh, my dear Georgiana," she cried again and took her friend by the arm.

Not desiring sympathy, Georgiana pulled her friend gently along and encouraged a slow stroll down the lane. "Listen…" she began, hoping to avoid reliving the recent rebuke of her parents. "I'm sorry I didn't tell you before…"

"Tell me what?"

"You'll probably find out anyway…"

"Tell me what, Georgiana?"

"I'm sorry if you have heard…" she stopped, planting her feet to the floor.

"What is it?" implored her friend for the third time.

"Thomas proposed yesterday," her eyes were half closed waiting for an attack.

"I know, mama told me," her friend said calmly.

Georgiana opened her eyes and saw her friend smiling affectionately.

"Do not worry, I am not angry."

"But I should have told you this morning."

"Mama shared the news over lunch, she must have spent the morning with your mother."

Georgiana shouldn't have been surprised, news spread fast in Middleton; it always did.

"You must understand, I think they are planning a second proposal. I have told them I will say yes if it happens."

Annabelle squeezed her friends arm tighter. "Do you think he will ask you again?"

"I hope he does not, although I fear he shall. It was the pressure of our parents that made him propose the first time, that pressure isn't going to simply disappear." A long sigh escaped her mouth. "I do not want to marry him, Annabelle, but I cannot reject him again. My life depends upon it. I'm sure mama is close to sending me somewhere far away."

"She wouldn't Georgiana, no matter how much she might threaten."

The girls meandered further down the lane, arm in arm, trapped in their own thoughts until Georgiana suddenly pronounced. "I do miss Edward; he would know what to do."

"Write to him," suggested Annabelle.

"He cannot protect me from Portsmouth, which is the reason why my parents have sent him away. No," she said, resolutely placing her next step with more force. "I must face this myself." She hoped she sounded braver than she felt.

Annabelle rested her head on Georgiana's shoulder as they continued walking aimlessly forward.

"Did your father approve of the bonnet?" asked Georgiana, hoping a change of conversation would make the atmosphere more light-hearted.

"Only just," Annabelle lifted her head. "I must not buy another for a very long time, even if it is a gift." She pouted her lips in thought. "Maybe Samuel could buy one for me on his travels."

Samuel Hastings, Annabelle's older brother, had been sent away on the grand tour by their father. He had only been gone nine months and already his sister had sent many letters asking him to purchase a trinket or two on her behalf. If he were to keep every request, the young man would need an army to help carry it all the way home to Middleton Manor.

"I haven't an Italian one in my collection, I would be the envy of everyone when he returns." She giggled at the thought.

"I didn't realise he was coming home yet?" enquired Georgiana.

Samuel had been a good friend of Edward's and had been a regular visitor to Denholm Park before he had been sent off abroad to better himself among the masters. He was a lot more down to earth than his sister, who was often distracted by pretty objects and silky fabrics. Second to her own brother, his presence was dearly missed at Denholm Park, so the thought of his returning sooner momentarily lifted Georgiana's spirits, knowing as she did that Samuel would do what he could in Edward's absence to protect her.

"Oh no, he's away for at least two years," she said flippantly, not realising it injured her friend's hopes. "He's in Rome at the moment, if I don't ask him now, I'll miss out. Look…" she pointed directly down the lane towards a man on a horse. "Isn't that Mr Kirkby?"

Georgiana froze, pulling Annabelle back with her.

"What's the matter?"

"We should turn back," Georgiana exclaimed in panic. "It will only make matters worse if we meet again," she tried to spin around but her friend kept hold of her arm.

"Your father will not know – he is not here. Besides, if he is staying in the neighbourhood for several weeks you are bound to meet again, he is Sir Gillingham's cousin."

"How awkward it will be… No, I really must turn back." She struggled to release her arm.

"I don't think you have a choice," Annabelle caught her friend as she broke free of her clutch. "He has spotted us." She waved gleefully to the gentleman. "And he is trotting in our direction now."

Her friend was right, there was no possible way they could leave without giving offence and, since Georgiana was trained in the art of politeness, all she could do was wait for the gentleman to greet them and hope she could leave as soon as possible.

"Good afternoon ladies," Kirkby jumped off his horse and lifted his hat in welcome. "I was on my way to pay a visit to Denholm Park, Miss Davenport." He smiled and turned to Annabelle. "I do not believe we were introduced this morning?"

"This is my friend, Miss Hastings from Middleton Manor," Georgiana said trying not to make too much eye contact. Even though her parents weren't present, it didn't stop her imagining the potential consequences of such an unsolicited meeting. The Davenports had eyes everywhere, they would surely find out about this.

"Ah yes, I had the pleasure of meeting your father only an hour ago Miss Hastings, he came to visit my cousin."

The horse pulled on his reins and Kirkby tugged firmly to calm the animal's temper. "I see you are out for an afternoon stroll, so I will not disturb you any further, however before you walk on, may I invite you and your families to Gillingham Hall tomorrow evening for dinner? It was the reason for my coming to visit you. I would be honoured to get to know you all better." He particularly glanced in the direction of Georgiana.

"Thank you, Mr Kirkby," answered Annabelle whilst her friend stood uneasily by her side. "On behalf of our families, we would be delighted, wouldn't we Georgiana?"

"Yes, thank you, it is very kind of you, sir. I will mention it to my father and I am sure we will accept your very kind invitation."

Kirkby climbed back on his horse and swung around. "A good day to you ladies," he tapped his hat with a nod and galloped away down the lane.

"What a handsome gentleman," Annabelle gushed. "With pleasing manners too, you don't always get the two together and he seems to have eyes for you, Georgiana." She dug her friend teasingly in the ribs.

"Do not even jest, Annabelle."

"Though, I don't know how well it would go down with your mother."

"Not very well, I can assure you," Georgiana answered as she watched the small figure ride away into the distance.

9

Sophie

"Hey you!" A large burly gentleman came bustling down the High Street. "You're the new estate manager, aren't you?"

"Actually, it's my father," replied Sophie a little shocked by this man's aggressive posture. She had popped down to the village to run a few errands and hadn't expected a welcoming committee. To be honest, most of the villagers had so far left her alone, presumably because they were either completely ignorant of who she was, or they had grown so embittered towards the family that they just didn't care.

"The hedges need seeing too, fourteen months I've been waiting for them to be cut back; I can barely get my tractor down the lane."

"I'm sorry, Mr...?"

"It's Jones. I'm not impressed, you know," the man said wagging a finger in Sophie's face. "Every week I've sent word for them to be fixed and not a response."

"My parents only arrived four months ago."

"I don't care about that, get something done about it."

"I'll see what I can do."

"No - I want it done today, I'm not going to be fobbed off again."

"I'm afraid I can't promise anything, Mr Jones."

"Today!" yelled the man.

Sophie stepped back as drops of spittle from the angry farmer's mouth landed on her cheek. This man was getting too close for comfort, she had to think quickly. Snippets of lectures replayed in her head, but nothing of any use explained what she should do as she stood isolated on the edge of Middleton high street.

The farmer stood impatiently grinding his teeth. There was nothing for it, the situation needed calming and no one else was going to step in to the rescue. Sophie met his gaze full on – she must follow her instincts.

"Mr Jones," she began. "I will make sure it is done, although I cannot promise it will be done today." She stretched up to her full height to meet his broad, six-foot figure, determined not to be intimidated. "We have a lot of things to organise and improve on the estate and we have to order them in priority."

"Not getting my tractor into my farm is a priority."

"If I remember rightly Mr Jones, you said your tractor was *struggling* to enter your farm, not that it was an impossibility. I understand the frustration, but I'm sure a few extra weeks aren't going to see a dramatic rate of hedge growth."

This wasn't the response Mr Jones had pictured when he came charging over to the defenceless looking young girl. He snorted several times through his nose. Sophie gulped, keeping her eyes locked with his. Did it look like she might be winning?

"Just get it done," he grumbled.

"Of course, Mr Jones, I'm writing it in my notepad." Sophie took out her pad and started writing. At the top of the page, she saw the note she had neatly written at Morgan's farm. The perspiration, that had started minutes after the burly farmer had come trundling along, spread to her temples. She crossed the T and dotted the I. It was now or never.

"Actually… Mr Jones, I'm glad I've bumped into you, we need to have a meeting."

"What about?" he huffed, unrolling an olive-green flat cap from his pocket and flopping it on his square shaped head.

"Only about a small matter that's arisen. I wonder if you are free in the morning?"

"Might be."

"Good… Is ten thirty okay for you?"

"My wife will call me in if I'm in the fields."

"Actually, I wonder if we could meet at Morgan's farm?"

Mr Jones' expression stiffened. "I know what that's about. Don't count on me turning up."

"That's all right Mr Jones, I will pick you up on the way." Her tone was light hearted, pretending it wasn't a big deal, but it was. This was the very first issue she had to tackle alone. If this could be resolved, then perhaps there was a future for the estate. Was it really possible to salvage something from the wreckage and transform her father's future? Her stomach flipped with uncertainty as she realised her hopes hung perilously in the hands of this grumpy old man.

"I'll make sure I'm not home then – I don't need no lift."

Sophie skimmed over her notepad and chewed the pen. "Well, if that's the case I might have a slight problem making your hedges a priority. I do have a lot of more important things to see to first."

The farmer grunted his disapproval. "That's bribery."

"Is it?" said Sophie innocently.

"Fine. I'll see you at Morgan's tomorrow. I'll make my own way there."

"Fantastic." Her mouth turned into a tremendous smile. "It was a pleasure to meet you, Mr Jones."

He snarled and stomped away in his bottle-green wellies.

Arrange meeting with Mr Jones. Tick. Sophie put the lid back on her pen, immensely pleased with herself, and tucked the notepad back into her bag.

The sound of clapping behind her made Sophie twist around and she caught sight of the fruit and veg guy she had bumped into the other day, smacking his hands together in applause.

"Amazing," he exclaimed shaking his head in disbelief. "I've never seen anyone stand up to old Jones like that before, you certainly ruffled his feathers."

"Thank you…I think." She stood awkwardly, her cheeks heating up from the unexpected praise, she hadn't realised anyone else was watching.

"I didn't know you were one of the famous Hastings."

"Guilty, I'm afraid… although, I'm not certain what we're famous for doing."

"All the wrong things," the guy said looking half amused. "The Hastings have a long-standing reputation for doing nothing."

"I'm getting that impression as I trawl through the papers in the office. We've a massive hill to climb if the estate is going to run effectively again - that's if it's even possible. I can't imagine my parents have the money to fund everything that needs restoring and updating."

The young man slouched against a brick wall and rubbed his chin. "You are included in this family business, then?"

"That all depends on who you're talking to, I'm hoping to be passing through. I've just finished my degree and I'm home for the summer until I find a job."

"Ah - you're an academic."

"I'd hardly call land management an academic degree."

"Land management?" he frowned thoughtfully. "And you're planning on leaving?"

"I know," she scrunched her nose. "It does sounds rather odd."

"I'd say. Sounds like the perfect job laid out before you at the manor, lots of things to get your teeth stuck into. What about your father, will he get to grips with the estate in your absence?"

"He should be able to, he was a bank manager for thirty years. If my mother gets her way though, I will be a permanent fixture."

"Is she likely to get her way?"

"Probably, she normally does."

The young man paused, his lips pressed together as if contemplating something before glancing at his watch. "I really must be going," he pushed away from the wall." It was nice seeing you again..." he lingered purposefully to get her name.

"Oh, I'm Sophie."

"Oliver," he held out a hand for her to shake and nodded his head. "Well Sophie, until we meet again."

****

94

"Is your father not with you today, Miss Hastings?"

Sophie stepped out of her little azure blue car at Morgan's farm. "He isn't well, Mr Morgan."

When Sophie had sent her father off to rest, she had meant for a couple of hours, however George Hastings had not resurfaced again, apart from to seek solace in his dust-filled library. Even the mumblings and complaints from his wife hadn't forced him from his reverie. Sophie was worried. She didn't want him sinking too deeply, knowing how long it would take him to re-enter the world again if he did.

"Has he always been a quiet man?" asked Jack Morgan.

"At times." Sophie forced a smile to cover her anxieties. "Mr Jones should be here any minute."

"I cannot believe you managed to tie Jones down to a meeting." Mr Morgan chuckled in disbelief.

"Well, he's got to turn up yet."

As if on cue, Mr Jones came tumbling down the dried track covered with deep ruts from the farm's tractors in his four-by-four.

"Good morning Mr Jones," greeted Sophie cheerfully as the farmer heaved himself out of his car.

"Let's just get this out the way," the farmer grumbled without lifting his head in greeting.

"Shall we take a seat round the kitchen table, Mr Morgan?" It was agreed they should and they made their way into the little farmhouse with Mr Jones trudging miserably behind hunching his shoulders.

"It's like this, Mr Jones," Sophie said in a business-like manner, after they'd settled around the table with mugs of steaming tea. "The land you are currently using to graze your sheep is rightly Mr Morgan's."

"I'm afraid you are wrong."

"It's not what the deeds suggest." She handed him a large sheet and pointed to the field on the map. "It's a large portion of land, which is needed for the expansion of Mr Morgan's farm. I believe it was on loan until such a time as it was needed."

"Loan," he spat out disagreeably. "It's ours by right." He tapped the tip of his finger forcefully on the table.

"Have you got proof?" Sophie's outward appearance showed a person in complete control. It was one of her many skills: below the table her feet were flapping in fear, but on the surface, she was swimming gracefully along. It was her university tutor who had first brought this skill to Sophie's notice and ever since it had encouraged her to step into unknown situations with more confidence, knowing that what she felt on the inside wasn't necessarily on display for all to see. This meeting was no different. Underneath, nerves and doubt led her body to grow hotter and hotter and Sophie wished she'd worn a thinner blouse. If this discussion should go wrong then the estate would be tackling a court case and she feared her dad wouldn't have the strength to face such an ordeal.

"You don't need proof when you've got my word," cried Mr Jones.

"Unfortunately, your word doesn't tie up with the evidence." What would she do if this argument failed… did she have a plan B? Sophie's stomach flipped as she beat herself up for not being more prepared.

"Come on, Arthur," coaxed Jack Morgan leaning over the table, his gentle manner contrasting with his rival's hostility. "You know that's not your land."

"It's always been our land, Jack," Mr Jones folded his hands in childish protest.

"I've got the contract our grandfathers drew up. Look, isn't this your grandfather's signature?" Mr Morgan showed a scribbled name on a yellowing piece of paper and passed it along the table for him to see.

"It's fake," he mumbled and without looking thrust it back across the table.

Sophie felt the tension grip her from inside and looked across to Jack because she wasn't sure what the next move should be. If the two farmers got into a fight, this thing would never be resolved.

Much to Sophie's surprise Jack was as calm as could be. His shoulders were relaxed and his eyes were soft with care. "How can this be fake, Arthur? You can see the age in the paper."

"Where am I to put my sheep?"

"I'm sure Miss Hastings can find a solution."

He grunted. "Just like she's sorted out my hedges."

"Arthur, you know as well as I do the shortcomings of the estate, but give this young lady a chance, she's just got here. I think things could change for the better, if you let the new family do their job."

Mr Jones didn't reply and stared moodily at the floor.

"How about I come to your farm and discuss the problem with you, Mr. Jones?" suggested Sophie encouraged by the silence. Mr Jones seemed to be a man of reaction and she assumed no response was a positive sign.

"Don't bother, I don't want your help." Pushing the chair away, he hastily got to his feet. "My sheep will be gone within the hour."

Bending low, he came close to his rival's face. "You have my word, if that counts for anything." Finishing with a scoff, he removed himself and slammed the door, echoing his defeat and frustration around the farmhouse.

Jack Morgan walked Sophie back to her car. "That went better than I thought, I was expecting more of a fight."

She smiled, feeling a great sense of relief rush over her.

"You can't fight evidence, Arthur's clever enough to know he wouldn't win if we took it further. Although, I feel I must warn you, I don't think you've heard the last. Arthur Jones is not the kind of man who goes down without a fight."

"Dad!" A voice called out from around the corner of the farmhouse before Sophie could question Jack further on his caution. "Dad!"

Jack bellowed back. "Round here son!"

"Tim's left the top gate open again."

"Again?" Jack turned to the figure stomping across the farmyard wearing a blue and red checked shirt.

"The cows have all escaped. I wouldn't have bothered you, but we need a hand."

"Right before milking as well," Jack shook his head. "Where is the boy now?"

"Eating bread and butter in the pantry."

"Okay, I'm coming. By the way," Jack turned to Sophie. "Have you met Miss Hastings, she's the new estate manager's daughter?"

The check-shirted figure looked in her direction for the first time and smiled. "Oh, hello Sophie."

"I didn't realise you worked for Mr Morgan?" commented Sophie smiling at the pleasant surprise of seeing this new acquaintance again.

"Technically I don't." He patted Jack on the back and kept the arm around the man's shoulder. "This is my father – I live here. Have to earn my keep, don't I dad." He winked in mischief.

"Well, I never." Jack chuckled. "It's a small world. When did you meet? Miss Hastings hasn't been in Middleton very long."

"We happened to bump into each other a few days ago," answered Oliver with a knowing grin.

"You'll have to pop over for dinner one day, Miss Hastings. It will be lovely to get to know you better."

The offer was unexpected and she almost accepted with great eagerness. But she reminded herself to be careful, since technically the Morgans worked for her dad, it wouldn't be good to blur the lines between business and pleasure.

"Thank you, that's very kind of you to offer, if I ever have the time, I will. I've a list the length of my arm. Every time I tick something off another thing is added."

"The life of an estate manager, I'm afraid," said Jack. "You've not landed yourself an easy one to run."

"Tell me about it, and it's not even my job."

"You're not staying around then, Miss Hastings?" The farmer looked a little disappointed.

"I'm currently looking for a job, I doubt I will find one locally."

"Such a shame, you're doing a grand job," Jack rubbed his hands together. "Right, I must be going to catch my cows and give my youngest son a stern word or two. Have a good day Miss Hastings."

Sophie returned the goodbye and started back towards her car until she heard Oliver's voice calling out behind her.

"Sophie, you must stop for tea breaks."

"Yes, I suppose I do," she answered pulling the car keys out of her bag.

"Stop in for one tomorrow. We normally have tea at eleven, my dad's a man of routine… why not join us?"

Sophie contemplated the proposal. It was only a tea break, surely that would be okay? To be honest, she was beginning to feel herself drawn to the Morgans, both father and son seemed to exude a calmness and compassion unlike anyone she had met before. When she had bumped into Oliver, he hadn't blamed her thoughtlessness, but criticised only himself and Jack had displayed nothing but courtesy and respect, even though Mr Jones deserved a good reproof.

The offer hung in the air.

"Yes," she called across the farmyard. If the lines became blurred, she'd deal with it later. "I'd love to."

****

Sophie sat in the empty rafters with her notepad on her knee. It had been a busy afternoon and her trip to Morgan's farm now seemed a lifetime ago as she sat waiting for Rupert's polo practice to begin.

She wasn't certain what to expect. Part of her wondered if it was even worth turning up. Rupert was a good friend, despite the last few years of separation. They had a history together and nothing could change that. But his unwillingness to put any effort into life irritated her, it was a complete contrast to her own work ethic and to be completely honest, she would be impressed if he turned up on time, never mind join in the practice with his team mates.

Chewing a pencil, she flicked over a sheet of paper to see the one below and frowned. All afternoon she had gradually filled the notepad with brainstorms, key words were encircled with fluffy cloudlike shapes and arrows came shooting out from the centre, with an array of elaborate ideas, to save the estate. Sophie vigorously scribbled out a word, causing a hole to form in the paper and mark the page behind.

"Hey Soph." Rupert climbed the bleachers dressed in slimline white trousers, black boots tucked inside and an emerald green polo shirt with the number one embroidered in neat red stitching on the top corner. He kissed her on the cheek in greeting and she looked up from her work. "What's this?"

"Estate stuff."

"Soph," he groaned. "You're falling into her trap."

"Dad needs my help at the moment. I'm at a loss to figure out how to improve things for him…the estate's in a mess."

Rupert raised an eyebrow.

"I won't fall into the trap, Rupert. I'm not staying…that's the theory anyway." Sophie was trying to convince herself that Elizabeth Hastings would not win the battle. Surely, she deserved to have a life, one where she could make her own decisions?

"I'm telling you; you're playing a dangerous game…" He sat down next to her and nudged her in the ribs. "Not that I mind you staying around though, it's good to have you back." He whipped her notepad away. "Enough of this now."

"Hey!" Sophie protested.

"You are about to see the master of hard work dazzle and amaze you, my dear Soph."

"Oh, I am, am I?"

"Indeed you are, right over there." He pointed to the polo field in front of them. "And I don't want you to be distracted."

"All right." She grabbed the notepad back. "You have my full attention."

A call came from a group of men huddled together on the field. "Stop flirting Donaldson and come and play!"

"Keep your eyes peeled, Soph," Rupert said as he ran down the bleachers to retrieve a horse from one of his team mates.

Sophie unzipped her bag. Rupert was probably right; she was overly distracted by the estate and had to be careful not to form an attachment to anything or anyone. It was vital her mother didn't gain a foothold. She snuggled the notepad inside and was just about to slide the bag back onto the floor when something caught her eye - the two-hundred-year-old red diary. Since finding the little book Sophie had carried it around everywhere, reading little snippets at any opportunity.

Casting a watchful eye upwards, Sophie saw the polo team still grouped together, discussing some new tactic. There must be time for a bit of light reading before the practice really began in earnest, all Rupert was doing so far was standing and nodding – anyone could do that and it certainly didn't scream out hard work.

The worn diary sat on her lap and the breeze wafted the smell of musty old paper into her nose.

I don't know what to do. I'm bound by my own words to marry Thomas if he proposes again. Mama will not let me escape now. Why did I speak those words and tell her I had reconsidered my response? How foolish I am...

Sophie turned the page.

All I can do is hope and pray that Thomas doesn't have the courage to return his sentiments.

Sophie paused, trying to imagine what it must have been like to have every decision made for you. Actually, it wasn't that hard for her to imagine, her own mother being the dominant figure in her own life. At least she could express an opinion...though these opinions often crumbled to nothing in the end. She could easily empathise with this girl, even though two hundred years of history stood in her way.

I can't imagine Mr Kirkby has any form of emotion towards me, despite what Annabelle thinks, although there is something charming about his manners, a breath of fresh air in this stagnant place. I must be extremely careful, for we have been invited for dinner with him at the Gillingham's. My rejection of Thomas will not be publicly known and paying too much attention to Mr Kirkby would only welcome more unwanted gossip...

A movement in the corner of Sophie's eye told her the players were finally mounting their horses and readying themselves to play. With great difficulty she closed the diary and regretfully put it away in her bag - the life of this girl had hooked her. Sentence after sentence revealed so many parallels to her own situation. How the story of a stranger written so long ago could impact her in this way could not be explained. What Sophie did know, was the words Georgiana had written were fast becoming like a favourite book she couldn't put down.

Sophie had never seen Rupert play polo before. It was a sport he had taken up after moving to the countryside. She had heard he was good, but most of her information came from his mother and could easily have been embellished. Leaning forward and placing her elbows on her knees and her hands on her chin, she watched as the Friday night practice began.

She didn't really know the rules, but any distraction still lingering was speedily pushed out of Sophie's mind. Her eyes were mesmerised from the first moment. Rupert was a confident rider and he directed his horse with great confidence with one hand, whilst simultaneously controlling a polo stick with the other. The coach muttered an instruction, inaudible to Sophie, and blew his whistle. Sandy dust circled the air as the horses set into motion, almost colliding with each other as the players fought to gain control of the small white ball. A bearded guy made a mighty swing and Rupert gained control racing down the field at full pelt, tapping the tiny ball with great precision and accuracy.

Sophie hardly noticed the training had lasted for two hours. She almost had to rub her eyes to check she was watching the right person. Was that really her friend on the field before her? Was this *her* Rupert, the boy who took the easy option and whose body malfunctioned if it broke into a sweat?

"Ready, Soph?" Rupert's curly hair glistened wet from the shower he'd quickly rushed after the practice had finished. Sophie stood up and walked down the rafters to meet him.

"That was amazing," the words came out of her mouth before she'd even reached him.

"Enjoy yourself?"

"I had no idea you were that good…I mean, you were sweating," her eye twinkled with a flicker of cheekiness.

"I told you I can work hard; I've just got to find the right motivation… What?" he turned self-consciously, feeling Sophie's eyes burrowing into his face.

"Sorry," she looked away shyly. "It's just… I've not seen you like that before. I've only ever seen the lazy version of Rupert, I didn't realise this side of you existed."

"We've both changed, Soph. We last saw each other at eighteen, that was three years ago, dare I say - we're adults now."

Sophie considered his words. How much of her childhood friend had changed? A new light had shone on him tonight, what else was there to discover?

"I'm sorry, Rupert." She didn't know why she was apologising, but the voice inside her head suggested she had treated her friend a little unfairly since arriving home. "I thought you were the same old Rupert."

"Well, I'm that too, of course." He smiled warmly. "But only the good parts."

They reached Sophie's car and Rupert chivalrously reached across to open the door. He leaned forward and swooped in, kissing her softly on the cheek. "Good night, Soph."

Sophie felt a fluttering in her stomach as he lingered for a second before pulling away.

Sitting in the driver's seat, Sophie touched the place where Rupert's lips had brushed her cheek. What had just happened? She felt ambushed by a rush of emotions that had emerged out of nowhere. Never in their whole relationship had she felt anything other than friendship for Rupert. She shook her head in a daze and blamed the excitement of discovering something new about an old friend. Clutching the wheel, she muttered, "Do not form any attachments, Sophie Hastings. You are not staying."

10

Georgiana

There was a warm glow from the house as the Davenports arrived at Gillingham Hall. Thankfully it wasn't a cold night because the family had to wait to alight from their chaise, the drive being so full of other guests in their own carriages. Three more families were stationed in front of them and a small crowd of people flocked up the grand steps leading to the open front door. Clearly, what had been expected to be a small gathering had turned into a party of great extravagance.

"I did not realise you were inviting so many people to dinner, Charles," commented Lord Davenport as he made his way along the line and greeted his old friend.

"I wanted to introduce my cousin to our society. Do you think I've been excessive again?" Sir Gillingham chuckled. To his credit he was a very generous gentleman, but very often this led to simple gestures becoming far more substantial than necessary.

Kirkby stood further down the line wearing a simple, tightly knotted white cravat, offset against a crimson red waistcoat and black doubled breasted tailcoat. One by one the guests introduced themselves, many of the females swooning before him as his nervousness caused him to blush and produce a delightfully charming dimpled smile. With much relief the young man gazed down the line and caught sight of a familiar face.

"I am so very glad you have come, Miss Davenport." He could have kissed her on the hand when she reached him, so overjoyed he was to see her in the crowded room, but he managed to restrain himself. "It is always nice to recognise a face amongst so many strangers. Could I have the honour of the first dance, I would be very much obliged?"

Politely Georgiana accepted Kirkby's offer, although she feared it was a great error. People of her acquaintance would naturally expect

Thomas to request the first dance. Would standing up with Gillingham's cousin cause too many questions?

She flowed along with the other guests into the saloon. It was a grand rectangular room with a long ocean blue carpet rolling down the middle, exquisite tapestries depicting Old Testament stories hung on the walls and two marbled fireplaces burned warmly at either end, the shadows of the flickering flames dancing on the guests standing nearby. Despite the large dimensions, the room was bustling with people and there was not much room to move. The chatter of many conversations filled the air and Georgiana darted her eyes around in desperation to find Annabelle.

"Your dress is beautiful."

Georgiana jumped as Annabelle's hand tapped her on the shoulder. She had chosen to wear a short sleeved lavender dress, reaching to her ankles and hemmed with a delicate ruffle, it was new and her friend had not seen it before.

"What a grand feast, I did not expect such a party." It was clear the extravagant evening thrilled Annabelle completely. Her eyes sparkled taking in all the sights around her. It was as if she was in a treasure house full of dazzling jewels.

"We didn't expect such a welcome either." Georgiana was not as pleased as her friend: large crowds maximised the chance of doing something wrong. More people to talk to, greater opportunity for error, especially under the current circumstances.

"Sir Gillingham does take any occasion to show off… we all know that," said Annabelle, stopping a passing footman holding a silver platter and taking two sparkling wine glasses and handing one to her friend.

"He means well, but he does get carried away in the moment," said Georgiana distractedly sipping from the glass. She had spied her mother amongst the crowd and was hoping she wouldn't be seen. "Oh bother, what have I done now?" she mumbled once it was clear

Lady Davenport was heading in her direction. "I can't even lose her in a room full of people."

Annabelle, who had been distracted herself, trying to spy out new fashions from London, followed the direction of her friend's eyes, her merriment significantly reducing upon seeing Georgiana's mother now approaching them.

"She doesn't seem angry," Georgiana nudged her friend. "Do you think she looks cross?"

"How can you tell? She never smiles at anything."

Georgiana watched her mother with caution, this wasn't a social visit.

"I'm sorry," said Annabelle. "Even if you think she's not angry I'm not staying around to find out. Your mother scares me half to death."

Georgiana couldn't blame her, the piercing hazel eyes of Lady Davenport seemed to have this effect on most people, including herself. It was a shame that, being her daughter, Georgiana didn't have the privilege of disappearing promptly into the crowd as Annabelle now did.

"Georgiana," said Lady Davenport coming within hearing distance. Her voice was harsh, but it didn't convey the usual familiar shrillness. Still, Georgiana could feel her body becoming tense, ready to face whatever might be coming her way.

"Yes, mama?"

"Are the rumours true?"

"What rumours?"

"Mrs Compton tells me an announcement is being made tonight."

"An announcement?" Georgiana furrowed her eyebrows. She had no idea what her mother was talking about.

"Don't act as if you were stupid…" Her daughter's dumbstruck silence made Lady Davenport's irritation begin to bubble. "Speak child!" She stepped back and glanced around, but the chatter of guests around them covered her callous cry.

"I'm sorry, I don't understand."

"Your engagement," she huffed when Georgiana's face remained blank. "I don't know why you are trying to keep it a secret, I'm just glad you came to your senses."

Secretively she huddled close to her daughter. Georgiana stiffened, finding this close proximity to her mother a little unnerving. "We will have you married as soon as possible; we don't want this going wrong. It will probably be your only opportunity."

Confusion completely took over Georgiana and she moved her lips but failed to produce any sound.

"Look," continued her mother, taking her daughter's wine glass out of her hand and drinking the remaining wine herself. "There is your father, I will tell him the good news. I might just be proud of you for once."

Georgiana was almost convinced she saw a hint of a smile spread across her face before Lady Davenport slipped away into the crowds.

Frantic to find out what was going on, Georgiana searched for Thomas. They weren't engaged and she couldn't understand where her mother had got the information from. Had Thomas decided to confirm their unification without her permission? It was possible he could have gone directly to her father. No, she dismissed the idea, Thomas would never do that without informing her... would he?

She pushed her way through the crowds. Where was he? She felt like she was swimming against the tide and a drowning sensation began to overwhelm her.

The sound of a clinking glass met her ears making her freeze. The loud babble of the guests turned to a mumble. Heart beating loudly in her chest, Georgiana found the source. What was he doing? She looked around in panic as the other guests also turned their attention to the gentleman lifting a wine glass in the air. How could he do this to her? She had said no. It wasn't right. She couldn't do it. Her breath quickened. Once the announcement had been spoken aloud a verbal contract was made. In her mind, the wedding vows might as well

108

have been spoken. There would be no reversing the pronouncement, it could not be undone, too great a dishonour would befall her family if she were to break an engagement.

"Ladies and gentlemen..."

Georgiana took a deep intake of breath and held it there, not daring in her angst to breathe.

"I would like to make a rather special announcement..."

She caught the gentleman's eye as he smiled coyly before the crowd. In her distress Georgiana slowly shook her head, eyes wide with horror, in the hope she could convey a wordless message to her friend to stop.

However, he took no notice. "I, as from two hours ago, have been made the happiest man on the entire earth. I am engaged to my love and my best friend, Miss Annabelle Hastings."

The crowd clapped gracefully with pleasure and those who had a glass rose them towards the betrothed couple.

The clapping hands faded into the background as Georgiana stood motionless, the crowds spinning uncontrollably around her. Could this be worse than her own name being announced?

Coming back to her senses she immediately scanned the room. The nearest exit needed to be found as quickly as possible. An open door lay to her right, not far away from where she was standing. Cautiously glancing behind her, she caught sight of her mother half-way across the room. Her face was pale from shock, but when her eyes suddenly fixed upon her daughter, her skin turned crimson red as her blood boiled rapidly. She was livid.

"Excuse me...Oh, I'm sorry." Georgiana lifted her dress and raced through the guests standing between her and the open door, bumping carelessly into many of them. Upon reaching the exit she dashed through and slammed it shut behind her.

The room was quiet apart from her rapid breathing. It clearly wasn't being used for the evening's festivities as it was empty of people. Relaxing briefly, she rested her head against the back of the door, trying to catch her breath.

"Miss Davenport?"

Her head shot up; she hadn't seen the figure hidden in the corner.

"Mr Kirkby, I am ever so sorry. I did not mean to…" She looked uneasily behind her at the closed door, not desiring to re-enter the saloon in a hurry.

"Are you all right?" Kirkby asked coming across the room.

"Yes…" A fleeting smile came and went from her face as she thought the door handle was rattling open and she flinched.

"No, I can see you are not well." He came forward, his kindly eyes full of concern.

"I just need somewhere to be alone, away from the crowds. If I may?"

"Of course, follow me this way."

Without a thought, Kirkby led Georgiana out of the room and up a stairway.

"I think you will find this a good place for quiet reflection." He opened a door and guided her into the library, which was full of so many dark mahogany bookcases there was no need for wallpaper.

"Thank you," she touched her forehead which was damp from perspiration. "I will not be here long. I only need to compose myself."

"Was it the announcement?" Kirkby asked unexpectedly. "You were not anticipating it?"

Georgiana's silence caused him hurriedly to regret his forwardness.

"I'm sorry, I shouldn't have asked."

"No, no, it's okay," she said reassuringly.

"This is no business of mine but…" he hesitated, fiddling with a cotton thread hanging from his tailcoat sleeve. "May I say… you are a beautiful young lady and there will be other gentlemen. I know it might be hard to hear at present…"

Georgiana's sudden laugh stopped him.

"Have I said something wrong?"

"I'm not in love with Mr Compton, if that is what you think. Although I was supposed to be engaged to him."

Kirkby looked at her curiously.

"It's a long story. I am currently hiding from my mother; she did not know Thomas loved someone else… my best friend actually."

"You would rather see your friend have marital happiness over yourself? That is a very selfless act."

"I could not marry Thomas knowing the heart of my friend would be broken into many pieces and I would be the cause of it. But my mother… well, she wouldn't understand and does not forgive easily."

Kirkby's face became enlightened. "That's why you didn't explain my role the day you fell into the river, your mother would never forgive you for being undignified in the presence of a stranger."

Georgiana blushed. "You must think I am foolish."

"Not at all." He sat down on an empty mahogany brass inlaid chair, his soft emerald eyes portraying no sign of judgment at all. "Why would I think you foolish?"

"I am always bringing disgrace upon the family…" she said sitting down opposite Kirkby and resting her eyes on her lap. "That's what they tell me anyway."

"Who are they?"

"My parents and sometimes my sister." Her long eyelashes fluttered, delicately touching her fair skin. "If no one had seen me, the day I fell into the river, the scolding would be less."

Kirkby leant boldly forward. "I think it was a very wise and sensible thing to do." He then glanced thoughtfully at the library door. "You know, you're not going to escape your mother here. Didn't you arrive in the same chaise?"

111

"Yes, we did." Georgiana tilted her head back and closed her eyes, letting out a gentle sigh. "I'm going to have to face her sooner or later."

It was true, she couldn't hide forever, but just a few more moments in the tranquillity of the mahogany-panelled library would definitely be most welcome.

"Could I…" she began as she rose to leave. "Could I ask you a question?"

"Of course." He smiled gently as they walked slowly together across the room.

"If you don't mind me asking, why were you hiding alone?"

"Ah." His cheeks heightened in colour and he looked guilty. "I'm not used to such extravagant parties; my cousin had promised me a small gathering."

"Sir Gillingham is famous for going over the top. I'm sure the dinner started off small and in his enthusiasm he let it get a little out of hand."

"I can see that." He shuffled his feet now they hovered by the closed door. "You see, I come from a very simple background, Miss Davenport. I, erm… felt a little overwhelmed, if I'm honest." He ran a tanned hand through his golden sun-steaked hair.

"I understand. A crowd can be very overpowering when all you desire is solace."

For a few moments their eyes mirrored one another, both full of sympathy and kind-heartedness for the other.

Before many seconds had passed, the sound of footsteps on the landing stole Georgiana's attention away. It was probably a servant scurrying to light a fire, but it made her realise that maybe she had hidden away for long enough.

"I really should go. I do not want to make matters worse by being caught alone with you upstairs."

Georgiana left Kirkby at the bottom of the staircase, where the mahogany theme continued in the floorboards, the window panes and the banister. The hallway itself was deserted, apart from Thomas who was pacing the length of the room. He stopped as he saw the pair coming down the stairs and eyed Gillingham's cousin warily as he headed back into the saloon.

"Georgiana," he came across to her. "I've been looking for you."

"What on earth has just happened?" Her voice appeared harsher than she had originally intended. She should be delighted for friend's engagement, especially since she'd been urging him to do it for such a long time. But, before she could celebrate with him, he had to know she did not approve of his careless announcement.

"I'm so s-sorry," he lowered before her. "I wanted to tell you first, really I did…"

"But you thought you'd tell a whole roomful of people instead?" Crossing her arms, anger continued to overcome her happiness for him. "My mother thought you were announcing *our* engagement."

Thomas straightened up, his tall figure twice the size of Georgiana's ting frame. "W-why would she think that?"

"Your mother told her we were engaged."

"She must have misunderstood…I-I never said anything of the kind. I'm ever so s-sorry, Georgiana, but I was under the impression this is what *you* wanted. I thought *you'd* be happy."

The injured look in her friend's eye could not lessen her displeasure over his actions. Unlike her mother, she had told Thomas how she felt and in her mind the matter was now over.

"I am happy for you, Thomas. You know I didn't want to marry you, but you were supposed to wait."

"I know, Isabelle said the same."

"So, what happened?"

"I am a wealthy man…a wealthy man who is in love."

Georgiana was dumbstruck. He had not considered her at all. "What about me Thomas…the person you would have married if I didn't tell you to marry the love of your life?" Tears threatened to reach the surface as her friend's negligence hit her again. "I thought you were my friend?"

"I am, Georgiana. I just...I am sorry."

"You've said that already."

She knew her friend hadn't meant to cause her such misery, but his foolhardiness had cost her dearly. Georgiana could see his ardent love, which had been suppressed for so many years, had finally overwhelmed him, causing him to be blind to anyone else who might suffer from his moment of madness.

It was not supposed to have turned out this way. Annabelle had agreed to wait until a significant time had passed after Georgiana's rejection of Thomas. This was necessary to make Lord and Lady Davenport as placid as possible before hearing the news. They must not know their daughter had any responsibility for the betrothed couple's happiness. Blame would fall on her anyway, for being foolish enough to pass him up in the first place, but the fewer faults they could pin on her the better. But now, standing in the dark hall, she realised everything had been messed up.

It was only six months ago when Annabelle had admitted all. She had broken down weeping, begging Georgiana not to marry Thomas. When Georgiana declared there was nothing she could do, that she was set on a path of matrimony with Thomas Compton, Annabelle broke down again, lamenting because she could not marry the love of her life. It wasn't that Georgiana had no sympathy for her friend, but she had witnessed such displays of ardent affection before, which often fizzled away in the blink of an eye because she was a girl led by her emotions. Georgiana believed there was an element of truth to her friend's feelings, but how much Annabelle really loved him was uncertain and she was not willing to put her own life at risk for the sake of a passing fancy that might last one or two days.

To this opinion she kept, until she discovered Thomas held the same undying passion for Annabelle. Now that Georgiana was aware of Annabelle's feelings little knowing looks and gestures between the two became clear to her. Little gifts Thomas bought as an act of friendship roused her suspicions. At balls, he always danced first with Georgiana, then second with Annabelle, after his duty had been performed. Why hadn't she noticed any of this before?

When Georgiana confronted Thomas, he rejected the allegations as false. But she persevered until eventually he broke and admitted all. He had loved Annabelle for many years, but his faithfulness to Georgiana and his parent's wishes prevented him from acting upon any desires. This was the moment Georgiana declared she would not marry Thomas. How could she, when he was in love with her best friend? On a daily basis she would be a witness to their unhappiness and this was something she could not bear to see. Of course, Thomas disagreed and stood firm by his parent's choice for him and would propose as soon as his grandfather's inheritance became available to him, which happened to be the day after Emma's wedding.

"Oh Georgiana, isn't this marvellous." Annabelle came floating out of the saloon and folded her arm into Thomas', oblivious to the chaos his announcement had caused. "Now we don't have to hide any more, I was so worried Thomas would be forced to propose to you again, obviously I knew you would have to accept him if he did."

Georgiana stepped forward to kiss her friend's cheek and offered her congratulations. However upset she might be with Thomas, she was truly happy for her friend. In the course of the last few months, Annabelle had proved her love was steadfast and not just a frivolous notion that flickered away into nothing.

"Your parents must be extremely happy," commented Georgiana.

"They are overjoyed, especially since everyone was expecting you to have my dear Thomas. I am so very thankful you talked him out of it, thank you for being such a loyal friend."

The door to the saloon opened again and all three turned their heads to see who had entered the hall.

Lady Davenport stood before them. Her posture was so rigid she barely moved an inch and not a syllable escaped from her mouth, not that it needed to, as her face did all the talking. Bulging eyes pin pointed Georgiana in an instant and a sporadic twitch caused her nostril to flare.

Annabelle covered her mouth in sudden realisation. "Georgiana, I did not mean for this to happen."

"We all knew the consequences," whispered Georgiana. "There is nothing I could have possibly done that is worse than rejecting a match my parents had purposely planned for me." She looked across to her mother, lifting up her chin in readiness to receive her penalty. "You had better remove your bride-to-be Thomas, in case she gets caught in the firing line."

Thomas scampered away without further thought, his arm resting protectively around Annabelle.

The sound of guests resonated through the walls and into the hall, a hearty laugh vibrated and the violins merrily began to play a new tune.

"How dare you," hissed Lady Davenport into the silent room. "That should have been your name."

"He loves her, mama," she spoke quietly. "You cannot blame Thomas."

"I am not blaming Mr Compton; I am blaming you. Have I not taught you nothing? Catching a husband of Mr Compton's status is difficult, but not impossible. Emma succeeded. If you had said yes when he asked, this would never have happened."

A woman with flowing long curls tied high on her head came streaming out of the saloon. She smiled at Lady Davenport, who nodded her head in politeness and waited with great impatience for the lady to leave the hall.

"This is completely unacceptable, Georgiana, and if you think you will marry Mr Kirkby you can think again."

Georgiana was taken back by the accusation. Where had this come from, the thought hadn't even entered her mind? "I do not want to marry Mr Kirkby."

"He is not a suitable match for you and I will not allow it."

"I do not want to marry Mr Kirkby. We have only just met and I do not understand why you think this is the case?"

The saloon door opened again and the two ladies watched closely to see who would enter through it. Lady Davenport's mouth curled up with pleasure as her husband walked in, her daughter's admonishment could continue at full strength.

"Gather your belonging Georgiana, we are leaving. I am not going to be embarrassed all evening, everyone knew you were meant to marry Mr Compton. What a disgrace, you disobedient, child!" Most of these words were spoken in her father's usual controlled calmness, but his disapproval was evident when, in anger, he released the final word in a roar.

Lady Davenport rested a hand lightly on his shoulder. "Remember where we are," she whispered into her husband's ear, looking around to check no one had come out to investigate the shout.

"Meet us in the chaise, Georgiana," she snarled before retreating out of the hall with her husband.

11

Sophie

Knock. Knock.

"Dad?" Sophie peeped her head around the door. "Dad, I'm going to Morgan's farm. Want to come?"

"Not this time, Sophie." George Hastings turned over in bed and tucked the duvet protectively around his face.

"It would be good for you to get out. You've been in here three days."

"I've been in my library too," he said feebly.

"Please come with me. I need you to help me sort out this mess. I'm not going to be here forever… please, you need to see what I'm doing."

"I'll see what you've done when you leave."

"Dad…" she walked across and laid her hand on his shoulder.

He twitched his body away. "I'm not coming, Sophie."

Sophie stepped back in the darkened room. It was sunny outside, but the drawn curtains only let a crack of light shine through and all she could see was her dad's dark hair, speckled with a silver thread, poking out from underneath the duvet. A familiar tingling sensation filled her nose and she sniffed before moving silently out of the room. She would have stayed with him longer, despite the fact he didn't want to talk, but she was due at the Morgan's for tea at eleven.

"He's not still in bed, is he?" came the indignant cry of Elizabeth marching out to meet Sophie as she was climbing into her car.

"He's not well."

"He's fine."

"Mum, he's been in bed three days in a row."

"He's just being lazy. No Sophie, I'm not having it. He's sulking, that's all he's doing because he doesn't get his poor little retirement plan. He's coming with you even if I have to carry him out." She strutted up the single step into the manor.

"No! I'm telling you he's not well." Sophie chased after her leaving the car door wide open.

"He needs someone to shout him into action. I don't understand what's the matter."

"Then you must be blind."

The words made Elizabeth freeze in anger. "I beg your pardon."

"Can't you see? Dad didn't want this. Four months ago he was a year away from retirement... a retirement he badly needed."

"He knew the inheritance was coming, it was just a matter of time."

"Yes, but he never wanted it."

"It had always been our plan."

"No, it had always been *your* plan. Leave him alone, you'll only make things worse."

"I will do no such thing. He needs waking up."

"Mum, can't you see the signs."

"What signs?"

"It's exactly the same as last time."

"And what a farce it was last time."

"Oh, my goodness - how can you say that, he's your husband?"

"I know what's best for him."

"Do you?" Sophie couldn't believe what she was hearing. This was exactly why she had no respect for her mother. George Hastings was the kindest, most considerate man in her life and she could not forgive Elizabeth's treatment of him in the past or the present.

"Yes, I do," said Elizabeth obstinately.

"Then fine, go and shout at him. Go and do what *you* do best." Sophie strode out the house and got back into her car, slamming the door extra hard in her frustration. Pressing down the accelerator pedal as if she was a formula one driver, she made her escape.

The short ride to the farm helped calm Sophie down a little, but it wasn't until she was in the presence of Oliver and his father that she gradually began to forget about her altercation with her mother.

119

"Cup of tea, Miss Hastings?" asked Jack Morgan carrying a chipped maroon coloured teapot across to the kitchen table.

"Call her Sophie, dad," said Oliver a little embarrassed at his father's formality.

"I like to be professional... cup of tea, Miss Hastings?" he asked again and grinned at his son with a twinkling eye. Nothing would ever make him throw away his old-fashioned values, taught to him by his own father. He was adamant that what might be deemed outdated by his son was the only way to live.

"Stubborn is the word Sophie..." Oliver smiled light-heartedly. "And set in his ways."

There wasn't an ounce of offence taken between the two men and Sophie was baffled by such harmless banter: her home was devoid of such merriment since Elizabeth couldn't take a joke without becoming personally insulted.

"You wouldn't have me any other way... would you like a cup of tea, Miss Hastings?"

"I'd love a tea, thank you Mr Morgan. It's been a long morning."

The tea was poured with only a couple of drips escaping from the spout and Oliver produced an old flowered tin in front of her face.

"Cake?" he asked.

"Ooo, yes please."

Oliver laughed at Sophie's round sparkling eyes. "Watch out, we have a sweet tooth in the house, dad."

Sophie blushed, realising how much the cake was making her mouth water. "Is it that obvious?"

"Don't worry, we've lots more cake," grinned Jack kindly. "I've a bit of a sweet tooth myself..."

"A bit?" Oliver raised an eyebrow.

"Don't tell the girl all my secrets yet." He winked at Sophie and picked up a matching maroon milk jug. "Do you take milk and sugar?"

"Just milk thank you, I get enough sugar from the cakes." She took the steaming mug from Jack as he passed it across. "So, who's the baker?" She looked from Jack to Oliver, not really expecting either of them to have spent hours wearing an apron.

"Mrs Bevis - our housekeeper, she often takes pity on us," said Oliver, as he cut Sophie an extra-large slice and handed over a plate laden with moist lemon drizzle cake.

As she took a bite, a tangy explosion of citrus burst into her mouth. "Wow, will Mrs Bevis bake for me? This is amazing!" Immediately Sophie took a second mouthful.

Oliver laughed again, amused by Sophie's enjoyment of something so simple. "She's good, isn't she?" He was extremely proud of his housekeeper's accomplishments: Mrs Bevis had been with them for as long as he could remember and she felt like family.

"How's your father, Miss Hastings. Is he feeling better?" asked Jack, sipping tea from a spotty mug.

Sophie had been hoping her family members wouldn't come up in conversation, though she guessed it should have been expected.

"Unfortunately, he's still in bed." There was no way she could talk about her dad's illness, it was all too complicated and would inevitably lead to her recent argument with her mother, which was still too raw for her to talk about rationally. She looked down at her well-brewed tea and fiddled with the handle.

"Oh dear, I'm sorry to hear that." The elder man's eyes crinkled at the edges with genuine sympathy.

"He'll be up and about soon, I'm sure. So... has Mr Jones kept his side of the bargain?" She hoped the subject change wasn't too obvious, although she was interested to hear if the rival farmer had reared his head since his defeat yesterday.

"So far, he is behaving... you know, I can't quite believe it. That man's always up for a fight, you must be a calming influence on him." Jack chuckled. "But, enough about that." He reached for the tea pot to refill his half-empty mug. "This isn't a business call, we wanted to get to know you."

"Me?" she shifted self-consciously in her chair. "There's not much to know really."

"You came from London?"

"Yes." She swallowed the piece of cake she had been munching, which had suddenly become difficult to eat as her mouth had rapidly turned dry. "I grew up in London - I've just finished a degree in the city, actually." The moment the words left her mouth she regretted them. There was very little of her life she enjoyed sharing and she feared this topic would ultimately lead to questions she didn't want to answer.

"Oh really, what did you study?" The farmer leaned forward with great interest, taking another piece of cake from the tin which Oliver had left in the middle of the long table.

"Land management." She reddened slightly as she answered and could feel perspiration threatening to surface on her skin.

"Well, isn't that convenient, you'll be a lot of help to your parents, I can already see you're good at your job."

This needed clearing up, before he got the wrong idea. "Oh no, I'm not the estate manager - that's my dad, I'm just here for the summer." She gave a weak smile as she watched Jack's perplexed expression. She couldn't blame him, it sounded silly in her head too.

"You're not staying? If you don't mind me saying, I think you've landed on your feet, your father's inheritance arriving just as you finish your degree. Perfect timing I'd say."

"It's not quite what I'm looking for." Her fingers found the mug handle again and she looked away hoping he wouldn't probe further.

"Well, that is a shame." Jack was visibly disappointed. "It will be a great loss for the estate, that's all I can say."

Sophie appreciated the compliment. It was nice to know someone thought she was doing a good job and she sipped her tea using the break in conversation to ask a few questions herself. "Has your family been in farming a long time?"

"I'm the third generation to farm here, but my family have been farmers for many generations before that, it runs in our blood.

"Dad was born here, in the farmhouse." Oliver pointed to the room above their heads.

Jack chuckled. "I don't think I've been away from this place more than a week in my whole life." He leaned back on his chair. "Hopefully the fourth generation will continue the legacy."

Here was another parent dictating the future of his child and Sophie looked at Oliver to check his reaction. She'd sensed the Morgans were different, but maybe deep down all families were the same.

"Oh no," said Jack quickly clarifying his words. "Not Oliver."

"I've four younger brothers, Sophie. Charlie looks the most likely candidate, doesn't he dad?"

"I'd agree with that one. He's the one pioneering our organic produce," he explained to Sophie. "He didn't want to go to college, so he works full time on the farm."

"Didn't you say you worked on the farm too?" asked Sophie turning to Oliver.

"I do, but the future... I'm not really certain." He cast a subtle sideways glance at his father.

"I just want my boys to be happy." Jack tapped Oliver on the shoulder. "If they don't want to farm, they don't farm."

Sophie observed the older man carefully. This way of thinking was completely foreign to her. "Don't you want Morgan's farm to continue?"

"Sure I do," his soft silvery tone loosened the knot Sophie had felt tightening up in her tummy. "But if the farm doesn't continue with my boys, then another family will take over."

"What's the matter Sophie, you look puzzled?" asked Oliver.

"Oh no, it's just...nothing. It's nothing." She handed back the mug in front of her. "Thank you for the tea, I'd better be on my way. You can't believe the amount of work that needs doing."

"You are very welcome," smiled the kindly face of Mr Morgan. "Please take another piece of cake, we've got plenty. Wrap it up, Oliver."

Oliver walked Sophie back to her car after leaving Jack in the kitchen to clear up the mugs before heading back out onto the fields. "Thank you for stopping by, it's been good to have you with us."

"It was a very welcome and much needed break, it couldn't have been better timed actually." Her face clouded briefly as she thought about heading back to the manor containing her mother.

"Things not going too well?" he asked as they stopped beside Sophie's car.

Sophie couldn't help noticing that his soft, kind-hearted eyes mirrored his father's exactly.

"I can only imagine how messed up the estate is, it wouldn't be an easy job for anyone," he continued.

"It's a challenge... but it will be okay." She smiled bravely, attempting to hide her niggling anxieties. One thing she was not going to do was spill her heart out to Oliver Morgan. His sensitive expression was tempting her to say more than she wanted and she had to keep reminding herself he was still a relative stranger.

"You must miss your father's help. Is there anything I can do whilst he's off sick?"

Sophie was taken aback by another unexpected offer. "That's kind of you, but I'm not certain you can help at the moment." She couldn't allow Oliver a front row seat to view her shambolic family, and to be honest, the biggest difficulty she was facing at the moment was her mother, the never-ending problem that followed her through life. She doubted Oliver could do anything to change that.

"That's fine," he smiled, not offended by her refusal. "You know where I am if you need me. I hope you won't be expected to handle things on your own for too long… is your father very ill?"

"No, he's… it's complicated," Sophie faltered, not wanting to go into the details.

Oliver sensed her awkwardness. "I'm making you uncomfortable, forget I asked, I really didn't mean to pry."

"It's just…my father being ill…it's not the only thing making my life particularly unbearable right now."

"I'm really sorry to hear that," his sympathetic gaze struck her forcibly. Here was someone right here in front of her who was ready and willing to listen, she would be stupid to pass up this opportunity, because the reality was, when would this ever happen again?

Everything about Oliver screamed out authenticity and, without realising what she was doing, she continued talking. "I don't have the best relationship with my mum, in fact, she can be quite hard work at times."

"That sounds tough, especially when you have to work together as well," his eyes crinkled with so much compassion that Sophie had to look away, feeling overwhelmed by so much attentiveness.

She shrugged dismissively in a desperate effort to deflect how vulnerable she felt. "You know what mothers can be like."

When Oliver didn't say anything immediately in response, it was pretty obvious she had said something wrong.

"My, erm…" he focussed self-consciously on the dusty farmyard floor. "My mother died when I was twelve."

"Oh Oliver, I'm so sorry. If I knew I would never have said…"

"It's all right, Sophie," Oliver instantly turned his attention back onto her face. "It was a long time ago… and we have Mrs Bevis' cakes to see us through." He smiled warmly, trying to lighten the mood. "Don't look so worried… it's okay. Listen, I know you're really busy right now but…how about we grab a late lunch?"

Sophie wasn't expecting such an invitation, especially after her giant faux pas. "I think I can spare an hour later," she said looking at her watch, the ridiculously large pile of papers waiting for her back in the office looming in her mind.

"Wonderful. I'll pick you up at one."

Sophie drove home feeling like a weight had been lifted off her shoulders. An hour spent in the presence of the Morgan's had been like taking medicine for a headache and she felt prepared to face her mother again.

****

On her arrival home, Sophie stopped in the kitchen and leaned against the badly chipped kitchen counter, fighting contradicting thoughts. She took a jar of chocolate spread that had been left out since breakfast, grabbed a teaspoon, unscrewed the lid and helped herself to a heaped serving of sweet sugary goodness. She couldn't get Oliver out of her mind. A large part of her was desperate for lunchtime to tick around so she could see him again. But another part of her felt uneasy. There was something about the guy that made her want to reveal every deeply hidden secret, knowing they would be kept perfectly safe with him.

Never in her life had Sophie been so open and honest with anyone. Of course, she'd made friends, but apart from Rupert, she'd kept them all to a superficial level. No one was allowed too close for fear they'd see what her life was really like. She'd lost touch with her school friends years ago, and as for her university acquaintances, no one had surfaced since graduation.

An intermittent buzz from the defective doorbell roused Sophie from her reverie. She screwed the lid back on the jar, licked the remaining chocolate off the spoon and went to answer it.

"I've come to start the tiling, love." A builder wearing plaster covered jeans and chewing an old piece of gum stood on the front doorstep.

"You'll want my mum," replied Sophie. "But I don't think she's home." She assumed Elizabeth wasn't home anyway, confident she would have been sniffed out by now if she was. "Which room are you tiling?"

"The hall ones, love. I know what I'm doing, I quoted for the lady on Monday."

"Okay," she said a little uncertainly. If something went wrong it would be her fault for letting the builder start without her mother's permission. "I'll leave the front door open and you can get started."

"Thanks, love."

Sophie left the door ajar whilst the unshaven builder went to retrieve his tools from a dirty white van. Not wanting to hover over him she took herself off to the office. There was no point procrastinating, Sophie decided: the paperwork wasn't going to organise itself.

Chewing on a pencil and sitting cross-legged on the disintegrating carpet, Sophie held two different letters in her hand pondering which would be her next priority. An hour had ticked by and still the endless mountain of papers stood reared up in front of her, the topmost documents fluttering in the breeze that entered the office through a shoddy timber framed window.

"Sophie Hastings!" The sound of her name came hurtling down the corridor. "Come here this instant!" The bellow was followed by the echo of clopping heels marching rapidly in Sophie's direction.

Sophie's immediate thought was that the builder had messed up. Maybe he had laid electric pink tiles instead of the luxury Grecian marble ones Elizabeth had ordered. A wave of apprehension flooded inside her and she swung a head round ready to face her mother who now stood furiously in the doorway.

"You have gone too far this time," Elizabeth fumed.

"I'm sorry, but the builder said he knew what he was doing."

"This isn't about the builder; I've recently had a conversation with the vicar."

Sophie placed the two letters she held carefully on the threadbare carpet and calmly stood up. She knew what was coming and prepared herself to meet the inevitable onslaught with as much composure as possible.

"How dare you go over my head?"

"I take it we are talking about the community fete," Sophie replied coolly.

Elizabeth burst out in forced laughter setting her mouth straight as soon as the outburst had ended. "Yes, we are talking about the fete. It is not happening and I told him so... again."

"It needs to happen, mum."

"Who's in charge here?"

"It will be good for the community to get to know us."

"I don't want to know the community."

"I'm afraid being Lady of the Manor doesn't give you that choice," Sophie tried to speak kindly, but she couldn't help a hint of curtness escaping.

"You will do as I say and ring the vicar to tell him it is not happening."

"I will do no such thing."

They glared at each other in a standoff until Elizabeth suddenly removed a phone from her pocket and dialled a number, placing it to her ear and waiting for the ring tone to begin before thrusting it towards Sophie.

"Tell him," Elizabeth snarled.

Any desire to maintain an atmosphere of calmness had long since vanished and Sophie stood glaring at Elizabeth for putting her in this position.

Reluctantly she answered the voice greeting her on the other end of the phone. "Hi, Reverend Bishop." She plastered on a smile to help create a fake cheery tone. "It's Sophie Hastings here...yes, I'm extremely sorry... It will be sorted. I will ring early next week... Thank you for understanding and I'm ever so sorry... Goodbye." She hung up and pushed the phone back into her mother's hand.

"Did you cancel it?"

"Did it sound like I cancelled it?"

"Get out of my house!" Elizabeth yelled practically foaming at the mouth.

"If you are asking me to leave, who will look after the estate?"

"That's your father's job."

"Oh yes, he's going to be a lot of good to you locked up in his bedroom." Sophie stormed passed her mother and fled down the corridor.

"You're right, I don't want you to leave."

Sophie halted, if her mother valued her in any way, she wanted to hear it.

"Your skills are too vital to me. Cancel the village fete and we will say no more about it."

Sophie turned around slowly; in one moment all her anger was gone like a pin pricked balloon.

"Cancel it," Elizabeth glared unblinkingly at her daughter.

"I'll see what I can do."

Sophie retreated down the corridor, she wanted to be as far away as possible from her mother. The fete would have to be cancelled.

Sitting in a quiet corner of Middleton's local café, Sophie pulled the little red diary out of her bag. Instantly she felt her spirits lift as she took refuge in the only person who understood how she felt. She smiled to herself; different era, same problems.

The carriage ride home was punishment enough! Papa sat looking sternly out the window, ignoring me as if I didn't exist. Mama wouldn't utter a syllable whilst the coachman sat out in front, I could see her fury burning, intensifying with every passing minute. I sat opposite, not knowing where to look!

But then, on our return home something very strange happened. The chastisement I was expecting didn't take place.

Sophie read the words again and shuffled in her chair, her eyes scanning down the page...what had happened?

I know my mother was preparing to announce all manner of threats and vile words because her mouth half opened ready to fire, but when my father's butler stepped into the room with a cough, she snapped it shut in an instant, propriety hindering her once again.

"What is it Ridley?"

"I have a message, m'lady."

"Well, hurry up and give it."

Ridley cleared his throat again. "A Miss Barnet called. The young lady wanted to make you aware she was residing at the Middleton Inn." He lingered waiting for a reply, or permission to leave, but my mother's face had turned from boiling red to pasty white and she said nothing. My father finally told him to leave, otherwise I think he would have waited there all night. I was then ordered to my room, and although exceedingly curious to know what was happening, I ran lightly away before he changed his mind.

My Aunt Lucy's name is not spoken in our house. For what reason, I do not know. Her sins, however, must be great because it is practically unheard of for mama to skip a scolding of me, her youngest daughter, whom she would disown in a heartbeat.

A coffee was placed in front of Sophie and this jolted her back into the reality of sitting in the café. She checked her watch: there was still half an hour left before Oliver picked her up.

A sudden sweeping hand holding a handful of flowers appeared in front of her face. "For you Soph." It was Rupert.

"How did you know I was here?" she asked taking the flowers from him.

"I was passing by and when I saw your face, I recognised the look."

"The look?" Sophie frowned, what was he talking about?

"You've had a fight with your mother... am I right?"

"That's correct." Sophie was baffled at her friend's intuition.

"I thought you might need cheering up... hence the flowers."

"Thank you," she smelled the cheerful sweet peas. "They're lovely."

"What are you reading?" asked Rupert picking up the little red book as he sat himself down at Sophie's table.

"Oh, it's an old diary I found up at the manor. You know, the ones I found in the green room?"

"Sounds boring." He pushed it to the side and stole a sip of her coffee. "So, tell me, what happened with your mother?"

"We are not exactly seeing eye to eye about the village fete. I don't understand her sometimes, I really don't." She tapped Rupert's hand lightly as he went for a second mouthful of coffee and took back the mug. "She asked me to leave the house, until she realised how useful my skills would be to her... not how much she valued me as a person, but how much she valued what I could give her - skills that she isn't even using, may I add."

"I value you, Soph." Dragging his chair round to Sophie's side of the table, Rupert wrapped his arm around her shoulder and gave her a reassuring squeeze. "It doesn't matter what your mother thinks."

"I wished she appreciated me sometimes, you know."

"I know." He pressed his lips together sympathetically. "How about we get some lunch? Keep you away from the manor a bit longer."

"Thanks Rupert, but I can't, I'm already meeting someone. In fact, I must be getting home or I will be late, he's picking me up at one."

"He?" Rupert's eyebrow shot up quizzically.

"Yes, Oliver Morgan. Do you know him?"

"A little," he frowned. "Where's he taking you?"

"I don't know." She picked up her bag, not forgetting to put the diary back inside.

Rupert stood up with her. "I'll pay for your coffee."

"You should really since you've drunk half of it, but I've already paid."

"Oh... I'll walk you to your car, then." He chivalrously allowed her to walk in front and the little bell above the café door tingled as they left together.

"I'm only parked around the corner Rupert; I won't get lost," she laughed at him.

Rupert ignored the gibe. "Did you enjoy my polo practice last night?"

Sophie swallowed nervously and stared at the pavement. "Definitely, you were great."

His eyes lit up. "You really enjoyed it?"

"Yes, I did... I had no idea." She halted as they reached her car. "Well, thanks for the flowers."

"You're welcome." Sophie was certain she saw a hint of shyness in his smile and this set the butterflies flying in her stomach again.

There was a brief pause before she climbed into the car as it seemed neither knew how to say goodbye. Finally, Rupert chuckled nervously before shoving both hands into his pockets. "See you later, Soph."

With ten minutes to spare before Oliver appeared at the manor, Sophie arrived home and raced upstairs to check on her dad. Her hopes were raised when she didn't find him in bed, but they were only to be dashed when she found him in his library next door. He wore his brown striped dressing gown and was unshaven. As she entered the room, Sophie could see he wasn't reading anything, nor was he doing any work, he was simply staring into space and she could only guess for how long.

"Hi dad, how are you doing?"

"Sophie." His voice was hoarse as he whispered and he reached out to his daughter, clasping her hand tightly in his. The touch nearly brought tears to her eyes. No words needed to be spoken, the tightness of his grip said it all. Her dad needed help; he just didn't know how to ask.

Sophie sat with him for a few minutes before tearing herself away. She could have sat with him forever, guarding him from any more harm. Closing the door gently behind her, she found her phone and began to dial.

"Sorry I'm not available to take your call at the moment, but please leave a message after the tone. BEEP."

"Dylan, it's Sophie. Call me."

12

Georgiana

The last time Georgiana had seen Aunt Lucy was ten years ago. She was eight years old and had been walking into Middleton village with Edward. The rain was pouring down and she stood waiting patiently as her brother ran errands for their father.

"Come on then, Georgiana, I'm all finished. Let's go home before we're soaked to the bone, overwise mama will scold me for letting the world see you in such a state," Edward grabbed his sister's hand and they dashed through the shoppers, trying to miss the potholes full of muddy puddles.

"Excuse me... Edward!" came a distant cry. "Edward Davenport…"

The boy swung round, seeking for the person who had called his name. Out of the crowds a young lady emerged in front of them. Her bonnet was sitting drenched on top of her head and her hair curled out underneath, wet and bedraggled.

"Aunt Lucy!" cried Edward in surprise. "What are you doing here?"

"I was in the area," she sniffed, as a droplet of rain water trickled down her nose. "You've grown, Edward." She looked the boy up and down, it had been a long time since she'd last laid eyes on him. "Is your mother well?"

"Yes, she's up at Denholm Park. I'm not…" He paused to consider his answer. "I'm not certain if you'd be welcome."

"If there is a chance, I'd like to come."

"She might not see you; it would be a waste of a journey."

"I'll take the risk." She smiled and looked at the little girl by his side. "You must be Georgiana, how old are you now?"

"I'm eight, ma'am," Georgiana replied, her speckled copper eyes gazing widely at the lady whose dark blond curls now stuck to her wet face.

Lucy laughed lightly. "You sound like the offspring of my sister. You don't need to be so formal with me, call me Aunt Lucy."

Edward shivered. "Let us not stand about in this weather; you are welcome to join us, aunt."

Georgiana had not met her Aunt Lucy before, but Edward had talked about her frequently. He remembered her visits to Denholm Park when he was a young boy with great delight; Lucy never arrived empty handed and always played games with him. However, something happened when he was five and her expected return didn't take place. As Edward grew older, he supposed she'd had a falling out with his mother, though he could not fathom out over what and he had not set eyes upon his aunt again.

"Mama?" Edward knocked hesitantly on the parlour door. Lady Davenport summoned him inside and he left Georgiana and Lucy waiting outside in the hall.

"Yes, Edward?" She put her quill down on the writing desk where she sat and looked up at her son, waiting for him to speak.

"I thought you'd like to know we came across an old acquaintance in Middleton."

"Can I enquire whom?"

"She was desirous to see you and walked back to Denholm Park with us."

"Who, Edward?" she leaned forward in her chair with eyes piercing into her sons.

Edward gulped. "Aunt Lucy."

"Lucy is in my house!" Lady Davenport banged the table, causing Edward to flinch and she fought to retain her composure. "Where?"

"In the hall with Georgiana."

Without warning his mother abruptly rose and flew past her son, knocking over a candlestand in her haste. Fixing her eyes on Lucy she cried, "How dare you come here. I thought I told you never to set foot in Denholm Park again?"

Georgiana retreated and stood beside Edward, who placed a protective arm around his sister's frightened figure.

"Please, dearest sister..." begged Lucy.

"Do not called me "dearest sister": you have no right to call me "dear", you forfeited that right after what you did."

"I wanted to see you," Lucy's eyes became full to the brim with tears.

"Leave. You are not welcome here."

"Please..." Lucy begged again. "It's been nine years and I have not bothered you at all."

"Edward, call Ridley to see Miss Barnet out."

Edward obediently scurried away.

"Can't I just...?" started Lucy.

"No," interrupted Lady Davenport, who knew exactly what she wanted.

"A-a-ch-chew!" Georgina sneezed and stood shivering, dripping rain water on the tiled floor.

Lady Davenport spun round to face her daughter. She'd forgotten she was there and lifted her hand so suddenly that Georgiana shrank back in terror.

"Go to your room, child!"

The little girl didn't need to be told twice and she hurried up the sweeping staircase as quickly as her little legs could carry her.

****

Things had been quiet since the wedding and extravagant dinner at the Gillingham's. It was no surprise to Georgiana that she had been prohibited from seeing Thomas and Annabelle, and it was this absence of her friends, as well as a spate of bad weather, that kept her indoors more than she desired. Lady Davenport also wasn't straying far from Denholm Park. She was still lying low, afraid of society's wagging tongues that would be discussing her daughter's failure to secure her engagement to Mr Compton. So the days passed slowly for the two ladies who were forced to spend more time than they preferred in each other's company.

A letter from Emma writing to announce she would be visiting at the end of the month saw Georgiana surprisingly pleased. She had not missed her sister's company or cutting remarks, but a visit from her would mean her mother would be busy preparing the house for guests, and once they arrived, provide a useful distraction for all concerned, since Emma was supposed to be bringing along a large party.

Her sister's removal to another county upon her marriage to Mr Faversham had brought Emma into new society, and therefore Georgiana assumed the house guests would be her sister's new female acquaintances. This was why on the day of Emma's arrival, Georgiana was shocked to see three young men step out of the carriage, in addition to her sister and her brother-in-law.

"Mr Lawton sends his apologises, mama," said Emma stepping down from the carriage. "He was desirous of visiting but business has held him in London." She strode across and pecked her mother on the cheek in greeting.

"Good day, Lady Davenport," Mr Faversham bowed low to his mother-in-law. "It is such a pleasure to see you again." He turned to the first guest. "May I introduce my cousin, Mr Turner, my good friend, Mr Southerly, and his younger brother."

All three gentlemen lowered their heads respectfully to their hostess.

Mr Faversham then spoke to his acquaintances and said, "May I introduce my sister-in-law to you, Miss Georgiana Davenport."

The gentlemen repeated their greeting and stood expectantly as Lady Davenport opened her mouth to speak.

"Thank you for bringing such a large party to us, Mr Faversham. We have not had much company since you took my dear Emma

137

away from us." She turned to her younger daughter. "Georgiana, show our guests into the house."

It didn't take long before Georgiana realised the reason for her sister's visit. These gentlemen were here for her. Every waking hour of that day was spent entertaining her brother-in-law's acquaintances and even though she thought it was an impossibility, her mother became more demanding than ever before. One moment she was sent to take Mr Turner on a tour of the grounds, the next she was obliged to entertain the elder Mr Southerly on the pianoforte, followed by reciting a poem to his younger brother. Not for one part of the day was she left alone.

The following day Georgiana eventually found refuge in the parlour. She shut her eyes and breathed a sigh, enjoying the luxury of quietness and not having to make meaningless chatter. To her displeasure, the peace was rudely broken when the younger Mr Southerly entered the room and took a seat next to her. It was at this moment she wished to be more like her mother, possessing a fierce glare that could frighten anyone away in an instant. Instead, she smiled politely and thus welcomed the gentleman to speak.

"It has been a pleasure becoming acquainted with your sister, Miss Davenport. She is a very talented young woman."

"Yes… she is," said Georgiana with little emotion.

"I see you do not get on well with your sister?"

Her mouth instantly dropped open at his unexpected frankness. In the past, her polite responses, although clearly devoid of admiration for Emma, had covered up her true feelings perfectly well and this perception startled her.

"It is okay, Miss Davenport." He leaned closer to her ear. "I understand, I'm not partial to my brother either." Henry Southerly grinned and a twinkle flickered across his eyes as Georgiana shifted uncomfortably next to him. "From what I can see, you and Mrs Faversham are similar to Robert and myself… complete opposites."

"Y-yes," she faltered, staring down at her hands interlocked on her lap. "I suppose that is what we are."

"There you are, Georgiana," cried Lady Davenport as she came bursting commandingly into the room. "Why don't you take Mr Southerly to our orchard? I'm sure he would be fascinated by the selection and varieties of fruit we have there."

"Sounds fascinating," Henry said, turning his back on Lady Davenport and looking at her daughter with a humorous glint in his eye. It took everything within Georgiana not to snigger, Mr Southerly had not the least interest in spending his morning looking at fruit.

In obedience Georgiana led her guest out of the house. They followed a path leading through symmetrical flower beds, filled with roses of many colours.

Henry Southerly rubbed his hands expectantly together. "Now we have our freedom," he said. "What shall we actually do?"

"We must go and look at the orchard," replied Georgiana, a little surprised that there might be an alternative option.

"Do you really want to go and look at bunches of apples and pears?"

"Of course not, but that's where mama has told us to go."

"And do you always obey your mother, Miss Davenport?"

"Yes, of course," she spoke these words with confidence, slightly offended that he asked her such a question, until she thought of Thomas Compton and his impending marriage with Annabelle and she reddened slightly.

"Come on, Miss Davenport," Henry cried spreading his arms wide open. "Live a little and feel the constraints of parental supervision evaporate."

"She'd find out, Mr Southerly."

"So?" he said, lowering his arms.

"You don't have to deal with the consequences."

"What consequences?" He laughed.

"I'm not my parents' favourite person at the moment, Mr Southerly. The smallest mishap could be fatal."

He shook his head in disappointment. "Maybe you are more like your sister than I imagined."

The statement hurt Georgiana. This gentleman didn't know her. She was nothing like Emma, how dare he say such a thing.

"Maybe I am." She drew up her chin. "Would you still like to see the orchard?"

Henry Southerly walked moodily by Georgina's side, his opportunity to have fun having been taken away from him. As their conversation dried up, Georgiana wondered which of the three men had the largest fortune, the grandest connections and which one was intended to be Thomas' replacement. She was almost convinced that whilst she was busy entertaining the younger Mr Southerly, the other two gentlemen would be thoroughly interrogated by her mother.

They strolled around the fruit trees, neither speaking a word. Henry picked up an apple from the ground, rubbed it on his tailcoat and began crunching loudly. Georgiana watched at him. This man was unlike anyone she had been introduced to before. Not only did he speak his mind, but he seemed to have little fear of anyone or anything. He probably wasn't even scared of her mother…maybe he would be a useful ally to have around. She frowned, wondering how he had managed to enter Lady Davenport's inner sanctum.

"Why have you come, Mr Southerly?" she asked, when she could not work out the answer.

"My brother invited me." He threw the half-eaten apple over his shoulder onto the ground, the core rolling into the uncut grass. "I wanted a change of scenery. Come now…" he said suddenly becoming jovial again. "We have seen the orchard and fulfilled the orders of your mother, let us go somewhere else."

"We have barely stepped foot inside the orchard walls."

"But we have been here." He raised an eyebrow temptingly.

Georgiana gazed back through the orchard gate and towards the house. No one was watching. This was her opportunity: she would show him she was not like her sister. "All right, I'll show you the river."

That evening Georgiana sat with a book on her knee. To the outsider it looked like she was intently reading, however her mind was deep in thought. She was convinced Henry Southerly had no knowledge that he was included in a party of potential husbands for herself. There was no way her mother would want this young man associated in any way with their family. Firstly, he was the youngest son, not heir to anything important, and secondly, his frivolous nature would most definitely not be accepted. He must have joined the party by accident.

"Georgiana, come and join us at the table," requested Lady Davenport. "Put your book down, I do not know why you are sitting reading alone."

So off Georgiana went in obedience, her solitude not returning until she retired to bed for her mother worked her hard. She went from playing cards, to singing, to playing the pianoforte, to reciting a book of poetry, to making polite conversation with Mr Turner, with the elder Mr Southerly and then with Henry. The only respite came when Robert Southerly desired to recite a poem himself. By the time Lady Davenport gave her permission to withdraw upstairs she was completely exhausted.

Rolling over in bed the following morning, Georgiana groaned. The prospect of another day of parading in front of suitable bachelors did not fill her with much joy. She tucked the bed sheet over her shoulders and closed her eyes again. Her thoughts drifted to Edward. He had written several times since his removal from Denholm Park and Georgiana had diligently replied, leaving out matters that might cause him unnecessary anxiety. There was nothing he could do to help her situation; he could not come home to rescue her. However, as she lay in bed trying to shut out her woeful reality,

Georgiana sensed the only comfort would come from communicating her troubles to her brother.

With purpose she flung off the bed sheets and pattered across to the writing desk. Licking the tip of her finger she separated the paper and picked up her inky quill.

My dearest Edward,

I was pleased to hear your regiment think so highly of you already... though I cannot say I was surprised to hear of their praises.

There are many things I have neglected to tell you. You will shake your head at me when you read what has happened. I have purposely avoided telling you because I did not want to worry you when there's so little you can do.

Thomas Compton proposed to me the day you left for Portsmouth. You may think I am foolish, but I declined him. Mama did not take the news well, especially when he announced his engagement to Annabelle Hastings shortly after.

I am sorry to burden you with my wretchedness, however, I am currently surrounded by a house full of eligible bachelors. Mama is unbearable, if I'm not singing to one, I'm reading to another... how I long for peace and solitude! Apart from yourself, there is no other man on this earth I would happily welcome into Denholm Park...

Georgiana finished off her letter with other general matters before folding the papers together and stamping them with her seal.

A host of grey clouds sprayed down a persistent light rain all day, preventing anyone from leaving the house. After breakfast, Emma took herself off into a corner to write some letters, her husband took a seat with Mr Turner to discuss politics and business, Henry Southerly stared miserably out the window, scowling at the rain preventing him from frivolous pursuits and Georgiana had been positioned to converse with the elder Mr Southerly.

Robert Southerly was fifteen years older than Georgiana; he had an air of great propriety and didn't smile much. Apart from similar facial features, she could not understand how Robert and Henry Southerly were brothers at all, so little did they have in common.

Creating conversation with the man was also extremely difficult. Every attempt on Georgiana's side failed to ignite a lively dialogue and at each one-word answer from the gentleman, Lady Davenport glared over the top of her book.

"It's a shame about the weather, Mr Southerly," she said again for the third time, touching the side of her head where a dull ache was beginning.

"Indeed," was all Robert Southerly allowed to escape from his mouth.

Georgiana smiled helplessly; this man was not a conversationalist and Lady Davenport shot her another scathing look. What more did this woman want from her? She was trying her best!

"Do you ride much, Mr Southerly?" she asked plucking a random subject out of the air in desperation.

"Not much," he replied and went silent again.

"You do not like the sport?"

"I prefer riding in a carriage."

"Carriages are more comfortable, I suppose."

"Yes, indeed." He looked across to Georgiana and blinked, his face expressionless.

Georgiana smiled nervously and opened her mouth to speak once more, but had nothing else to say and was greatly relieved when Ridley entered the room to announce a visitor.

"Sir Gillingham and Mr Kirkby," he announced standing by the doorway.

As had become customary on his visits, Sir Gillingham promptly made excuses and made his way to find Lord Davenport in the library, where he would stay until he ended his visit. This left Kirkby sitting awkwardly on the sofa next to Georgiana, feeling the watchful eyes of Lady Davenport on him as quietness filled the room.

"Play the piano, Georgiana," Lady Davenport's shrill voice commanded and meekly Georgiana did as she was told. As she pulled back the piano stool to position herself, the noise of the legs scraped along the wooden floorboards, echoing around the silent room.

The tension began to ease as each person focused their attention on the musician, whose melodious song filled the air. At the end of her piece Georgiana's heart began to race, for some reason she dared not stop playing and the final note lingered in the air.

"Play again," ordered her mother. So Georgiana played again…and again and again. She was not allowed to stop until Sir Gillingham reappeared to collect his cousin.

As Lady Davenport politely wished good health to Sir Gillingham and his family, Kirkby used the distraction to conveniently shuffle across to Georgiana, who had used the opportunity to remove herself from the instrument.

"Rather crowded in here," he whispered nonchalantly into her ear.

"Yes, we are a big party at the moment," she replied in low tone, not wishing to reveal the reason for their many guests.

He stared down at Georgiana who was rubbing her strained hands. "Your fingers will be tired after all that playing."

"A little."

He coughed shyly. "I am very glad to see you survived your refusal of Mr Compton."

"William!" The two looked immediately up as Sir Gillingham broke in. He had finished his goodbyes to Lady Davenport and was ready to go.

"Good day, Miss Davenport." Kirkby tilted his head and without looking in Georgiana's direction, followed his cousin out of the room.

13

Sophie

"Oh, you're back, are you?" came the peevish voice of Elizabeth.

Sophie snapped her phone shut, annoyed that Dylan hadn't answered her call. "Don't worry, I'm not staying long," she muttered, keeping her head low. "I'm out for lunch."

Elizabeth ignored the comment and barged past her daughter into the library. "George, I need you this afternoon to talk about renovations." She hauled open the faded gold curtains and sunlight gushed into the room making her husband squint. "The architect is coming at two and I need you looking presentable."

"Send my apologies," George said gruffly, clearing his throat and rubbing his eyes. "I won't be there."

"Oh, you'll be there." George didn't say a word in response and slowly closed his eyes as he sat in his chair. "It's an order."

"Mum," said Sophie following her back into the room. "Just leave him alone."

"George…" Elizabeth lowered her body, face level with his. "Stop moping around. Get up. Get dressed. Enough is enough."

"Mum!" Sophie said louder, pulling her mother's intimidating figure away from her father.

"No," Elizabeth shook her daughter's hand away. "I'm not having it. He's sulking, that's all your father's doing, because he doesn't get his poor little retirement plan. Well, I'm sorry, but that's life George. L.I.F.E. Life. Be downstairs at two." She spun on her heel and stormed out without further comment.

George continued to sit motionless, his eyes shut tight.

"Dad, she doesn't mean…"

"Please leave me, Sophie. I want to be alone." He rubbed the bridge of his nose as he leaned an elbow on the chair arm. "Shut the curtains on your way out."

Sophie leaned against the library door again after shutting it closed behind her. A single tear trickled down her cheek. She wiped it away and gave a sniff. This was too big for her to handle alone. She lifted her phone and dialled again.

Sorry I'm not available to take your call at the moment but please leave a message after the tone. BEEP.

"Dylan, it's Sophie *again*. Call me, please... It's about dad."

****

"Is everything all right? You seem a little distant."

"I'm sorry..." Sophie had been staring at her watch periodically throughout her lunch with Oliver. Two o'clock was looming closer and she knew her dad would not be downstairs discussing colour schemes with the architect. Her tummy tightened as she anxiously contemplated how Elizabeth would respond. "What were you saying again?" She felt like the worse lunch companion in the world, her concentration was appalling.

"I was rattling on about a sick cow," Oliver shook his head and laughed. "No wonder your attention is elsewhere. I'm not much of a conversationalist, am I?"

"Don't be silly, I find sick cows very interesting." She paused to reconsider what she'd just said. "Okay, maybe not... I'm sorry, it's nothing to do with you. My family's going through a tough time, I've a lot on my mind."

Oliver's warm smile immediately vanished as he looked at his lunch companion. He leaned forward, his forehead wrinkled with concern. "What's the problem?" As the words shot out, he suddenly pulled back. "I'm sorry, I'm really not trying to be nosy."

Sophie smiled across at him. "It's okay, I could do with a listening ear." She was surprised by her reaction, when earlier Oliver's questions had left her feeling too exposed for her liking. But now she didn't care. Her fifth attempt to call Dylan had failed and Oliver's welcoming face screamed out at her to confide in him instead.

"I'm all ears," said Oliver taking a bite from his chicken baguette, which was oozing with a smoky barbeque sauce.

"It's a long story..." She looked away, her confidence fizzling away, maybe baring all to Oliver Morgan wasn't such a good idea after all. "I wouldn't even know where to begin."

"Well, you could start by telling me why you keep looking at your watch... got a hot date you can't miss?"

Sophie laughed. "No, it's my dad."

"Your dad's your hot date...mmm, that's interesting." Oliver grinned.

"You know that's not what I mean," said Sophie momentarily forgetting her unease and allowing her threatening perspiration to recede.

"I'm sorry... go ahead, you said it's about your dad?"

"You know my dad's not well..." Oliver nodded as he chomped away and as Sophie watched him, she could feel the heat rise into her cheeks again; this wasn't an easy topic to talk about, she needed to take a deep breath and say it as quickly as possible. "You see... he, erm...he struggles with mental health."

"I'm sorry, that can't be easy." He put down the baguette and wiped his sticky fingers on a napkin before focusing his attention solely on Sophie.

Sophie had to take a sudden intake of breath as Oliver's empathetic eyes burrowed into her face. Their deep sapphire tone had the potential to knock her completely over. She was so close to tears; it would not be good to break down in the middle of their lunch.

Casting her eyes onto the red and white checked table cloth she dared to continue, remembering the chaos from her past so vividly. "About ten years ago he suffered from depression, quite badly actually. It took him a long time to recover."

147

"He did recover?"

"On the whole he did, but now...I can see him falling into it again."

"Since he's taken on the estate?"

"That's when he started changing. You see, last time my brother was here to help, I was only eleven at the time."

"Your brother, he's older than you?"

"Yes, he was sixteen when it all happened. He nursed dad back to health and managed to keep me afloat too. This time it's just me and mum."

"It must be really tough seeing him struggle again...and for your mum too."

Sophie's slumped form became instantly rigid, hearing her mother receive undeserved sympathy. "Yes, I'm sure it's hard for her."

Oliver sensed the icy tone and sat back a little, making Sophie immediately regret her reaction.

"I'm sorry," she said quickly. "Mum and I don't often see eye to eye, you know what it's like." Her hands shot to her mouth: how could she make the same mistake twice? "Oliver, I didn't think..."

"It's okay, my mum died a long time ago, I don't easily get upset." He reached across and touched her arm reassuringly. "Why don't you and your mum get along?"

"We never have, or at least, I can't remember a time when we did. She wants perfection and I never meet the standard."

"It can't be that bad, can it?"

"Believe me, it is... why do you think I studied land management?"

Oliver considered the question. The answer was obvious. "Ah..."

"I only did it because it's what *she* wanted."

"What did you want?"

The question caught her by surprise.

"It doesn't matter." She quickly batted away the question. What did it matter what she wanted? She never got a choice and it was too late anyway, now she was stuck on a track leading to a mind-numbingly boring career which only made her mother happy.

"Of course it matters," Oliver exclaimed a little too loudly, so that the lady sitting behind him was caught off guard and spilt her tea into the saucer. "Tell me," he said, with a little more consideration for the other customers. "What would you like to do?"

"It's nothing interesting." She poured a drop of milk into her cup, even though the little teapot for one was empty. "Let's talk about something else."

"What is it Sophie? I'd really like to know."

Cautiously lifting her head, she met his attentive gaze. "You'd really like to know?"

"Yes."

"Educational Psychology," she spurted out hastily and winced not wanting to hear his response. "It's stupid, I know, but…"

"Who said it's stupid," said Oliver leaning forward again.

"I studied psychology for A-Level and loved it," she explained, encouraged by his genuine interest. "Part way through the course we did a module about children, I knew then that's what I wanted to do." The excitement rose in her voice as she spoke, no one had ever taken an interest in what she wanted before, since everyone around her generally bowed down to the authority of her mother.

"That sounds great, Sophie."

"Land management doesn't provide much opportunity for working with children."

"Erm, no… it doesn't. Do you enjoy working on the estate, at all?"

"Not really. I've found the last three years of my life rather dull if I'm honest. But with a mother like mine, you've got to pick your battles. My brother's a conservationist, if you didn't know."

"Ah," he said again. "I see."

"My mum is not a sensitive lady." She picked up the dessert menu. "She can see my dad is ill, but she still shouts at him in an attempt to

149

snap him out of it. I fail to see how she loves her family when all she seems to care about is herself, or what we can offer her."

"I'm sure there's love somewhere."

"If there is, she doesn't show it."

Oliver caught the eye of a waitress. "Cake?"

Sophie's eye lit up. "Chocolate fudge cake, warm with ice cream, please," she grinned at Oliver's amused smile.

"Just a coffee for me," he said to the waitress, who wrote down their requests and headed back to the kitchen. Sophie stared at him in surprise. "I didn't inherit the sweet tooth," he explained. "Give me a sausage roll or a ham sandwich and I'll be a happy man."

"More cake for me then." Sophie laughed, feeling the atmosphere lighten. "Anyway… that's enough about me. How about you?"

"What about me?"

"What do you really want to do? You said you don't see your future on the farm."

The waitress reappeared, placing a milky coffee before Oliver and a large serving of moist gooey cake in front of Sophie.

"Dad would support me whatever I did," he said, stirring the foamy topping. "Charlie was a natural at farming and so expanding into organic produce was a great idea for him, but dad would never force me to stay if I didn't want to." He stopped and sipped his drink, licking the foam off his lips.

"You didn't answer my question."

"I didn't?" he said in innocence, his mouth curving up into a half smile.

"No, you know you didn't," said Sophie laughing.

"Okay, okay…" he put down his coffee. "I'm waiting to continue my education, but I can't fund it right now, so I'm stuck here whilst I'm saving up." He shrugged. "Nice cake?"

"Delicious… but you're not getting away with it that easily." There was no way she was going to be the only one squirming on this lunch date. "What is it you want to do; you still haven't told me?"

Oliver pressed his lips together, obviously deliberating if he should let her into his secret. He looked around. "Don't tell my dad, he doesn't know…"

"My mouth is sealed."

"What I'd really like to do…" He spoke more to his coffee cup than to Sophie. "Is teach children who can't attend mainstream education, kids who have been kicked out, the ones who don't have it easy. Actually…" He lifted his eyes to hers and paused with an amused expression. "It sounds like we'd make a good team."

"How?"

"You'd support them mentally and I'd help them academically…it's a shame neither one of us is living the dream."

"Can't your dad help you financially? I'm sure he would if he could."

"Oh, he would in a heartbeat, in fact he'd go into debt to fund it, but I know he could never afford it. Teaching means a degree and then an extra year on top of that. Dad would never forgive himself if he couldn't send one of his sons to university, if that's what they wanted to do. I've actually been saving up for the last few years, although I'm still a long way off. Farm wages aren't the best, as you can imagine."

"You should tell him. Even if he can't help you financially, he'd be pleased you have a dream."

"I'm not certain I'm ready to tell him yet." He wiped the edge of his foamy cup and licked a finger. "Phew, I wasn't expecting our lunch date to make me feel so vulnerable." He laughed, flapping his t-shirt up and down, allowing the air to cool him down, as he did so, something caught his eye. "What are you reading?"

Sophie wondered what he was talking about until he pointed to the old tattered diary in her open bag.

"Oh, I don't think you'd be interested," she said, remembering Rupert's indifference.

"Try me… is it a first edition?"

Sophie reached down and picked up Georgiana's diary, cradling it to her chest and suddenly feeling protective over the life of a girl she knew nothing about. If he had anything negative to say, she didn't want to hear it.

"It's, erm… it's a diary of a girl." She passed the book tentatively across for Oliver to examine. "I found it at the manor."

"Who is she?" Oliver carefully flicked through the browned pages.

"Her name is Davenport, but as far as I'm aware the Middletons have been at the manor for centuries, so I don't know how it ended up there. I found a box full: her whole life is written down." She relaxed a little as Oliver's face became buried inside the hard-backed diary.

"This is amazing… the date is 1819. What a time capsule!" he exclaimed. "Listen to this… *I'm not certain what to do. Aunt Lucy has visited Denholm Park and I am so desirous to meet her again. We correspond regularly, in secret obviously, mama is never to know. I haven't set eyes upon her since I was eight years old when she asked if we could become better acquainted, her exclusion from the family having always prevented it before. I was curious to take her up on the offer and sought out Edward for advice. He encouraged me to write to Aunt Lucy, as long as mama never found out, because that's what he had done since he was five old years old.*

"On Edward's recommendation I wrote to my aunt and over the years she has become my confidante and my friend, a woman whom I greatly admire and respect. Except now she is here in Middleton and if I seek after her, mama will surely find out… and then what would happen?" Oliver looked up. "What does she do?"

"I don't know, I haven't read further yet. I'm hoping she visits this long-lost aunt; she seems to be the only person except for her brother who actually cares for her. Her mother doesn't sound pleasant at all."

"Sounds like your mother," he said with a glint of humour in his eye.

Sophie chose to ignore the comment.

"Exactly!" her eyes lit up, had Oliver seen the similarity too? "Don't our lives appear to be very similar?"

"Do you wear corsets too?" He smirked.

"That's not what I meant." She laughed and took the diary back out of his hands. "Listen to this... *Mama had me playing the pianoforte for two continuous hours. I was allowed no pauses to find my music and no stopping to ask for requests. Each and every time I finished a piece, she glared with slit eyes in my direction and I knew I had to immediately begin again. Her game didn't fool me. She would do anything to avoid my socialising with Mr Kirkby. Thomas Compton was her favoured match, the one she had chosen. This newcomer is not her choice, therefore his presence in our house is undesired. This is why I have retired to bed with very tired fingers and a throbbing head."* Sophie stopped and shut the book excitedly. "Do you know Rupert Donaldson?"

"I've heard of him. Everyone's heard of everyone in Middleton."

"He's *my* Thomas Compton."

Oliver wrinkled his forehead, wondering if his lunch guest had just turned crazy in front of his eyes.

"My mother wants me to marry him."

"That's…mmm, interesting."

"Her two goals in life have been to become Lady of the Manor, which she has accomplished, and to witness Rupert Donaldson become her son-in-law."

"Surely she wouldn't make you marry someone you didn't love?"

Sophie didn't answer. Oliver didn't know her mother. She was capable of anything.

"At least I can argue with my mother, which is something this girl isn't allowed to do." She fingered the diary. "I wish I knew more about her."

"Maybe we should do a bit of investigating, I bet there's something that would shed some light on who she was and how she's linked to the manor. I'll come and help you look, if you'd like?"

"I wouldn't want to waste your time, Oliver. You're busy on the farm." She picked up the little red book and pushed it back into her bag.

"I do have free time, Sophie. I don't live in the cow sheds."

"But you don't want to spend it at the manor."

"Why not? I'd like to help; it's really fascinating."

Sophie hesitated. He seemed to be genuine… actually, everything about him seemed genuine.

"Only if you're sure." She rooted around in her bag for a pen and scribbled down a number on an unused red napkin. "Ring me when you're next free, I'll probably be in the estate office, I seem to live in there at the moment."

"Sounds like a plan to me." He smiled warmly. "I'll be there when I can."

14

Georgiana

Lord Davenport had decided to plan a hunting party for his male guests. He did it reluctantly, preferring his own company to that of young men he hardly knew, but his wife insisted that he should. This meant the gentlemen were to be absent from Denholm Park for several hours. Georgiana was greatly relieved to be presented with an opportunity for some much-needed time alone and promptly excused herself to run some errands in Middleton, overjoyed that she was able to escape the company of her mother and sister as well.

It felt such a freedom to be walking along the potholed lanes unaccompanied and she revelled in the luxury of isolation. Soon, all her errands were completed and she began the trek back down the little high street towards the lane that would lead her home.

Right at the end of the high street stood the Middleton inn. Curiosity caused Georgiana to slow her pace and glance up towards the lead windows. Would Aunt Lucy still be there? If her mother had visited on the night of Gillingham's dinner she would have been chased out of town for sure.

A sudden wet foot drew Georgiana's attention to the deep puddle she had stepped into and she shook it dry. She had to make a decision.

Glancing to either side revealed her end of the high street was deserted. A few shopkeepers were outside seeing to their wares, but no familiar faces revealed themselves and so tentatively, Georgiana tentatively walked across and pushed open the creaking inn door.

"Excuse me," she asked timidly, trying not to touch the sticky worktop. "Is there a Miss Barnet staying here?"

"She checked out this morning, miss," said the innkeeper polishing a tankard with a white cloth.

"Thank you, sir." Georgiana turned away from the counter a little deflated. She had only just missed her. She had known it was highly unlikely her aunt would be there, but all the same, she had hoped her assumptions would be proved false.

"Georgiana?" A woman carrying a large leather case appeared from a dimly lit passage by the bottom of a staircase. "Is that you?"

"Aunt Lucy?" Georgiana instantly recognised the dark curly blond hair and hurried closer to the figure, who grasped her in an embrace and kissed her cheek in greeting.

"What a surprise! I thought I'd missed you," cried Lucy, now holding the girl at arm's length and taking in her elegant figure with a face full of pleasure. "Come on..." She grabbed the case she had abandoned on the floor and took Georgiana by the arm. "Where is the nearest tea room?"

Sitting at a table far away from the window, Georgiana sat with her aunt sipping a cup of tea out of a dainty porcelain cup.

"How well you have grown up, Gianna," exclaimed her aunt, using the abbreviated version of Georgiana's name that only she ever used in their letters. Georgiana remembered Edward once calling her by the nickname and was immediately put to rights by their mother, "We do not use abbreviated versions of our names, we are not common men, Edward. We gave you a name and we expect you to use it in full."

"You have not aged a bit, aunt," said Georgiana thinking how strange it was to be sitting face to face after years of only writing. "You look exactly the same as when I was eight years old."

"What a compliment!" smiled Lucy, beaming from cheek to cheek. "To have not aged in ten years." She sipped her tea and watched Georgiana over the rim of her cup. "Your mother came to see me."

"I feared she might have driven you out of Middleton before I had chance to find you."

"She did try and not so politely asked me to leave."

"Why didn't you go?"

"Because I wanted to see you." Lucy had never told her niece why Lady Davenport had disowned her from the family and although extremely curious, Georgiana never asked. "I decided I would leave today whatever happened, it was becoming too much of a risk. I dare not think how your mother would respond if she found me to be here…and you have to live with her, you poor thing." She gulped down the last bit of her drink, leaving the tea leaves floating around the bottom and dabbed the corner of her mouth with a cream cloth napkin. "I'm sorry our time together has to be so short: I was hoping to see you sooner."

"I have been detained at Denholm. Mama is trying to find me a husband and I am currently surrounded by every eligible bachelor possible. It is not easy to escape their company." As Georgiana spoke, she saw her aunt's appearance change; her beaming smile had vanished and she sat gnawing her lower lip. "What is it aunt?"

Lucy reached across and grabbed her niece's hand. "Before I go, there is something I must ask you. You can say no, please don't feel like you have to say yes." Georgiana felt her stomach clench and without realising, clasped her aunt's hand tightly in return. "Gianna… would you consider coming to visit me, in London?"

"Visit you?" Georgina felt alarmed. How could she visit London when she was barely allowed out of sight of her mother? It would not be allowed, not even given consideration. It felt silly to even think of it as a serious possibly.

"Yes, come and visit me, Gianna. We would have such fun together."

"Mama would never…"

"I know…" She wrapped both hands around Georgiana's and squeezed them tenderly, in an attempt to stop hearing the truth, even though she knew her suggestion was outrageous. "But… she might say yes, we won't know if you don't ask. I enjoy our correspondence, Gianna, but I want more than just letters. I want to spend time with you, I want to hear your voice and be an aunt to you."

"You are an aunt to me and a very good one."

"That is kind of you to say." She fixed her gaze earnestly on her niece. "Would you consider asking? I know you would have to brave your mother and I will not force you."

"Do you think there's a chance mama would consider it?"

"I cannot answer that, all I can say is you would be warmly welcome in my home and you would be able to stay as long as you are able."

"I would need an escort, that's assuming mama would even let me, I could not travel alone and Edward is in Portsmouth."

"I have many friends who could meet you half-way, if your father could start you off on your journey with a servant...please consider asking, Gianna." Lucy leaned forward, her eyes now pleading.

"I would have to find the right time to ask, I am not mama's favourite person right now. It might take me weeks to raise the question, and even then, she might not allow it."

"I understand… do not feel pressured," Lucy released her hands, pulled on her gloves and rose up from the table. "Promise me you will write, either once you've asked her, or if after contemplation, you decide you cannot approach her."

"Of course, aunt."

"Look," said Lucy peering out the far window past the other customers sipping their teas. "There is a coach. I must leave now; I do not want to be standing in the open too long."

"Mama is at Denholm and papa is hunting, you should be fine."

"But still, I must be careful." She hastily fastened the three buttons on her pelisse coat. "I am so pleased to have seen you, Gianna." She picked up her case and guided her niece briskly out of the tea room.

Georgiana saw her aunt safely onto the stagecoach. There was much for her to contemplate as she made her way back down the high street and she slowly meandered in the direction of Denholm, caught up in her own thoughts.

"Miss Davenport!" A gentleman's voice broke into her thoughts and she heard someone come up behind her. She circled dreamily around, pulling herself back into reality.

"Mr Kirkby." She smiled warmly. "What a pleasure to see you again."

He tipped his hat and caught his breath after running part way down the high street to catch up with her. "I see you have escaped the confines of Denholm Park?"

"With much relief, yes I have."

"There was quite a crowd when I was last with you. Can I take a guess the party is for you?" he looked half-amused.

"Is it obvious?"

"I presumed it was the result of you declining Mr Compton."

"You are correct, mama has lined them all up."

"Have you had any proposals yet?"

"Surprisingly, I have not. However, I'm bound to have at least one before they leave."

"When are they to leave?" he asked with interest.

"I'm not certain, but soon I hope, they're beginning to outstay their welcome."

"I am sorry I added to the number the other night," he said apologetically.

Georgiana looked awkwardly down at her feet, one still slightly damp from stepping in the puddle outside the inn. "You were a very welcome, uninvited guest."

Kirkby smiled, pleased with her reply. "Actually, I am glad I bumped into you, Miss Davenport. I wanted to tell you I will be returning home at the end of the week."

"Oh, so soon?" she said visibly disappointed.

"My mother is getting married again," he explained. "I wish to be present at the ceremony."

"I'm sorry, I didn't realise your mother was widowed."

"Yes, sadly my father passed away about a year ago. He was in the navy - I did not really know him, most of his time was spent at sea." He paused, considering how frank he should be next, but if he didn't speak now, he was afraid his opportunity might be lost forever.

"It is a shame my mother's marriage has come about so quickly, I have been enjoying getting to know you, Miss Davenport." He cleared his throat and looked away, trying to hide the pink tint suddenly spreading across his face. However, he soon regained his composure and returned his gaze as the hue disappeared. "Although, I see there is a bit of competition to gain your attention, this makes me believe my success will be limited." He raised an eyebrow and looked at her questioningly.

Georgiana glanced around her in panic. She shouldn't be here. Everything she had ever been taught about respectability swam about in her head. This wasn't how it should be. Mr Kirkby was putting them both in harm's way, speaking in such a forthright manner. But, despite her dismay, Georgiana stayed. It would have been easy to run away and to keep her dignity intact, however, she needed to hear more.

"Maybe I'm mistaken," Kirkby continued when he got no answer. "But I don't think your mother likes me… or does she always make you play piece after piece on the pianoforte without a break?" His mouth curled up at the corners, as he was clearly entertained by the memory: however, he too was aware their current position could lead them into serious trouble and his mirth soon disappeared.

"My mother is a very harsh woman," Georgiana spoke in hushed undertones, for fear someone might overhear and report back. "She does not take kindly to people who threaten her authority."

"I am threatening her authority?"

"She thinks I have designs to…" Georgiana looked bashfully away. "Marry you."

"I take it I'm not on her list of potential husbands. Your parents are not forward thinking. Do you not get a say in your own future?"

"My mother is very strict and it's been worse since my brother has left home to join his regiment."

"I'm surprised he's been sent off to the army."

"Since turning eighteen my mother's desire to rid me from her home has increased dramatically. Edward was slowing the process down by protecting me, so they had to remove him from Denholm Park."

"That's outrageous." His voice rose, causing Georgiana to dart her eyes around in alarm, she could not afford any unnecessary attention. "What have you done that's caused such dislike?"

"I've had the audacity to breathe."

Kirkby stepped back in agitation. "I must say this, Miss Davenport, and I know it goes against all rules of courtship to be acting in this way…" He took her hand lightly. "You deserve to be loved: I see you do not get much of it."

The warm touch of his hand felt reassuring, but Georgiana knew she had to let it go.

"I'm used to it," she whispered, her eyelashes shyly fluttering down onto her cheek.

"You should not have to be *used* to it." He gripped her hand, sensing she was about to let go. "I have watched you since my arrival here… you are one of the sweetest, most accomplished ladies I have ever met. You are caring, thoughtful and considerate. You have courage to stand for truth, even if all around you has fallen into foolishness." His head lowered in sadness. "It is a shame, therefore, that I will miss my chance." He let her hand fall.

"What do you mean?" Georgiana murmured overcome by his words.

"It sounds like you will be engaged when I return."

She felt a sudden stab of sorrow. It was true, her mother would ensure one of the men residing at Denholm Park would be her husband, it was a foregone conclusion. A carriage trundled passed them, but she felt so disheartened, that this time she did not care who might have been watching.

"I know our acquaintance is young, Miss Davenport," continued Kirkby. "Nevertheless, I feel I must ask you to not accept a proposal from any other man in my absence."

"If I am offered a proposal of marriage, I don't know that I can decline. We have only just met and I cannot cross my mother again. She lined up Mr Compton for me, who I rejected, and now she has set up three more, if I refuse them too, I…"

"Can I presume," he broke into her meandering thoughts, "That you will consider my request, since you have not outwardly declined my proposition?"

"I will consider it, but as I've said, I have no say over my future."

Her answer was good enough for him and as there was a small group of shoppers heading their way, they reluctantly parted company.

Georgiana did not find the walk home as pleasant as the journey into Middleton. Her emotions were in a whirl and solitude now became her enemy as she allowed her doubts and anxieties to attack. Lady Davenport would never accept this man, so it would not do to pin any hope on him. His promises would end in nothing and she would be left with a broken heart. Yet it was tempting to consider life by his side, with no oppressive voices in her ears and no restrictions. Her daydreams were rudely dispersed by visions of her aunt and she let out a groan. Two impossible requests with inevitably two undesirable consequences.

15

Sophie

"I know you're the estate manager, but I don't understand how we can do this without your mother's permission."

"You've got *my* permission, isn't that enough?" Sophie sat in the rectory desperately trying to persuade the vicar to hold the community fete in the grounds of Middleton Manor.

"I really need your mother's consent. I'm not having any embarrassing confrontations if I set up on your good word and Mrs Hastings comes out to have a quarrel."

Inspired by her nineteenth century counterpart, Sophie was determined to win one fight against her mother and prove to herself that it was possible to reclaim her own life. Each time she read a passage from the yellowing diary she could see Georgiana finding a piece of hidden confidence. From her rejection of Thomas Compton's proposal of marriage, to her considering an engagement to Mr Kirkby, she could see Lady Davenport's hold slowly being loosened, even if the girl didn't see it herself. Surely as a young woman living in the twenty-first century, Sophie had the ability to make her own decisions about her future too.

"I understand your concern, however I believe it needs to be at the manor if this estate is going to thrive, we need the community on our side."

"I agree, however I cannot allow it to happen... not this way." The vicar stood up with determination. "I'm sorry Miss Hastings." The battle was over; her mother had won again.

Leaving the church offices behind Sophie felt completely deflated. Where did she go from here? If her mother was going to call all the shots, what was the point in her being here?

Looking ahead, she saw a small crowd of people gathering together for the weekly market day. Rupert had told her it was very popular and was worth a visit in order to see the delights of

Middleton's local industries. She followed the small swarm of people to the open square which stood behind Middleton's row of high street shops. It was a large space filled with fifteen or twenty different stalls, some with massive awnings for protection from the elements and some being only standard tables with collapsible legs.

As Sophie wandered along, she wondered if Jack Morgan had a stall in the market place and her heart lifted at the thought. So far, Oliver hadn't appeared at the manor, although she was determined not to be too disappointed, excusing his absence because of his busyness on the farm. Dylan still hadn't returned her calls and she felt helpless watching her dad spiral head down into imminent danger. Even though she wouldn't purposefully seek him out, bumping into Oliver might be just the thing she needed.

At first Sophie couldn't see anyone selling fruit and vegetables. She was sure Mr Morgan had a stall, thinking back to the day she'd bumped into Oliver. She assumed he must have been carrying the crates to the market. Continuing her search, she found no sign of the Morgans anywhere and her shoulders drooped. As she prepared to retrace her steps, a lady wearing a puffy-green body warmer caught her attention and Sophie wondered why this person had decided to wear swelteringly hot winter attire in the midst of summer. Suddenly the lady crouched down to view some second-hand books in a cardboard box and Sophie gasped, tucked away in the corner of the square, with one of the biggest crowds, was Mr Morgan serving punnets of fruit to delighted customers.

"Good morning, Mr. Morgan. How are you today?" chirruped Sophie once she'd ploughed her way through the throng of people.

"Miss Hasting," Jack Morgan's eyes lit up in recognition and Sophie could tell he was genuinely pleased to see her. "How lovely to see you. Can I tempt you to some strawberries? Charlie's done an amazing job with them, such sweet little things." He took a punnet of strawberries and dropped them into a paper bag without waiting for an answer.

164

"Thank you." Sophie sniffed the open bag. "They smell delicious. How much?"

"On the house."

"No, really, how much? I can pay."

"On the house," he repeated with a smile and turned to serve another customer as Sophie popped one of the strawberries into her mouth.

"Good, aren't they?"

She quickly swallowed the juicy sweet fruit, seeing Oliver walking towards her with an armful of crates. "Yes, they're amazing." She licked her lips. "Best strawberries I've ever tasted."

"My brother's a genius when it comes to producing fruit." He dumped the crates full of potatoes down on the ground and stretched his back. "I'm sorry I've not managed to come to the manor yet, I haven't forgotten. One of dad's herdsmen has been off ill and I'm covering for him, I seem to be working night and day at the moment."

"Don't worry about it." She shrugged her shoulders and tried to sound blasé, even though she had spent a lot of her time wondering why he hadn't called.

"How are you doing?" he looked self-consciously down at his dirty hands and rubbed them clean on his top.

Now she was standing in front of him, the need to offload all her worries didn't seem appropriate. This was not the time or place to discuss her problems. Oliver was working, she couldn't bother him now.

"I'm fine," she said.

Oliver stood up straight, folded his arms loosely and scanned her face. "I don't believe you."

"I'm fine, Oliver… really I am." Even Sophie could hear her high-pitched voice wasn't going to convince anybody. How did he know her so well…hadn't they only just met?

He leaned his face closer, scrunched up his nose and continued his scrutiny. "Nope, you're not convincing me." He looked at his watch. "Give me an hour and I'll be finished."

"Oliver, I'm fine."

"I'll see you in an hour, okay?" He waited until she confirmed the arrangement before he picked up one of the crates and walked away to help his father.

Sophie decided to explore the rest of the market whilst waiting for Oliver to finish on his father's stall and she stopped at a table covered with handmade bags. Picking one up, Sophie saw it was skilfully hand-stitched with a mixture of deep maroon, cream and dusty pink tones, all beautifully blended together.

"Did you make this?" Sophie asked the owner, who was sitting hand-sewing behind her stall.

"Yes," the middle-aged lady replied, pushing a pair of scarlet-coloured glasses back on top of her nose. "I've handmade all of these from my little cottage. It's just something to do in my spare time and gives me a bit of money."

"They're lovely," Sophie glided her hand smoothly over the material. "I wish I could do something like this."

"Thank you, Miss Hastings… it just takes practice."

Sophie looked up from the bag. "I'm sorry, I don't think we've met?"

"We haven't, but everyone knows you."

"They do?"

"The new estate manager, aren't you?"

"Well, technically that's my dad…" she said trailing away. What was the point? Even people she didn't know thought it was her job.

"Either way, you're doing fantastically well." The lady smiled encouragingly.

"Oh… thank you very much." The compliment caught her off guard, she wasn't certain what she had done that had been so amazing.

166

"One bag for the lady please." A hand swooped onto Sophie's lower back, as a second hand reached across the table of bags and handed over a ten-pound note to the stall holder.

"Rupert! You don't need to do that: I can buy one myself."

"I insist, my treat to the best acting estate manager in Middleton," he winked charmingly as Sophie thanked the lady. They turned away from the stall and began winding through the crowds of shoppers together.

"So, my dear friend, what are you doing on this fine day?" Rupert asked, steering Sophie away before she stepped on an unseen toddler sitting unexpectedly on the concrete floor.

"I'm ever so sorry," stammered the boy's mother upon realising her son was in everyone's way. "Bailey, come here."

Rupert kindly lifted the boy up by the hand and passed him back to his mother. Sophie didn't miss the gesture and found herself staring after the child, instead of listening to Rupert's repeated question.

"Soph…" He poked her. "I said, I didn't expect to see you down at the market, considering all the paperwork you keep telling me about at the manor."

"Oh!" She pulled her focus back. "I had a meeting with the reverend and thought I'd potter into the market whilst I was here."

"And…?" He looked questioningly at his friend.

"No, I didn't win. The fete will not be at the manor."

"You can't blame him Soph."

"I know, it's just…"

"You're not going to win every fight."

"I don't get to win any fights."

"The vicar will hold the fete somewhere else. It doesn't mean you can't go along."

"That's not the point Rupert, everyone will know the Hastings refused to be hosts. It won't reflect well on us."

"You're overthinking this, Soph."

"I'm not." Her skin prickled in frustration. This was exactly why she'd rather confide her anxieties to Oliver Morgan. Rupert rarely took anything she cared about seriously.

As they reached the last stall, Rupert's six-foot figure looked hopefully down at her. "May I interest you in lunch?"

"I can't, I'm afraid," she said checking her watch. "I'm meeting someone in ten minutes."

Rupert looked disappointed. "Oh... who?"

"Oliver Morgan."

"Again?"

"Yes. Is that a problem?" she asked, sensing a resentful tone in his voice.

"No... no... no, of course not," he repeated as if he was trying to convince himself it wasn't a problem. "I'm missing your company, that's all. I want all the Sophie time I can get before you are whisked away from me on some brand-new career path. Friday night then...?" he said. "Let's do something Friday night."

"That sounds good, I could do with a night out. I tell you, if I close my eyes, all I see is mounds of letters flashing in the darkness. Is there a cinema close by?"

"Yes, in the next town, it's only a twenty-minute drive - Ah, hang on a minute..." he tutted in realisation. "My mother has planned a party Friday night and has requested my presence, I'd completely forgotten." An idea suddenly hit him and he jumped animatedly in front of Sophie. "Here's an idea... come with me."

"You mean as your date; don't you think Maisie might have a problem with that?"

"I mean as a friend. It will be great."

Sophie wasn't certain. The idea of crashing someone else's party didn't fill her with great joy. "What's the party for?"

"My gran's 90th birthday."

"Oh Rupert, I can't gate-crash that."

"Of course you can, you're practically family anyway…please!" He pouted his lower lip as they continued walking.

It wasn't her ideal night out, but Rupert's puppy-dog eyes weakened her ability to reject him again. "Okay, I'll come… as long as your mother won't mind."

"Not in the slightest." He grinned. "Remember she does want you as her daughter-in-law."

Sophie laughed. "That's true."

She glanced at her watch again. "Sorry Rupert, I need to go, but I'll see you Friday at…?"

"8pm."

"Great. Formal dress or casual?"

"Formal, of course." Rupert shot her a dazzling smile, making dimples surface in his cheeks.

Sophie's tummy flipped and she had to dart her eyes away. How could you go from finding someone so utterly irritating to completely desirable in the matter of one conversation? She wondered what on earth was happening to her - this was Rupert, her best friend…who had a girlfriend.

She waved goodbye and walked quickly away, trying to compose herself before meeting Oliver.

****

Sophie's mobile rang as she climbed up into Oliver's van. He'd suggested escaping the crowds of Middleton and driving was the quickest way to do this.

"Something wrong?" He turned on the engine and caught sight of Sophie's frowning face next to him.

"I don't know."

Oliver checked his mirrors and pulled out into the road.

"I've just received an email from Marie, you know, the lady who runs the recruitment agency on the high street?"

"I know the lady, her husband is a teacher at Middleton primary. He teaches Tim. What's the problem?"

"Listen to this…" Sophie scrolled down her screen. "She says, sorry the interview wasn't what I wanted, but to let her know if I'm still interested and she'll keep searching for me."

"I didn't realise you'd been offered an interview."

"Neither did I."

"Must be a mistake. Give her a ring and find out."

"It's all right," she said beginning to put the phone away in her bag. "I'll do it later."

"You don't need to be polite on my account, Sophie. Ring her."

Hesitating, she dialled the number.

"Hello. Can I help you?" said Marie's voice on the other end of the phone.

"Yes, actually - I wonder if you can. I've been sent an email about an interview I declined, but I don't know anything about it."

"Let me look in your file, what's your name please?"

"Sophie Hastings."

Loud typing could be heard over the phone. "Let me see…you've definitely had an interview offered, just give me one moment…ah yes. I rang through earlier and was told you were no longer looking for work."

"Are you sure you're talking about Sophie Hastings? I am still looking for work."

"Yes, I'm looking at your profile in front of me now."

"Oh… well, there must have been some mistake. I'd still like to be considered for any jobs that come up in the future."

"Of course, I'm sorry for the misunderstanding, things like that don't normally happen."

Sophie reassured her it wasn't a problem and rang off.

"Sorted?" asked Oliver.

"Y-e-es," she said slowly, gazing suspiciously at the phone in her hand before shoving it into her bag. "Just a mistake on the system."

"That's good."

Oliver indicated at the end of the high street and turned into a tiny lane running through the fields. "So…going back to my question earlier… how are you?"

Sophie opened her mouth and inhaled ready to answer, but Oliver spoke again before she had chance. "And I mean, truly how are you…?" He waggled a finger towards her whilst keeping his other hand firmly on the wheel. "Not just surface level nonsense. "I'm fine" won't cut it."

She laughed lightly. "You've trapped me now, Oliver Morgan."

"Someone's got to ask the tough questions," he grinned.

It had been a long time since someone had cared enough to ask Sophie how she really felt and had stuck around long enough to listen to the answer. Her friends at university never truly understood, they knew parts of Sophie's home life but never pressed for more details and Sophie chose not to give any away.

Being away from home for three years, with a couple of fleeting trips over the holidays, had allowed Sophie to ignore things for a while. With Elizabeth safely at a distance, she could easily forget how little control she had over her own life, and regular phone calls to George pacified her guilt over leaving him alone. However, since arriving in Middleton, she had immediately felt overwhelmed by her overbearing mother and frightened by her father's mental decline. Things could no longer be overlooked.

"It's dad…" she finally said gazing straight out of the front window at an elderly lady walking a bouncing cockerpoo in the fields. "I'm really worried about him and I don't know what to do. My brother hasn't responded to my calls and I don't understand why he's not rung me back. He and dad have this amazing relationship, he knows how dad works and whether he says one word or twenty, dad listens to him," She touched a hand to her head and breathed deeply. "And then I always end up shouting at mum."

"Your mum must be struggling too, if your joint efforts aren't helping your father get better."

Sophie scoffed. "Mum isn't helping, her bedside manner has a lot to be desired."

"She can't be that bad, Sophie."

"Don't try and stick up for her Oliver, she's only got herself to blame if her husband is in the depths of despair. You've read the diary I showed you, let me just say my mother is Lady Davenport personified."

"I'm sorry, I didn't mean to offend you. Of course, I don't know your mother, but I can't imagine it's easy for her."

Sophie folded her arms and glanced sullenly out the window and they drove on in silence.

"When did you notice a change in your dad?" Oliver asked, trying to get the conversation started again.

"That's what I don't understand," Sophie said, springing back into life. "The day I arrived home from uni, I could tell dad was really trying hard to be positive. For weeks I had been anxious to see him face to face, I knew the inheritance would have taken a massive toll on him, but his outlook was cheerful. Then, the next day, it was as if a switch had been flicked and he was gone. Something must have happened overnight, but I don't know what."

"Have you tried asking him?"

"Do you think I should?"

"It might help." He paused in thought. "Maybe you need to see it like a physical illness."

"What do you mean?"

"Knowing the cause could help you treat the symptoms."

"I haven't thought about it like that before."

Oliver lowered the gear as they trundled up a steep hill. "Do you want me to come and visit him?"

Sophie glanced at him as Oliver focused on the road straight ahead. Had he just offered to come and help? "But... you don't know him."

"I know, but a little normality might give him a respite from whatever thoughts are haunting him. I'd be very happy to come, if you think it might be helpful."

"That's kind of you," Sophie sat back and peered out of the window. "Where are we going?"

Oliver chuckled. "I wondered when you'd ask... I'm not certain actually."

"You mean you're lost?"

"Oh no, I'm not lost, I've lived here my whole life. What I mean is..." He smiled. "I got lost in our conversation... I am concentrating on driving, honest."

Sophie sat up in her seat, this seemed like a good opportunity to lighten the atmosphere. "It's probably a good time to play the *spontaneous game*, then."

"The *spontaneous game*... what's that?"

"Me and Dylan used to play it. After he'd passed his driving test, he would take me out at the weekend and every time we got to a junction, we would choose whether we'd go left or right, with no aim in mind whatsoever, we'd simply see where we ended up. Of course, there are probably more interesting things to discover in London, but I'm sure Middleton and the surrounding countryside have a few hidden gems."

"Let's find out, shall we?" He drove on to the next junction. "Okay, do you want to turn left or right?"

They turned right and for twenty-minutes they drove around the countryside until they ended up at an old watermill.

Sophie enjoyed the afternoon relaxing in Oliver's company. He was so easy to talk to, there was no hidden agenda or a feeling that she had to impress. As they laughed and chatted about anything and everything, all thoughts of her strange new emotions for Rupert evaporated from her mind.

"I didn't know this place existed," commented Oliver as they sat on a grassy bank, watching the enormous wooden wheel endlessly rotate in the steady flow of river water.

"That's the beauty of the spontaneous game." Sophie smiled broadly. "Middleton does have a hidden gem."

"Indeed, it does." He lifted a hand and gently took hold of Sophie's, interlocking his fingers with hers.

****

Sophie felt the happiest she'd been for a long time. On her arrival home she nimbly trotted up the stairs to check on her father. His curtains were still drawn and a wiggle under the duvet showed Sophie he was fast asleep. Even though she knew sleeping so late into the afternoon would mean he was likely to lie awake for endless hours that night, Sophie did not have the heart to wake him. His face seemed so restful as he slept with all the strains lifted. Once he had woken, she knew the huge weight would return and she felt more relaxed knowing he was having a momentary respite from his struggles.

Quietly shutting the bedroom door, Sophie made her way to the estate office. The familiar mountain of papers greeted her and she flopped down on the chair behind the desk.

As she flicked through a couple of new letters her mother had left on the desk from the morning's mail, a flashing light on the answer machine caught her eye. She pressed the button.

"New message received yesterday," said the well-spoken recorded voice.

New message? Sophie was puzzled, there hadn't been any messages yesterday, she had checked. She put down the letters in her hand and listened intently.

"This is Marie from the recruitment agency in the village. Just ringing to let you know we've found you an interview…"

So, they did ring. Sophie naturally went to press the delete button, the message was unnecessary now…but as her hand reached across the desk, something caught her attention as Marie continued speaking. "Please give me a ring…"

"Hello, can I help you?" a new voice sounded on the recording.

"Yes, I'm ringing for Sophie Hastings."

"That's my daughter. She's not home."

"Can I leave a message for her?"

"No need, I can tell you personally she's no longer looking for a job."

"Oh?"

"She's got one."

"I'm sorry, I hadn't been told; I will update my details. Thank you very much for your time. Good day."

Sophie could picture the smirk of satisfaction that would have spread across Elizabeth's face as the answer machine beeped, "End of messages."

Furious, she marched into the main house to find her mother.

"I've already got a job!" Sophie yelled upon seeing the top of Elizabeth's head poking over a chair in the lounge.

"I beg your pardon, Sophie?" said Elizabeth, so unalarmed by her daughter's display of aggression, that she continued coolly with her knitting.

"I've already got a job?" Sophie repeated now facing her mother sat in the chair.

"Have you?"

"Don't play the innocent, mother." Sophie's nostrils flared.

"I'm not, I simply don't know what you are talking about?" She calmly placed her knitting on a side table and looked attentively at her daughter.

"You told Marie I've already got a job."

175

"I did?"

"I have evidence, it's on my answer phone."

"Oh."

"Yes… oh." She crossed her arms waiting for an answer.

"It must have been a misunderstanding," Elizabeth picked up her ball of wool and began clicking the needles together again.

"I – AM – NOT – STAYING!" Sophie shouted slowly and clearly so any fool would understand.

"I think you will find, Sophie darling, that you are. I've invested too much to allow you to go. You can be estate manager, now your dad is useless. I'll get a contract lined up to make it official."

Sophie looked at her mother, mouth gaping open, not knowing where to start first. "Number one… I'm not going to be your estate manager; I am simply helping dad out until he's back on his feet… and number two, how dare you say dad is useless? Have you given up on him completely?"

Elizabeth gave her a wearied stare. "He's no good to me in this state, Sophie. He won't sign any cheques, or listen to the plans I have for renovations. Last time it took him thirteen months to recover, I'm not waiting for him this time, therefore, he is useless to me. You will be estate manager."

"I'm not going to be estate manager. I decline the job."

"I'll put the contract on your desk and we will have a meeting tomorrow morning to discuss getting builders in to start the kitchen diner… I can't cook in there anymore, it's disgraceful. We'll also phone the bank so you can be a named signatory."

"Are you even listening?" Sophie spoke in disbelief as she watched her mother calmly cast on a new colour of wool. "I'm your daughter - it's our family home, you can't give me a contract and also, have you forgotten… I – DON'T – WANT – THE – JOB!"

"It's your duty to stay."

"Send for Dylan then because by your definition, it's his duty too."

"I am not sending for your brother."

"Then I'm not staying."

"Dylan is a busy boy; his life is elsewhere now."

"Great, what you're saying is I don't have a life. Thanks very much."

There was no point staying. This conversation was helping no one. Sophie spun immediately on her heel and marched towards the door, stopping only when her mother spoke. "If you leave, you will no longer be welcome in my home."

"Oh, for goodness sake… not this again?" Sophie swivelled to face Elizabeth. "This is childish. Why can't I choose my own life? You told me what to study, you told me who to be friends with, you told me what hobbies I could have… when will it end!"

Elizabeth waved a hand in the air, unimpressed by her daughter's outburst. "The conversation is over, Sophie. Whatever you decide, let me know. I don't want to waste unnecessary paper printing off your contract."

Sophie laughed hysterically. "Whatever I decide? Yeah right, mum. As if I've ever been able to make a decision before in my whole life."

She waited for a response, but got none. Elizabeth ignored her completely, showing no sign of remorse or distress as she serenely continued with her purl stitch.

16

Georgiana

Kirkby had written to Georgiana within the first week of his absence. It filled her with a strange mixture of joy and agitation. She feared the consequences if her mother found out a gentleman was corresponding with her in private. Yet, on the other hand, each letter he faithfully wrote taught her more about him. Each page she read made Georgiana realise this man had won all her favour. His daily correspondence became something she relied upon most dearly. It kept her sane when Emma's visit was repeatedly extended. No one had proposed and Georgiana believed their stay would continue until someone plucked up enough courage to do so.

"Let's take a ride," announced Henry Southerly one morning. "It is such a glorious day; it would be a shame to miss it."

Even his elder brother didn't protest, the desire to escape the confines of the house overcoming his hatred for riding.

They waited for their horses to be prepared and, with the exception of Lord and Lady Davenport, the whole party rode out together. Georgiana felt an increased sense of safety in numbers, being alone with any of the gentleman might result in her receiving an unwanted proposal.

Mr and Mrs Faversham rode out in front. Emma had barely spoken a word to her sister since her arrival home, apart from, with a hint of a smirk rising at the corners of her mouth, to give commiserations over losing Thomas. Next came the two Southerly bothers riding together in the middle, leaving Georgiana to ride alongside Mr Turner at the rear.

"The Denholm estate is extremely pleasant, Miss Davenport," Mr Turner commented as they sauntered casually along.

"It is particularly pretty in the autumn," she replied conversationally. "It is my favourite time of year."

"I can imagine the scene." The older man spoke seriously, setting his lips firmly together.

Mr Turner was a thoughtful man, who smiled little. The sound of his voice was monotone and greatly wanting in emotion, although he did not have a reluctance to speak like Robert Southerly and so Georgiana decided he was the lesser of two evils.

"Has it been in your family long?" he asked.

"For three generations."

"It is a shame the line will end."

Georgiana glanced across. She wasn't certain what he meant. "End?"

"Your parents only having daughters. I assume the estate is not entailed to the female line."

"I have a brother, Mr Turner. He is the heir to the estate."

He looked flustered and hurried to correct his error. "I did not realise, please accept my apology."

"There is no need to apologise. My brother has recently joined his new regiment in Portsmouth, which is why you have not meet him."

"The army - an excellent career. I considered it once."

"You didn't think it worth pursuing?"

"I decided to invest my money in property."

"How many properties do you own?"

"I have recently purchased my fifth in London. I consider my purchases very seriously and do much research into my transactions." He then went on for the next five minutes to discourse about the particulars of buying and selling, giving his companion no opportunity to converse.

Georgiana's eyes began to glaze over as she politely nodded and smiled in all the right places, the lack of modulation in his voice as it droned on made her begin to feel extremely sleepy.

"That is why I decided to buy Gladstone House," he continued. "It was a risk, nonetheless I think it was one worth taking."

"Indeed." She stifled a yawn as she cantered beside him on her horse.

"How are you at galloping, Miss Davenport?" called back Henry Southerly, breaking into her lethargy.

"Quite good, Mr Southerly. Why?"

"Let's liven up this ride and have a race - sadly my brother will not join me." He rolled his eyes towards his brother, who had his eyes fixed directly on the path before them.

"I will not join you, Henry," said his brother crossly. "Because this is neither the time nor the place."

"Live a little, Robert" coaxed Henry.

"This is exactly why I brought you with me," his older brother hissed from the corner of his mouth.

Henry laughed and turned back to Georgiana. "My brother, Miss Davenport, thinks I'm too free and spontaneous, that I don't take a single thing seriously and that I should grow up. What do you think?"

"I think there is room in life to be both serious and spontaneous, depending on the situation," she replied.

"Bravo," cheered her brother-in-law from the front. "Well put, my dear sister. That will sort out these two squabbling children."

"Miss Davenport," continued Henry ignoring Mr Faversham's comment. "Tell me then, is the current situation one for spontaneity or seriousness?" He pulled a quizzical face as he spoke the last word.

"That depends on how far you are expecting us to race."

"To the trees." He pointed to a small copse in the distance. "Just over there."

"Henry," warned his brother. "Miss Davenport is not going to race you."

"Indeed, she is not, Georgiana knows better than that," piped up Emma, who sounded more and more like their mother every day.

Georgiana frowned. Emma was not her mother and it would definitely liven up the party. Riding next to Mr Turner was not entertaining in the slightest.

Henry saw her wrinkled brow and gave a questioning stare.

"Will you give me a head start?" she whispered as Mr Turner turned his head away under the pretence he couldn't hear.

"It is the gentlemanly thing to do." He spoke with a twinkle of rebellion in his eye.

Georgiana chewed her lip, considering if what she was about to do was foolish. Before Thomas had proposed, she would never have dreamed of defying her parents, or even social protocol, in the way she had done recently. When Henry winked discreetly at her, before twisting his body to face the riders in front, her resolve was strengthened. Maybe she could have some amusement in life without getting into too much trouble.

"My horse could do with a good run, Emma," she shouted, hardly daring to breath for fear of being caught. "He is getting frustrated from the slowness of our trot."

"We will be stopping soon, Georgiana. Ride him then," said her sister irritably.

"He cannot wait."

Emma huffed. "Oh, very well, give him a run - only do not go far."

The plan had worked.

Moments after Georgiana raced out from behind the back of the party, Henry Southerly left the group too. She heard his brother shouting after him over the top of galloping hooves. Georgiana stayed in the lead for a while, but Henry's mare was taller and stronger and eventually he overtook her. They stopped their horses by the edge of the copse; laughing in delight.

"Thank you for the head start, Mr Southerly," said Georgiana regaining her breath.

"It was a pleasure. You gave me a fine race; I wasn't certain I'd catch you."

"You are a good horseman." She patted her horse to calm him down. "What is it?" she asked noticing Henry was staring at her. "Do I have mud on my face?"

"No," he cleared his throat. "I am actually surprised you went ahead with the scheme; I did not think you capable of defying the rules."

"Maybe I'm not as similar to my sister as you first thought."

"Georgiana!" scolded her sister when the rest of the riding party caught up with them. "What has got into you? You would not have dared do something so improper before I left home, just wait until I tell mama."

"Mrs Faversham, do not be too harsh on your sister," jumped in Henry. "It is my fault, I simply took advantage of the opportunity before me, it was simply a bit of harmless fun. Your sister did not know I was going to pursue her."

Emma looked through suspicious eyes towards her sister. "Is that true?"

"Of course," said Georgiana innocently, trying not to dart her eyes towards Henry and give their game away.

"Very well," said Emma after some consideration. "Do not do it again Mr Southerly. You should not be compromising my sister in such a way."

"I'm sorry, Mrs Faversham." He tilted his head charmingly towards her. "It will not happen again." Emma tugged her horse away, missing the rebellious grin Henry pulled at his partner in crime, who struggled to stifle a giggle.

Mrs Faversham swung back upon hearing the snigger.

"Bless you, Miss Davenport," Henry spoke up mischievously. "The sun is very bright today."

On their arrival home each of the Davenport's guests departed to change their mud splashed riding attire. Georgiana performed the task with particular speed, with the intention of hiding before the others reappeared again. Her plan was successful and she managed to steal away to the formal gardens, but it was not long until she was discovered and her mother could be seen charging towards her.

Georgiana's spirits instantly drooped when she heard her mother's jarring cry. "Georgiana. A word, please."

"Yes, mama." The young girl met Lady Davenport half-way down the garden path.

"I do not want you spending any more time alone with Mr Southerly."

"Which one?" Georgiana asked, although she knew full well which brother her mother was referring too.

"Henry Southerly - the younger one."

"Why not?" she asked apparently in all innocence.

"He is not good company for you. Emma tells me he was not invited on this trip to Denholm Park. His brother, desirous of removing him from the temptations of the capital, brought him along unexpectedly. He is not a virtuous man, Georgiana. Do not go near him."

It was a shame. Henry Southerly was the most interesting man amongst her sister's guests. The other two were exactly the type of potential husband her mother would choose for her, solemn and dull.

"If he talks to me, I cannot be rude and ignore him." This she pointed out, knowing her mother would not allow any discourtesy.

"Of course not, I have bred manners into you, you shall talk to him, but coldly. You are not to encourage him if he makes advances."

That evening Mr Southerly the elder came, took a seat next to Georgiana and surprised her by initiating a conversation.

"I have come to apologise for my brother's behaviour, Miss Davenport."

"Oh, there is no need to apologise, Mr Southerly. He was only searching for some amusement. No harm has been done."

"The problem is this *amusement* you speak of, could have done a lot of damage to your reputation. I take things like that very seriously. A young lady's virtue is not to be trifled with."

This was the most Georgiana had heard the man speak. His brother's shortcomings were clearly a subject of distress for him. "Please do not worry, as I said, no harm was done."

"Such an innocent, child," he muttered to himself and shook his head.

How rude, thought Georgiana. This man might be ten years her senior, but he had no right to demean her like that.

He continued. "Henry does not realise harmless pleasures can be fatal, that once an impulse is acted upon, it cannot be undone. His role as the younger son has left him lacking much in maturity."

Georgiana didn't answer. She had nothing else to say on the matter and glanced across to Emma, who had been coaxed into playing the piano by her husband.

"Will you delight us with your music tonight, Miss Davenport?" Robert Southerly asked moving on from judging his brother. Georgiana confirmed that she would play after her sister had finished.

"I find your tones very soothing and extremely easy to listen too. You are a very accomplished lady."

"Thank you, Mr Southerly."

"One day, I would enjoy your entertainment in my own abode. The pianoforte I have is exquisite and only takes kindly to accomplished players. Your talent would sound incredibly well on it."

"You are too kind." She smiled awkwardly. Was he now referring to their potential marriage or, did he presume she'd simply visit him on a trip to see her sister?

"Maybe you could do us the honour of playing now. Your sister appears to have completed her performance."

Self-consciously, Georgiana walked over to the pianoforte and began to play, noticing the eyes of Robert Southerly never leaving her face. The sound of her playing caused others to end their conversations, being attracted by her captivating notes.

"Keep on playing," demanded Lady Davenport, as Georgiana finished her first piece and pushed the stool back to leave.

"My throat is dry, mama. I need a glass of water."

Her mother puffed out in irritation. "Hurry up and get one, there are people waiting to listen."

On returning to the room Georgiana was greeted by Mr Turner. "Such sweet melodies you sing, Miss Davenport. I would never tire of hearing them."

Her stomach immediately tightened upon hearing another gentleman's discreet designs of marriage. "Thank you, Mr Turner."

She attempted to walk straight past him back to the piano, but to her distress, she could not shake him away.

"I live alone, Miss Davenport, it can be very lonely sometimes."

"I can imagine, sir." She glanced fleetingly at the piano, hoping he would pick up on the signal and leave her alone so she could play.

"Every so often, my good cousin Mr Faversham invites me on his travels."

"That is very kind of him."

"I am not a man who particularly enjoys my own company," his monotonous voice droned on. "My poor mother died last year, leaving me all alone."

"I am sorry to hear that."

"My only brother sailed to America not so long ago."

"What an amazing adventure," she beamed, wondering if she could get the man to show delight rather than be so melancholic.

"I do not think so," he said, his chin raised high with disapproval. "Foolish, I'd say."

Georgiana had had enough. She smiled politely. "If you will excuse me Mr Turner, I believe my mother would like me to play another set."

"Oh yes." He half bowed before her. "Yes – please do."

Georgiana sat down at the piano and made herself comfortable in the hope she could stay there for the remainder of the evening.

"Mrs Faversham, why don't you play again?" piped up Henry suddenly. "I'd like to have a dance and I believe married women are not disposed to do much dancing."

Emma looked horrified and flashed her eyes towards her mother. "I do not play much now I am married. I have played once tonight, that is enough for me."

"Nonsense," cried her husband, unknowingly thwarting his wife's plan to keep Henry Southerly away from her sister. "You practise night and day. I sometimes think you play it in your sleep. Come - you play beautifully."

Emma was reluctantly led by Mr Faversham to take Georgiana's place. The sisters glanced uneasily at Lady Davenport's emotionless face. Both instinctively knew she was furious with Henry Southerly for getting in the way.

"May I?" Henry bowed before Georgiana and reached out his hand.

Georgiana could do nothing else but accept it.

"Am I wicked, Miss Davenport?" he asked with a twinkle in his eye after the music had started and was loud enough to cover their conversation.

"You know full well you shouldn't have asked, Mr Southerly."

He laughed as they spun in opposite directions and met again in the middle. "I'm sorry, but this party is so dull. You cannot deny it."

Georgiana agreed. "My mother forbade me to have anything to do with you after the incident this morning."

"Did she?" He looked amused. "You are dancing with me now."

"I didn't have much choice; I would be chastised for being rude if I publicly declined such an innocent sounding offer."

He laughed again and they skipped to the left and then the right repeatedly.

"You dance well, Miss Davenport, even though there is a distinct lack of other dancers."

"It has been drilled into me - dance well, sing well - both have been repeatedly whispered into my ear since childhood."

Their arms crossed together and they spun genteelly in a circle.

"I hear you have been taken away from the temptations of London."

"Is that what you heard?" He chuckled.

"It is why I'm not to associate with you."

"My brother always paints such a grim picture… that's why he and Mr Turner get on so well. I must say one thing I am particularly grateful for, that Robert's voice does not drone on so depressingly as that other man, he does put me to sleep."

Georgiana could not help laughing, but a quick glance at their audience told her at least one pair of eyes were piercing through her and she quickly drew her mouth back into a straight line.

"So, which are you to marry?" Henry asked bluntly.

"Marry?"

"Yes." He locked his arm around her and they turned together. "From what I observe your mother is pushing both in your way. So, which one will you choose?"

"Neither one has proposed, Mr Southerly."

"It will come," he said as if he had some inside knowledge that she didn't. "I can't speak for Mr Turner, but my brother has been seeking a companion for a while. He wants to increase his income; I believe you'd come with rather a nice dowry and good connections. We would be brother and sister, Miss Davenport. Imagine the fun we would have," he raised his eyebrows playfully and bowed low as the music ended.

187

"Once is enough, Emma" commanded Lady Davenport quickly. "There are not enough dancers. It does not seem right."

"Of course, Lady Davenport," said Henry in all innocence. "I simply couldn't fight the urge to dance."

"Try your hardest to fight it then, Mr Southerly," she said sternly. "For you will not be dancing again during your stay at Denholm Park."

17

Sophie

Another cold bowl of soup was left outside the door. George Hastings had not eaten anything all day.

"Dad," Sophie tapped on the door and opened it a crack. "You need to eat."

"I'm not hungry, Sophie."

George was in the library again. Dust particles could be seen floating in the air from the single beam of light which was entering through the drawn curtains. It wasn't a large room and the tall mahogany bookcases stacked against each wall made it feel even more confined, reflecting George's claustrophobic state of mind. He sat on a two-seater brown leather sofa, covered with numerous rips, facing an unlit fire place.

Sophie shivered. It might have been mid-summer, but the light-starved room had a distinct chill. "Will you drink a cup of tea if I bring one?"

He didn't answer.

"Dad?"

George touched his aching head. "If you bring one, I'll try, pumpkin."

It was the best she could ask for and she made her way down to the kitchen, the warmth of the sunlit landing immediately warming her face.

Dialling her brother's number again, she pattered down the stairs. It had become a familiar routine to listen impatiently to each repeated ring only to receive no answer at the end. She needed him, what was he up to?

Carefully selecting her father's favourite mug with a picture of a huge golden trophy labelled *Number One Dad*, Sophie absent-mindedly squeezed the teabag against the side of the cup, lost in her own thoughts. A ring on the front door bell roused her from unwanted reflections and, taking the over-brewed tea in her hand, she went to answer it.

A smile from the visitor met her puzzled expression. "I promised you I'd come. Is it a good time, I can come back if it's not?" It was Oliver.

She stood back to let Oliver in, his unexpected arrival giving her momentary relief from the burdens she had been mulling over.

"Thought I'd say hello to your dad, if that's okay?"

Sophie smiled and led Oliver towards the stairs. "You can pass him his tea... no wait." She took a sip and pulled a face. "He can't drink this, it's cold." Abruptly, she raced back towards the kitchen, splashing tea on the floor and stepping on Oliver's toe. "I'm sorry," she gasped. "Are you okay?"

"I'm fine... but I'm not certain you are?" He scrutinised her face. "Are you doing okay?"

Sophie felt a squirming inside. She almost blurted out automatically that she was fine, desiring to deflect the all too intimate question away, but she knew such an answer would not pacify him when she saw Oliver's soft stare waiting patiently for an answer... a truthful answer.

"I'm not going to lie; it's been a tough few days," she met his gaze head on.

Oliver gently took her hand and Sophie could say no more as she fought an overwhelming urge to burst into tears.

"Everything will be okay," he whispered squeezing her hand tightly.

Sophie swallowed hard as the warmth from his touch sent a wave of emotion rushing through her. Her life had become so devoid of a reassuring hand, that she'd forgotten how valuable a friend like Oliver could be.

After a few moments, he took the tea from her hand and sipped it. "It's fine, not too cold at all. Which way am I going?" He started walking up the stairs.

"Turn left at the top and it's the room in the corner. I'm not certain if he wants visitors, shall I check first?"

"It's okay - if he doesn't, I won't push."

Sophie let Oliver find his own way, trusting him completely to deal with her father sensitively. She had no fear he would overstay his welcome or force himself in if he was not wanted.

Glancing at her watch for the fifth time that hour she watched the clock hand as it slowly ticked around. She had expected Oliver back within minutes, assuming her dad would not welcome someone he did not know. Now an hour had nearly gone by and she sat in the office, having barely completed any work.

"So, this is headquarters."

Sophie jerked her head to see Oliver's good-humoured face poking its way through the door.

He came into the room and handed across an empty cup. "I'm to give this to you," he said, clearly pleased by the look of bewilderment on Sophie's face. "I'm also to ask if there's any more soup available for the patient?"

"How did..." she was lost for words. "Oliver, that's amazing, thank you."

However, her admiration soon disappeared when a pair of very recognisable heels were heard clopping down the corridor. Sophie swung in the office chair to face the door, her eyes narrowing as she waited for it to open. "You're about to meet my mum - I'm going to apologise in advance."

Oliver rested a hand on her shoulder as he stood above her. "It will be fine."

Sophie wished she had Oliver's confidence.

Elizabeth ground to a halt when she entered the room and saw Oliver standing next to her daughter.

"I see you've decided to stay." She took great care to focus all her attention on Sophie, ignoring the unknown male figure as if he didn't exist.

"Not necessarily," said Sophie crossing her arms in defiance.

"Don't take too long deciding, I need to advertise if you're leaving."

Finally, she stared at Oliver, unable to overlook him any longer. She eyed him suspiciously up and down. "Who are you?"

Sophie's eyes widened in horror. How could her mother be so rude?

"Oliver Morgan. It's a pleasure to meet you Mrs Hastings," Oliver cordially held out his hand, but Elizabeth ignored it.

"Who, may I ask, is Oliver Morgan? I've not heard of you." Her nose wrinkled in the air as if she'd suddenly sniffed an unwelcome scent.

Sophie was fuming, but for Oliver's sake she attempted to speak with as much composure as she could possibly muster. "Mum, this is Mr Morgan's son."

Elizabeth shook her head innocently, her expression one of incomprehension.

"Morgan's farm... he's one of our estate dairy farmers." Sophie clenched her fists tightly as she waited for an answer.

"How's Rupert? I've not seen him here recently."

Sophie glared at her mother. She had completely disregarded Oliver and brushed him to one side, as if she had never asked who he was.

"I don't have to live every waking moment with Rupert Donaldson."

"That's not what you used to think." Elizabeth gave a sly smirk. "Couldn't get you away from him at one time, could I, Sophie? Let me know if you're staying, I wouldn't want to waste money redecorating your room if you're not." Without saying anything further she smugly retreated from the room.

"Wow," whistled Oliver, when the clopping heels could be heard no more. "She's intense."

"That's a kind way to describe her. I could think of many other words that would suit her better." Seeing a pile of letters before her, Sophie picked them up and skimmed through them to calm her anger. She hated her mother for suggesting there had been something between herself and Rupert. It was none of her mother's business who she spent time with and Sophie was determined not to let her ruin this new friendship with Oliver, just because he threatened Elizabeth's own selfish plans.

The phone rang, putting an end to her brooding. The caller ID flashed before her, she couldn't quite believe what she was seeing. "It's Dylan... I'm sorry, Oliver, I need to take this."

She walked out into the corridor, clutching the mobile to her ear. "Dylan, where on earth have you been?"

"I'm sorry, Soph. I've been busy," Dylan said apologetically on the other end of the phone.

"Busy? Dad's not well, I told you so in the message. What can take priority over that?"

"I can't come right now, Soph. I'm sorry."

"Dylan, dad needs you - *I* need you. Please... he's not doing well." Sophie's throat felt dry and she gulped quickly trying to manufacture a source of moisture. Was her brother being serious? It sounded like there was a real probability he wasn't coming to help her.

"Work's really busy right now," continued Dylan.

"Can't you get some time off?"

He didn't answer.

"Dylan, ask for some time off, explain to them there's a family emergency."

"I can't just make up an excuse, Soph."

"It's not an excuse, Dylan." She snapped back angrily, holding the phone close to her mouth as she paced up and down. "Please don't tell me you're going to leave me here alone."

"Don't say that, Soph."

"Here's some news for you - if you don't come, I *am* alone." Tears threatened to escape from her eyes once again. He couldn't do this to her.

"You've got…"

"Don't even say it," she cut him off. "You know mum is a comfort neither to myself nor dad."

"I'm sorry," he said again, the hurt in his voice obvious.

"Thank you very much Dylan, you've been a great help." Her emotions told her to hang up the phone and collapse, sobbing right there in the draft ridden corridor, but she fought the urge, knowing a falling-out with her brother wouldn't help the situation.

"Come on, Soph. You know I'd be there if I could."

Sophie didn't answer, too upset to trust herself to speak.

"Say something, Soph."

She sniffed. "If that's your decision then there's nothing else to say."

"I'll ring you and check how he's doing."

"I don't need a phone call, Dylan. I need you here."

"I just can't right now," his voice raised briefly in agitation. "I'll call you, Soph."

He rang off.

Sophie blinked at the phone in her hands. He hadn't even bothered to give a real excuse.

Oliver looked expectantly at her as she re-entered the office.

"He's not coming…" She spoke in disbelief. "I can't believe he's not coming."

Oliver didn't say anything. He simply stepped forward and wrapped his arms around her, resting his head on top of her chestnut brown hair.

Sophie allowed a single teardrop to trickle down her cheek and closed her eyes tight, leaning lightly on Oliver's chest and listening to the calming beat of his heart.

"Oh… I'm sorry. I didn't mean to disturb you."

Sophie sprung away and hastily wiped her cheek dry. "Rupert, what are you doing here?"

"Just thought I'd pop over."

He hovered by the doorway, not wanting to intrude, but at the same time, not retreating either.

"I believe you know Oliver Morgan." Sophie felt awkward and she scolded herself for feeling so, there was no need for her to feel uncomfortable about having another male friend besides Rupert.

"Yes, I do," Rupert nodded his head and watched Oliver carefully.

"Did mum ring you?" asked Sophie questioningly. How likely was is that Rupert's visit had been concocted in pure innocence, so that he should conveniently show up when Oliver was here?

She watched Rupert perch himself on the desk and fiddle with a pot full of ballpoint pens.

"Yes, your mum phoned, said you needed assisting with…" He trailed off without finishing his sentence, put the pens back inside the pot and promptly lifted his head. "So, my dear Soph… how can I help you?"

"I'm going to go Sophie," interrupted Oliver who was already edging out the room. "I'll call you later."

"You don't have to go, Oliver." Sophie stepped towards him, but he held out his hands to stop her coming closer.

"It's okay, dad will be expecting me back." He scanned Rupert thoughtfully out of the corner of his eye. "I'll see you later."

Sophie waited for the door to shut behind him. "Well, thanks Rupert," she couldn't help sounding cross, if his visit had been a coincidence she would apologise later.

"What?" He sounded innocent. "I haven't done anything."

She shook her head and slumped down into the chair. "Dylan's not coming."

"I didn't know you were expecting him."

"Dad's not doing well, Rupert. I need Dylan to be here, you know how vital he was last time in nursing dad back to us."

"He's not that bad, Soph. You can deal with it."

"I don't think I can and mum's not exactly helping."

"Chill, Soph." He jumped off the desk and rested his hand on her shoulder. "You're making life into a major dilemma when it doesn't have to be."

Sophie jumped up from her chair and brushed his hand away. "Depression is a major dilemma, Rupert."

"He's not that bad."

"For goodness sake," she muttered under her breath and stormed over to the door and opened it. "I think maybe you should go - I don't need your help. Mum only phoned you to get rid of Oliver."

"What?"

"I told you they still want us to be together. I think you need to remind your mother about Maisie."

"I think I do," he moved slowly to the open door. "Don't sit there moping all day, Soph." He kissed her cheek. "I'll see you later at gran's party."

"Party?"

"You said you'd come, Soph."

"Oh…is it Friday all ready? Yes, of course I'm coming."

"Great." He smiled and moved away down the corridor.

Sophie's heart felt heavy as she heated up a bowl of soup and carried it up to George. A terrifying sense of loneliness swept over her and she scurried away to find sanctuary in her own room, after the warmed soup had been delivered. The power Elizabeth had over her life felt immense and Sophie wondered if she would ever be able to break free from it.

Cradling the little red diary close to her chest, she sniffed the ageing papers and closed her eyes. Georgiana was the only person who fully understood.

Thomas and Annabelle were married today. Mama would not attend the ceremony. All day she stalked me with her eyes, jutting out her jaw and flaring

196

her nostrils rapidly. I cautiously stayed away. One step too close today would be extremely foolish indeed.

"I wish I could have your courage," whispered Sophie to the empty pages open before her. "You rejected your mother's plan and so far, you are winning... why can't I do the same?"

I am yet to receive a proposal. I often wonder if declining Thomas was the right thing to do, for by now I would be free of my mother and secure in the home of a man I trust and respect. If I have to accept Mr Southerly or Mr Turner my life will change little, my freedom will be no greater because my mother has chosen the matches to benefit only herself. The only man who might change things for me, I fear I will never have.

The day's entry ended. Sophie blinked rapidly to clear away her watery vision and she touched the page of the book open before her. "If I was standing next to you, Georgiana," she murmured. "I would urge you to take control of your life - it's yours. No one else has the right to take away your choices."

If only she could take her own advice and cast off the restraints of her own mother. As far as she could see, the only way to achieve this was leaving the manor entirely, hiding away and removing herself from the family. Her shoulders drooped. If this was the only way to gain such freedom, then why was she still here?

18

Georgiana

I hope all is well with you my dearest Georgiana. William Kirkby wrote in his most recent letter. *I will be returning soon now my mother is married. I am sorry I cannot be present to shield you from two unwanted proposals. Please, I ask, keep strong, I am on the way.*

Georgiana's spirits rose as she read Kirkby's words. A strong admiration for the man had grown during their correspondence. However, she could not be certain if Kirkby's intention to propose would materialise on his return to Middleton, or if she would accept it if he did. Whatever might happen, she began to fret as the two chosen bachelors prepared themselves for the journey home.

Lady Davenport had begun to make subtle hints in order to remove the party from Denholm Park. Waiting for the gentlemen to propose in their own time was producing no results and she felt it her duty to try and force at least one proposal by limiting their remaining days in the county.

Georgiana feared there was no way to avoid the event since both Mr Southerly and Mr Turner had been hovering around her both day and night, although neither had been successful, or courageous enough, to isolate her long enough to express any marital sentiments.

Not a soul lingered in the morning room as Georgiana crept through the door. All was surprisingly quiet and with a sigh of relief she set up her writing equipment. She had decided it would be a good idea to write to Aunt Lucy, explaining that so far, she had not plucked up enough courage to approach the subject of her visiting London.

She tapped the quill lightly against her cheek, desperately trying to think of the right words to break the news to her aunt who would inevitably be disappointed.

"Ah, Miss Davenport."

Georgiana's body tensed at the sound of Mr Turner's voice. She had been so lost in her own thoughts that she had not heard the handle turn and the door open. Plastering a polite smile on her face, she quickly assessed if an exit was possible, but the gentleman stood between her and the only door.

"It is not often we get to be alone." He touched his damp forehead with a handkerchief which had been previously stuffed up his sleeve. "I am glad to have found you, Miss Davenport. There is a matter of great urgency I wish to discuss with you."

Georgiana straightened her posture, readying herself for what was to come. She should have hidden better.

"I don't know what business you could have with me, Mr Turner."

"I fear I am against the clock - our departure is near." He warily looked behind his shoulder before laying a clammy hand awkwardly on top of Georgiana's. "I am normally a man of many words, but on this occasion, I believe long speeches are unnecessary. I simply ask you this…marry me?"

"Mr Turner…" she began.

"I do not expect an immediate answer," he broke in promptly, almost as if he expected her to decline.

The sentiment softened Georgiana towards him, thankful he had allowed her some space to contemplate her answer. "Thank you for your offer, Mr Turner. You are right, such a request needs careful consideration."

"I agree." He released her hand and took a step backwards. "I realise you do not know me well; however, your mother is

199

adamant we will make a good match and I am inclined to believe her."

Lady Davenport had been whispering in his ear, she knew this would have been the case. "If my mother said it, then I have no doubt of its accuracy, Mr Turner."

He nodded his head and began retreating out the room. "I will leave you to deliberate our future."

The room became silent and Georgiana dropped her head into her hands, squeezing her eyes shut as her mind brought up images of Kirkby. If she said yes to Mr Turner, the promise of Kirkby would be no more.

A cough behind broke into her thoughts.

"I beg your pardon, Mr. Southerly," she said upon opening her eyes and lifting her head to see the gentleman stood before her. "I did not hear you enter."

"I was under the impression you were sitting all alone and I thought I'd give you some company." It was the elder Southerly who now seated himself beside her.

Georgiana smiled and said nothing, fearing a single word spoken in error might lead to something she did not want to hear.

"It's a pleasant day," he commented nervously.

"Yes, it is."

"The bread at breakfast was simply delicious."

"My mother sends a boy to Upper Cranleigh every morning."

"Indeed, such a long way to go for bread."

Georgiana shifted uncomfortably; something felt strange. It was not like Robert Southerly to ask so many questions in an attempt to begin a conversation.

They sat in silence.

"Miss Davenport," he said finally breaking the irksome silence. "I cannot sit here any longer. I must declare my love for you. I cannot waste this opportune moment. I cannot see you receive an offer from anyone else. For you are the most beautiful lady I have ever set my eyes upon."

He got down onto the floor, kneeling before her. "Will you accept my offer and marry me?"

Her mother had done it again. She could just imagine Lady Davenport congratulating herself, two proposals in a matter of minutes.

"Mr Southerly… I thank you for your offer, it is not one to be taken lightly. I therefore ask for time to think over my decision." The excuse had worked for Mr Turner, why not for Mr Southerly too?

"Yes, of course," he practically stumbled backwards, appearing shocked by her answer. Georgiana swore he had been convinced of an immediate acceptance, but she was not going to humour him in this way.

Sombrely he bowed his head. "I will await your answer, Miss Davenport."

He left the room, leaving Georgiana stunned by the rapid speed of events.

Lady Davenport burst into the room. A large prominent indigo vein throbbed on the left side of her neck as she halted directly in front of her daughter, her warm breath wafting directly into her face. "Two proposals and you have accepted neither!"

"I have not declined either man, mama." It was imperative her mother knew no decisions had been made, that she would accept one of these men, it was just a matter of deciding which was the better match.

"You have not said yes, therefore you have declined them." As her mother breathed out angrily, flecks of saliva fell onto Georgiana's cheek, where they remained, since she dared not wipe them away.

"I am considering their proposals."

"Not good enough. Have you failed to remember what will happen if you refuse the next offer brought before you?"

Georgiana kept quiet, her hands turning white as she gripped onto her chair in terror. She had never been so forthright with her mother before.

"Oh, I see..." Lady Davenport's fierce face smoothed out in realisation. "It's him, isn't it?"

"I- I don't..."

"Don't act as if you don't know, Georgiana!" she shouted. "You are hoping to receive a proposal from Mr Kirkby. Mr Turner and Mr Southerly are respected men of great status and I have done much research into their families to prove this is the case. What do we know about this Mr Kirkby?"

Here was the opportunity to stand up for herself, Annabelle had married the man she loved, why couldn't she? "He is Sir Gillingham's cousin, mama."

Lady Davenport tutted, but said nothing so Georgiana continued. "Sir Gillingham is of high status and has been our dear friend for as long as I can remember. Surely he would not associate with anyone so inferior to your own ideals."

"Mr Kirkby is unknown to me."

"I believe he is an honourable man."

"What proof do you have?"

Georgiana stood open mouthed. She had no evidence or argument to prove her mother was wrong.

"Exactly. You have none, child. You are fortunate, therefore, that I have found out information about your so called 'honourable man'. On his arrival into our county I considered him as a match for yourself, as I would any other bachelor entering the neighbourhood. But on conferring with our dear friend Gillingham, I instantly disregarded him and told you so immediately. You believe you know who Mr Kirkby is, but you do not... he is not the cousin of Sir Gillingham." She smirked seeing Georgina's distraught face; she would have no daughter of hers triumph over her judgement.

"The two gentlemen will leave on Friday, Georgiana. You must accept one of their offers before they depart. Am I understood?"

"Yes, mama," Georgiana whispered, drooping her head so her chin touched her chest.

Lady Davenport sauntered smugly out of the room.

With shaking hands, Georgiana snatched a fresh piece of writing paper and swung her knees under the writing desk.

My dearest William,

I am greatly distressed. My mama has just informed me that your identity is false. I believed you to be the cousin of Sir Gillingham, however I am told you are not. I do not understand, you introduced yourself in this way. I am sure there is an explanation. Please write immediately. I have within the hour received two proposals. I will be forced to receive the hand of Mr Turner or Mr Southerly before they return home on Friday. Send a clarification - I beg you.

As ever yours...

The letter was sent immediately.

Georgiana waited the next morning, pacing up and down in anticipation for the post to arrive. She felt great relief when Ridley finally tucked a folded and sealed letter into her hand.

However, after seeking solace in her own room and flipping over the paper, her joy wilted upon seeing the inscription. It was not Kirkby's untidy scrawl.

My dear Gianna,

I cannot wait much longer to hear from you. Have you been successful in asking your mother?

Georgiana groaned, remembering the unwritten letter to her aunt lying unfinished on the writing desk. She scurried downstairs with the purpose of ending her aunt's waiting.

It didn't take long to complete the letter and Georgiana found herself back in the hall in searching of Ridley.

"Who is that letter for?"

Georgiana jumped. She had pushed open the door into the dining room searching for her father's butler and had met her mother directly behind it.

Lady Davenport slipped the letter from her daughter's fingers and read the name of the recipient. "Lucy Barnet... explain, child."

Georgiana felt the blood flowed from her face. It was not worth lying, her mind could not think of any plausible reason why she should be in touch with her aunt.

Her eyes locked on her delicate silken shoes. "I-I was planning a visit to London."

"I can't hear you!" her mother bellowed.

"I was planning a visit to London," Georgiana spoke a little louder with a noticeable wobble in her throat. Whatever courage she had found earlier had now obviously departed. "Aunt Lucy lives in London and I thought I might…"

"You will do no such thing. How do you even know my sister, you should have no contact with her at all?"

"Edward said…"

"Edward said what?" In her rage Lady Davenport seized Georgiana by the shoulders.

"It was a long time ago, mama," she said trembling and trying to step away. However, her mother's grip on her dress was firm. "Aunt Lucy sent me a letter. Edward said it was acceptable to reply."

"When?"

"I was eight."

"Since you were eight!" Lady Davenport thrust her daughter away with so much force that Georgiana stumbled and landed backwards on her wrist. "You are not to contact her, do you understand? Lucy Barnet is not part of our family, and may I add, there is nothing on this entire earth that will induce me to let you out of my sight. You will not run away to London or elope…"

"That was not my intention," Georgiana winced as she rubbed her injured wrist.

Her mother bent down, their noses inches away from each other. "You are on the verge of being engaged. I will not allow anything or anyone to stop this."

A creaky floorboard turned both their heads. Henry Southerly loomed at the top of the stairs, clearing his throat. "Am I interrupting something?"

"No," said Lady Davenport rising up. "We have finished," she took the letter with her and removed herself from the hall, not looking back once.

"Are you well, Miss Davenport?" Henry rushed to help her off the floor and examined her wrist.

"I slipped," she said weakly.

"Did you have a disagreement with your mother?"

"It's a daily occurrence, Mr Southerly."

"I am sorry to hear that."

Her reluctance to speak further made Henry make no further enquiries. "Do you have an ice-house?" he asked still examining the damage.

Georgiana confirmed that they did.

"I will fetch some ice for your wrist, it will help with the swelling." Gallantly he left to seek out Ridley.

Georgiana sat cradling her wrist. It had been a long time since she had been physically hurt by her mother. She had hoped those days had ended forever in her childhood…clearly, they had not. The sooner she could escape Denholm Park the better. The question was, who would take her away?

19

Sophie

Sophie had found the royal blue ball gown hiding away in her wardrobe. She had worn it five years ago for her school prom and it had been brought across in the move with the rest of her belongings.

She sighed as she sat on the edge of her bed and stroked the light cotton material, watching the silver sequins bordering the neckline sparkle as they caught the light coming in through the window. She remembered choosing this dress. A shopping trip had been arranged with Elizabeth to try on a pre-chosen outfit. However, to Sophie's delight, an unexpected sprained ankle prevented this. Dylan stepped in at the last minute and his sister dragged him around every shop until she found the perfect dress, one that was completely different to the pale lilac, long sleeved gown her mother had picked out for her.

Blue had always made her eyes pop and the sleeveless bodice made her feel like a princess. For once, she had made a decision all on her own. Sixteen-year-old Sophie had made a promise to herself that day; this would be the start of reclaiming her life. But here she was, five years later and she was still trapped in a world where Elizabeth called the shots.

The long zip down the side ran smoothly as Sophie fastened up the dress in front of a tall freestanding mirror. The mirror was useless really, there was a crack running from top to bottom and three quarters of it was covered in a faint cloud, leaving few parts clear enough to see your reflection. Sophie twisted her figure in attempt to see how she looked. Her mid length chestnut hair was twirled into a neat bun, a single silver grip adorning the side, the figure-hugging dress flowed down her long legs and stopped just before the battered wooden floor.

She gnawed her lip anxiously, it didn't feel right leaving George sat at home in his robe and darkened room, but he had begged her to go, not wishing to let his unhappiness infect his daughter.

Respecting her dad's wishes, it wasn't much later that she found herself tapping on the Donaldsons' front door.

"Wow, you look stunning." Rupert kissed her on the cheek and welcomed her into his parent's home.

She stepped into the hallway, which was dominated by an impressive crystal chandelier spiralling down from the ceiling, and Rupert took her shawl. Looking around she observed a distinct lack of people.

"It's very quiet Rupert. Where is everybody?"

"Funny story, actually," he said laughing lightly.

Sophie raised her eyebrow, recognising the laugh. Something was not quite right and Rupert was to blame.

"Turns out all of gran's friends clubbed together to buy her a gift of a lifetime."

"Oh... what was that?"

"A parachute jump."

"What... you've got to be kidding me?"

"Gran's a bit of a daredevil... anyway, then they whisked her away on a two-week cruise around the Mediterranean. So..." he clapped his hands together.

"What you're trying to say is, she's not here."

"Which means... she's not here."

"Didn't her friends tell you what they were planning, surely they were invited to the party?"

"I believe some invites got lost in the post."

"What about the guests who did get their invitations, how come they didn't turn up?"

"Ma cancelled with them and we will rearrange."

"Thanks for passing on the memo, Rupert." She snatched her shawl back from his hand, but quick reflexes meant he kept hold of the end.

"Don't go, Soph. I thought we could spend the evening together anyway – you know, have a catch up."

"There's not much I can do in a dress like this. I wish you'd told me."

"We've loads of food going to waste, stay and have dinner with me...please. You can eat in a posh dress, can't you?" He stuck out his bottom lip.

"Oh, don't pull that face, Rupert Donaldson," she pointed a finger reprovingly at him, but she couldn't stay angry with him and she let go of her shawl. "Fine, I'll stay."

"Great... if you will follow me, madam." Rupert half bowed before her, slipping an arm around her back to guide her out of the hallway.

The dining table had been set with tall golden candle holders lining the middle of the long emerald green table runner. There was space to seat at least twenty people and Sophie felt a little lost sitting at the end, viewing the empty places. Rupert pushed the door open, carrying two plates of steaming hot food and placed one before Sophie. Automatically, she inhaled the delicious aromas wafting up into her nose.

"This smells incredible, is it duck?"

"Duck with a red wine jus," he said sitting down opposite Sophie. "Your gran was going to be spoilt. She's missed a treat."

"We like to spoil her... you're only ninety once."

He reached across and lit the candles in front of them. "It's been really good seeing you again, Soph. I know we lost touch during uni."

"Friendships are for different seasons. Some last a lifetime, others dwindle away." Her knife slid through a piece of tender duck as he laid the matches down to one side.

"Which one are we...a lifetime, I hope?"

209

The piece of duck dangling on Sophie's fork landed quickly in her mouth as Rupert leaned forward waiting for an answer. What was she going to say, and more importantly, what did he mean by asking it? Rupert was a really important part of her life, she didn't want to lose him, but the pressure and guilt she felt from her mother breathing down her neck was beginning to taint their relationship. An easy solution to her problem would be to avoid seeing him altogether, but she couldn't tell him that.

He waited for her to chew, an excessive number of times, before she swallowed and smiled nervously. "Time will tell, I suppose. How's Maisie?" The subtle change of topic allowed her underarm to momentarily pause its surge of perspiration.

"She's busy with work at the moment, our timetables keep clashing."

"Is that because your life is so hectic and you haven't a moment to spare?" She smirked in amusement, laughing at her friend. The reality was, that even though Rupert had completed his degree with the highest standard possible, he was still to start his job hunt, knowing a graduate program would fall easily into his lap and he spent his time sitting idle and enjoying life to the full.

"She's busy, Soph," he said again, his cheeks colouring slightly.

"I understand that, I only thought you'd go visit her and make the effort. She lives in Scotland, doesn't she?"

"Yes, but it's complicated." He frowned and started hacking away at his duck.

"Don't take it out on the duck," Sophie teased. "Everyone goes through relationship problems. What does she do?"

"She's a teacher."

"Isn't it the summer holidays?"

"She teaches summer school... Wine?" he held up a bottle with a grin.

"No thanks, I've got to drive home."

"Very sensible," he said putting it straight down again.

They continued eating and chatting with the candles flickering and dancing before them. Sophie wiped her lips with the tip of her napkin, laying her cutlery side by side on the empty plate. "What's for pudding, chef?"

"Still got a sweet tooth, I see?" Rupert laughed. "Actually, I was thinking, how about some music before we eat pudding, let the duck settle a bit, eh?"

Sophie agreed and he headed over to an old-fashioned record player. "This was gran's, we brought it out of the loft for the party." The sound of crackling, soft jazz swept through the air as Rupert connected the needle with the record. He bowed low to Sophie. "Can I have this dance, madam."

She gladly accepted and they stepped lightly in time to the music as he held her close. The scent of his spiced aftershave drifted up her nose and she rested her head softly on his shoulder. After such a long day it was nice to be held in the arms of someone who felt so familiar.

Rupert brushed a loose piece of hair behind Sophie's ear as the song came to an end, his sparkling cobalt blue eyes suddenly trapping her gaze. The music faded away into the background and neither of them noticed the jumping needle indicating the record had now ended. The aroma of his aftershave seemed to grow stronger and her thoughts became hazy. Down the hall the grandfather clock chimed the hour of ten.

Sophie jerked away. "Goodness, is that the time?" She released herself from his clasp. "I should be going home."

"Don't rush away Soph." he reached for her with his hand. "Stay."

"It really is later than I intended to stay. It was a lovely meal, thank you for inviting me."

"Sophie Hastings leaving before pudding," he grinned. "That's unlike you."

"I'm sorry, Rupert."

She left the dining room looking for her shawl. Rupert directed her to the hat stand in the hall where it was draped over a hanger.

Rupert took the matching royal blue shawl and wrapped it over her shoulders. "I owe you a pudding then… meet me tomorrow for coffee and cake?"

"Maybe… I'll call you; I don't know what my plans are yet." She could barely look him in the eye as she scurried out of the front door.

The cool air met her face and she shook her head trying to clear her thoughts. What was going on? Every time she was near Rupert her heart ended up leaping towards him. In fact, she wouldn't be surprised if her mother had hired Cupid to shoot his arrow through the two of them. She was not attracted to him…was she? It wasn't possible, she didn't spend hours dwelling on him in his absence. Actually, there were times his thoughtlessness irritated her to the bone. But still, there was something… if only she could put her finger on what it was.

Utterly exhausted, Sophie intended to head straight to bed on her arrival home. However, her plans were changed when, pulling up on the drive, she saw a beam of light glinting from the estate office. Someone had left the light on. With a deep sigh she supposed she'd better turn it off, any saving on electricity would help the estate finances.

With blurry eyes Sophie plodded through the manor. When she reached the office, she slipped her arm through the half open door and switched the light off, only to immediately switch it back on again. A ripped envelope on the desk caught her eye and she swung the door wide open and walked across to inspect it.

Sophie took the letter, her tiredness instantly vanishing as she hurriedly scanned the words in front of her. She read them over and over again, trying to understand what she held in her hands. Not knowing what else to do, she reached for the mobile in her pocket and scrolled frantically through her contacts.

"I'm sorry it's late," she said, after listening to the dialling tone ring endlessly. For a moment she worried no one would pick up.

"Sophie… Is everything okay?" asked a concerned voice on the other end of the line.

"No… not really. I didn't know who else to call."

"I'll be right over."

Twenty minutes later Oliver stood by Sophie's side. The letter was still firmly in her hand as she scanned it again, desperately searching for hidden clues that might answer the questions swirling around her head

"It's dated the day after my arrival home from uni. This was the trigger… it must have been."

"Why would he not say anything?" asked Oliver wrinkling his forehead and examining the contents of the letter over Sophie's shoulder.

"I don't know."

Nothing made sense to her. If her father was hiding such a secret, it was no wonder he'd slipped into his current mental state. Slouching into the office chair, she rested her head in her hands. "What a mess?"

"Nothing's going to change overnight, why don't you get some sleep, it's late."

She lifted her head to meet his sensitive sapphire eyes willing her to rest before facing the challenge that lay ahead. "I can't sleep, not before I've spoken to dad."

"Will he be awake?"

"He suffers with insomnia when he's depressed so he's likely to be awake."

Sophie rose up to leave the room, but she hesitated. "Will you come with me?" It sounded so stupid to ask Oliver this, to see her father who she had no fear of, but she needed the strength of a friend, she felt too weak to handle the situation alone. "It's just…"

"You don't need to explain, I'm right behind you," he reached out his hand and slipped it into hers. "Come on."

Sophie tapped on George's bedroom door and Oliver stood behind.

"I'll wait out here," he said. "Shout if you need me."

Sophie was constantly amazed by Oliver Morgan. He seemed to understand exactly what she needed, without her having to ask. Having the privacy she desired, but knowing the reassurance he was close by, was exactly what she wanted.

The second tap on the door was met with another silence. Twisting the handle, Sophie tiptoed into the room, her mind a mixture of emotions. The stillness seemed to suggest her dad was sleeping, which would do him good. But, if he was sleeping now, she would have to wait until the morning to talk with him, which would probably mean she would be the one suffering from insomnia overnight.

"Dad," she whispered. "Are you awake?"

She retreated when she realised his bed was empty and signalled for Oliver to follow her to the library. Repeating the exercise, she knocked lightly on the door. "Dad?"

No response, she didn't wait to tap on the door again, this time she went straight inside. No one was there and she spun towards Oliver, feeling her body tremble. "He's not here either."

"Don't worry, I bet he's in the bathroom."

It was a good idea, but he wasn't. Sophie began to panic. There weren't any other places he could be.

"He's gone, dad's gone." She stood helplessly watching Oliver poke his head into a couple of the empty guest rooms.

"He can't be far, let's keep looking. I'll continue searching the rest of the manor while you get changed, shall I?"

"Get changed?" Sophie couldn't understand what he was talking about until she saw Oliver scanning her royal blue ballgown. "Ah… yes." She had forgotten all about her evening with Rupert and she blushed slightly.

Sophie told Oliver to meet her in the car and raced along to her room to throw on an old baggy t-shirt and grey jogging bottoms. Scooping up her rucksack, she caught sight of herself in the clouded mirror. She looked tired and her hair, which earlier on had seemed so elegant, now fell messily around her face. She blinked twice. Maybe she needed to ring Dylan again? There was no doubt Oliver could support her, but what about her father? George didn't know Oliver; would he know how to handle him when they found him? Only Dylan would know what to do, now she knew her father was bankrupt.

20

Georgiana

It was the day before Emma's departure and Georgiana paced the Denholm gardens. Sleep had evaded her that night. Tossing and turning fitfully, she made every effort to slip into a blissful slumber, but it did not arrive. Five days had passed since she had written to Kirkby and this worried her. From the time he left the county to attend his mother's wedding, he had been a very reliable correspondent, sending two or three letters a week, sometimes even four, and now he was suddenly silent. Georgiana could only presume their friendship had come to an end, that the answer she was waiting for could not be revealed owing to the many shameful secrets it was potentially hiding.

It was unfortunate for Georgiana that such an event had happened at this time. All her hopes had rested on Kirkby. He had become a source of hope, a light in the darkness and her only way of escape. She did not know how their marriage would come about, nor could she fathom how her parents would even accept the match in the first place. However, no word from Kirkby meant she had to choose Mr Turner or Mr Southerly, whether she liked it or not.

In Georgiana's opinion both men were dull and neither would allow her much freedom. Mr Turner lived alone and had few relatives or acquaintances. Her life would inevitably become one of continued loneliness, especially since he owned a large remote property on the Yorkshire Moors. There would be little or no social contact to give relief from her isolation.

Robert Southerly, on the other hand, lived in his family home, not many miles away from a market-town. She reasoned that Henry Southerly would be there for entertainment, whose light-hearted character she was becoming particularly fond of. Gentlemen of his type had always been excluded from Georgiana's acquaintance, never before had she met anyone like him, until he slipped through the crack. The younger Southerly intrigued her, he was more than just a frivolous young man and she would enjoy getting to know him in a less formal setting.

Pausing on her tour around the gardens she made her decision and took a deep breath. It wasn't ideal, but she could see no alternative. Keen to get the deed completed she turned on her heel, intent on finding Mr Turner. She hurried swiftly through an old brick archway and immediately bumped into Ridley.

"I beg your pardon, Miss Davenport. A letter has arrived for you."

With thanks Georgiana took the letter and waited for Ridley to retreat before turning it over. The sight of Kirkby's scrawl took her breath away, its timing could not have been better planned. She ripped open the seal, tearing the paper in her haste.

My dearest Georgiana,

It has brought me much heartache to keep you waiting for an answer; for this, I ask your forgiveness. Today I am travelling to be with you and I will give an explanation of what has caused you distress. I know this does not clarify anything for you now, but please, have faith in me, it can all be explained and I'm hopeful of still being worthy of your hand… I pray I will not be too late.

As ever yours…

Georgiana lowered herself down on a well-placed bench. It was not the answer she had hoped for. He hadn't denied or confirmed anything. What was she to do now? Re-reading the letter, she reassured herself that there was, at least, an explanation… but what was it? She needed an answer.

After sitting and contemplating for several minutes, it seemed right to continue her search for Mr Turner. She could not marry him, no matter what happened with Kirkby. There was still a whole day to accept Robert Southerly, if Kirkby made no appearance.

It was not a pleasant conversation, nonetheless, Mr Turner accepted her refusal like a gentleman and kept himself out of her way for the remainder of the day. Lady Davenport walked around with a proud look on her face, believing Georgiana was about to accept Mr Southerly's offer - he was always the one she preferred, he had a larger income and grander connections. Therefore, Mr Southerly attached himself to Georgiana like a piece of string; no matter where she was, he always seemed to find her.

Evening came and still Georgiana held on for Kirkby to appear. She held on, needing to hear his explanation before resigning herself to her fate. As the hour grew later, Georgiana's weary eyes could hardly keep open. Ignoring the watchful eye of her mother trailing her out of the room she said her goodnights. It was possible Kirkby had been delayed and would arrive during the night, she could still accept Mr Southerly's proposal in the morning if he failed to show, and so calmly she entered the hall and began climbing the staircase.

"Miss Davenport."

Georgiana's heart thudded and her hand froze to the banister. Why had he followed her, could he not see she was not ready to give her answer?

"I do not wish to rush you, but I need to know what you are thinking. I do not believe we will have another opportunity to be alone. We are due to leave early on the morrow."

"Mr Southerly, I..." Georgiana faltered. This was not her plan. There was no excuse in her mind which would allow her to say no and if a yes was spoken, then that would be it.

"I know you have declined Mr Turner," said Robert reaching for her hand. She nearly pulled it away, but politeness prevailed and she allowed him to escort her back down the stairs.

"It is true, I have declined Mr Turner, but..."

"But?" he stepped away, still holding onto her hand. "Please do not trifle with my heart, Miss Davenport." His cry was passionate and he looked away.

Georgiana was shocked, she did not think he loved her this much... or if in fact he loved her at all. This marriage would be one of convenience, on both sides, she was not trifling with his heart at all. "I need to be honest and explain that I am having great difficulty making a decision. I require one more night to make absolutely certain accepting your hand is the correct thing to do."

Robert shook his head and let Georgiana's hand fall to her side. "It is as I feared."

"I… I do not understand?"

"It is my brother, isn't it?" His shoulders hung low.

"Your brother?" What was he was talking about; how did Henry have anything to do with this?

"You cannot marry me because you are in love with Henry. I know, I have seen the looks you have shared together. You are afraid it will be too torturous to have him as your brother-in-law, knowing you can never share your love. I cannot say I blame you, Georgiana, but I am saddened we cannot unite together for we would have made a good match. I will now save you the heartache of talking." He gallantly lifted her hand again and kissed it gently. "I bid you farewell and please do not be troubled, we part in good faith."

Bowing courteously, he left Georgiana speechless at the bottom of the stairs.

Two proposals and neither one accepted. What had just happened? She wasn't in love with Henry. What should have been a moment of relief was one of fear knowing her mother would surface any moment. Frozen to the spot, she did not even dare to run upstairs to the sanctuary of her bedroom. This was something she could not hide from.

"You have declined both gentlemen! What is the meaning of this?" Lady Davenport came charging in the hall.

"I'm sorry, mama," Georgiana felt her body tremble. "I…"

"Enough, I do not want to hear your excuses. I don't know what you are planning, child, but I can tell you now, if you do not reverse one of your marriage refusals, I will do everything in my power to make your life a misery. If you are still contemplating a marriage to your beloved beau, all I will say is that you are forbidden to accept his proposal, and if he comes to see your father, he will not be accepted."

Georgiana clung to the banister as her mother crept closer. "I did not intend to go against your wishes, mama. I have not purposefully rejected both gentlemen, but can I say…" She gulped, fear should have stopped her, but she had to go on. "Mr Kirkby is a good match, even if he is not Sir Gillingham's cousin."

"He can have connections with the king for all I care. I will choose your future husband and only I…"

A cough broke Lady Davenport's speech and Ridley's shadow hovered silently in the corner of the room.

"I am sorry to bother you m'lady. A letter has arrived for you."

"At this time of night?" snapped Lady Davenport over her shoulder.

"It appears to be of some urgency." He came across and placed the sealed document into his mistress' hand before slipping away.

Georgiana stood still with her heart beating rapidly, waiting for her mother to continue…but she didn't. Instead of hurling further abuse, Lady Davenport's face was drained of all its colour as she scanned the contents of the paper in front of her.

"Mama, is everything okay?" Georgiana asked cautiously.

No answer was given and the next thing Georgiana knew, she was flinging out her hands hurriedly towards her mother as the elder lady fell crashing to the floor.

It was a miracle Lady Davenport wasn't injured. The commotion had been instantly heard and with the assistance of Lord Davenport and Mr Faversham, they carried Lady Davenport into the parlour. Georgiana stood uncertainly to the side as Emma tried to revive her mother with smelling salts.

"Can you hear us, Lady Davenport?" asked her son-in-law, perching before the elder lady.

Suddenly her eyes flickered open and she looked hazily around at the faces crowding her weakened figure. Her gaze rested on

Georgiana. "She needs to go," she whispered putting a hand to her aching head.

"Who, Lady Davenport?" asked Mr Faversham looking in Georgiana's direction.

"Her…" she slithered a hand out and pointed a shaking finger at her daughter. "Get your bags ready, child."

"Wh-where am I going?" asked Georgiana beginning to panic as she felt the eyes of everyone on her.

"Georgiana!" bellowed her father. "Your mother has asked you to leave, not to ask questions. Now go!"

Georgiana had never seen her mother react in such a way to a piece of news before and she wondered what could have been contained in the letter. Fleeing to her room in direct obedience, she pulled a trunk out from under her bed. It was covered in dust and she wiped it clean with her hand. It had been a long time since she had travelled anywhere, five years ago maybe, when she had visited her cousins with Edward. She lifted the lid and began filling it with items. It wouldn't be a surprise if she never saw this room again. Under current circumstances, she was uncertain her mother would ever send for her back once she had left Denholm Park.

A tap sounded at the door. Georgiana ran lightly across and crouched low by the keyhole.

"Who is it?" she whispered.

"Miss Davenport? Are you there?"

"Mr Southerly?"

It was Henry. She stood up and opened the door ajar. "What are you doing up here?" Her eyes darted up and down the landing. "You will get me in even greater trouble if you are found by my room"

"I know… I wanted to check on your welfare. What is going on?" he asked.

"You are asking the wrong person. I have no idea."

"Your mother is downstairs in hysterics."

221

"I have never seen her like this before, she is always in perfect control of her emotions."

"Have you rejected any more men?" He grinned mischievously.

"That is not funny, Mr Southerly. I am in serious trouble and I do not know why."

"I'm sorry." He touched a finger to his lips and straightened out his smile. "That was inappropriate of me. I do not do well in serious situations; it is my disposition I'm afraid."

"You must go back downstairs, Mr Southerly. I cannot emphasise the uproar that will commence if you are found in my quarters."

"I will find out what is happening and report back to you."

"Why are you even bothered about me? You are escaping Denholm Park tomorrow, go – be free of us."

"You deserve the right to know what is in that letter and I have a feeling you will not be told."

"Do not feel obliged, we will not become family. I am not about to bring shame upon you."

Henry scoffed loudly. "You think I care about that… I am the one who is famous for disgracing our family, you need not worry about that. Didn't you accept Robert?"

"Things didn't quite go to plan and I don't suppose it has helped my mother's condition. I am not engaged and have managed to decline all the offers laid out before me."

"You did this intentionally?"

"Not entirely."

"Do you know where your father will send you?"

"If I knew what my offence was, I might begin to comprehend where he might send me."

"Do not worry, I will seek you out if I find any information which concerns you."

"Thank you," She formed half a smile. "It is very kind of you and much appreciated." For a brief moment she allowed her eyes to linger on his before he awkwardly bade her farewell and retreated back downstairs.

Georgiana continued to place her most priceless processions inside the trunk, although she did not have many. Her mother had always bought Emma fine clothes and trinkets and rarely spent her fortune on her youngest daughter. She did not want to leave anything behind for fear she would not return. Inside, Georgiana slipped a pile of letters from Edward and a gold chain she had been given as a young child, but most importantly, she collected together her diaries, so many had she filled over the years. They were a source of encouragement and reminded her of the many struggles she had overcome and helped her hope for a better future.

Lottie walked in when Georgiana was locking the trunk with a tiny metal key.

"Are you ready, Miss Davenport?" her mother's maid asked as two footmen appeared to take her trunk away.

"Where am I going, Lottie? I cannot be travelling through the night?"

"The carriage is waiting for you outside. Your mother has instructed that you are to travel immediately."

Georgiana followed the footmen downstairs, pulling on her long cream gloves. Lord Davenport was waiting for her in the hall.

"Papa, I do not understand what is happening? Please," she begged. "Can't you tell me?"

"Your mother has been taken ill and you are the cause." His deep bushy eyebrows drew together and he would not look at his daughter.

"How am I the cause?" she asked as her father marched her to the front door.

"There are rumours that have been spread. You do not need to know them."

He handed her a letter. "Your uncle is not expecting you, but give him this on your arrival…and do not bring further shame upon us, Georgiana, otherwise there will be much trouble indeed."

21

Sophie

Sophie and Oliver searched through the night. They hunted all over Middleton and the surrounding estate, but no clues could be found to help locate the whereabouts of George Hastings.

"Where can he be?" Sophie rubbed her tired eyes. Dawn was beginning to break on the horizon and she felt worn and beaten.

"Time for home, Sophie," Oliver tapped her shoulder and headed back towards the car expecting her to follow.

"I've got to keep searching."

"You're no good to anyone if you haven't slept. Besides, your mum will be waking up and she needs telling."

"She won't care," Sophie mumbled kicking a small pebble with her foot.

"You don't know that," Oliver came back towards her.

"Okay, I'll correct myself - she'll only care when she realises dad's bankruptcy means no manor for her."

"She can't be that heartless."

"Just wait and see."

"All I'm saying is give her the benefit of the doubt."

"I've done that before and it's backfired on me." She crossed her arms, too exhausted for politeness.

"You're tired," he said not taking offence and tugging at her elbow. "Come on, let me take you home."

The need to find her dad battled against her need for sleep. In the end, she knew her friend was right, her limbs would not carry her much further anyway.

When Sophie finally made it into bed, she didn't sleep long and woke with a start a couple of hours later. Blindly reaching down the side of the bed she pulled up Georgiana's diary and sat up, rubbing her heavy eyes and trying to focus on the blurry handwriting.

Uncle greeted me warmly, although he found it incredibly strange that I had travelled through the night with no prior warning. His affection towards me soon changed after he had read the letter from my father. I do not know what had been written, but whatever it was had not put me in a good light.

I have immediately written to Mr Kirkby informing him of my exit from Denholm Park to my Uncle Barnet's house - I am hopeful he will arrive here soon.

She felt sorry for the girl, having been sent into exile and not told why. Everything appeared to be going wrong for both of them and she frantically read through the entries, trying to find a small glimmer of hope. Finally, still searching an hour later for her nineteenth century friend's silver lining, Sophie forced herself to go downstairs and make breakfast.

Elizabeth walked into the kitchen and saw her daughter sitting at the table, dark circles under her eyes. "You don't look well Sophie. If you are contagious, don't come near me, I am very busy at the moment and do not wish to be sick."

Sophie was suffering too much from lack of sleep to battle against her mother's insolent tones. She wearily pushed out the seat opposite her with her foot. "Sit down, mum. There's something you need to know."

When Elizabeth heard her husband had disappeared, she didn't appear too bothered and was about to leave until Sophie pushed the letter under her face. "His financial advisor has recommended he declares himself bankrupt."

"Bankrupt?" Elizabeth ogled at the paper and sat down, trying to process this new information. "I don't understand... how does he have no money? He never told me!"

"He has mum - repeatedly. The manor is expensive to run and all the renovations you are doing cost money. He was only a bank manager, not a millionaire."

"He should have been saving so he was ready. Your father knew he was next in line."

"He had a family to raise and bills to pay."

"So, he's decided to run away, rather than face the facts."

"He's not run away."

"Where is he then?" Elizabeth scraped back the chair and stood towering above her daughter.

"I don't know…but I know dad isn't a coward, if that's what you're inferring."

"He's left his wife and daughter to deal with *his* bankruptcy: that's cowardice."

"It's not just *his* problem, mum. We're family, we face these things together."

Elizabeth huffed and didn't respond.

"He's depressed, running away might seem like the best option – he can't think straight."

"You don't need to defend him, Sophie," snapped her mother. "Your father makes his own decisions and he needs to face the consequences."

"It's not his fault you're bankrupt!" Sophie shouted banging the table with her fists as she rose. "It's your fault."

"My fault?"

"Yes! Dad's a good steward with money and you've been spending faster than the estate can bring money in. You can't spend thousands of pounds and expect a continuous supply of money. He had to give up his job to be Lord of the Manor. You seem to forget he has no income and the estate is in such a mess that very little money is being made. If you bothered to take an interest in anybody's life but your own, you would have noticed that."

The room went silent apart from the dripping tap.

"Have you quite finished?" asked Elizabeth icily, tapping her foot and folding her arms firmly across her body.

"Oh, we've finished… for now." Sophie thrust the chair under the table and turned her back on her mother as she stormed out the room.

"Sorry I'm not available to take your call at the moment but please leave a message after the tone. BEEP."

Sophie threw the phone into her bag. It was the fifth time she'd tried to call her brother that morning with no response. She tapped her finger irritably on the counter having escaped to Middleton's café to purchase a caffeine-filled beverage before she went back on the hunt for her father.

A sharp fall of rain five minutes earlier had made the air feel fresh as Sophie stepped out of the coffee shop holding an insulated disposable cup in her hand. She looked at her watch – it was half past nine. Jaw clenched firmly with determination, Sophie took the phone out of her bag again. Her brother wasn't going to hide himself from her today.

"Hello, Historic Surveyors. How can I help you today?" The woman's over enthusiastic greeting grated upon Sophie's already frayed nerves.

"Could I speak to my brother please, he works for you. His name is Dylan Hastings."

"Dylan Hastings?"

"Yes, he's one of your surveyors."

"I'm sorry no one works here called Dylan Hastings."

"Are you certain?"

"I can check for you, but we are a small company and I don't believe we have anyone by that name. Will you hold please?" A cheesy pop song played over the line and Sophie blew through gritted teeth and checked her watch again. This was wasting time.

A few moments later the receptionist returned. "I'm really sorry, Dylan Hastings doesn't work for us… maybe you've got the wrong number."

"Oh, that's strange. Thank you for your time anyway."

Sophie frowned at the phone in her hand. This was definitely the right number.

She phoned Dylan's mobile again.

228

"Sorry I'm not available to take your call at the moment but please leave a message after the tone. BEEP."

"Dylan, I don't know what you're up to… ring me - ASAP!"

"Excuse me, are you Miss Hastings?"

Sophie spun round to see the face of a stranger, olive skinned, clean shaven and dressed in a freshly pressed business suit.

"Yes, can I help you?" She looked at the man in confusion as he handed her a large brown envelope. "What's this?"

"You've been served." The stranger gave no further explanation and disappeared as quickly as he had appeared. Feeling her legs wobble underneath her, she curiously opened the envelope and scanned the documents inside.

Rupert, who had been passing by, saw his friend from across the road and raced to grab Sophie as she staggered backwards. "Whoa… are you okay, Soph?"

He looked around and guided her to the nearest bench, which was surrounded by enchanting asters and chrysanthemums. Sophie clasped his hand and held it tightly.

"What's wrong, Soph?"

"You won't believe this… he's suing me."

"Who?"

"Mr Jones." Her voice wobbled as she spoke.

"What?" Rupert snatched the document and scrutinised it in disbelief. "He's suing you for negligence, he can't do that."

"Apparently he can." She burrowed her head deep in her hands. "I don't need this right now."

"Don't panic, Soph. Ring your dad, let him look over it. It might not be as bad as you think."

She closed her eyes. "I can't, dad's missing."

"Missing?"

"He's bankrupt," she said, lifting her head up and staring straight ahead.

"You're kidding me: I said he should have sold the manor. Why didn't you tell me?"

"I only found the letter last night. Oliver Morgan has been helping me look for him."

"Oliver Morgan…Soph, you could have rung me." He sounded hurt.

"I'm sorry Rupert. I don't know why I didn't call you…"

"It's okay." He took her hand, but his thoughts were elsewhere. "Listen… I need to go."

"What… now?"

He let go of her hand and got up from the bench. "There's something I've got to do."

"Rupert, I'm sorry I didn't call you…please, don't go."

"I'll call you, Soph."

That was about right, Sophie thought, when things got tough Rupert Donaldson didn't stick around for long. He never was very good in an emergency. She remembered one summer when she had visited the Donaldsons, how a poor little elderly lady had fallen in the street. Nobody had seen it but she and Rupert. They had immediately raced off to see if the lady was all right. Sophie had stayed with the lady to help her, but Rupert left them behind when he had a sudden memory of promising his mother that he would pop into the fruit shop to buy some oranges. Whatever feelings of affection she had for her childhood friend now evaporated as she watched him flee down the high street. She needed someone whom she could trust.

She shoved the brown paper envelope into her rucksack. Any thoughts of Mr Jones now needed to be pushed right to the back of her mind because finding her dad was more important.

Sophie called into every shop and business she could find on the high street, asking everyone she saw if they'd seen George Hastings and flashing a recent photo of him on her phone. No one had seen him or heard of his whereabouts.

"Where are you, dad?" she muttered under her breath as she stepped out of the estate agents, the final building in the high street. Up and down the road, people were busy going about their everyday lives. Sophie watched them, feeling completely and utterly helpless; she couldn't believe any of this was happening. She didn't think Georgiana's situation was so troubling now, whatever the cause of her exile, because the girl's blissful ignorance made Sophie slightly envious. A tingle crept into her nose, but her mobile buzzed loudly before a single tear could be shed.

"Hi Sophie." A sheepish voice sounded down the line.

"Dylan... what is going on? I've tried to call you."

"Listen, before you shout at me – which you have every right to do... I think we need to meet."

"I can't right now, Dylan. I've more important things to see to... like, I don't know - dad disappearing."

"Just come Sophie. I'll explain everything... please."

There was an earnestness in his voice which caused Sophie to agree. Dylan gave her the details of where to find him.

"It's two hours away, Dylan," she exclaimed after typing the location into the map on her phone. "I need to be searching for dad, I can't waste time."

"It's important, Sophie. Dad will be fine. I'll see you soon." He hung up so his sister couldn't argue with him anymore.

She would have called him back immediately, if a text hadn't flashed on her screen. It was Oliver, checking up on how things were going.

Searched has stopped. Dylan wants to meet. I'll be gone for a few hours. S x

Ten seconds after Sophie pressed send her phone rang again.

"I'm coming with you, Sophie."

"Oliver, you've done so much already - you need to work."

"I've asked permission, dad's got plenty of hands this morning. I'll come and pick you up."

She couldn't argue with that.

231

They drove along the winding country lanes until they reached the motorway. Sophie stared out the window, her teeth gnawing her lower lip.

Oliver stole several glances across at her as he kept his focus on the road ahead. "Are you doing okay?"

Sophie didn't respond.

"We'll find him," he said with as much confidence as he could find. He couldn't deny he was concerned himself.

"I don't know if I can handle anything else, Oliver."

"You don't have to handle anything else."

"Something's not right...I can't understand why Dylan wants to see me now when I haven't seen him for over a year."

"I'm sure there's a perfectly innocent explanation... Sophie?" She'd turned her face away and cast her eyes gloomily out of the window.

"There is something else..." began Sophie. "Arthur Jones is suing me."

"What!" cried Oliver.

"For negligence."

Oliver gripped the steering wheel and they both became silent.

A pub sign signalled their arrival and Oliver pulled into a parking space and turned off the engine. "Let's find your dad first," he said speaking gently. "See what Dylan has to say and then we'll deal with Mr Jones...okay?"

Sophie nodded as she held her lips firmly together - she had to be brave, her dad was counting on it.

Together they walked across the car-park. The sun was dazzling behind the old Tudor building, so the figure walking out towards them from the old pub at first appeared like a silhouette.

Sophie squinted - it was Dylan.

Confusion muddled her emotions as she considered how to greet her brother, she wanted to shout at him, hit him and run into his arms, all at the same time. However, the choice was taken away from her when Dylan stepped to the side and revealed a second man behind him.

Sophie gasped. "Dad?"

22

Georgiana

"I still don't understand why you are here," Mary Barnet said again, with a mouth full of pins. She had decided that morning one of her gowns was the perfect fit for her cousin.

Georgiana stood in the middle of Mary's bedroom on a tiny wooden stool, whilst her cousin pinned the hem.

"Mary, I've told you many times now - I cannot tell you what I don't know myself."

"Aunt Jane has banished you?"

"No, Mary, my mother has not banished me."

"But you've been sent away under a black cloud." Mary pushed another pin through and stepped back with hands on her hips. "That should be okay…try walking."

Georgiana cautiously stepped down. She had already been stabbed several times that morning: she had forgotten her cousin had never been a good seamstress.

"So…why hasn't Mr Kirkby come to rescue you?"

"I don't know, Mary."

Georgiana reached the mirror and lifted the dress so she could see her toes. "I think it's still a little long."

"You'll have shoes on," Mary tutted. "But if Mr Kirkby loves you…"

"No, Mary, I haven't said he loves me."

"Sorry, I mean, if you love him…"

"Mary, I haven't said I love him."

"You're confusing me."

Mary started unbuttoning the round fabric buttons at the top of Georgiana's back. "I'll leave the gown for Rosie, she's mama's lady's maid, she'll soon get it sewn up."

Mary neatly draped the gown over the bed as Georgiana got changed.

"Okay, let me try again. Aunt Jane sent you here because she doesn't want you to marry Mr Kirkby, whose proposal you've accepted?"

Georgiana pressed her lips together. She had not seen her cousin for many years and had forgotten how slow she was to grasp new information. Mary Barnet was a kind girl, only a little older than Georgiana, but she did not have much sense.

Georgiana explained again about the letter her mother had received and how this had been the catalyst of her arrival in her uncle's home. She repeated that she had had two proposals, neither of which was from Mr Kirkby and both had come to nothing.

"You live such an exciting life," sighed Mary.

"I do not call it exciting," replied Georgiana, the events of the night before still resonating in her mind.

"I've never had one proposal and here's you with three."

"All unwelcome, Mary."

The two girls made their way down the stairs and into the garden room.

"Mama," cried Mary, as she skipped into the room. "Have you heard? Cousin Georgiana has had three proposals!"

Georgiana's cheeks turned rose pink.

"Indeed?" Her Aunt Charlotte's eyebrow rose greatly in height. "And you are still unmarried, Georgiana?" The lady attempted to keep a stern glare, but could not, and ended up smirking, the corner of her mouth rising up at an angle, as the girls sat down.

"I have hemmed up my old cotton gown for Georgiana, the one with the pretty blue daisies."

"That is very kind of you, Mary."

"I've left it for Rosie to sew."

Her mother nodded. "Mary."

"Yes, mama," said the girl, eagerly coming to the edge of her seat. "Go and find Rosie now. Your cousin might be in need of a gown quickly – I do not know how many she was able to bring with her." Mary happily obliged and sauntered out of the room.

Charlotte turned to her niece. "How bad is your mother, Georgiana?"

"I have never seen her so ill before."

"Is it true you have declined three gentlemen?"

"Yes, but it has not entirely been my own doing."

"No good comes from meddling in other people's affairs, remember that Georgiana and do not become like your mother."

Georgiana chose not to reply. There had always been a bitter rivalry between the two ladies. Lady Davenport had never forgiven her aunt for marrying her older brother. Charlotte's family had been shopkeepers, until her father had risen through the ranks of the navy. Her aunt had known nothing but luxury, which had come as a consequence of her father's good fortune, but Lady Davenport looked down upon them and discredited them as social climbers.

Hearing her niece had defied her sister-in-law gave Charlotte great satisfaction and she greatly enjoyed listening to Georgiana's account of the three different episodes which had resulted in no engagement.

Mary eventually bounded back into the room and the girls spent the morning drawing and catching up on news. Although Aunt Charlotte could be equally as austere as her mother, Georgiana had always found the atmosphere in her uncle's house to be less oppressive than at Denholm Park. She felt more at liberty to express an opinion and could breathe freely without being scolded. In the afternoon, Georgiana requested if she could take a solitary walk whilst Mary visited a friend; her Aunt Charlotte readily agreed.

Georgiana breathed in the fresh air. It was a pleasant day and the chirruping birds lifted her spirits. She ambled along the pathways, contemplating the events that had led up to her removal from Denholm. It had all happened so quickly that it was quite difficult to remember the sequences of events. What really puzzled her was the contents of the letter sent to her mother.

236

The winding country lanes were dry and cracked as Georgiana continued her walk, this part of the country had suffered from little rainfall and a downpour was desperately needed.

"Help, someone!"

The faint cry of a young girl broke into her musings. Georgiana darted her eyes hastily around, but could see nobody. "Hello?" she called softly, her voice not travelling far in the open air.

"Is someone there?" a young girl called.

"Y-yes," answered Georgiana.

"Please, come quickly."

"Where are you? I cannot see you." Georgiana stood on tiptoes trying to see into the farmlands.

"In the field, behind the hedgerows... hurry."

Georgiana looked around and noticed a gate in between the hedges where the girl's voice had been calling from: she unclasped the lock and hurried into the field.

"Over here!"

Georgiana saw a hand waving over rows of golden wheat. She lifted up her dress to run faster and followed the girl into a small orchard.

"What's wrong?" Georgiana queried, kneeling down and looking with concern at a small boy who was holding onto his ankle in great pain.

"I think he's broken his foot, or something worse," the girl explained anxiously. "He fell out of the tree when we were collecting apples."

"Let's take a look shall we." Georgiana smiled kindly at the pair. "What's your name?" she asked the boy.

"Edward, ma'am," he said quietly, stifling a sob.

His sister piped in. "He's my little brother, ma'am... and I'm Eve."

"My brother's called Edward too," replied Georgiana softly. "Can I take a look at your ankle, Edward?" The boy nodded and wiped his runny nose on his sleeve. Examining the ankle, she could see it was swollen, but further diagnosis was beyond her skill and she could not tell if it was broken.

She looked up. "Where do you live, Eve?"

"It's a mile to our farmhouse. Ma sent us out to pick fruit so she could make a pie."

Georgiana sat back, apart from farmland, there was no one and nothing else in sight and she realised she could not leave them there alone. "Eve," she asked. "Can you carry the basket?"

"Yes, ma'am."

"Good. Edward, if you put your arms around me, I'll carry you home."

It felt like a long mile. Edward was very good and didn't complain once, even though his ankle must have been throbbing. At first, he appeared lightweight, but very soon Georgiana's back began to ache and the humidity in the air was drawing all her energy away. Finally, Eve pointed out a little brick farmhouse with ivy growing up the side.

As they entered the farmyard a middle-aged lady wearing a cream coloured apron came rushing out. "Eve," the lady called, wiping her floury hands. "What has happened?"

"Edward fell out of the apple tree, ma. I told him not to go so high."

"Come, come," the lady said, as she rushed Georgiana, who was still carrying Edward, into the farmhouse. "Put him here, my dear." Georgiana did what she was told and the children's mother immediately examined her son's ankle.

"Eve, go and fetch a cloth drenched in the coldest water you can find - we'll try and help the swelling go down." She bent and kissed Edward's head, stroking his fair hair. "Just a sprain by the looks of it. How did it happen, Eddie?"

"I wasn't messing around, ma. I promise."

His mother cast doubtful eyes over her son before turning to Georgiana. "Thank you, ma'am, for your help, it was very kind of you. Will you stay for tea? You look worn out."

Georgiana was relieved to receive the invitation. "I would be very grateful; the weather is very tiring today."

The lady moved away from her son and began busying herself at the stove. "My name's Bessie." She smiled warmly at her visitor. "I've not seen you before, are you visiting family?"

"Yes, I'm visiting my uncle. My name is Georgiana Davenport." She tottered over towards the kitchen so she didn't have to raise her voice. "You've got a lovely farmhouse."

"It's been in my husband's family for generations, bit on the small side with so many children running around, but it's warm and cosy when the hearth is blazing."

The downstairs consisted of one room, stove and table in one corner, fireplace and chairs in the other. Eve tumbled back into the room with a dripping cloth and began tending to her brother.

"Let Eddie hold onto the cloth, Eve," said Bessie. "You go and wash the fruit and then we can start on the pie."

Eve obeyed her new orders and Bessie spoke to Georgiana again. "It was only a matter of time before Eddie hurt himself... he's a mischievous one is that boy. He can't sit still for a second, always climbing and jumping on things. All my children work on the farm and he's old enough to pull his weight."

"Have you got many children, Mrs..."

"It's Simms, but call me Bessie. I have five sons and two daughters. Eddie's the youngest." She placed a cup of tea on the table along with a buttered slice of bread and ham. "Sit down, Miss Davenport."

"You do not need to feed me as well; I would have been quite satisfied with the tea." Despite her polite protest, Georgiana was incredibly thankful. She felt ravenous after carrying Edward so far.

"I like to look after my guests. Come on, sit down." Bessie kindly pulled a solid wooden chair out from under the table and beckoned Georgiana to sit down.

After eating the final piece of bread, Georgiana got to her feet, thanked Mrs Simms for her hospitality and explained she needed to be getting home, otherwise her uncle and aunt would worry where she was.

"Do you have to leave so soon, Miss Georgiana?" asked Eve coming back into the farmhouse with a basketful of washed apples.

"There's a storm brewing by the look of those clouds," said Bessie stopping by the window. "Miss Davenport does not want to get caught in a downpour, Eve."

"Will you come back again?" asked Eve, her eyes open wide with expectation. Georgiana was uncertain what to say and looked up at Eve's mother.

"You are more than welcome," said Bessie, who had begun to knead out pastry for the pies. "Whenever you'd like."

"Come and eat leftover pie tomorrow. Ma always makes too much," said Eve with a greedy sparkle in her eyes.

"That's true," agreed her mother with a chuckle. "I like to send my children to bed with full stomachs. If there's leftovers I know I've done my job well."

"Please, say you will come Miss Davenport," begged Eve as she laid the basket on the farmhouse table.

Georgiana said she would try and visit, however, she couldn't promise anything. Who knows what might happen in the course of a day, her mother might summon her home or Mary might have other plans? But Georgiana knew she would attempt to return if at all possible. She had never been in such an unusual place where she had been instantly valued and her presence eagerly desired.

The storm did arrive, though Georgiana managed to return before the rain began to fall.

"I am so very pleased to have your company, Georgiana," said Mary, as they were sitting resting that evening. "It was such a surprise to see you this morning." She leaned over and whispered, too loudly, in her cousin's ear. "Your Mr Kirkby has not arrived yet?"

Georgiana felt heat rush into her cheeks and she smoothed down her dress in embarrassment. "He's not *my* Mr Kirkby."

"Is this a beau you are whispering about, cousin Georgiana?" It was Tobias who spoke, Mary's older brother, and he lifted his head with interest.

"Yes," said Mary, excitedly clapping her hands as Georgiana grew hotter and hotter.

"He isn't my beau, Mary," she said trying not to make eye contact with anyone else in the room.

"Who is this Mr Kirkby?" asked her Aunt Charlotte who had been similarly intrigued.

"He is no one, aunt," said Georgiana hoping to squash their interest.

"He must be someone, otherwise you would not be so rosy in the cheeks. Is he approved?"

Georgiana knew instantly what her aunt meant. "My parents have deemed him unacceptable."

"But you wish to marry him?" Charlotte questioned further.

"No, Mary has misunderstood. Mr Kirkby is a friend. There has never been a proposal made or any expression of affection between us."

"Why would you expect him to arrive here then, if he does not love you?" asked Tobias.

Georgiana glared at Mary. She did not want to be having this conversation: news could easily travel from her uncle to her mother with remarkable speed.

"I am not expecting him, cousin."

"But Mary said…" began Tobias.

"Does he know you're here?" asked Charlotte talking over her son.

"He is a friend, I wrote and told him of my departure, but there is no reason for him to appear."

Throughout the conversation her uncle had been sitting by the fire giving the impression he was reading contentedly. Georgiana knew he was not: her uncle had not turned a single page. He was listening, retaining all necessary information to regurgitate it back to her mother. Her aunt may well disapprove of Lady Davenport, but her uncle was quick to bow down to her dominance, still living in subservience after his marriage twenty years ago.

The door opened and the butler came in with a message. Her uncle left the room and Georgiana's heart pounded in her chest. It was imperative to steer the conversation in a safer direction.

"Did you go to London last season, aunt?" she asked, but her efforts were fruitless.

Her uncle returned immediately into the room with his mouth set straight. "You have a guest, Georgiana."

Colour drained from her face, petrified that it might be Kirkby. Although she was anxious to see him, his presence would make her situation ten times worse.

She made her way through the connecting rooms and into the hall, where she saw a man who had been drenched from head to foot after coming from the raging storm outside.

"Mr Southerly..." she gasped in surprise as the gentleman turned to face her. "What are you doing here?"

"Miss Davenport," Henry Southerly stepped towards her and bowed his head civilly. "I hope I find you well."

"Yes, I am very well."

"That is good to hear."

Georgiana didn't say anything, but waited expectantly as the butler removed Henry's wet cape and took it away to be dried.

"I told you I would investigate and I have discovered a great deal." He paused, searching around him. "Is there somewhere you can sit? I fear my news may shock you."

Georgiana led him into the lounge, where she then sat, perched on the edge of a mustard yellow chair. She was amazed Henry had found out so much so soon, it had barely been twenty-four hours since her banishment.

"My intention last night had been to ride straight to London, where rumours generally start...but stopping at an inn for refreshment, I overheard stories that I can only presume must have been written in the letter your mother received. I am sorry to say, you were correct in assuming the contents were about yourself."

"No one knows me outside of Middleton who could possibly start any false talk about me. What did you hear, Mr Southerly?"

"The rumours, I'm afraid, concern your parentage."

"My parentage... I do not understand?"

"Apparently." He stepped back in agitation. "I am sorry to bring you such shame, Miss Davenport."

"Shame? I know of nothing that could bring me shame."

Henry looked across at her, very conscious of the innocence which her features expressed. It hurt him to speak of such things in her presence, but it was only right that she should know. "The rumours suggest you are illegitimate."

A wave of relief rushed over Georgiana and she smiled. "Oh, we know they are only rumours. I am the youngest of three. There can be no question of my parents not being married, anyone who knows our family can refute anything that is being said."

"Miss Davenport." He knelt before her, resting his arm on his knee. "The rumours are not about your parents."

"Then what are they about?"

"You are the illegitimate child... of someone else."

The room immediately started spinning and it took a few moments for Georgiana to steady herself. "So...whose child am I?" she finally asked.

"I could not find out. As I guessed, the gentlemen in the inn had first heard the rumours in London. I must travel to the capital to find out more. Do you have any contacts there at all?"

"No, I have no links and have never visited. Mama has always denied me any connection with the place. Surely these are only rumours, they cannot be true?"

"My fear is that there is some truth to them, simply because of the way your mother reacted to the news."

"I should write to my Aunt Lucy and ask if she has heard anything."

"Why would your aunt know anything?"

"She lives in..." Realisation dawned. "Aunt Lucy lives in London - I do have a connection."

"Your Aunt Lucy is your mother's sister?" asked Henry, piecing together the relationship.

"Yes, there was a rift in the family many years ago."

Henry scratched his chin. "How many years ago?"

Georgiana counted the years in her head, recounting what her brother had told her. Surely Henry couldn't be suggesting Lucy was connected with the rumours. "Nineteen years ago, or thereabouts."

"Pardon me for asking." He looked away a little embarrassed. "But how old are you, Miss Davenport?"

"I'm eighteen... you do not think?"

"It's just a thought."

"The dates don't add up. I was born a year after the rift, and mama would never take an illegitimate child into her home, it would bring devastation to her social position. No," she shook her head in resolution, trying to shake it all away. "I'm sure it's all rumours."

"As I've said, rumours are often based on truth, Miss Davenport. I am known as a rogue in many of my parent's circles and although

244

many of the stories are untrue, they are not completely based on falsehood."

"What do you advise me to do, Mr Southerly?"

"I suggest you write to your brother and ask him if he has any further details. In the meantime, I will go to London and continue the search."

23

Sophie

"Sophie, come and sit down." Dylan took his sister by the hand and guided her to a booth, tucked away in the corner of the old Tudor pub and next to a large open-hearth fireplace.

"Would someone like to tell me what's going on?" Sophie asked, focusing first on Dylan and then on her dad. Neither wanted to speak first and cast guilty looks at each other. "I thought you were missing, dad, I've been searching high and low for you and you've been with Dylan all this time, and you…" She pointed accusingly at her brother. "You didn't even call me to tell me he was okay."

"I know it looks bad Sophie," said Dylan.

"Don't state the obvious, it does look bad… and while you're at it, maybe you could explain why you don't work for Historic Surveyors, like you've always told us." Sophie sat back and folded her hands impatiently across her chest.

Dylan fiddled with the salt pot, unscrewing the lid on and off. "I'm not certain where to start, so much has happened."

"At the beginning might be a good idea," Sophie snatched the salt away and banged it down hard on the table. There would be no squirming away this time, she expected answers.

"Dad came to me a few weeks ago, he told me his financial advisor had advised him to declare bankruptcy."

"You could have told me, dad." Sophie felt hurt. Her thoughts flew to Georgiana who was never told anything, her entire life ordered by other people. Did they not feel like she could be trusted? She was an adult, for goodness sake, living in the twenty-first century, she had a right to know if her family was falling apart.

Catching sight of the dark circles underneath her dad's eyes, her frustration diminished: she couldn't be too harsh with him, no matter how furious she was with Dylan.

"I didn't want to worry you, pumpkin." Sitting next to Sophie at the end of their small wooden table, George was able to reach across and stroke his daughter's hair. "And… there is another reason I went to your brother and not you." He looked resolutely towards his son. "We need to tell her Dylan; she's found out half of it anyway."

"Tell me what?" If it was something horrendous, maybe she didn't want to know. She meant what she had said to Oliver on the car journey there, she didn't think she could handle anything else.

Dylan tilted his head back and drew in a deep breath before he faced his sister. "You're right Sophie, I don't work for Historic Surveyors… I never have. In fact." He picked up a circular paper coaster and began folding it over, since the salt pot was now out of reach. "I'm not even a surveyor… I'm a lawyer."

"A lawyer?" exclaimed Sophie. "Dylan, you need a law degree to be a lawyer."

"That's correct… I have a master's degree in law."

"No, you don't. I've seen your degree certificate hanging on the wall."

Dylan put down the neatly folded coaster, now in the shape of a triangle and looked straight at her. "It's a fake, Sophie."

"Fake?" she looked at her brother, whose face was deadpan - he was serious.

"I told mum I would study conservation, but I secretly enrolled in law… only dad knew." Sophie opened her mouth to speak, but Dylan didn't give her chance. "That's why I couldn't come home when you asked. Mum's been nattering me to come back home since they moved into the manor, kept insisting she would employ me as her conservationist. I had to make up all these excuses to get her off my back, eventually she got in a huff and won't talk to me anymore." He leaned forward in his chair. "I'm so sorry, Soph, that I couldn't come home when you asked. Mum would be asking all these questions I wouldn't know the answers to and then she'd find out I'd lied."

Sophie rubbed the bridge of her nose, just like her dad did in moments of great stress, trying to make sense of what she had heard. "You mean, all these years you've been a lawyer?" She couldn't get her head round it. Her brother had been living his own life, a path he'd chosen, his own qualifications and career. If she'd known, would she have had the guts to do the same? There was a good possibility his secrecy had cost Sophie her freedom. "I don't understand why you didn't tell me?"

"The fewer people who knew, the better, I suppose."

"I'm sorry we didn't tell you, pumpkin," said her dad, his eyes crinkling in the corners as his mouth curved round in sympathy. "When I realised how close to bankruptcy I'd become, I got in touch with Dylan. He's been advising me, you see, and then he asked if I could bring all my financial documents to him: he needed to see them in order to advise me fully."

"But I thought you'd run away; I was worried sick."

"I was hoping to return before anyone noticed I'd gone."

"I found your letter in the office."

George stretched his arm around her. "It's been such a burden keeping this secret from you, Sophie. The day after you came home was the day the letter arrived. The weight of it broke me, thinking of the shame it held and how I've let you all down... I couldn't overcome it."

Sophie rested her head on his shoulder. "You haven't let us down, dad. Besides, we're here to help, no matter what... aren't we Dylan?"

"Absolutely." Dylan smiled and Sophie sat up to reach for a crisp from the bowl, which had been placed on the table by a waiter sometime during the course of their conversation.

"Are you suggesting dad declares bankruptcy?" she asked munching away.

"I think it might be the best option. You've a lot of creditors demanding payment you can't give."

"I told your mother to stop spending, but she wouldn't listen."

248

"I told mum it was her fault, too," said Sophie eating her fourth crisp, she hadn't realised how hungry she was. "She can't get away without taking the blame."

George sat bolt upright. "You told her I am bankrupt."

"I had to dad, I thought you'd gone and I had no idea where you were."

"I bet she wasn't impressed," commented Dylan, who knew too well what the effects of his mother's disappointment could be like.

"Not one bit."

"Well, that's not going to be a joyful conversation when I get home," George said gloomily.

"Mum would find out sooner or later and she needed to know, otherwise she'd keep on spending money you don't have. I think it'd be best to let go of the manor anyway." She turned to her dad. "You have to admit she has got worse since moving in - it's become an obsession."

"You're right." George stood up. "Let's go and face the music, Dylan has all the documents he needs now. How did you get here, Sophie?" I

In all the confusion, Sophie had forgotten about Oliver and looked around for him in darkened room. She strained her head to see beyond the other customers, all enjoying their ploughman's lunches – the special for the day.

Two tables away, sat Oliver, biting into a huge chunk of bread, cheese and pickle. He looked up, realising the eyes of the Hastings' were all focused on him.

"I recommend the ploughman's… I didn't want to interrupt a family meeting," he muttered with his mouth full in explanation of his half-finished plate.

****

"Have you told him?" asked Oliver, casting a cautious look at George Hastings sleeping in the back seat of the car.

"About Arthur Jones? I can't Oliver, he's got enough on his plate."

"He really needs to know." Oliver checked his mirror and indicated to change lanes. "Jones is suing the estate of which your dad is legally the head."

"Your father did warn me he'd surface again."

Sophie had been considering what to do about Mr Jones. She could easily crumble and allow the circumstance to beat her, but as they had been driving along, the little red diary had poked out from the top of her bag and she found a new courage. Georgiana could have let her spirits be crushed, but she didn't. Being banished from her family, losing the man she loved and facing harmful rumours, none of these could defeat her.

Sophie turned to Oliver with a look of determination. "I'm going to meet with him and sort this all out, I will not let him trample all over us because he has a few overgrown hedges and he's lost land that didn't even belong to him."

"Be careful, he'll twist your words and use them against you, he's a crafty old thing."

She slumped back in the passenger-seat. It wasn't the reaction she'd expected. Immediately, she reconsidered her declaration, there was no way she could do this alone.

"But... I'll come with you."

"Would you?" Sophie's eyes widened in hope.

"Two are better than one, you'll have someone to record the conversation and I've known Jones since I was a boy, I'll be able to tell when he's bluffing and when he's not."

They discussed a strategy during the final part of the journey and concluded that if the meeting didn't result in their favour, they would consult Dylan for advice, now Sophie knew he was an expert in law, rather than in precious antiques, collectables and heritage buildings.

Oliver pulled up on the drive and George snuffled, waking up as the engine vibrations ceased.

"Sorry kids, I wasn't much company for you," he said rubbing his eyes.

"You needed the sleep, dad. I'll see you later, Oliver."

A surprise offensive is what they needed with no time beforehand for the enemy to collect his thoughts and mount a second assault. Oliver would have driven Sophie round to the farm immediately after dropping George off, but Sophie was anxious about sending her father in to his wife without backup, and wanted to support him first.

As Sophie and her father stepped into the hall, Elizabeth was there waiting for them, like a lion ready to devour its prey. The sound of her tapping foot echoed around the walls.

"I think we need to talk, Liz," said George directly, stepping closer to his wife with arms slightly widened in surrender.

"I'm surprised to see you, George. I thought you'd abandoned us to deal with the trouble you have caused."

"Let me correct you right there, mum," Sophie advanced promptly towards her mother's smug figure, until her father reached out an arm and stopped her getting any nearer.

"None of this is dad's fault," she continued behind the barrier of George's firm grip. "Don't lay blame where it doesn't belong."

George patted Sophie's back. "That will do Sophie."

"She can't speak to you like that, dad."

"Enough," said her mother sternly. "I want to speak to your father alone."

Sophie hesitated. There was no way she trusted her mother, not while her father was in such an unstable state.

"It's okay, pumpkin, you can leave us. Your mother and I have got a lot of things to talk over."

It hadn't been Sophie's plan to leave him alone and she glared at her mother, whose victorious smirk caused the hairs on her skin to rise in irritation. The relationship between Sophie and Elizabeth had never been great, but it had never been this bad before.

Sophie exited the hall and walked into the lounge. She sat down by the old harpsicord, one of her mother's many excessive purchases since arriving in Middleton, and absent-mindedly walked her fingers up and down the keys, keeping an ear out so she could rush in to rescue her father, if necessary. If George had to declare himself bankrupt, her mother would never forgive him and who knew what the future would hold for them all.

Her father eventually reappeared without a scratch. He didn't reveal any of the conversation he'd had with his wife and Sophie didn't ask, but searched his worn face for signs of stress.

Adamant he was okay, George retired to his room to rest. Sophie could only hope he would emerge again and not be sucked back within its dark and musty walls.

****

"Everything all right?" Oliver asked as they met again that afternoon. Sophie nodded and changed the subject because the reality was, that she didn't know if everything was all right.

Walking down the farmyard Sophie's tummy began to churn and she hugged her notebook closely to her chest.

"You need to know," said Oliver. "Mr Jones is a fighter and he isn't going to back down quietly." His hand hovered over the brass door knocker as they came to a standstill outside the farmhouse door. "Are you ready?"

Sophie nodded and he rattled the bronze lion head.

Mrs Jones answered the door and smiled widely when she saw Oliver. "Hello, Oliver. What can I do for you?"

"Good afternoon, Mrs Jones. We need to speak to your husband; it is a matter of great urgency."

"He's out with the sheep." She looked at her watch. "But he normally comes in for a cup of tea afterward, I'm expecting him any time now."

"We'll wait, if that's okay with you."

"Of course, I'll put the kettle on."

When Arthur Jones opened his back door, he scraped his muddy wellies on the mat and hung his khaki waterproof on the peg. A sheepdog scurried past his legs and sat panting by his food bowl.

"I'll get to you in a minute, Jed. Let me put my feet up first." The old farmer grunted, tottering to the table before stopping in his tracks at the sight of two figures sitting around his kitchen table. "What do you want?" he snapped.

"Good afternoon, Mr Jones," smiled Sophie ignoring the raging nerves in the pit of her stomach. "I've come to discuss our dispute." She pushed the brown envelope containing legal papers across the table towards the farmer.

"Dispute?" questioned his wife pottering back to fill the kettle again with water. "What have you done this time, Arthur?"

"He's suing the estate for negligence, Mrs Jones," explained Sophie.

"You can't do that, dear," cried his wife, as Mr Jones slumped into the chair at the head of the table.

"I can and I will…should have been done years ago."

"Mr Jones, I understand that my predecessors badly neglected the estate. I agree with you, however you are not giving my family chance to change things."

"You've been here nearly four months, Miss Hastings - I have seen no change."

"There's a lot wrong with the estate, it's going to take years to see it working at its full potential."

"Take a look out of the window," said the farmer stabbing a finger in the direction of the courtyard. "Those hedges need lopping: they're becoming a health hazard."

"Oh Arthur," exclaimed Mrs Jones, pushing a mug of steaming tea in front of him. "I've told you time and time again, do it yourself. Don't bother the Lord of the Manor with such a small matter. You have the equipment, don't you?"

"That is not the point, it is the estate's responsibly, not mine."

"Mr Jones," said Oliver, joining in the discussion for the first time after letting Sophie take the lead. "Filing a law suit against the estate is not going to help anyone, in fact it will make it even less effective than it is already. Continue with the case, by all means, but the estate's efforts will go into fighting you and not into making the changes that are so desperately needed. I know the estate has neglected you, and I understand your frustrations, but you need to give Sophie a chance."

Mr Jones huffed and slurped his tea.

Sophie leaned forward: "Let us make a deal, Mr Jones." The farmer's eyebrow arched at the intriguing suggestion: she knew he was listening. "Give my family a year to prove ourselves; change doesn't happen overnight, as you know. If, on the anniversary of my parent's arrival in Middleton, you have not seen sufficient results, and you still insist that we are neglecting you and not performing the duties that rightly belong to us, then by all means, sue us for negligence. But I ask you, please drop the case against us as of this moment, otherwise we will be of little help to you."

Sophie sat unblinkingly, waiting for a response. Mrs Jones also stood still, with a dripping mug and tea towel posed in the air, waiting for her husband's response. The clock ticked on the wall and the sheepdog growled softly under the table, impatient for his meal. All held their collective breath.

"I will consider your proposal, Miss Hastings," Arthur finally mumbled.

"Thank you, Mr Jones," Sophie nodded. It was the best she could hope for, the stubborn old man had begun to retreat and now it depended on how much he was willing to surrender.

On her arrival home Sophie was uncertain what she might face. A run in with her mother could end in disaster and finding her father still tucked away in the darkness would only add to her worries about him.

A mumbling of voices greeted her as she entered the hall and she walked curiously towards the sound, stepping into the lounge.

"Rupert…I wasn't expecting you?"

Her friend was standing by the fire place. When he saw Sophie, he smiled with satisfaction across to the second unexpected guest in the room.

"Mr Donaldson?" she questioned.

Sophie's face was one of bewilderment, which increased further when she saw her father sitting opposite. He smiled broadly at his daughter with eyes that glinted in pleasure.

24

Georgiana

Henry Southerly had been in London for several weeks and Georgiana had heard no further word on the rumours involving her parentage, or if he had managed to confirm their falsehood. In all honesty, Henry had left without much hope of disproving them and so, she did not expect a happy ending.

Meanwhile, as she waited to hear news from the capital, she split her time between Mary and Bessie Simms. Wiping condensation from the damp window, Georgiana stared miserably out into the rain as yet another bout of wet weather confined her to the house, frustrating her greatly, for she much preferred the company of Bessie to her cousin. It was fortunate that the Barnets were still completely ignorant of her new acquaintance. If her uncle ever discovered an association with the Simms family it wouldn't be long before her mother found out and the friendship would be quickly squashed. Fraternising with farmers' wives was below the Davenport's social status and would not be accepted under any circumstances.

"What is the matter, cousin?" enquired Mary who was working on her embroidery.

"I wanted to go for a walk, but it looks like the rain will stop me."

Mary sighed and put down her work. "Yes, life is dull, isn't it? I should ask mama to throw a ball..." She sat up suddenly. "Maybe we could ask *your* Mr Southerly to come along." She giggled.

"Mary, when will you learn these gentlemen do not belong to me. Mr Southerly did not come to propose. How many times do I have to tell you?"

"He left very promptly."

"He had an important errand to run."

"Or, he was too overcome by your refusal."

Georgiana ignored her cousin's mirth and turned her attention back to the rain pattering on the glass pane.

"Play for me!" asked Mary, after realising her teasing words were no longer having an effect. "Your playing is superior to mine and I might learn something."

Georgiana walked across to the pianoforte to oblige her cousin. There was nothing better to do anyway, and she needed a distraction.

Half-way through the second piece a footman entered, halting Georgiana's melodious notes to announce a visitor. The ladies stood up and Mary flattened down her dress, preparing herself for the caller, who had not been named.

A gentleman walked in and took off his hat.

"Good day," he nodded. "I am sorry to intrude: I was hoping to speak to Mr Barnet."

"My father is in his study," replied Mary. "Please, wait here and I will fetch him."

"You are most kind."

The gentleman stepped back as Mary passed by him and waited until her footsteps could be heard moving away before he turned to Georgiana, who was still standing behind the piano.

"I am so very pleased to have found you here." He moved closer, casting a cautious look over his shoulder. "How are you?"

Georgiana remained motionless, her mouth set straight.

"You are cross with me for not coming to you earlier?" the gentleman asked as the piano acted like a barrier between them.

"Did you get my letter?" Georgiana asked quietly. "The one explaining I had been removed to my uncle's house?" An undelivered letter, she thought, would at least give some excuse for the delay.

"I did not receive anything - you've got to believe me. After arriving at my cousin's home, I learned a rift had occurred in your family and that you no longer resided with your parents." He looked back towards the doorway again and lowered his voice. "Am I to hope from your current position that you are not currently engaged?"

"I am not."

The gentleman did not know how to respond to this news, seeing his companion's indifference towards him, but he had no time to enquire further since the door he had been carefully watching creaked open and they both darted their eyes towards the figure who had entered the room with Mary.

Mr Barnet looked suspiciously at the gentleman. "Can I help you, sir?"

"Good day, Mr Barnet. I was passing your neighbourhood and wished to make my introductions to yourself."

Mr Barnet glared at him, waiting for further details.

"My name is Mr Kirkby; I am an acquaintance of your niece." He boldly reached out a hand to the stern-faced Mr Barnet, who appeared offended by the gesture, but reluctantly gripped the hand anyway.

"How did you know she was here?" Barnet asked, glaring at Georgiana as if Kirkby's arrival had been her mastering.

"My cousin - Sir Gillingham, he told me."

"How fortunate for you." Mr Barnet had the same spiteful features as his sister and Georgiana shuddered when his eyes darted rapidly between herself and Kirkby.

"Would you like to stay for dinner, Mr Kirkby?" piped up Mary, eagerly thinking she was doing her cousin a great service.

"No, Mary, I…" began Georgiana.

"I am sure Mr Kirkby has better things to do with his time," commented her uncle with all the congeniality he could muster through gritted teeth.

"Not at all," smiled Kirkby, either not noticing or choosing to ignore the unwelcoming tones of Mr Barnet. "I would be delighted."

"I will tell mama." Mary raced off in delight, unaware of the trouble she had caused. The three stood awkwardly together as Mary's head peeped immediately back in. "I forgot to say, papa. Bristow desired an audience with you."

"Whatever for?"

"He did not say… something to do with…something…" she snorted. "I should listen more." She giggled and skipped away again.

Mr Barnet stood uncertainly, clearly debating within himself whether his niece should be left alone with this gentleman.

"I will be back shortly," he grunted, glowering meaningfully for a final time at Kirkby before marching out of the room in search of his butler.

"He knows!" Georgiana exclaimed, her eyes wide with alarm.

"There is nothing to know about."

"Mama must have written to warn him about you. Did you not see? My uncle did not want to leave us alone?"

"I did see his reluctance and I know it was foolish of me to accept an unwanted dinner proposal, but I needed to see you. You deserve an answer to your question and then it will be in your hands to decide whether you believe me." He lowered his head. "I do not know how my tale has been twisted by your family."

"Sir, I do not know anything."

"That places me in a better position." He looked up hopefully and took a breath. "Firstly, I ask for your understanding as to why I waited so long to reply to your request for information. If your uncle was as severe as your parents, I feared a letter might be intercepted, so I waited until I could visit you in person. Unfortunately, Sir Gillingham's carriage needed an urgent repair and when it was free to use the coachman fell ill, otherwise I would have travelled to you sooner."

"The carriage is not your own?"

"My family does not own such luxuries."

"I was under the impression it was yours."

"That is because it was the impression I gave." He shook his head. "Georgiana, although I have not lied to you, I have not been completely honest."

259

"So, this is the famous Mr Kirkby," Aunt Charlotte came bursting into the room with a clap of the hands and curtsied before the gentleman. "My daughter informed me of your arrival."

"It is a pleasure to meet you," bowed Kirkby.

"The pleasure is all mine; I am intrigued to acquaint myself with a gentleman my sister-in-law despises so much."

Kirkby cast a concerned glance towards Georgiana as Mary came back into the room.

"Cousin Georgiana, you must play for us while we wait to eat. Have you heard my cousin play, sir?"

"I have." Kirkby smiled. "She is extremely accomplished."

"I agree." Mary hurried to her cousin and pushed her back onto the piano stool, crouching low to her ear. "This is your chance, cousin. Catch him with your enticing notes and magical voice."

Georgiana clenched her jaw in irritation, she did not want to catch Kirkby. How many times had she repeated this to Mary? Catching this gentleman would cause even greater complications, ones she now did not wish to endure, no matter how much she cared for him.

The hours slowed down as the day moved towards dinner. At no point had Georgiana been left alone again with the visitor and their conversation was left frustratingly unfinished.

Finally, dinner was served, although it did not bring much relief and it was filled with awkward silences, where every chink of cutlery against a plate or bowl could be heard distinctly. Mr Barnet and Tobias cast numerous warning glares towards Kirkby, whilst Mrs Barnet sat and ate in a very conceited posture, almost laughing that her sister-in-law was being defied by this gentleman sitting in her niece's presence. In ignorance, Mary was the only one to chatter and chirrup away about fashion, balls and which of her friends she wanted to visit on the morrow when the rain had stopped.

After dinner, Georgiana sat perched on the edge of her seat in the drawing room, gnawing at her nails and waiting for the gentlemen to enter.

"They will not eat him, Georgiana." Mary laughed.

"I cannot understand what my sister-in-law disapproves of in this gentleman, he is handsome and incredibly charming. Has he come to make you an offer of marriage?"

Her aunt's bluntness shocked Georgiana. "No aunt, he hasn't."

"But he has promised her one," slipped in Mary.

"Mary!" cried Georgiana. "Aunt, he has promised me no such thing."

Mrs Barnet arched an eyebrow with interest. "If he were to propose, what would you do?"

"I would not accept."

"Why ever not?

"You know why aunt."

Charlotte tutted. "I hope when the time comes, I allow my children a choice. Yes, I may suggest certain matches, but I would never force marriage upon anyone, it is such a backward way of thinking. However, perhaps you are wise Georgiana, it is not a good thing for a young lady to be estranged from her family because of one bad decision." She finished by raising the opposite eyebrow, hinting at what might become of her niece if she went against her mother's wishes.

Finally, the door opened, but only Mr Barnet and Tobias walked through, Kirkby did not follow.

"Come, Georgiana," her uncle bade her and she followed without delay, only stopping when they arrived at the library and she was summoned to sit down.

"Your friend has left and will not be returning," her uncle began and sat down behind his desk. "The gentleman uttered his regret at not being able to wish you goodbye in person, but I declined his request to see you again. It is no surprise he has turned up on my doorstep, your mother warned me about Kirkby with great urgency on account of his low family connections. I have forbidden him to step foot inside this house again and, if in the unlikely event he finds you alone, which I will do everything in my power to make sure he does not, you are not to accept a proposal under any circumstances. If you are foolish enough to go against what I am telling you now, you will be immediately disowned by your family and you will be asked to leave this home and not to return to your parents. We must protect our family honour - you shall not taint us, Georgiana. Do I make myself perfectly clear?"

"Yes, uncle."

"You may go."

Georgiana left the library feeling dejected. She had not expected a proposal from Mr Kirkby, although it was likely one would have been made if he had been given the chance, and she felt the pain of losing something she knew she could never have. No part of her life had ever been controlled by herself and the tiny light that indicted a hope of change had been snuffed out. Her future felt uncertain, but there was one thing she knew for sure; she would never see William Kirkby again.

25

Sophie

Life had calmed down immensely in the weeks which followed the discovery of Dylan's secret. Sophie had to admit when she heard the words, "Roger has approached us with an interesting offer," she wondered if her dad was being taken advantage of and prepared herself to fight on his behalf… but a fight wasn't necessary. It turned out Roger Donaldson had come on a rescue mission.

"Did the meeting go okay last night?" asked Sophie when her dad came into the kitchen whistling a catchy pop song he had heard on the radio that morning. It was good to see him happy again, though she still caught him with the odd glassy eyed look every now and then. But on the whole, she could say with confidence that George Hastings was on the mend.

"Yes, it did. Those Americans are lovely people. They have every right to demand so much for their money, but they are satisfied merely with an annual visit," George poured himself a mug of coffee from the pot. "We've fallen on our feet, Sophie."

"Did you get in touch with your financial advisor?"

"I did. Bankruptcy is a mere memory."

Sophie was sceptical at first when Mr Donaldson had suggested the idea of American investors. She could not think why someone would want to donate their hard-earned cash to an old English house they had never visited and a family they didn't know. Mr Donaldson had simply said the sole motivation was passion for British history and culture.

Roger Donaldson's American roots meant he had many contacts in the States, a handful of whom had a particular interest in English culture. He could not personally understand the attraction, but he was very willing to help out a friend and make further enquiries if he desired him to do so. To Sophie's surprise, he already had two or three interested parties who wanted to invest in the manor. Of course, Roger added, investment wasn't for everyone, some investors requested very little of the owners, but others would want the property open to the public. Sophie was worried her dad was getting his hopes up, she knew her mother would never allow strangers to trail through her home and, if this was a breaking point, the whole arrangement would fall through instantly.

After a few video calls it appeared George Hastings had found exactly the business-partner he was looking for and the weight he had been carrying on his shoulders lifted. The couple from Oklahoma had a long-standing fascination with English history and their only demand was to use the manor when they holidayed in the UK once a year. Other than that, they agreed to finish the restoration and help fund the general upkeep, if the Hastings committed themselves to reorganising and updating the estate so part of it would become self-sufficient.

The change in George was amazing, he began involving himself in estate affairs again and Sophie gradually saw his dark circles replaced by a healthy glow as he caught up with lost sleep and built up a healthy appetite.

Elizabeth was pacified too and continued planning her colour schemes and restoring expensive pieces of furniture. This made Middleton Manor feel strangely harmonious. Even more so since Sophie had stopped her job hunt for the time being and reluctantly signed a temporary contract which her mother had shoved under her nose. Helping George in the office was her priority, he was doing so much better and had bounced back miraculously well, but she didn't want the task of managing the estate to overwhelm him. Once everything felt more under control, she would leave, the downside being she had to put up with her mother for a little while longer.

"You seem to be spending a lot of time with Oliver Morgan," commented Rupert one afternoon. Sophie had bumped into him down the high street and he had naturally tagged along beside her, taking charge of her shopping bags.

"Yes, I suppose I am."

"Is there anything you need to tell me?"

The playful glint in his eye irritated Sophie slightly. "No, nothing at all."

"Isn't that him over there?" He pointed across the road to a brick building that hosted the local adult education centre.

"Yes, I think it is," she said straining to see as far as her friend. She pondered what Oliver was doing. He hadn't told her he was taking any courses, though she had not known him long, there was probably a lot she didn't know about him.

As if reading her thoughts Rupert spoke. "I wonder what Mr Perfect is doing... thought he knew everything." He pulled a face.

"Rupert, you're not jealous, are you?" Sophie nudged him in the ribs and laughed.

"No, of course I'm not. He's just spending a lot of time with you, that's all."

"You can't have me to yourself every waking hour!"

"I know that, Soph. I'm only looking out for you."

"Thanks Rupert, but I can look after myself. Hey, how's Maisie?

"She's good, thanks"

"I'd still like to meet this mysterious girl."

"Well, you're in luck, she's coming to visit."

"That's great," said Sophie slightly shocked. "I would love to meet her. She seems to be a good influence on you."

"What makes you say that?"

"I meant it when I said there are a lot of very likeable traits you've developed since we last met and I'm assuming she's got something to do with it."

He reddened slightly and stared down at the floor.

"Are you embarrassed?" she said laughing. "That's not like you."

"I do have a sensitive side, Soph... maybe that's one of my new likeable traits?" He tilted his head to the side and caught her eye.

"Must be." She smiled. "So, when's she coming?"

"I'll let you know. She hasn't confirmed the details yet."

They stopped outside the café. "I'm going to get a coffee; do you want one?" asked Sophie.

"Wish I could, but ma has got me running errands." He handed back Sophie's bags and produced a scrunched-up shopping list out of his jeans pocket. "I'd better make a start."

Two weeks have passed since I last set eyes on Mr Kirkby and he hasn't been seen or heard of since. I must say, I am a little surprised, though maybe I was wrong about the feelings I thought he had for me. Presumably he has left the county and has decided to give up trying to claim my hand...

Sophie stirred her mocha repeatedly. Kirkby did not seem like the kind of man to be scared away by austere uncles. But now, he had left this girl trapped... the only glimmer of freedom extinguished. She read the passage again. Wait a minute... she licked the froth from the spoon...was she trapped too? Living in the manor meant she was in her mother's domain; how much was Elizabeth orchestrating behind the scenes? Before she knew it, Rupert would be her fiancé and she would be a permanent member of staff.

"Is this seat taken?"

Jolted out of her terrifying thoughts she looked up and saw Oliver smiling down at her and holding a travel mug in his hand. "How's Georgiana?" He tapped the top of the book.

Sophie was impressed, he had remembered her name.

"We still need to go searching for answers, don't we?"

"Yes, but there's no rush, I'm busy with the estate at the moment anyway," she tucked a lock of hair behind an ear. "I saw you at the adult education centre, I didn't know you were on a course."

"I'm not, my brother asked me to drop something off." He sat down and placed his mug on the table. "How's your dad?"

"He's doing well, better than I expected. His financial expert says if he's careful he might not have to file for bankruptcy after all."

"That's great news. Must have taken the pressure off a bit."

"It's keeping mum quiet."

"How's things going with your mum?"

"My mum?" She tilted her head and frowned slightly, sensing he appeared a little nervous. "The same as usual, I suppose. Why are you asking?"

"I'm just…" He looked up, his eyes earnestly finding hers as he took hold of her hand. "I know it's none of my business, but I'm concerned about you, if I'm honest."

"Concerned about me… whatever for?"

"You don't seem to have a good relationship with your mother."

"What gave that one away?" She laughed, shrugging off Oliver's worries.

"Sophie, I think you need to take it seriously."

"Oliver, it's the way it's always been. I'm used to it."

"But, don't you want to change things?"

"Not really. I know what she's like."

"I don't want you to regret not trying." He looked away. "You only get one mother."

A sudden rush of sympathy flooded over Sophie and she placed her free hand on top of his. "Oliver, you didn't get to have a relationship with your mum, and I'm really sorry if seeing how I am with my mother upsets you, but I'm afraid nothing can change it. How old were you when she died? I can't remember."

He frowned. "We don't need to talk about it - just promise me you'll consider making an effort with her."

"Okay, if it's that important to you, I will." Although, she seriously doubted she would come to a different conclusion. Elizabeth and herself would never see eye to eye, they were so different, being related by blood was the only thing they had in common.

"I hope I'm not interrupting anything?" Rupert had appeared out of nowhere and was looking suspiciously at them holding hands.

"Hi Rupert," Sophie slid her hand away from Oliver. "You can't have finished all those errands already?" She pulled another chair towards the table for him to sit down, but he refused.

"No thanks, I only came to tell you Maisie is coming tomorrow."

"That's great, bring her round to the manor, I'd love to meet her."

"Absolutely. Well, I'll leave you to continue your coffee." He immediately left the shop, leaving the bell above the door to tingle quietly away.

"He doesn't like me much," said Oliver, casting his eyes out of the window and trailing Rupert down the high street.

"Who, Rupert? He's an old friend, very protective."

"I can see that." He picked up the travel mug. "I must be off as well. I'll see you around Sophie."

****

The next day came and Sophie busied herself in the office. Half of the paperwork had now been sorted and the room was beginning to look strangely uncluttered. With barely a break for a cup of tea, Sophie worked tirelessly all day. It wasn't until evening came that she closed the office door behind her and realised Rupert hadn't appeared with Maisie. She dialled his number.

"Hi Rupert, everything okay?"

"Hey Soph. Everything's fine. You?" He seemed unaware of why she had called.

"You said Maisie was coming today."

"Oh yes, she's been delayed, I forgot to ring you... her uncle died."

"Oh Rupert, I'm sorry. I know you were looking forward to seeing her."

"Don't worry about it… listen, since you've rung, I've no plans... do you want to do something?"

Sophie checked her watch; it was getting late. For some reason every time she spent time alone with Rupert it seemed to stir unwanted emotions within her, especially in the evening. She didn't want to put him in a compromising position and besides, she really liked Oliver and she didn't want to mess that up.

"I can't tonight… I'm spending some time with dad."

It wasn't a complete lie, although the event hadn't been planned. Her dad had been working hard, putting all of his energy into pleasing his new investors, and it had been in the back of her mind to make sure he rested.

"Tomorrow then? Let me take you out for ice cream… my treat?"

Lunch would probably be all right, less romantic and more people around…it sounded safer.

"Okay," she said. "Text me the time and place."

"Will do, Soph, I know you can't resist a good ice cream. Good night."

Sophie laughed. "You know me too well, goodnight Rupert."

Seconds later, the sound of Elizabeth's shoes came clacking down the corridor. "What are you doing here?" she demanded when she reached the office.

"I live here mum," Sophie calmly ignored her mother's hostility, pushing past her as she made her way towards the lounge.

"Dorothy said you were meeting Maisie today," continued Elizabeth, walking at a steady pace next to her daughter. "I thought you'd be with Rupert."

"She couldn't make it."

"Poor boy. Go over and comfort him, Sophie."

"He's fine mum."

"Her poor uncle died. A good friend would go and give comfort."

"It's not Rupert's uncle."

"I'm sure he's grieving with her."

"Mum, I've just phoned him, he sounded fine."

"It's all a cover, he's a sensitive boy."

Sophie could feel the tension rising inside of her like a pressure cooker. She was about to release the mounting pressure by opening her mouth and letting rip with an uncountable number of unpleasantries, but she was stopped when a figure of Oliver loomed large in her mind.

All afternoon she had been trying to work out why her friend had been so insistent on her mending the relationship with her mother. She couldn't understand why it was so important, it didn't affect him. Whatever the reason, Sophie realised as her mouth hung open ready to fire off harsh words, that Oliver's opinion mattered to her and so, for his sake, she had to make an effort.

"Actually, mum... I, err - thought we could watch a film together... maybe?"

A perfect thing to start with - no talking required.

"A film?" Elizabeth wrinkled her nose as if she had not heard of such a thing before.

"Something girly maybe," Sophie said ignoring her mother's response. "Or would you rather watch an action film?"

By this point they had walked into the lounge and Sophie had crossed the room and was crouching by the DVD unit, viewing their possibilities.

Elizabeth picked up a glossy magazine from the coffee table. "I haven't got time for that, Sophie."

"Oh, I'm sorry," Sophie looked up. "Have you got plans?"

"Yes, I've got a very expensive mud mask to try out."

"Can't that wait until after we've finished." She picked a DVD from the shelf. "This one is only an hour and a half."

"No, it can't wait - but we know Rupert is free. Go and spend time with him."

"We never do anything together, you'll still have time to do your face mask." She glanced at her watch. "It's not too late."

"I don't want to waste time watching a pointless film. I'll ring Dorothy to tell her you're coming, make sure Rupert is still at home."

"Stop forcing him on me!" Sophie rose to her feet. It took everything within her not to throw the DVD on the floor in her anger, or worse, at her mother.

"Don't tell me you like that Oliver chap because I don't see a future there."

"Why not?"

"Farmer's wife? That's not you…that's not the Hastings."

Sophie couldn't believe she was having this conversation; had she momentarily been sucked into Georgiana's life? Elizabeth sounded just like a stubborn-headed, autocratic, nineteenth century mother.

"How can you say that? Our family isn't better because we own a manor and they own a farm."

"You've got a lot to learn, Sophie."

The resemblance to Lady Davenport was eerie and Sophie watched Elizabeth move towards the door with the magazine tucked under her arm.

"Actually, the Morgans are better than us," Sophie called after her. "I've never felt so relaxed and welcome by anyone before. There's no judgement… or back chat."

"It's all a show, Sophie." Laughed Elizabeth amused by her daughter's naivety.

"No, it's not - it's really not." Sophie's eyes began to well with tears and she charged out of the room. She'd had enough. Oliver didn't know what he was asking her to do, spending time with this woman was impossible. She'd tried it and it hadn't worked. Forging any kind of relationship with Elizabeth was out of the question. This woman had ruined her life and showed absolutely no remorse over it. She could never forgive her. A wall had been built so high between them that nothing could penetrate it, not even the good intentions of Oliver Morgan.

26

Georgiana

No one had seen or heard from Kirkby for two weeks. Finally, after what seemed like an eternity, it was deemed safe for Georgiana to be out alone without a chaperone. You could tell her uncle was a little cautious, but her aunt was less concerned and talked him into letting her niece have some freedom. Whether this was because she cared for Georgiana's well-being, or because she wanted to see her sister-in-law squirm if Kirkby did reappear, it wasn't certain. But Georgiana was incredibly thankful to escape the watchful eyes of her uncle and get a rest bite from her cousin.

It was a cold morning and the sun had not yet warmed enough to dry the ground. Small droplets of water rested on the shrubs as Georgiana passed by. She allowed the fresh breeze to revive her spirits and was immediately reminded of the day she met Mr Kirkby.

Automatically she headed towards the farm. It had been quite a time since her last visit and she had missed the companionship whilst being trapped inside the house, surrounded by people who only cared for themselves. Such a negative environment had naturally led her to become too focused on her own troubles: the uncertain rumours about her parentage, the banishment from Denholm Park and her separation from the only man who could have taken her away from all of it.

The comforting smell of freshly baked bread greeted her as she rounded the corner into the farmyard.

"It's Miss Georgiana!" A girl cried from inside, her excited tones carrying through the open window. The front door opened and Eve appeared. "I thought we would never see you again."

"I'm so sorry I've not been earlier, there's been trouble at my uncle's."

"Come in, ma has made bread."

Eve grabbed Georgiana's hand and pulled her into the open plan farmhouse. Her eyes squinted as they adjusted to the darkened room and she saw the bulky figure of Mrs Simms carrying a large loaf of bread onto the table with her children scurrying behind trying to get a seat.

"Okay, okay, you'll all get a piece… Georgiana." Bessie smiled across when she saw Eve leading the girl towards the table and sitting her down in a chair. "How nice to see you, will you join us for tea?"

"Thank you, I will. How is Edward's ankle?"

"It's fine, miss," said the little boy himself climbing onto her lap. "I can jump again."

"Edward," scolded his mother. "Take your own chair."

"Yes, ma." The little boy obediently jumped down and sat next to one of his sisters.

"Can I help, Mrs Simms?" Georgiana rose wanting to make herself useful.

"Pour the children a cup of milk, will you, and call me Bessie, for goodness sake, Mrs Simms makes me sound old."

Georgiana took the pitcher of milk from the side and poured milk into each of the cups held out by the thirsty children.

"Eve," Bessie turned to her daughter. "Take a plate to Mr Simms." She passed across an empty plate and turned to Georgiana. "Sometimes my husband works so hard he forgets to stop and eat."

The girl filled the plate with food until it looked like a mountain.

"Don't forget the milk," cried her mother and Eve ran back for the pitcher she'd forgotten.

Bessie clapped her hands over the noisy chatter of the children. "Come on everyone, back to work."

Georgiana watched, impressed by the children's obedience, within seconds they had left the farmhouse and quietness descended.

"You said all your children work on the farm?"

"Yes, they all have jobs to do, and then in the afternoons I sit with them to do their letters and numbers. That is apart from the eldest, too grown up for that now. We have an acquaintance who was trying to better him, but I don't think it will work out."

"Why is that?"

"It was kind of him to try, but I think we are all happy the way we are, no need to climb up society's ranks, if you know what I mean."

"I know what you mean Mrs Simms…"

"Bessie, please."

"Sorry… Bessie." She blushed, not being used to such informality. "I've been wealthy my whole life and I can tell you from experience, it's not for everyone." She lowered her eyelashes and the older lady watched as she saw a sadness creep over the girl.

"I'm sure it's not," Bessie placed a soft hand upon the girl, making her look up.

For a moment, Georgiana could swear the eyes she was looking into held stories which could greatly sympathise with her own. However, whatever these tales were, Bessie chose not to share them.

"Now then," Bessie stood up and wiped both hands on her charcoal dress. "If you're staying, I can find you a job as well, if you'd like."

Georgiana felt honoured to be asked, as if she was one of the family. At home her duties were to perform on command and to be genteel, there was no sense of purpose in anything. Doing something useful gave her great excitement.

"What can I do?" she asked with eager eyes.

"Ethel!" called Bessie and a girl of about twelve years old ran into the farmhouse. "Take Georgiana to do the milking."

"Yes, ma. Please follow me this way, Miss Georgiana." The girl smiled and led her away.

Georgiana sat back and wiped her sweaty brow: they had milked all twenty cows.

"You'll feel it tomorrow," said Ethel, taking away the milking stools.

"I think you're right," said Georgiana stretching out her back. "That's not an easy job. How do you manage it?"

"Your muscles get used to it. When I first started, I was in agony."

"Do we need to carry the milk to the farmhouse?" She began lifting up the handle before Ethel stopped her.

"No, the boys will come and do that."

Georgiana cleaned her hands on her dress and stared at the stains of mud. She laughed. "If only my mother could see me now, I'd not live to see another day."

Ethel opened the door to the milking shed. "Really? We always look dirty, it's part of the job. Ma doesn't mind, she says it shows we've been working hard."

They walked back to the farmhouse together where Bessie was outside tightly gripping to a bat and whacking the dust out of a rug hanging over a line. Georgiana turned to thank Ethel, before speaking to her mother. "I must be going, Bessie. Thank you for letting me loose on your farm. I don't normally get the opportunity to be useful."

"You know you are always welcome, whenever your uncle and aunt can spare you." Bessie gave the rug another bat, but stopped before she could beat it further and looked out beyond the yard. "I still can't get over him wearing a tail and hat." She smiled cheerfully and waved energetically to a figure in the distance. Ethel, who had been standing quietly next to her mother ran to meet the newcomer, who embraced her in his arms and ruffled her hair.

"Hurry up William," called Bessie. "There's someone I want you to meet. Georgiana, this is my eldest, the one I was telling you about."

275

"Well, well, it is a small world, Miss Davenport."

William Kirkby walked up to Georgiana, a large wide smile spreading across his face. He bent low and kissed her hand.

"Are you already acquainted, William?" asked his mother

"Indeed, we are ma. I take it your uncle does not know you are here?"

Georgiana was speechless. She kept looking from Kirkby to Bessie in utter shock, his presence had been completely unexpected.

"Miss Davenport, would you come and sit down," Kirkby said, seeing her dazed expression and leading her by the arm back towards the farmhouse. "Ma, put the kettle on. I think I've some explaining to do."

****

Georgiana knew she'd be late home and she fumbled with her bonnet when it was time to leave in haste.

"I will walk part of the way with you," announced Kirkby, whilst she hurriedly said goodbye to his mother and two of his sisters.

"I am sorry if I misled you in anyway," he said gallantly when they were walking along the lane which led out of the farmyard.

"You haven't misled me in the slightest, I completely understand why you didn't say anything."

She had to admit that, at first, she was shocked by his revelations, but she had allowed him to speak before she made any judgement. As he continued his story, her initial distress vanished and she watched his anxious face with great interest. He really wanted her to trust him; she could tell this by the number of times he glanced across to Bessie for support.

"Sir Gillingham was trying to better me for my father's sake," explained Kirkby again locking the farm gate behind him.

"I understand. He is a kind man to do so."

"Unfortunately, however kind a man he is, I am no longer allowed on his estate. His good will has ended."

"It was not his doing." She spoke softly trying to defend her family's ever loyal friend.

"I know…" Kirkby looked away. "I'm afraid I bring too many low connections for his neighbours to bear."

Georgiana cringed inwardly, she knew he was talking about her mother, only he was being too polite to mention her by name.

Back in the farmhouse, Kirkby had revealed what his late father had written in his will. Displeased with his own efforts during his lifetime, the late Captain Kirkby had written that his eldest son, William, was to be guided by his good friend, Sir Gillingham. No one knew how the two men had become friends, but on his death Sir Gillingham had honoured the will and readily agreed to take Kirkby under his wing.

"Why do you call him cousin when you are not related?"

"Sir Gillingham was concerned a newcomer in town would raise too many questions, that certain members of your community would research my family connections upon my arrival and would then turn an unfavourable eye upon me, which would defeat the objective of introducing me into a higher society. If I was to be rejected, I might as well have stayed at home. Therefore, he suggested I refer to him as cousin, the Gillinghams are a well-respected family, no one would question my roots then."

"Except my mother."

Kirkby sighed compassionately and offered an arm to his companion who gratefully accepted.

"She can sniff out low connections from a great distance." Georgiana laughed sadly.

It turned out that Lady Davenport had directly asked Sir Gillingham about his "cousin" when she was contemplating if he was a good match for her daughter after the downfall of Thomas Compton. Unfortunately for the young pair, Gillingham, being a man of integrity, had told her the truth and nothing on the whole of the earth would allow her to unite the Davenports with such a man.

"Do you resent your mother for her decision to marry Mr Simms?" asked Georgiana as they sauntered down an uneven trail.

"Not at all," he said without hesitation. "I know it lowered our status, but she is happy and with my father she was not. Ma had been miserable for years; I watched her suffer with no means to help her. What good are rank and high standing if your life is wretched? Mr Simms is a good man and looks after her well. My father did not love her, he gambled and drank away all our money so we lived in poverty, and then beat my mother when he came home from sea. Joseph Simms is the complete opposite and I don't care if he's only a farmer, he's welcomed my family into his home and cares for them as if they were his own."

Georgiana was uncertain how Bessie, once a highly esteemed sea captain's wife, had come across the gentle farmer after her husband's death, but she asked no questions. She already held the woman in high regard, but now she knew Bessie had disregarded society's firmly drawn boundaries and found herself living a life of great contentment, she stood in awe.

"So, where does this leave you?" she asked, trying to figure out how low Kirkby had sunk in rank, after all, his father had still been from a reputable occupation, despite his questionable reputation.

"In love with a girl above my station," he turned away, bashful at his own forwardness. "I know this is an impossible decision for you to make, but I have to ask you, because if your uncle realises where my mother lives, I'm afraid I will not get this opportunity again." He stood still and took a breath, regaining his disposition as he did so. "I must ask you, dearest Georgiana, for your hand in marriage. It would give me no greater joy than to have you as my wife."

The sound of the birds flitting in and out of the hedgerows met Georgiana's ears as she contemplated her answer. "I am uncertain how to answer you."

"I understand," Kirkby stepped away. "It was foolish of me to ask."

"No, you do not understand." She took his arm and pulled him back. "My heart is telling me to say yes; the way you have talked so distastefully of what my parents esteem so highly has given me hope to believe there is a better life for me. If my marriage didn't hold so much importance to my family, I would take your hand and not look back. But I have already been warned, numerous times, against marrying you. I would be disowned from my family and I do not know where that would leave us. Can you afford to marry, for I am certain not to bring a dowry with me and you are an unestablished young man?" she faltered. "Sorry to be so direct, but I must be wise about this."

"Please don't be sorry, at least one of us must think with her head. Let me tell you my intensions and maybe then you might have more confidence in my ability to provide for a wife. Now that my time with the Gillingham's has come to an end, I am going into business. I cannot farm and my father's poor reputation would not give me any foothold in the navy. I have few savings, but can promise you I will work hard to achieve some wealth. We can establish our first home with ma on the farm. She has already agreed, she knows you will be a great help to her and will enjoy your company. I will come and go as business calls. I believe we will be happy there until we can afford our own dwelling." He stopped when he saw Georgiana chewing anxiously on her lip. "What is the matter.... is there something else?"

"I'm afraid there is... you may still want to reverse your proposal."

"Nothing would see me do such a thing."

"You need to know about the rumours that have been spread about me... unless you have heard?

"Rumours?"

Georgiana told him all she knew anticipating he would leave soon afterwards.

"My dear Georgiana, I do not care who your parents are, remember my mother married below her station and it does not bother me. I know it goes against convention, but I love you and nothing can alter that."

He loved her. She hadn't heard such words fall out of anyone's mouth before. Her heart ached because of the choice that lay before her and she promised to consider Kirkby's proposal, but the great implications an acceptance would have for her and her family might prevent the answer from being yes.

Kirkby sympathised greatly and encouraged her to be certain before answering and in the meantime, he would simply begin his business venture and start earning a living.

By the time she arrived home it was nearly time for dinner. Charlotte had covered for her absence and made her husband believe Georgiana had retired to her bedroom after returning home with a headache.

"I am so very thankful," Georgiana whispered to her aunt as she entered the hall and removed her bonnet. "I got waylaid."

"Be careful, Georgiana," Charlotte hissed back in hushed undertones. "You do not want to bear the wrath of the Davenports. I have witnessed first-hand what they can do and it isn't something I would wish on you."

The warning lingered in Georgiana's mind. It would not be a pleasant time if she turned against her family's wishes, but she could not help dwelling on the life she could have with Kirkby. Although the initial impact would be devastating, once the waters had settled, she would be left with a loving husband, an accepting mother in the form of Bessie and a life full of so much freedom, that she began to

280

consider the sacrifice of her social status was worth it. In the end, she decided to write to Edward. The decision she was thinking of making was not one to be taken lightly and she needed guidance and a wise head. Edward was the only one she could think of to fit this description.

Later on, as they were resting after dinner, Henry Southerly arrived once again at the house. He spent the evening with the family, charming Georgiana's aunt and speaking often to her uncle.

"What a handsome gentleman," whispered Mary, who was sitting next to Georgiana and looking across toward Henry playing cards with Tobias.

"Yes, I suppose he is," commented Georgiana observing Henry's smooth olive skin and dark engaging eyes.

"I wonder why he has come back?"

"He went to London to investigate the rumour; he promised to return with information."

Mary half smiled knowingly. "Oh, he did, did he?"

"What's are you suggesting?"

Mary smiled goofily. "He loves you."

"He does not, Mary."

"Why would he investigate something so damaging if he did not love you... you're blushing," Mary elbowed her subtly in the ribs.

Georgiana touched a hand to her cheeks. "For heaven's sake, don't talk so loudly, he might hear you... and remember I didn't ask him to do anything."

"That supports my point further. He is either trying to disprove the rumour to make you a more desirable match, or he is trying to attract your attention."

"Uncle would never agree to a marriage between us, mama has already warned me I am not to marry Mr Southerly under any circumstance."

"Why not?"

"He does not live an appropriate lifestyle."

"He seems very endearing tonight, maybe he's changed."

"In a few weeks, I don't think so Mary."

The girls both sat up straight when Mr Barnet stalked across the room towards them.

"A word, Georgiana." He spoke without making eye contact and left the room directly.

Having followed her uncle into the connecting hall, Georgiana stood nervously waiting for him to speak.

"I believe on a previous occasion you had been told you were not to marry Mr Southerly."

Georgiana felt her cheeks blush again... had he heard the conversation with Mary? She knew her cousin was speaking too loudly. "Mama forbade it: I would not go against her wishes."

"Well, I un-forbid it. If he proposes you are to say yes."

"But mama said..."

"Your mother has agreed for you to marry the next man who asks you if he is from a good family. We cannot afford for you to marry Kirkby; his station is too low and we must protect you from him. Henry Southerly will calm down with a good wife by his side and his family is socially acceptable to your mother. If he asks, you are to say yes."

Mr Barnet did not wait for an answer, obedience from his niece was automatically assumed and he slipped back into the drawing room.

Georgiana stood there speechless. Her mother was still taking charge all the way from Denholm Park. Would she ever be free of her? She lingered for a few moments, not wishing to re-enter the drawing room.

The door creaked open and Henry Southerly came out. "I have much to tell you, Miss Davenport. If you have a moment now you are alone, I can tell you my findings."

"Of course." She was a little reluctant to be on her own with Henry after the news her uncle had just given her. Who knew what plan her mother had up her sleeve? "Have you proved the rumour false?" she asked hopefully cutting straight to the point.

"I have not."

Georgiana felt deflated, she had believed his return signalled the arrival of a more positive report.

"I am sorry to bring you such bad news, but it is as we feared. You were taken in by your parents as a new born baby and they claimed you as their own."

"I do not understand why they would do that." She shook her head in confusion. "My mother is the last person to taint herself with any kind of immorality."

"From what I can see, Lady Davenport did it to protect the family."

"Our family?"

"When I went back to London it was to seek out one person in particular, the only name you gave me as a possibility."

"Aunt Lucy?"

"The very person. Nineteen years ago, she found herself unmarried and pregnant. Having no mother of her own, she turned to her eldest sister for help. Lady Davenport had to cover the whole affair by pretending she was pregnant with a third child and removing herself away to convalesce somewhere far away, no one was to know the baby was not her own. After she had helped her sister to give birth, nine months later you were brought home and proclaimed a Davenport. Your Aunt Lucy was then disowned and banished from your mother's presence forever as her punishment for nearly ruining the family's good reputation."

"So, let me get this right... Aunt Lucy is my mother." She sat down on a small Chippendale chair positioned behind her. "I cannot believe this... but it explains so much."

"Your aunt wished me to request that you visit her immediately in London."

"I cannot go immediately... but I shall write to her promptly."

Henry hovered, looking as if he wanted to say something else.

"What is it, Mr Southerly?"

"I do not wish to burden you more, Miss Davenport. You have had quite enough to take in. I will leave tomorrow, maybe we could take a walk together before I leave?"

"Yes, of course. Thank you for going to such great lengths to discover my history."

"I would do it again in a heartbeat, Miss Davenport." He bowed.

If her uncle had not recently suggested a proposal might be on the horizon, she would never have considered it for a second. Nothing in Henry's manner suggested he was in love with her, but when she considered it, he was the first man her family had chosen that she could possibly see herself marrying. Though she believed he would not make a very good husband, since his nature did not seem to suggest he was ready to settle, he had proved himself responsible. If he did propose, Henry would certainly be the safer option.

Her heart ached. All she wanted was Kirkby and she felt trapped knowing she had an impossible decision to make. Who should she choose… William or Henry?

27

Sophie

Sophie scraped the bottom of her ice cream tub with a neon-green plastic spoon. Rupert walked alongside her smiling in delight.

"Nice?" he asked.

"Delicious. You certainly know a way to a girl's heart." She grinned and gave her spoon one final lick. They had met for an ice cream as planned the previous evening. Sophie hadn't been able to decide which flavour to choose, so Rupert had treated her to all three – chocolate heaven, strawberry cheesecake and lemon meringue.

"The way to your heart Sophie Hastings is sugar - I don't know if all girls are that easy to please."

"Maisie isn't a sugarholic then?"

"No, she's not." He whisked away Sophie's empty container and threw it in a passing bin. "So, this Oliver Morgan…"

"Yes?" Sophie rolled her eyes, waiting for another big brother like speech.

"He looks after you, does he?"

"Rupert, he's not my boyfriend. We just hang out. We're getting to know each other - that's all."

"I know… but you do like him?"

"Why are you asking?" She eyed him suspiciously. "I've told you before I can look after myself."

"I'm just interested, Soph."

"If you didn't have a girlfriend, I'd really start to believe you're jealous."

"Jealous!" He snorted. "I've told before you I'm not jealous. I'm looking out for you, we're best friends, aren't we?"

"Of course we are and it's appreciated, really, but I don't even have Dylan breathing down my neck."

"That's because he's not here."

They continued down the road talking about the recent renovations at the manor and Rupert's latest polo triumphs.

"It's a shame Maisie couldn't make it down, I was looking forward to meeting her."

"We'll have to arrange it for another time," he said shoving his hands inside his pockets.

"Is she not coming down at all over the summer?"

"Probably not, she can't afford to fix her car... that's why she didn't make it this week."

"Oh, my mum said her uncle had died."

"She did? Actually... now you mention it, her great uncle passed away last week, poor girl was quite upset.

"I'm surprised you aren't going to see her, give her some comfort, especially since you haven't seen her since you finished uni. That was a couple of months ago now."

"I can't at the moment Soph." Rupert darted his eyes away and rubbed the back of his neck.

"Why ever not? You're not busy, all you do is play polo and run errands for your mother."

"I'm teaching polo to the juniors."

"There are other teachers, Rupert."

"And there's other stuff."

"Like what?"

"Just stuff, Soph."

Sophie narrowed her eyes suspiciously as the massaging of his neck intensified.

"Surely she could come down on the train to see you, even if her car is broken."

"She can't afford it: trains are expensive and she's coming all the way from Scotland."

"Not even with a railcard?"

"She's not as well off as us, Soph."

"If she's struggling financially, I'll pay for her."

"She won't accept handouts." He switched hands and touched the other side of his neck.

"Having problems with your neck, are you?"

"Hmm?"

"Your neck?"

"My neck?"

"You're rubbing it as if it's hurting."

"Oh," he looked guiltily at his hand. "Polo injury."

"It seemed all right yesterday."

"I slept on it in a funny position."

Sophie abruptly stopped and grabbed Rupert's sleeve, preventing him moving any further. "Look at me Rupert."

He wouldn't.

"Rupert." She skirted round him and studied his face. "You're lying to me."

"What?" He laughed lightly. "Why would I be lying to you?"

"You tell me." She folded her arms.

"I'm not lying, Soph." He tried to walk on, but Sophie refused to let go of his sleeve.

"I know you Rupert and I know when you're feeling guilty about something. I can only presume you're lying."

"Well, you're wrong." He released his arm from her grip and stormed away.

Sophie hoped her accusation was right, otherwise she'd just been the worst friend on the planet. She stared after him... he was hiding something, she was certain of it.

"When you massage your neck, that's a sign you're lying..." She started power walking after him. "When you stole sweets from Mr Patel's corner shop, you did it then, when you got caught cheating on your mock SAT paper in year six, you did it then. When you..."

"Enough!" he shouted and spun round to face her. "Enough," he repeated more calmly and walked towards her; his shoulders slumped - the game was up. "You're right."

287

"Right about what?" The sense of triumph about being right didn't last long. What was he going to reveal to her? He'd never lied to her before… what was so important that he should start now?

"I lied about Maisie - I made her up."

"You…you what?"

"I made her up, Soph."

"You're telling me she doesn't exist - why on earth would you do that?"

He couldn't look at her.

"Rupert?"

"To make you jealous, okay?"

"Make me jealous… I don't understand?"

"This was not how I wanted to tell you, Soph."

"Tell me what?"

He moved agitatedly around on the spot and grunted. "It was our mothers' idea."

"Oh, I see - the plan of the mothers', I can't believe they managed to persuade you to do it, you know what they're like."

"I didn't need much persuading."

Sophie searched his eyes. He seemed so vulnerable and she realised she had never seen him like this before. For a second neither said a word, until Rupert took a deep breath.

"I… I like you, Soph."

Sophie laughed and tapped him jocularly on the shoulder. "Of course you do, we're best friends."

"No, you don't understand. I mean, more than like…" he reached out and grabbed both her hands in his. "I love you, Soph."

Sophie froze. Whatever was going on around her faded away, the screaming toddler in the background, the dog sniffing at the lamppost… what had he just said?

"I love you Sophie Hastings… I always have."

"Always have… what do you mean?" She slipped her hands out of his hold. How was she supposed to react to this sudden acknowledgement? They'd come out for ice cream; it was supposed to be safe.

"I knew it when we moved to Middleton."

"When you were twelve!" She couldn't hide the shock in her voice... she had no idea.

"I missed you, Soph. My heart was broken, I couldn't settle, I couldn't' eat and I lost sleep. It wasn't until I confided in ma that she told me what was happening - that I was in love with you."

"You can't love when you're twelve."

"I did."

Sophie stepped back and touched her forehead, trying to process this sudden change in their relationship. "So, let me get this straight. You've loved me since we were twelve, then we've met again this summer and you decided it would be a good idea to lie to me?"

"Lie is such a strong word, Soph." He reached out to take her hands again, but she flinched away.

"What would you call it?"

"Extension of the truth."

"Oh, baloney, Rupert. It can't be an extension of the truth when there isn't any truth to begin with."

This time Sophie marched away. She wasn't going to let him off the hook because he said he loved her.

"Soph. Sophie... come back!"

Rupert raced after her, spinning her around when he caught up. He stepped back and saw a lone tear escaping from her water-filled eyes.

"You're crying... why are you crying?" he asked softly and gently wiped the teardrop away.

Sophie didn't speak. What could she say? Her mind was flooded with a host of thoughts all competing against each other.

"I only lied because I love you, Soph... Soph?" He bent his knees so their eyes were level. "Speak to me, Soph."

"It's just that... I was beginning to..."

289

"To what?" He brushed her hair behind her ear. "Is there a chance you feel the same?"

"No...maybe. I don't know."

Oliver was amazing, but she had suppressed down her feelings for Rupert because she thought he had a girlfriend. Would her reaction to those thoughts have been different if she knew?

"Maybe we need to find out," Rupert lowered his voice and stroked her hair again, before carefully moving closer to her.

Automatically Sophie pushed him lightly away. "No, Rupert." She wiped an eye on her sleeve. "Just because you've said you love me doesn't mean we're a couple, and it doesn't mean it undoes the fact you lied to me."

"I didn't say it did."

"You were moving in for the kill."

"Oh Soph, don't put it like that."

"I need some time to think."

"Sure, of course. Take your time."

"That means you give me some space, Rupert."

"Of course."

"Real space."

"Yes, Soph. I've said yes."

"Not poking your nose in and spying on me."

"Spying?"

"Don't sound so innocent. I know that's what you've been doing... the other day you had errands to run so you couldn't join me for coffee, but you saw me and Oliver through the window and along came your fictitious phone conversation with your "girlfriend"," she gasped suddenly as another realisation hit her. "Your gran's ninetieth birthday... I bet she never went skydiving at all!"

"Don't," he said looking embarrassed.

"And when my mum phoned you, that day at the manor, and you came across in all innocence..."

290

"You don't want him, Soph," he half shouted waving his arms in the air.

"I take it you are referring to Oliver." She folded her arms defensively.

"He's not right for you."

"How do you know?"

"He's just not… I'm right for you. Can you imagine how happy our mothers will be when we announce our engagement?"

"Whoa, wait right there…engagement? Rupert, we haven't even been on a date."

"But we know each other like the back of our hands. What dating needs to be done?"

"Erm, being best friends is a bit different to being in a relationship."

"No, it's not. The best relationships are based on friendship."

"We can't go from friends to engaged overnight Rupert; it doesn't work like that. When I said I'd think about it, I meant dating, not marriage."

"Well, I'm offering marriage."

The floor started to spin around her. She had just been eating an ice cream, an innocent indulgent ice cream and the next minute, bang…was she being proposed to?

"Sophie Hastings." He took her hand and knelt with one knee on the cold cobbled pavement.

"Rupert," she said calmly but firmly. "Stand up, what are you doing?"

"I've loved you for so long, the way you talk, the way you look, even the way you breathe. I can't stand to be apart from you for another minute. Let's give our families, and each other, a happily ever after. Soph, will you…"

"Rupert," she glared at him, warning him to stop.

"Marry me?"

Sophie's heart beat rapidly in her chest and she looked up and down the high street fearing passers-by might be watching. She gently removed her clammy hand out of his grasp.

"I'm not answering you, Rupert." Tear after tear rolled down her face as she whispered the words.

"You've got to give me an answer," he exclaimed quickly grabbing a hand back.

"I can't."

"Then think about it...please. Sophie...please." He looked straight into her eyes, almost pleading. He wasn't having her on, he really meant this.

"Can you take me home now please," Sophie said looking away.

Rupert rose up and in a trance like state they walked slowly away, in a silence which continued all the way home, until Sophie stepped out of the car. She bent her head back inside Rupert's Lamborghini.

"I will think about it, Rupert. I promise you, I will."

28

Georgiana

As predicted, Henry Southerly proposed the following day. He had come of his own accord, nobody had sent him or pressured him into it. He declared Georgiana was all he had thought about since leaving Denholm Park and was greatly encouraged when Robert revealed he had been rejected. The revelation of her parentage didn't worry him, it could be hushed up easily enough. Her uncle seemed pleased with the match, he had already spoken with him on the subject, and so he was convinced Lady Davenport would soon follow suit.

Georgiana listened patiently. Hearing proposals was becoming second nature to her.

"Mr Southerly, I do not know what to say," she said after Henry had finished speaking.

"At least that's not a no." Henry laughed nervously; it was the first time Georgiana had seen him look so uncertain of himself.

"No, it's not a no, but I'm afraid it's not a yes either... at least, not yet anyway."

"What are your concerns?" he asked and with hands locked together he leaned forward.

They were sitting in the ornate drawing room, facing each other on opposing sofas. Georgiana was impressed by the question. He wasn't trying to sweet talk her or persuade her into something she was uncertain of and this lifted him higher in her eyes.

"I know we are expected to marry at a word from our parents, whether we love our match or not," she began.

"Ah, you are concerned because you do not love me?" he said bluntly.

She felt a little awkward being so forthright about her feelings. "Well... yes." She reddened slightly. "Can you honestly say you love me? We have not known each other long, nor have we spent a lot of time together."

"You are one of the first people not to judge me and to speak to me as an equal, I truly believe you will make me a better person. If we spend time getting to know each other, I think we will find ourselves very much in love."

Did he love her? He had dodged the question.

"Will you refrain from saying no just yet?" he asked.

"I consider that a good agreement." Georgiana smiled and excused herself, there was so much to consider. It was possible she could be happy either way, but deep down she knew, there was only one gentleman who would make her truly complete.

Their agreement seemed to appease her uncle too, and Henry was invited to extend his stay. This unsettled Georgiana and led her to anxiously contemplate what communication there had been between her uncle and her mother. How long would they keep Mr Southerly trapped as their guest? She feared he would only be released on her acceptance of his offer, and in this way, her hands were tied.

Immediately Georgiana wrote to Kirkby, he must be informed of this second proposal. In reply, he wrote he was not surprised that she had received another offer, and understood the pressure she was under to accept. He didn't press her for an answer to his own proposal, but instead told her about the successes he was having in establishing a business, and how his sisters missed her and requested she return to the farm as soon as possible.

The days marched on and every so often Georgiana would find time to escape the confines of her family and Henry Southerly, the presence of the latter being not unwanted, but the pressure to respond lingered unfavourably in the atmosphere. On these rare occasions, she would hide away at the Simms's farm and be engulfed by the children as soon as she arrived, momentarily helping her to forget the turmoil she felt inside.

Eventually Kirkby had to head off for London, he had news of a good business opportunity and didn't want to miss an opening. He promised to write, which he did the very day he arrived, describing in detail every part of his trip and how much he missed her. Georgiana continued her visits to the farm in his absence. She felt wholeheartedly like she was becoming one of the family and felt totally and utterly accepted, unlike anything she had experienced before.

One day her uncle announced he was taking Henry hunting. Georgiana considered he was probably attempting to bring about a second proposal, since the first one had come to nothing. She could not think why else he would spend time with a gentleman who had originally been so unacceptable to the Davenports.

The event caused Georgiana to realise it was time to make her decision. Deep down she knew what she needed to do, but a lack of confidence stopped her doing it. She needed some guidance and Bessie was the only one who would understand. Making excuses for a solitary walk, Georgiana headed to the farm. It had become a familiar route and took her no time at all following the shortcuts she had discovered.

On her arrival at the farmyard Bessie came hurrying out the house, locking the door quickly behind her. Georgiana knew instantly something was wrong, the usual welcoming smile being replaced by a flustered face.

"What's the matter, Bessie?"

As she walked closer Georgiana could tell she had been crying, which was unusual, for the woman was normally so in command of everything.

"It's our Eve," Bessie said stifling a sob and dabbing her damp cheek with the apron tied around her wide waist. "You must leave, Georgiana. The doctor has confirmed she's got smallpox."

"Oh goodness, is there anything I can do to help?"

"Stay away from here for a start, otherwise my William will never forgive me if anything happened to you."

Hesitantly, Georgiana obeyed. She didn't like leaving her friend in such a state and she worried about the health of the children, dwelling in the large room below the sick girl. Any one of them could start with the symptoms next, one after another they could fall victim.

When did Kirkby leave? She fretfully tried to work backwards, counting the days. Had he left before his sister became contagious? Come to think about it, she was yet to receive a letter from him and he was normally such a diligent writer. Perhaps he was ill too, and she blamed herself for not asking Bessie when she had the chance. Her fears haunted Georgiana all the way back to her uncle's. In fact, she had no idea how she got home, having no memory of the lanes and stiles she took.

Thankfully the house was quiet when she arrived back and so she was at liberty to scribble a few lines to Bessie, reiterating how she would help in any way possible, promising to stay away and asking to be kept informed of any news. Next, she wrote to Kirkby, desiring him to write immediately to inform her of his good health.

When searching for a footman to post her letters she was shocked to hear her uncle's voice calling her into his library as she passed by the room.

She walked cautiously inside. "Uncle, I thought you'd gone hunting and would be absent for the day?"

"We cut the expedition short on account of an old shoulder injury resurfacing." He steepled his hands as he leaned both elbows on the dark mahogany desk. "When were you going to tell me your new friend's son was Mr Kirkby?"

Blood drained from Georgiana's face. How had he found out?

"Have you accepted an offer of marriage from the gentleman? Is this the reason why you are delaying your acceptance of Henry?"

Her head drooped towards the floor and she chastised herself for procrastinating. The life she wanted had been right in front of her, but she had been too scared to grasp hold of it.

"Speak child!" shouted her uncle in exactly the same tone as her mother.

"I have not accepted anything."

"So, he has proposed?"

"Yes."

"And you've said no?"

Georgiana swallowed. How had she found herself in this position again? "I have not said yes or no."

Mr Barnet banged his hand on the table. "Will you not learn, child? You are forbidden to leave this house. Is that understood?"

She nodded.

Nothing was mentioned about accepting Henry and upon his request she exited the room. Now her only decision was, could she bear to be Henry's wife for the rest of her life? He was lively and youthful now, but would he look after her and stay by her side, or would he be drawn further away into the temptations of London, because marriage wouldn't mean this side of him would end? Her worries continued as she pondered how, as the younger son, Henry would support her, since he had indicated no designs of embarking upon a respectable career and currently lived off the wealth of his parents. She closed her eyes and felt her heart grow heavy. Maybe the letter addressed to Kirkby in her hand needed to be rewritten, informing him he should stop corresponding because she had finally been forced to accept Henry's offer.

The days grew tedious locked up inside the house. The first thing she would do each morning was to open the bedroom window as widely as possible, so she could feel the breeze blow softly on her cheeks. The air was becoming incredibly stale inside. Having endured a week of imprisonment she began to feel weary and her head beat hard. The only joy she received was a letter from Kirkby informing her he was well.

"Please can you ask my uncle if I can take a walk around the gardens if Mary supervises me? I really need some fresh air; the stuffy house is not doing me any good," Georgiana asked her aunt one day. The late summer heat was becoming quite oppressive, the rooms lacked air and she felt like she was living in one of her uncle's greenhouses.

"Yes Georgiana," agreed Charlotte. "You do not look well."

With permission granted she took a daily walk around the grounds with Mary, but still she did not feel better. Her head continued to ache and it quickly spread down to her back.

On the day she heard the news that Eve was recovering and no one else in the household had suffered, Henry Southerly approached her as they were all taking tea together.

He sat down beside her. "I'm going to need an answer soon," he said staring straight ahead and sipping his tea.

When she did not answer he looked across. "Georgiana," he gasped suddenly seeing her reddened eyes and pallid skin. "You do not look well."

"It is the heat and as you know my uncle has banished me inside with only one small walk a day."

"You should take rest. We can talk later." He smiled, but his eyes revealed much anxiety.

That evening the family were together again after dinner. Georgiana had rested all afternoon and had eaten little, but the politeness inbred within her forced her continue to socialise, despite feeling physically unable, instead of retreating upstairs to bed.

"Georgiana, will you play for us?" asked her aunt who also delighted in her niece's musical ability, her own daughter not playing quite so well.

Georgiana stood up, her head swimming. She was uncertain if her legs could carry her to the piano stool.

Seeing her unsteadiness, Henry sprang up from his chair. "Are you well, Miss Davenport?"

Georgiana informed him that she was, but taking the first step towards the instrument her ears began to ring and black circles swirled in front of her eyes, blocking out her view of the piano.

Henry reached out his hands and grabbed her before she hit the corner of a side table. Muffled voices rang around her as Henry confirmed she was ill. A hand touched her clammy forehead and a voice followed informing everyone she had a fever. Then came the distant sound of Aunt Charlotte summoning Tobias to carry her up to bed.

29

Sophie

Sophie didn't sleep well that night. She tossed and turned reliving the events of the evening before. What bothered her most about Rupert's proposal was the fact that twice he had mentioned about making their families happy. This was the only reason he gave – she was right for him because it would please their mothers.

This is what it must have felt like... or partly anyway. Marrying because it pleased the family. No love involved. No choice. It just benefitted, financially and socially, the family. Georgiana must have felt like a trophy on display, waiting to be handed over to the best competitor. She was certain Rupert loved her, but how much had he been manipulated by his mother... or by her mother?

It was only now she could fully empathise with her nineteenth-century friend. How to put off the acceptance or even refusal of the proposal was her main concern. She would have to face Rupert at some point... even her mother when she discovered the news. However the longer she could escape that scene the better.

The proposal had also brought the question of Oliver into her head. So far they were friends, with the hint of something more not having materialised. The question was... did she want more? If she chose Oliver, she'd lose Rupert for certain. On the other hand, accepting Rupert would mean the end of her relationship, wherever it was heading, with Oliver. Could she let the possibility of something more go?

"Good morning, Miss Hastings," said Mr Morgan.

Sophie plodded across the farmyard in a pair of green wellies. She had to see Oliver and confront him about their future. It was the only way she could make her decision.

"We weren't expecting you. To what do we owe the pleasure?"

"I've come to see Oliver, is he here?"

"He's in the kitchen preparing to head out into the fields. If you hurry, you'll catch him."

Sophie didn't hang around to chat as she normally would, but instead rushed over to the farmhouse.

"Hello?" She knocked on the kitchen door that was already half-open.

"Hey Sophie." Oliver gave her a broad smile; he was visibly pleased to see her. "What are you doing here?"

"I was passing and thought I'd drop in."

She stood in the doorway a little uncertain whether to enter or retreat. Now she was here, her tummy knotted with nerves and she rapidly reconsidered her visit; discussing Rupert was not a good idea.

"I was heading out to the fields. How about lunch later?" He swung a messenger bag over his shoulder.

"Yes, of course." She twisted round to retreat, but concerned her abruptness had been too rude, spun back quickly, almost stumbling into the farmhouse. "Erm, lunch sounds good, thanks... I'll see you later." She could feel her body heating up, embarrassed that she had come at all.

"Sophie?" questioned Oliver. "What's wrong?"

"Nothing... everything's fine. I'll see you later."

"You can't fool me, come and sit." He stepped closer, trying to gently tug her into the farmhouse by the elbow.

"You haven't got time. You've got to get into the fields."

"Sit!" He ordered and she gave up the excuses and sat down at the end of the old wooden table. Oliver positioned himself next to her, waiting for Sophie to explain her strange behaviour.

"So... do I need to guess, or are you going to tell me?" he said eventually, when she remained silent.

"I don't know what to say," she began not wanting to make eye-contact. "I don't even know why I came."

"Is it your dad?" Oliver asked beginning the guesses.

"No, he's doing really well."

"Your mother?"

"She's always a problem."

"You're too harsh on her." He sat back heavily in his chair and folded her arms across his chest.

Sophie felt her skin tingle, why was he always defending her mother when she made her life such a misery?

"You don't know her."

"I think if you just tried…"

She wasn't standing for this. She rose, placing both palms flat on the table. "I did try, Oliver. I thought about what you said, I made the effort and she turned me down."

"You did?"

"Yes, last night."

"And you're just going to give up because the first time didn't work?"

What more did he want, had he not heard her say she tried?

"She doesn't want to spend time with me and she never will, so there's no point trying. I'm not being turned away time and time again."

Oliver was quiet and he sat still, trying to read Sophie's face.

Sophie huffed. "I'll be on my way; you should be in the fields."

As she was walking out of the kitchen with her back to Oliver, he called out after her. "Have you forgiven her?"

The question came out of the blue and she turned back. "What for?"

"You tell me."

"I can reel off a list, if you'd like."

"You're holding onto things you need to forgive."

"How do you know?" she shouted feeling her emotions wobbling and beginning to lose control. There were a lot of things she needed to forgive her mother for, but for some reason, it irritated her that Oliver was asking the question. Elizabeth didn't deserve pardoning for all the times she'd hurt her.

"Sophie," he lifted his hands. "Please don't get offended."

"Too late," she pursed her lips.

"Sophie…" He tried walking towards her, but she moved away.

"I'm not forgiving her until she shows a bit of remorse about how she's treated me for all these years."

"Sophie," he spoke softly again and slowly took her hand. "Sometimes we need to forgive so that we can move on. You're not saying what your mother did was right, but you're not going to move on in life until you've let go of the things that have hurt you the most. You might not be able to change your mother, but you can change who you are."

"I can't forgive her," she said close to tears.

"Then…" He paused deciding if he really wanted to say the next words. "I'm not certain where that leaves us."

"What do you mean?"

"I don't think I can watch you live your life in this way."

"I tried Oliver." She had come to find out what their future had in store, but this wasn't the answer she had expected.

"I think you need to try again."

"You don't understand… how can you? You haven't a mother like mine."

He let go of Sophie's hand and let it flop to her side.

"You're right, I haven't a mother - I wouldn't understand." He pushed past her. "I'm late for work, Sophie. Let's reschedule lunch - I'll see you around."

Sophie drove home in a daze. What had just happened? Rupert hadn't even entered the conversation and they ended up falling out. She let out a gasp… she'd fallen out with Oliver – the most caring, kind-hearted person she knew. It was possible she had just ruined the best relationship she'd ever had.

Entering the estate office, Sophie slumped down onto the swivel chair behind the desk.

"Tough morning?" asked her dad, walking in with a pile of files. When she didn't say anything, George circled round her. "Pumpkin... what's wrong?"

"I've had a fight with Oliver." She spoke as if she was trying to understand what had happened herself - she still couldn't believe it.

"Oh, I'm sorry, but I'm sure it will soon blow over," he said casually, assuming it was some minor falling-out and went over to the filing cabinets and flicked through the papers inside. "He's a good boy, he'll come to his senses. What was it about?"

"Mum, actually."

"Oh?" Absent-mindedly he rolled shut the filing cabinet and came back towards his daughter. Anything to do with his wife was a sore subject and immediately he knew their fight wasn't over something trivial.

"He wants me forgive her." She spoke quietly focusing on her stubby fingernails.

George pressed his lips together. "Very wise, I think."

"What?" she flashed her eyes towards him and straightened up in the chair.

"You're not happy Sophie, anyone can see that. Your mother is the main reason why, isn't she?"

"Of course she is, but I can't change that dad, I wish I could."

George crouched down low beside his daughter. "You have every right to hate your mother, she's over-controlling and judgmental, amongst other things. What I think Oliver is trying to get you to consider is that fact you can change your attitude even if your mother doesn't change hers."

"I just feel so trapped all the time." Sophie folded her arms around herself and hugged them tight. "Why did you marry her, dad?"

"Who... your mother?" The question had caught him off guard.

"Yes, I've always wondered. You don't exactly strike me as a happily married couple, never have come to think of it."

George pulled up a rickety wooden stool sitting in the corner of the room and sat in front of his daughter, taking hold of her hand. "Sophie, you've got to understand when I met your mother she was like a completely different person."

"She must have been, otherwise I don't understand at all."

"Sophie…"

"I'm sorry… go ahead."

"You didn't know your grandmother, she was nothing like your mother, in fact they couldn't have been much more different. Doris had no involvement in your mother's life at all - she didn't even come to our wedding. Your mum was desperate for someone to appreciate her and then I came along and give her the security and love she'd longed for her whole life. You wouldn't believe it, but she was so thankful for what I'd done and we fell in love and got married." He smiled at the memory, until a new thought cast a shadow. "The year her mother died was also the year she gave birth to you and something changed inside of her. Suddenly she wanted to give you and Dylan everything she never had, she wanted to be included in every decision, every activity and every breath that you took. Except she went about it the wrong way because she didn't have an example to follow. She meant well and I kept telling her she was becoming too overbearing, but she didn't listen. I urged her to seek counselling and tried to show that her poor parenting skills were a cry for help. She needed to grieve for her mother and the childhood she never got to have… but she didn't listen." He shut his eyes briefly, remembering how his wife had changed in so short a space of time and how little power he had to stop it.

"Are you telling me she's done nothing wrong?" asked Sophie, narrowing her eyes.

"No, I'm not saying that. She's got a lot of things to answer for… my depression being one of them. It pains me to see her as she is, when I know who she was before. I struggle to watch her destroy her relationship with us and it hurts me daily. I know what she was aiming for… she intended good, Sophie – these "things" she does, her purpose was to draw you closer, not push you away. I'm not justifying her, but I want you to consider that there's a reason behind it all."

He paused and contemplated if what he wanted to say next was necessary. But one look at his daughter told him that it was, he couldn't allow her to continue on a path that would ultimately lead her to destruction.

"I know you don't want to hear it, pumpkin… but I think Oliver has hit the nail on the head. If you can forgive your mother then it might allow you to be happy. It doesn't take away what she's done to you, it might not even change her attitude and could be something you have to continuously fight against your whole life; but it will set you free. I'm afraid your unwillingness to forgive has trapped you and taken away your joy, because all you see before you, are the things she's done wrong. You've set yourself on a path that's only taking you deeper into bitterness and now you're on the downward spiral, you're stuck. I can see you're placing the blame on your mother and using her has an excuse, but you have the power to move on. Lift up your eyes, pumpkin and see that there's more. There are good things to see, fix your eyes on those."

****

Sophie woke the next morning after another broken night's sleep. Images of Elizabeth traumatised her, George's words boomed repeatedly in her ear and Oliver became a taunting figure towering above her. Waking in a sweat she rubbed her aching head, and being unwilling to re-enter such an unsettling dreamworld, she forced herself out of bed, got dressed and went in search of some much-needed pain killers. One thing was certain, if she wanted to have any normality in her life, steps needed to be taken to face her fears head on.

The medicine box was empty when she found it, making her first stop of the day the Middleton pharmacy. There was no way she could work with such a pounding head.

Stepping out of the pharmacy, she pushed two white tablets out of their foiled case, chugged back a swig of water and swallowed, hoping they would do their job. Clattering sounds to her right reminded Sophie it was market day and she knew Oliver would be there right now setting up his father's stall. Her headache was an easy problem to solve, but her fight with Oliver not so simple to fix. She cared about what he thought and hated the fact that their next meeting would be awkward and without his warm, welcoming smile. This was something that could be changed now, if she had the courage to face him.

"Hello there, Sophie. You're becoming quite a feature at our stall."

"Good morning, Mr. Morgan," Sophie's stomach knotted. "I guess I can't keep away from your amazing produce."

Jack Morgan elbowed his son, who was standing next to him, in the ribs. "I don't think she's just talking about my apples and potatoes."

Oliver didn't smile and he placed down three heavy crates with a bang.

"Sophie, maybe you could tell him carrying all those crates will do his back in before he's forty; he doesn't listen to his old man, but I think you'd listen to you," Jack winked and wandered off behind the back of a large cream awning circling the stall. He was obviously oblivious of their fight.

"It's true you know, it's not good for your back." Getting no response, Sophie tried to break the tension and picked up a shining pink lady apple. "These are my favourites." She smiled, digging inside her pocket to find a bit of cash and held it out to Oliver.

"No, no, my girl - it's on the house," piped up Jack coming back with a clipboard and pencil in his hand. "Right, I think that's

307

everything." He turned to Oliver. "Now remember, Mrs Trenton is coming to collect an order, keep an eye out for her and dash to the van as soon as possible, it's a big order and we don't want to keep her waiting."

"Yes, dad." Oliver rubbed his hands together and blew through them, the warm summer mornings were gradually drawing to a close and there was a light chill in the air.

"You need some of those fingerless gloves," commented Sophie.

"Na, I'm fine," he said without looking at her.

"No, you're not, your hands are chapping already, I can see."

"It happens every year - I'll survive," he grumbled hiding both hands inside his pockets.

What was the matter with them... they'd had one argument and now they had to disagree about silly insignificant things as well? Sophie stood there awkwardly, holding the apple in her hands, feeling too self-conscious to bite into the sweet juices she knew were lurking underneath its skin. She was beginning to think she'd just leave: Oliver was clearly not in a good mood and discussing yesterday was probably not a good idea, it would only make things worse.

"So..." he suddenly grunted. "Have you thought more about what I said?"

"You mean, about my mother?" Obviously, he meant her mother, she winced at her own stupidity.

"Of course, do you think I wasn't going to mention it?"

"No, I was just..."

"Trying to avoid the topic?"

"Well, yes if you put it that way - you don't exactly seem to be in the best of moods to discuss anything."

Oliver stood there, his face emotionless and arms folded across his chest. "And...?" He was waiting for her to explain.

"And what?" Her skin began to prickle; he wasn't making this easy.

"I wasn't blowing hot air yesterday, Sophie. I meant what I said."

"You would really break up our friendship if I did nothing about it?"

"Sophie, it's important to me."

"She's not your mother."

"No, she's not, however she affects you and well…" He stepped closer, out of range of his father's listening ear, and softened his tone. "I care what happens to you."

"To be honest, I haven't seen her recently to do anything else about it."

"You live in the same house, Sophie."

"It's a manor house, it's big enough to get lost in."

"Good excuse."

He bent down to the crates piled on the floor and began taking out bunches of streaked green bananas and placing them on the wooden table that lay between himself and Sophie.

"It's not an excuse, Oliver."

"Oh, so you are planning on doing something about it then?"

"Maybe…" she said not committing herself.

Oliver chucked a handful of bananas down onto the table in frustration. "Sophie, I'm not messing around here."

"The relationship between me and my mum is perfectly normal, it's the way it's always been."

"Your normal isn't normal and it's zapping all your life away."

"It's normal for us. So, I don't get on with my mother, do you get on with yours?" she gasped as the words shot out of her mouth in instant regret. She had done it again. "I'm so sorry Oliver, I didn't mean that, I wasn't thinking."

Oliver wouldn't look up and continued unpacking the bananas.

"No, I mean, I'm really sorry, that wasn't kind of me."

"Forget it, it's okay," he turned away and brought forward a crate of soil-covered potatoes.

"You don't seem okay about it?" Whenever his mother was mentioned Sophie had noted his defences always shot up.

Oliver slammed the potato crate on top of the empty banana box and stared intensely at her. "Just promise me you will sort it…" He wasn't going to take his eyes off her until he got an answer. "Promise me, Sophie."

"I- I…" What could she say to him? Maybe she should have decided exactly what she wanted before speaking to Oliver, because right now she had no idea. "I'm not going to lie to you… I'm not certain I could ever fully make amends with my mother."

"Then I can't see you anymore." His words shocked Sophie as they flew out of his mouth.

"Why not Oliver, this is silly."

"I'm not going to sit and watch you do this to yourself."

"Do what?" cried Sophie.

Oliver looked up and gestured for her to speak more quietly, customers were slowly beginning to creep out of their doors and he didn't want to present an unprofessional front. Making a decision, he hurried around the front of the table and caught up Sophie with his arm, leading her behind the awning and away from the eyes of an unwanted audience.

"I can't sit and watch you neglect a relationship with your mother that you could easily fix. Don't you realise how lucky you are to have the opportunity to be able to do that? You say you want her approval, but you're not willing to make the sacrifices to get it. I understand you don't get along with her, and that's fine, but not everyone has the same chance as you. I'm afraid if you don't make the effort, you'll regret it; your life will be full of arguing and upset as you try and claim the acceptance and love you truly deserve, but will never get."

Sophie was speechless. What Oliver had said was so similar to her father's description of Elizabeth's early life, who also desired to be accepted and loved by her mother. Quickly, she pushed these thoughts back, her mother didn't deserve sympathy. In fact, if she thought about it, what Elizabeth had done to her was worse because she understood the heartache of never receiving approval from a mother and yet, here Elizabeth was years later, doing exactly the same thing to her own daughter.

"It's a two-way relationship, it's not my fault if she won't meet me half-way," Sophie said loosening her tongue.

"You haven't allowed her to meet you half-way. You tried once, failed and gave up. There is so much hurt there, you have to keep fighting through it until you see a breakthrough. Let's face it, forgiveness isn't a one-time thing, is it? The memories will linger and haunt you and there will be days you'll slip back into bitterness. The only way you'll heal anything inside yourself is to forgive and forgive again – repeatedly."

"Why bother trying when I know she'll throw it back in my face each and every time."

"You don't know that; you've got to at least try…and I'll be here to pick up the pieces." He gently placed a hand on her shoulder. "I mean it Sophie; I'm not going anywhere."

His words gave her so much security, but there was a niggle at the back of her mind which she had to voice because, if she failed to meet his expectation, where would that leave them?

"But our relationship shouldn't be built on conditions, Oliver."

"I'm only doing it because I care."

Why was he being so stubborn? Sophie could put it down to only one thing. "Listen Oliver, I'm sorry you lost your mother and you can't have a relationship with her. I'm sure she was amazing… if she's anything like you - but you don't know *my* mother. We've never had a relationship and she's never wanted one. I had a nanny to look after me when I was little, a childminder after that, I'd be sent off to holiday clubs for practically the whole of the summer… actually, she even sent my brother to boarding school - so it's not just me she's messed up. I really don't know why she had children; she doesn't care about us."

Oliver snorted through his nose. "Then I'll see you around, Sophie." He turned his back and stalked away towards the stall.

"That's it?" Sophie stared after him, mouth open in amazement. "You're just walking away."

"Aren't you?" he said looking over his shoulder.

"Oliver, come on."

He turned, but didn't walk back. "There must be one thing you could do, just one thing that shows you're willing to make the effort with your mother."

An image of Rupert flashed before her. "There might be one thing," she said slowly.

"Do it then...for us." A silence filled the gap that stood between them.

"Oliver, I..." she trailed away.

"I understand you don't want a relationship based on conditions, I don't either, but surely you can see why this is important to me?"

"I don't actually."

"Don't what?"

"See why it's so important to you that you're almost obsessed with it."

"Obsessed..." He laughed. "Caring about you is an obsession now?"

"Don't flip it back onto me." She stopped herself promptly in order to calm her flaring emotions. Under no circumstance did she want what she was about to say next to sound like an attack. "I'm not surprised you struggle; losing your mum at such an early age can't have been easy. Have you ever talked with anyone about it... maybe you have issues you haven't dealt with yet? There are people who can help."

Oliver reeled back, feeling for the brick wall that lay to his side. He leaned against it almost becoming unaware of Sophie's presence.

"Oliver? Oliver, are you okay?" Sophie stepped cautiously closer. "Oliver?"

He shot up when she got too close and Sophie thought he was going to take flight. As she was considering whether she should go after him if he did run, he suddenly twisted round to her in anguish.

"I lied to you, Sophie."

Blood drained straight out of Sophie's face, she didn't believe the words - *Oliver Morgan* and *lie* could never go together in the same sentence.

"You…you lied to me?" Her voice was barely audible, anxious about what he might reveal.

"I'm sorry," he ran fingers through his fair hair. "I've always done it and when you came along, I didn't see the need to change my story. I had no idea we'd grow so close."

"What are you talking about?"

"My mother…" He paced up and down in agitation before stopping in front of Sophie. "I told you she died when I was twelve - I tell everyone she died when I was twelve… but she didn't die."

"She didn't?"

"No." He hung his head in shame. "No, Sophie. She didn't." He came and sat beside her on the wall and took her hand. "What I'm about to tell you, I've told no one else. Only my father and brothers know the truth. My mother - she ran out on us. When I was twelve years old, she ran away from her family and we haven't seen her since."

"Why didn't you say? People would understand."

"They wouldn't. If a guy says his mother died when he was a boy, all he gets is sympathy. But, if a guy says his mother abandoned him, all he gets are questions and to be honest, I got fed up of answering the questions. My dad eventually made up the story she died in a car crash because I struggled so much… I couldn't handle it, my behaviour at school was shocking and in the end I…" His cheeks reddened and he looked away. "It embarrasses me to tell you this…I was suspended one too many times and was eventually expelled."

Sophie took hold of his hand and squeezed it tight, wishing she could take these memories away from him.

"As you can imagine, my exam results were a train wreck; it's pretty impossible to learn in an environment surrounded by unwanted and uncivilised children. My GCSEs weren't worth the paper they were written on."

Sophie knew what he was going to say next, it didn't take a genius to work it out.

"My dad let me work on the farm. I was so mad with myself for allowing my life to become so messed up, I was only sixteen years old. I worked hard for dad, he deserved it after the nightmare I'd put him through. When I was eighteen, I decided to retake my GCSEs and then followed straight into my A Levels. The other day, when you saw me, I was collecting my final exam results... I wasn't doing anything for my brother. Financial restrictions aren't the only reason I haven't completed a degree yet, you kind of need qualifications to pass the entry requirements." He stared straight down at Sophie's fingers interlocked with his and stroked her thumb. "I'm sorry."

Sophie felt a strange peace. She should be cross with him after he had hidden so much from her, but she wasn't. "Oliver," she said gently. "You can't hide from it forever."

He finally moved his head up and she returned his gaze. "Can you tell me there is not a single question fluttering in your head?" he asked.

"Yes, I have questions, but I don't need to know the answers and I certainly don't think any less of you."

"That's not what I've experienced. You don't mourn when your mother leaves you, you feel shame. A mother should be there when you're sick, when you finish school at the end of the day, when you've done something foolish - a mother should be there and mine wasn't... isn't."

At this point he twisted his whole figure to face her. "Don't you see, Sophie, you have this amazing opportunity to make the relationship with your mother work, whatever she has done to you. Be angry with her and tell her so, but try and change it for the better - she's the only mother you have. I can't tell mine how angry I am with her, how much she's messed up my life. I can't tell her because I don't know where she is, but you know where yours is. For years I held a grudge and laid the blame on her for everything that went wrong with my life. I was cross with the whole world… but my father never was." He shook his head and laughed lightly. "Good old dad… I remember one day, I came home from my alternative schooling for unruly children, and shouted at him for no reason and I roared until my voice became hoarse. I had never cried so much in my life and he simply stood there and listened to it all. That evening he came into my room and as I lay in bed his hand stroked my hair. He told me how much he loved me, however, I needed to realise that until I forgave my mother things would never change. He promised me I wouldn't be letting her off the hook, but by doing so I would start to set myself free me from the bondage of bitterness I'd allowed myself to become caught in. It wasn't until I listened to these wise words that things began to change. It wasn't easy, and there are still days when I struggle."

"Oliver! Where are you?" Jack Morgan called out from the front of the stall. "Mrs Trenton is here."

Oliver took one last look at Sophie and released her hand, without saying another word he left, disappearing from view as he stepped in front of the awning.

30

Sophie

Sophie raced home; her mind full of conflicting thoughts. Accepting Rupert was the only way to begin to making amends with her mother, Elizabeth wouldn't take notice of her any other way. Her purpose in doing this would give her Oliver, however the very act of becoming Rupert's fiancé would inevitably take him away. She needed some advice, but George and Dylan were her only confidants, neither of whom would understand.

On arriving home, she dashed to her room and took out the box full of diaries from underneath the bed. Only three remained unread and she settled down to read them all with the hope of finding an answer. There was no way she could make a decision until she knew what Georgiana had done. Would she choose the man she loved or accept the man selected by her family?

I cannot write any longer, my body aches all over. I can barely pick up my quill to write, my fever is so great. Aunt Charlotte has quarantined me in my room. I am not too concerned, the red spots which have appeared on my tongue have appeared only because of my fever. I remember a similar thing happening to Edward when we were children - I am certain it is just a trifling cold.

And that was the end - the final diary. Sophie looked around frantically to see if one had dropped out and searched through the empty boxes. The diary in her hand was half written, which was highly unusual because Georgiana always used every single page possible. Sophie flicked through the empty pages. There was nothing else.

The green room was nearly finished and a fresh coat of pale green paint had only been applied by the decorator the day before. It was the smell of this new paint which hit Sophie as she ran through the door. The room had been completely emptied apart from the four-poster bed and an ottoman which stood at the end. Sophie rummaged through the wooden panelled ottoman, but this was empty too, apart from a few paint brushes and pieces of sandpaper. Underneath the bed was bare as well. In desperation, she pressed her face against the wall and tried to look behind the ancient radiator. Nothing. There were no more diaries anywhere. She flopped on the bed and fought the urge to cry. Her friend had left her, the only person who knew exactly how she felt had gone. What was she going to do now?

Footsteps brought Sophie back to reality and she sniffed, attempting to send her tears into retreat. The steps could be heard coming up the grand stairs case and along the balcony, soon a voice joined them, "Soph… Soph?"

It was Rupert.

"I'm in the green room," Sophie shouted wiping her running nose with a sleeve.

"What are you doing in here?" he asked stepping into the room.

"Just admiring the makeover." She feigned a smile. "Looks good doesn't it."

"Amazing," he agreed and stood there a little shyly, waiting for Sophie to continue the conversation. It was the first time they'd spoken since the proposal.

The silence carried on until they both began speaking at the same time and they laughed nervously.

"You go first," said Sophie. In all honesty, she didn't know what to say anyway.

"I haven't seen you since…you know," Rupert looked down at the newly carpeted floor. "I need an answer… I don't want to wait any longer."

Sophie thought there would be more time and watched Rupert closely, a lock of curly hair had fallen onto his forehead as he avoided her gaze. She couldn't keep him waiting, it would be too cruel… but saying no would break his heart. Then again, saying yes would break hers. Surely she could still be friends with Oliver… couldn't she? That's if Rupert wasn't too jealous. It would show Oliver she was serious about restoring a relationship with her mother, although it did mean sacrificing their relationship, but it would make the majority of the people she cared about happy. She exhaled deeply. "Yes, Rupert. I will marry you."

At first, he gasped in disbelief and then his face lit up. "Really, Soph?"

"Yes, really."

He rushed towards Sophie and pulled her close, producing a diamond ring from his pocket and slipping it onto her finger.

****

Elizabeth and Dorothy were soon busy planning the biggest engagement party Middleton had seen for years. When the new couple had announced their news, Elizabeth bounded across to Sophie and gave her daughter the first hug they'd shared for years. Everyone appeared happy, but Sophie noticed her dad kept himself in the background and said little about an occasion she thought he'd be so pleased about. After the initial excitement had passed and everyone was engaged in happy chatter and drinking champagne, George came up to his daughter.

"Congratulations, pumpkin." He said the right words but his expression didn't match.

"You don't seem very pleased, dad."

"I'm happy if you are." He raised his eyebrows. "Are you?"

"It's probably not a question we should analyse."

"Oh Sophie," he shook his head in disappointment. "Why have you done it?"

"She wanted me to." Sophie eyed Elizabeth, standing by the mantlepiece with her head tipped back and laughing heartily at something Rupert had said. "It was the easy option." She shrugged her shoulders. "It makes everyone happy."

"What about Oliver?"

"What about Oliver, we've only ever been friends."

"I respect Rupert, I do, but I can't see you being happy with him…not in the same way you'd be happy with Oliver."

George's intuition shocked Sophie. She'd never discussed her feelings with him, but he'd seen Oliver was special to her in a way Rupert could never be.

"Oliver wanted this."

"Really… this?"

Sophie wasn't convinced either. "He wanted me to make things work with mum, accepting Rupert has started the ball rolling."

"But this is your life Sophie."

"It's the first time I've made her happy dad, truly happy."

"By letting her control your life? It's not what I wanted for you, Sophie."

"Rupert is a good friend, we'll be okay."

George didn't say much else, if this was his daughter's decision, he wasn't going to talk her out of it.

****

A week flew by and it was market day again. Sophie hadn't seen Oliver since her engagement and she didn't fancy running into him. She cashed the cheques for the estate as quickly as possible, her intention being to flee the high street before any stallholders came to set up. However, her planned failed, when directly outside the bank Oliver had parked up and was unpacking crates from the back of the van.

Banging the back doors shut he looked up and saw her. "I hear congratulations are in order," he said without emotion.

"You've heard then?"

"Yes, I've heard Sophie." He picked up a crate full of vegetables and clattered it on top of another. "My dad got a save the date card for the engagement party of the year."

319

"My mum has invited the whole estate," she said feeling like she had to give a reason for Jack Morgan's invitation.

Oliver moved to a third crate which was wedged into the one beneath and he shook it vigorously to loosen it, before throwing it onto the ground with extra force. He glared angrily at Sophie. "When I said do whatever it takes, I didn't exactly mean marry the biggest chump on the face of the earth."

"I'm sorry Oliver, but it's what my mother has always wanted, it's been arranged since we were small. Marrying Rupert is the first step in restoring our relationship, isn't that what you wanted?"

"That's not what I meant - I wanted you. I thought that was obvious, we could have worked through it."

"You were ready to bail on us, as far as I could see, if I couldn't fix things with my mother."

"No Sophie, I said you needed to try."

"I did!" shouted Sophie.

Oliver shook his head. "If your mother rejected you, I would have been there to support you, but trying once and giving up isn't making the effort." He stomped round the side of the van and shut the driver's door which had been left open. "Marrying Rupert isn't fixing anything, Sophie. She's still got all the control - she's living your life."

"I didn't know what else to do," she said through the tears which had started to fall. "You didn't exactly give me many options."

"You could have told me."

"You didn't want to hear."

They stood facing each other and both knew their words were forcing them further apart.

Oliver sighed. "There's no point arguing, it's done now and can't be undone." He picked up the pile of crates, steadied his feet and gained his balance, before passing Sophie, who stepped out of his way. "I'll see you around Sophie."

31

Sophie

I will rest now in the hope I feel better tomorrow. Sophie kept reading and re-reading the same words. Did Georgiana feel better… how was she to know? The diary gave no more information - there was no more. She flicked through the remaining empty pages once again in desperation to find a single note from Georgiana, however once again there were none.

I will rest now in the hope I feel better tomorrow. What had happened to her… she couldn't have died, could she? Tears began to trail down Sophie's cheeks. It was the morning after her encounter with Oliver and she felt miserable. She knew it was late in the morning, it was possible that lunch had been and gone, but she couldn't rouse herself to move and sat hunched up on the floor by the bed.

Once Georgiana's diary had given her comfort, but now, the written words only added to her sadness. What had happened to the girl? Their stories were so scarily similar that Sophie needed to find out if Georgiana had married Kirkby and defied her family in a way she had failed to do. If her regency friend had taken control over her life, maybe she could too…it might not be too late.

With a flash of determination, Sophie wiped a teardrop from her cheek and reached across the bed for her laptop. After typing in her password and waiting for it to load up, she brought up the search bar and started typing in the symptoms she knew Georgiana to have – fever, headache and red spots on the tongue. She held her breath and the results proved her worst fear to be true. Having been in such close proximity to Eve, it was very likely Georgiana had contracted smallpox. The article before her wasn't very encouraging and reiterated that smallpox was one of the deadliest diseases known to mankind. Sophie shook her head – no, she wasn't having it, Georgiana couldn't have died from such an awful sickness.

Thrusting her laptop onto the floor Sophie searched for her black trainers with the pale pink laces, fastened them up and swiped up the half-written diary, before rushing out of the room. It was crazy how someone who lived two hundred years ago affected her so much. Her rational mind told her Georgiana had died eventually, whether it was from this disease or something else, otherwise she would be the oldest living person on the planet. Sophie knew this, but there was a deep aching within her which wouldn't go away until she found out some answers.

"Where are you going in such a rush?" called Elizabeth from the newly renovated morning room.

"Out!" called Sophie from the hall picking up her car keys from a tall three-legged wooden stand.

"Out where?"

"Just out. I'll be back soon."

"I'm only asking, Sophie." She sounded offended and Sophie rolled her eyes, retracing her steps back towards the morning room door. Oliver's words still echoed distinctly round her mind; they couldn't be ignored. Where once she would have bristled and fired back, now she took a deep breath and smiled pleasantly.

"I've got some work to do, that's all."

"Work?" Elizabeth perched her glasses on the end of her nose, pausing her knitting to look up at Sophie.

"Something for Rupert," Sophie lied.

"Be quick, I need you to be here when the electrician comes later."

"Why, where are you?"

"Having tea with Dorothy."

"Can't you have tea here? I don't know how long this will take me."

"Here?" She sounded shocked that Sophie had even suggested it.

"We do have tea, mum, and cups and saucers too."

Elizabeth ignored the comment. "Be back by two, there's a good girl."

Sophie clenched her jaw, attempting to squash the rude remarks she desperately wanted to fire at her mother, who had already turned her attention back to the wool and needles.

Driving much too fast down the country lanes, Sophie sped towards Middleton. Much to her pleasure a parking space opened up on the road outside the library and she spun the wheel and yanked up the hand brake. Grabbing her bag from the passenger seat she flew inside and headed straight for the reception desk.

"Hello, erm... I wonder if you can help me?"

An older lady wearing purple framed glasses on a chain, smiled and held up one finger to summon Sophie to wait. "Won't be a minute, darling."

Sophie smiled back, but impatiently tapped her foot.

"Yes, yes, we do printing. Colour is a pound... mmm, yes? Black and white is fifty pence. Okay, thank you for calling." The lady hung up and wheeled her chair towards Sophie. "How can I help you?"

The phone rang again.

"Oops, won't be a minute, darling." Much to Sophie's irritation the lady answered it again. Wasn't she next in line, didn't she understand this was an emergency?

"Yes, story time is on a Friday afternoon... Pardon? Two o'clock... No, it's free. Okay, thank you for calling." She put the phone down again and look up at Sophie with another smile. "How can I help you, darling?"

Unbelievably the phone rang again.

"Oops, we are busy today - won't be a minute."

Sophie jutted out a hand and held it over the phone, preventing the lady from answering it as it continued to ring. The lady looked at her with eyes narrowed, her smile suddenly disappearing.

"Please can you answer my question, I was here first?" said Sophie.

"Sorry, I can't do that."

"Why not?"

"It's not good customer service."

"Ignoring me is not good customer service."

The phone continued to ring.

"Can I kindly ask you to wait over there. I will be with you as soon as I can," she pointed to a row of green cushioned chairs.

"Really?" huffed Sophie.

The lady waited for Sophie to remove her hand and picked up the phone. "Good morning, sorry for the wait." She glared daggers at Sophie and waved her off towards the chairs. "How can I help you?"

Unbelievable...she wasn't waiting around all day. Turning to the left Sophie walked up the stairs, she'd find what she wanted herself.

In front of her lay a set of double doors with a sign reading "reference library". Sophie walked in and the scent of old books wafted straight into her nose. A young girl pulling a trolley appeared, stopping every so often to put a book back on the shelf.

"Excuse me," Sophie whispered in consideration of the other library users. "Do you have any archives in this library, I'd like to do some research?"

"You want level two. Go to the information desk up there and they will help you with what you need," said the girl with the trolley.

"Perfect, thank you." Relieved that there was at least one member of staff who was helpful, Sophie went up to the second floor.

"Here are the microfiches," said a man with a very nasal voice, whose top was slightly too tight for his figure.

"Micro what?" asked Sophie. She had easily found the information desk and was being shown how to use the archives since it was her first time.

Like a flight attendant, the man pointed to each specific filing cabinet in turn. "Microfiche - sheets of film containing information. We have newspapers, marriages, births, deaths and other miscellaneous documents, you can find them here."

"Oh, thank you. I guess I need to start with the deaths."

"That depends on what you are looking for," the man said seriously, pushing a pair of thick, black rimmed glasses back up his nose.

"I'm trying to find out if someone died."

"Then deaths would be a good place to start."

If Sophie hadn't been so stressed, the sound of this man's voice and his solemnity, would have cracked her up laughing. Rupert would have found him hilarious and mimicked him for weeks, causing Sophie to burst into giggles every time a re-enactment came about. The familiar knot tightened in her stomach, she did have good times with Rupert, perhaps marrying him wouldn't be so bad.

"Which year are you looking for?" the man asked in a drone.

"I'm not certain."

"Roughly?"

"1819 or 1820."

"Then you need to be here." He opened up the central filing cabinet. "Only take one microfiche at a time and make sure you return it to the correct place." He walked rapidly away, his job done.

Sophie stood there for a few moments. The long table in front of her held seven microfiche readers, two of which were already occupied. At one sat a bald man with wisps of light grey hair circling over his head like a Mr Whippy ice cream. He was looking intently at his screen through a monocle. At the other end of the table, a middle-aged lady sat scribbling away into a notebook, filled to the brim with papers and documents. Every so often she would look up, roll the film on the screen round and continue writing.

Sophie peeped inside the filing cabinet and found a little grey plastic box labelled "Derbyshire Deaths 1815-1821". This should be it. Gently, as if it were a thin leaf of glass, she lifted it out of the cabinet with a racing heart, wondering if what she held in her hand would reveal Georgiana's fate.

Pulling out a chair, Sophie sat at one of the readers and placed her bag down by the side. How did it even work? She looked dumbly at the machine in front of her and felt around the edges of the reader for some clues. Come on, she had a degree, how hard could it be?

"Erm, excuse me," Sophie whispered leaning towards the balding man sitting two readers away. "I wonder if you could help me?" The man ignored her and continued ogling through his monocle.

"You won't get anywhere with Pete."

Sophie spun her head to see the notebook lady getting out of her chair and coming across. "Once he's got a microfiche in his hands, you'll get nothing out of him. Let me show you."

"Oh, thanks."

"We don't often see young folk in here. Doing a bit of research for school?"

"I'm researching a bit of family history." This wasn't completely true; Georgiana wasn't a Hastings, but somehow her dairies had ended up in Middleton Manor, there must be a link between the two families somewhere.

"Good for you. It's interesting to know where you come from. Have you got your microfiche?"

Sophie passed across the little box filled with small sheets of clear film. The lady took one out and pointed to the handle that needed to be pulled out in order to place the film underneath a piece of glass. She gently pushed the handle in, and magically, scrawls of joined up handwriting appeared on the screen.

"Just move the handle round to find what you're looking for. Microfilms are different, if you want me to show you, just holler, I'm over there." She smiled at Sophie and walked back to her seat.

Sophie stared at the screen - now she had to think. Opening the diary, she reminded herself of the date of Georgiana's final entry - the twentieth of February 1820. She looked at the screen and squinted her eyes, it was blurred. Searching the reader, she found a dial to bring the screen into focus. Her eyes adjusted and she moved her face closer, trying to figure out what the handwriting said, its large loops and messy appearance making the names hard to distinguish. She found a date. 1816 - too early. She moved the handle around and came to the end of the document - still 1816. She looked back to the little box, it was full of small pieces of film. She was going to be there a while.

Ten minutes later she finally found the first document for 1820. She took a deep breath and started moving the microfiche from side to side, scanning for the name Davenport. Whenever she saw the letter D her heart beat a little faster for fear of what she would find. Suddenly, her hand stopped dead still and she grasped onto the handle, she had seen the name Davenport in the corner of the screen… did it say smallpox? She closed her eyes, now the moment had come she didn't want to know. Peeking one eye open, Sophie finally looked along the line and breathed out with relief. It read Thomas Davenport, aged 3. It wasn't Georgiana.

Diligently she kept looking, trawling through film after film, but nothing surfaced. She even went further and upon reaching 1825 sat back feeling deflated on her chair.

"No luck?" called the notebook lady.

"I can't find what I'm looking for."

"Probably looking in the wrong place then. I always find the information is somewhere, you've just got to find it."

Sophie half smiled in response to this unhelpful advice. She'd had enough and placed the box of microfiches back inside the filing cabinet, collected her bag from the floor and walked out of the room. Her head began to ache again, most likely from squinting too long at the old-fashioned handwriting.

She walked outside into the bright sunshine and paused outside the library, considering what her next step might be.

"Penny for your thoughts?" whispered a voice interrupting her reflections and making her jump.

"Oliver, I didn't expect to see you."

Oliver looked sheepishly away. "Listen, I'm sorry about yesterday… I didn't sleep a wink last night. What's done is done and

I'd hate to lose you from my life… is there a possibility we can still be friends?" He reached out a hand expecting a hand shake in return, which Sophie gave him. Their grasp lasted a little too long and Sophie pulled reluctantly away. Being friends was probably not impossible, but it wouldn't be easy.

"You look like you've got the weight of the world on your shoulders," he said looking at her strained face.

Sophie sighed. "I feel like I do."

"What's the matter?" asked Oliver his forehead creased in concern.

"I'm all right, don't worry about it… it's stupid."

"Tell me, nothing's stupid."

She held on tightly to the diary which was in her hand and hesitated.

"Come on, Sophie. Please let me help."

Her eyes drifted down to the little red book and Oliver followed her gaze.

"What's happened to her?" he asked.

"How did you know?" she asked faintly.

"I know her life means a lot to you and you're also holding onto that diary for dear life." He nodded towards the book.

Sophie looked down: her knuckles were white from holding on so tightly. "The problem is she just stops writing and I can't find any more diaries. I have no more information…and I don't know what happened." Her eyes began to well up and she breathed deeply trying to stay in control of her emotions.

"It's okay." He placed an arm gently round her shoulders without a thought that she was now someone else's fiancé. "Slow down… you do realise that she died over two hundred years ago, don't you?"

Sophie wiped her eyes and laughed, not missing the twinkle of humour held in his voice. "Of course I do… but, I need to know happened, I don't know why, I just do."

"I can tell you why."

Sophie looked at him with interest. How did he know?

"You're so used to letting other people make your decisions that you're terrified of making a mistake. You're fighting within yourself. You want to take a stand and determine your own future, but fear is holding you back. Georgiana's life is so much like yours that you want her to decide for you. If you can discover what she did then you can do the same, saving the anguish of deciding for yourself."

Sophie opened her mouth to speak and Oliver stepped back slightly, the way things had been going between them lately, he was expecting a sharp come back.

"You're right, Oliver. How did I not see that?" she said baffled.

"You were too close to see it." He looked towards the diary. "Now tell me what's happened to her."

"But you just said…"

"I said, don't let the girl make your decisions, not that you shouldn't find out what happened to her. I think you need to know and give yourself some closure, otherwise you'll be forever wondering."

The knot in her stomach unravelled slightly and Sophie smiled at him, Oliver was the sweetest guy she knew… and she had let him go, but at least they were still friends.

"I know she got smallpox in 1920," she began. "But there's no record of a death."

"Who else is involved, did she marry Kirkby?"

Sophie was a shocked he'd remembered so much detail of a girl who meant nothing to him. "Erm, no… would that matter?"

"Name changes." He grinned. "You're no historian, are you?"

"Apparently not."

"If she survived, she would have got married. Who else did her parents want her to marry?"

"There was a Henry Southerly."

"Okay, she could have been either Kirkby or Southerly, and probably married quite quickly after recovering if her family had anything to do with it." He rubbed his chin. "I've got an idea. Do you want a ride?" He pointed to his van that was parked on the roadside just behind Sophie's little blue Corsa.

"Hey, Soph!" a yell came urgently down the street "Where are you going?" Sophie looked up after taking a few paces towards the parked van and saw the accusing bellow coming from her fiancé's mouth.

Rupert jogged up breathlessly. "Are you off somewhere?"

"Oliver's helping me with some research."

"Research… what research?"

"Just a personal thing. Nothing important."

"Personal?" he wedged himself between Sophie and Oliver, wrapping a possessive arm around his future wife. "If it's personal then I'll help."

"Don't worry, Oliver's got an idea that might help."

"Might help? Soph, I'll find you an idea that *will* help. Besides," he bent down towards her ear. "Personal is my business, you're *my* fiancée, remember."

"I'll be going, Sophie," said Oliver, looking uncomfortable.

Sophie felt too helpless to stop him and watched his hunched figure walked away.

Rupert turned to her after watching the van door bang shut. "So, my lovely fiancé, how can I help you?"

Sophie released his arm and stormed away in the opposite direction.

"What… what's the matter?" He ran after her. "Soph?"

"Stop it, Rupert?"

"Stop what?"

"Don't act the innocent."

"I'm not."

She spun round and wagged a finger crossly at him. "Oliver is a friend. He is not a threat. Understand?"

"Whoa!" Rupert held up his hands. "I'm only trying to help and as I said, if it's a personal matter, it's my business, not his."

"He was only trying to help."

"Yes, I understand, but I want to help too... if you'll let me," he bent his head low and flashed a pair of sad puppy dog eyes in Sophie's direction. "Will you let me?"

She breathed out heavily, there was no good reason why she shouldn't include him. "Okay... I'm trying to do some research on this diary."

"Diary?"

"Yes, the one I found at the manor... you remember?" His face remained unenlightened, but she continued anyway. "The girl stops writing and I wanted to find out what happened to her."

Rupert took hold of the musty diary using the tips of his fingers and stared at the cover. "Not this again, why are you wasting your time, Soph? You should be busy planning our wedding."

"I'm not wasting my time. I find it interesting."

He shoved the diary back into Sophie's hand. "Put it away and let's go have lunch. I'm ravenous."

"Rupert, you said you'd help me."

"Only if it was something worth helping with."

"I don't believe you." She shook her head. "I should have gone with Oliver."

"You should have done no such thing. You know your rightful place is with me."

"Rupert, stop being so possessive. You have me, okay, you won." She stormed away again. "And don't follow me," she called without looking back.

32

Sophie

"You couldn't find Georgiana Kirkby or Georgiana Southerly?"

"Sorry Sophie, I spent all day at the parish church and couldn't find a thing in marriages or deaths."

"Thanks for looking anyway, Oliver." Sophie swirled the straw which stood in her milkshake. Oliver had asked if they could meet so he could update her on their mission to find Georgiana. "She can't have disappeared," she said. "And most of the manor is cleared, I doubt I'm going to find anything else."

Over the last few weeks Sophie had focused her energy on devouring the manor for any information she could find, leaving George in charge of the majority of estate work. Clearing out room after room, she'd done multiple trips to the tip, the charity shops and the auctioneers, but had found nothing.

"You've done a good job, Sophie," said Elizabeth that evening. "The manor is finally looking presentable."

Sophie had to double take, was her mother giving a compliment?

Elizabeth came across and handed a brown envelope into Sophie's hand. "You can sign it when you get a moment."

"Sign what?" Sophie opened it up and peeped inside.

"Your contract."

"My contract?"

"You'll be staying in Middleton now you're marrying Rupert."

"We've not discussed anything yet, mum."

"You'll be staying." In Elizabeth's mind there was no room for discussion.

"Even if I am staying, I might look for another job."

"Where else would you work?" She laughed. "What a silly notion!"

Sophie watched as Elizabeth sat back down and sipped a mouthful of coffee which had been perched on the side table. Oliver was right, she had let people make her own decisions for far too long.

"Actually, no."

Elizabeth lifted her head. "Pardon?"

"I said no, it's not a silly notion. Rupert and I will make our own plans, when we are ready."

"Rupert told me you'd be staying in Middleton."

"Well, Rupert hasn't told me."

"He also said he'd be encouraging you to work on the estate."

"It's funny how he's had none of these conversations with me." Suddenly, she felt a calm wash over her and she knew what she had to say. "I'm in control of my life, not you... not even Rupert. We should have dealt with this a long time ago and I'm sorry we let it get so far."

"What are you talking about, Sophie?"

"I can see you have my best interests at heart, but it's too much. You've never let me choose anything; you picked my qualifications, my career, you've even chosen my husband. Please, just for once, can you let me decide?"

Elizabeth huffed.

"Mum, I don't mean to offend you, but if I don't say something our relationship will be beyond repair. Dad told me about grandma."

"What do you know about that?" she snapped.

"I know she wasn't a good mother to you."

"You're comparing me to her?"

"No, not at all," she took herself over and sat next to her mother, balanced on the edge of the sofa. "Thank you for being so involved and concerned about the things I do, but I'm grown up and I deserve my own life. I'll always come to you if I need advice, but apart from that, I'm asking for you to take a step back."

Elizabeth stood up abruptly and began walking away.

"Where are you going?" asked Sophie.

"I can see when I'm not wanted."

"That is not what I said at all."

Elizabeth hovered by the doorway.

"I'm just trying to say…" Sophie took a breath, whether or not it would be received with grace, it was vital she uttered the next few words in the hearing of her mother. "I forgive you and I want us to start afresh."

"Forgive me!" shouted Elizabeth. "You forgive me! I have done everything for you, Sophie - you are extremely ungrateful, and may I add that I've done nothing wrong."

"Mum, you're not listening. It's not just you - I'm sorry for my part too. I've never really considered your feelings, why you've been like you have, or even appreciated the fact you want to be so involved in my life… I hope you can forgive me too?"

"Who on earth have you been talking to… what drivel has penetrated your ears?"

"Mum, it's not drivel."

"It's that Oliver Morgan, isn't it? You shouldn't be seeing him anymore, you're with Rupert."

This wasn't working. The process had started, however, forgiving her mother didn't mean she had to stay in the same room with her. "For goodness sake, I don't know why I bothered," Sophie muttered, pushing past Elizabeth and escaping up the stairs two at a time.

****

"You're very quiet," commented Rupert as they were eating breakfast the following morning. He had taken Sophie out to eat and was cutting into a piece of bacon. "Is this about the other day, because I'm sorry I acted so jealously."

"Oh, don't worry about that," she said quietly and without a smile.

"Then what's the matter?"

"Nothing... it doesn't matter." She sipped her strong tea, feeling weary. She couldn't remember the last time she'd slept properly.

"Please, tell me."

"These pancakes are delicious," she said, running a fork full of pancake through a generous helping of maple syrup and taking a bite.

"You're dodging the question, Soph."

"It's only the usual stuff with my mum, it will pass."

"No, it's not the usual stuff with your mum, because you would be shouting by now." He took her hand from across the table. "You seem sad, that's not like you. Talk to me."

"I'm okay... really. Tell me how your polo training is going."

"Good, thanks." He frowned. "You know, Soph, I'm going to be your husband - I wish you'd confide in me."

"I will, Rupert. I'm just not ready yet. Okay?"

"Okay... only promise me you'll tell me when you're ready."

When Sophie arrived home, she should have headed straight to the estate office, knowing her dad would already have started work for the day, but she couldn't face it. What was the matter with her? All she wanted to do was hide under the bed covers and never come out again.

Walking aimlessly around the manor Sophie came into the long gallery. Since the restorations had taken place, this room was becoming one of her favourites. As the name suggested it was incredibly long and Sophie enjoyed imagining how the ladies of the house would have taken their daily walks up and down the room on rainy days when they couldn't get out. The six windows along one side allowed a vast amount of light to flood into the room, brightening up the dullest day. Along the other side were rows of portraits, many of them being Hastings ancestors who had lived there in the past. Their new American investors wanted each painting in the manor cleaned, and at the end of the room where Sophie had entered, there were three empty spaces on the wall. Each space was tarnished with dirty dark mucky marks in the shape of the missing portraits which had been taken to be restored.

Sophie walked up to the first painting hung high on the wall and stopped to admire it. It was a lady, wearing a cream regency style dress, sitting upright on a reclining sofa with a fluffy tan coloured dog lying at her feet. It was covered in a layer of dirt that had been built up over years of neglect.

She stared at the figure in the painting, her gaze focusing directly into the middle of the girl's eyes which because of the artist's skill seemed to look directly back at the viewer. She had rosy cheeks and her brown hair was tied back in a bun, with ringlets rolling out around her face. She looked calm and peaceful, the window painted behind her was open and it let in rays of sunshine. Sophie looked down to the brass plate sitting at the bottom of the frame and wiped it clean with her hand so she could read the inscription. Gasping, she fixed her eyes back on the girl before her and fumbled around in her pocket for her phone.

"Oliver, come quick!" Sophie shouted excitedly down the phone after dialling. "I've found her."

Knowing exactly what she meant, Oliver raced round to the manor immediately, leaving half the cows unmilked.

"She's a Hastings, come and look!" She waved Oliver across as he entered the long gallery. "Look!" She pointed up to the painting and Oliver followed where her hand was pointing.

"Georgiana Hastings," he read wiping the remaining dirt away. "We don't know it's her, Sophie."

"It must be, Middleton isn't a big place. How many other Georgianas would there have been?"

"It was a popular name at the time," he said still staring at the painting as George walked in.

"Good morning, Oliver." George smiled, looking at his daughter with interest. "We haven't seen you for a while."

"How are you doing Mr Hastings?"

"Not bad, thanks."

"I thought you were in the office?" said Sophie.

"I was, but this painting has an appointment with the restorer in half an hour. Actually, I'm glad you're here Oliver, I could do with your help to get it down, they're deceptively heavy and I struggled with the others."

Oliver readily agreed to help and they manoeuvred themselves into position on either side of the painting.

"Have you got your side, Oliver?" shouted George, straining as he pulled the portrait off the wall, the golden gilded frame suddenly weighing a tonne.

Oliver confirmed that he had and as they moved it off the wall together a small wad of paper moved behind it and came fluttering down to the ground. Sophie bent down and picked it up. It was definitely old and the yellowing pages indicated it had been hidden there for some time. Sophie flipped it over and there before her, in an old-fashioned script, was the name Georgiana.

"What is it, pumpkin? It must have been stuffed behind there for decades."

Oliver watched Sophie as she studied the paper, holding it like a precious gem in her hand.

"Open it," encouraged her dad who knew nothing about Georgiana, but always enjoyed a good mystery.

Sophie looked at Oliver for reassurance and gently began to open the folded pages with a racing heart, she felt incredibly apprehensive about what she was about to read.

My dearest Georgiana,

I cannot believe after all these years I am writing another letter to you. May I first congratulate you on your marriage - I know this took place more than five years ago and my compliments are a little late, but I send my congratulations all the same.

I need to tell you; my heart is filled with much grief as I write this. I think about you daily and if I close my eyes, I can still see your face. However, it's important for you to know I am happy - I married a sensible wife who cares for me deeply and keeps a good home.

I feel there is a need to explain my silence... why I never came back for you. The second ma wrote and informed me of your illness I rode immediately to you, not stopping for lodgings or nourishment. Upon my arrival I first checked on Eve who was recovering well, although extremely pox marked on her face. With my spirits in turmoil I came straight to your uncle's home, I did not care if he turned me away - I needed to know how you were suffering, if you had overcome that horrid disease, or if you had succumbed to its deathly nature.

When I arrived, I found your family entering a chaise — I can only assume they were evacuating their contaminated home. I yelled to announce my presence and galloped over to meet your uncle who had come across to greet me. When I enquired how you were, he told me...I can still feel the pain as I relive the words he spoke - he told me you were no longer living on this earth.

I mourned - for a long time. Not even my dear mother could console me. My life crumbled and I became lost - I had to learn to live without you, my dear, dear, Georgiana.

But alas, I have received news you are still alive! I could not let another day pass by without writing to you, and although we are too late to be together, I wish you the utmost happiness in life and pray that one day our lives will cross again.

Yours forever,

William Kirkby

Sophie had begun reading the letter out loud, but choking with emotion half-way through: Oliver had to take over.

"Why am I so upset?" she sobbed.

George looked concerned as Oliver wrapped her in his arms. "It's okay, Sophie. It's not the ending you wanted."

"They told him she was dead." She moved away from Oliver and wiped the falling tears away from her eyes. "How could they do that?"

"Look at the positives, she married and look..." He pointed to the painting standing up against the wall. "She looks happy, Sophie - you don't know that she was unhappy."

338

"But she loved Kirkby... how long did she wait for him to return, only for him not to reappear? You see, this is what happens when you let your family control your life... they stole her future from her." Fresh tears fell and Oliver comforted her, both looking out at the painted girl and neither saying a word.

"Do you think there are any more letters behind the other paintings?" Sophie asked eventually with a sniff and leaning her head on Oliver's shoulder.

They checked - but there were none.

33

Sophie

The sound of hammering roused Sophie from her sleep the following day. It had been another restless night and she did not feel refreshed at all. She pattered over to the window, rubbing her sleepy eyes and opened the shutters. On the grassy area in front of the manor a group of men were putting up an awning and setting up a stage with a sound system. A couple of women were tying up bunting and her mother was smack bang in the middle of it all with a clipboard in her hand. What was going on? She pulled on a hooded jumper over her head and slipped on a pair of wellies over her polka dot pyjama trousers.

"Mum, what's going on?" The morning was chilly and as Sophie stood on the grass, she folded her arms around her waist and rubbed them to keep warm.

"It's the day of the village fete." Elizabeth trailed her finger down a list on the clipboard.

"I'm sorry… what?" asked Sophie her brain still waking up.

"The village fete," her mother repeated.

"Mrs Hastings?" Sophie turned to see the vicar plodding across to them. "Is it okay for the stewards to set up the car-park on the top field?"

"Yes, that will be fine, but not near the orchard, the gardener reseeded the grass yesterday and I don't want it ruined."

The vicar nodded and left them, talking into his walkie-talkie.

"I'm sorry, what is going on?" asked Sophie, feeling as if she was in a dream.

"You told me it would be a good idea."

"You told me to cancel it, which I did… weeks ago."

"Well, I uncancelled it and it's today."

"Why didn't you tell me?"

"It must have slipped my mind."

Sophie stared at her mother in amazement. The gesture hadn't gone unnoticed, this was her way of apologising.

"Stop gawping, Sophie. I need your help and you can't do that in your pyjamas." She scanned her daughter up and down. "Go along and get dressed, there's lots to do."

An hour before the fete was due to start Jack Morgan arrived.

"Where do you want us, Sophie?" he asked, poking his head out the van window.

Sophie consulted the plan she had been given by her mother. Not only had Elizabeth agreed to host the fete at Middleton Manor, but she had also taken on the job of organising everything too.

"Down by the walled garden, Mr Morgan. Did you know about all this?" she asked.

"We were only told the location yesterday. The vicar was going to hold it in his back garden. Who knows how he would have squeezed everything in there, it's barely large enough to swing a cat."

He drove on round to the walled garden and Sophie continued to make sure the stallholders had everything they needed before the public arrived.

Very soon the estate was filled with every single person from the local community. Children ran around with painted faces, chasing balloons and eating candyfloss. Farmers from around the county had brought their finest livestock to compete against each other and judges were marking the baking contests in one of the many marquees. The fete was bursting with happy families and a buzz of excitement. Wherever Sophie went people introduced themselves and congratulated her on the most successful fete they had had in many years.

"There's the star of the moment," beamed Oliver, who had spotted Sophie in the distance and headed straight across. "You've done a great job."

"Thanks, but I've had nothing to do with it - it's all mum's handiwork." She looked self-consciously at her feet. "Listen, I really need to thank you."

"Whatever for?" he asked as they began walking together through the crowds.

"You were right, about giving my mum a chance and forgiving her even if she didn't want it. I hadn't realised how trapped I had become."

"I'm really pleased for you... what?" he asked, seeing she hadn't finished.

"I've realised something else you were right about as well."

"Any one hearing this would think I'm right all the time." He laughed before listening to what she had to say.

"When I found out Georgiana had married neither Kirkby or Southerly, I began to realise how much I relied on a person whom I'd never met, and never would meet, to set the course of my life." She paused reflectively as they continued walking together. "There are things I've been pushed into that need to change, otherwise I'm never going to be happy."

They stopped by the Morgan's farm fruit and veg stall and Oliver turned to Sophie. "I'd better go and help dad... I'm sure you'll make the right decision." The look in his eyes told her he knew exactly what she wanted to do...but would her courage fail her in the final second?

Sophie continued wandering around the fete on her own in the hope of finding her mother. Eventually, she found her in the manor. Elizabeth stood in the empty lounge looking out the window at the fete full of merry people.

"Mum, why are you inside all alone?" asked Sophie.

"I needed a break from the crowds."

"It is a bit busy..." Sophie paused. "Why did you do it?"

Elizabeth came away from the window. "Do what?"

"Allow the fete to be held here, when you were so set against it."

"Someone once told me it would be good for community relationships and I dismissed the idea without thinking of the impact it would have. I've recently realised my mistake."

Sophie felt a rush of sympathy for her mother, admitting she had been wrong was not easy for her. "Thanks for changing your mind, it's been a fantastic success and you've done a great job as host."

Elizabeth smiled. "I've something for you, wait there and I'll go and fetch it."

Sophie waited for her to return, wondering what on earth it could be, her mother never gave her presents.

"Here..." Elizabeth returned carrying a cardboard box in both hands. "I found it when we first arrived, they looked worth saving, so I did," she handed them over. "Then your dad told me about your discovery yesterday and I wondered if they might be from the same girl."

Sophie sat down with the box on her knee and undid the flaps. It was full of little notebooks all identical to the dairies she had read. Reaching inside she took one out, and upon opening it, recognised the writing straight away. They belonged to Georgiana.

"Mum, I ...I don't know what to say."

"Consider it the first step of a very long awaited apology."

Sophie looked up. Was she dreaming?"

"It's not going to be easy for me to change, but a lot of things you said were true...it all started because I didn't want to become my own mother...now look at me, she's the very person I've turned into."

"You're the complete opposite to grandma."

"Yes, I am, but I'm afraid I've spread just as much damage," Elizabeth started to leave the room, having made herself far more vulnerable then she had intended.

"Mum," Sophie called - this was her chance. "I don't want to marry Rupert."

"Of course you want to marry Rupert." Elizabeth laughed lightly.

"It's not what I want."

"Nonsense, if it's not what you want then why did you say yes?"

"To make you happy, to change things for the better."

"You've got cold feet, Sophie," she said continuing out the door.

"No, mum. I haven't," Sophie stood up as Elizabeth re-entered the room. "I like Rupert, he's a good friend, however just liking is not a good enough basis for a marriage."

"Have you told Rupert this?"

"Not yet. I wanted to tell you first."

"You are going to cause us a lot of embarrassment, the engagement invitations have been sent out, the announcement has been in the newspapers."

"I'm not happy. You've made the decision for me, but I've finally realised it's my life and I want to choose who I marry."

"So, who do you want to marry?" Elizabeth asked suspiciously.

"There isn't anybody else I want to marry right now, but I'd like the choice in the future."

"You're not going to marry Oliver Morgan."

Sophie's calmness began to seep away. "You're not listening, mum. I'm not going to marry someone else instead, I simply want freedom to choose my husband, freedom to choose where I work and where I live and not feel guilty because it's not what you want. Don't you trust my judgements?"

"I knew this would happen and it all started when I let you choose your own university; I told your father a precedent had been set and that one day it would be thrown in our faces."

"You don't get it at all," cried Sophie. "It's got nothing to do with the fact I didn't go to Oxford or Cambridge - I don't know why I bothered explaining it to you."

"Everything all right?" Rupert poked his head around the door after hearing yet another loud conversation between his fiancée and future mother-in-law.

"You should hear this, Rupert," said Elizabeth spitefully. "Your fiancée doesn't want to marry you."

Sophie's face drained of colour and she staggered.

"What's she talking about, Soph?"

"I'll leave you to it," said Elizabeth with a smirk and clopped away in her heels.

Sophie plonked down on the chair behind her and buried a head in her hands. "I'm so sorry Rupert."

"Sorry about what?"

"I don't think I can marry you?" she closed her eyes immediately, hating herself for doing this to him. "I should never have said yes. I don't love you Rupert and I can't go into marriage based on friendship alone."

Deflated, Rupert sat next to Sophie. "Why did you say yes?"

"To please my mother. You know it's what she's always wanted and for once, I wanted her to be proud of me. You don't want to marry me. We'll be miserable."

"I won't be."

"How much do we really have in common?" She took his warm, familiar hand. "Growing up with you was amazing and you'll always be my best friend, but we've changed… a lot."

Rupert raised her hand and kissed it. "You did say you can't go from friendship to marriage overnight."

"You do understand, don't you?"

"Is this about Oliver Morgan?"

Sophie opened her mouth ready to squash the suggestion.

"No, no," he said quickly holding up his hand. "I mean, yes, I've been jealous of him, but you like him, don't you?"

"Breaking things off with us has nothing to do with Oliver. It's to do with me, making my own decision."

They chatted some more and eventually returned to the fete together.

"I'll see you around, Soph," Rupert kissed her on the cheek. "You can't get away from me that easily."

Sophie smiled, pleased that although he was clearly disappointed, he hadn't stormed away like her mother had done.

As predicted the fete was a big success. By the end of the day, after everything had been tidied away and every one had gone home, Sophie fell into bed with the cardboard box besides her. She closed her eyes. It had been a good day and for the first time she looked positively into a future which could be anything she wanted it to be. She took out a diary and smiled, ready for a reunion with an old friend.

She stayed up longer than she had planned, reading and re-reading details of Georgiana's life she didn't know about. The first entry began four months after her recovery from smallpox and many questions were answered as she read page after page. Eventually, tiredness caught up with Sophie and she fell asleep, with a hand propped under her chin, an elbow resting on the pillow and the diaries lying all around her.

34

Georgiana

Georgiana sat resting in a chair. The journey had tired her more than she had expected.

"Drink this, Gianna. It will refresh you a bit."

"Thank you, Aunt Lucy," she hesitated. "Am I all right to call you aunt?"

"Certainly, I wouldn't expect you to call me mama."

"I'm so thankful to you for allowing me to stay." Georgiana sipped her tea. "I didn't know where else to go."

"We're family, Gianna. I wasn't going to leave you alone, as some seem to have done."

Georgiana had been extremely ill. On the night her fever took hold, her Aunt Charlotte came upstairs to check on her niece, only to find the rash rapidly spreading across her body. Panic had spread through the household and it was decided the family would seek refuge in her uncle's second home, by the next day all the arrangements had been made. They took every member of staff with them, apart from the nurse hired to stay with Georgiana and look after her wellbeing. After this day Georgiana never heard from them again.

Once Georgiana had recovered from the worst of the disease, she wrote to her mother asking if she could be retrieved and brought home to Denholm Park, but she received no reply. She wrote again, asking if she could forward her uncle's address and again, she got no reply. It appeared she had been abandoned.

One day the nurse came and told her she was leaving at the end of the week. Upon hearing Georgiana had survived, her uncle was to stop her wages – the nurse's services were no longer needed. Realising she was about to be left alone, Georgiana's first thought was to write to Bessie Simms. However, she quickly reconsidered this, knowing she was so weak as to be a hindrance to the busy mother and wife.

If only Kirkby could come and retrieve her, he would nurse her until strong enough to be useful. It was strange she had not heard from him since her illness started. He had been away on business, but always dutifully corresponded. With sadness she considered that, maybe he too, had used the smallpox as an excuse to part ways, as Henry Southerly seemed also to have done. This gentleman had already written to her in order to reverse his offer, he valued her dearly, but on reflection, he wasn't ready to support a wife through the trials of life.

Edward would be of no good to her, Georgiana thought as she searched her mind for anyone else who might possibly rescue her. He lived in the barracks and would never be allowed to have a convalescing sister live with him. There was only one person left who might help - Aunt Lucy.

Lucy replied promptly, relieved to hear from her, although she had not heard Georgiana had been unwell. She hastily arranged transport and travelled herself to pick up her daughter.

"You are not angry with me, Gianna?" asked Lucy the next evening as they sat comfortably in each other's company before the roaring fire.

"I'm sure I should be," said Georgiana lazily. "However, I feel too relieved. I spent my whole life wondering why I didn't seem to belong and now I know, it's because after all this time I belonged with you."

"And now you're here." Lucy reached over the arm of her chair and squeezed Georgiana's hand. "How I've missed you, pretending to be your aunt for all these years…and an aunt forbidden to see you as well, it has been excruciating. However, enough of the past." She bent forward and stoked the fire. "My life is now complete."

A knock was heard at the door and Georgiana wondered who it could be at such a late hour. Lucy went to find out, a few low whispers were heard before she came back in.

"A visitor for you, Gianna." She grinned and moved out of the way to reveal a gentleman.

"Edward!" squealed Georgiana and rushed over to him, arms open wide and crying tears of gladness onto his tailcoat. "Oh, I've missed you." She wiped her eyes on her sleeve. "What are you doing here?"

"Our regiment is now based only an hour away from London and I've taken leave. I thought I'd come and visit my favourite sister." He held her at arms-length. "Let me see you… you're still very pale."

"The journey was tiring for her, Edward," explained Lucy.

"Sit down, Georgiana. Please, you need to rest."

She did as she was bidden, but perched eagerly on the edge of her seat with great excitement at seeing her brother again.

"Have you heard the news?" she asked. "About me and Aunt Lucy."

"I have, Aunt Lucy told me herself when she wrote to inform me you were coming to London. It all makes sense now, so much sense."

"We are cousins then, not brother and sister," her smile faded as she spoke.

"You will always be my dear little sister - nothing will ever change that. I wrote to mama, she deserves to know what has become of you, even though it was her who ordered your abandonment."

"Have you heard back?"

"Not yet. You do realise you will never be allowed back home, even if she does reply? The Davenports cannot be tainted by anything impure. Mama has always been convinced you would bring about our family's downfall - it is all she's ever known."

"I do not particularly desire to return to a home where I am not wanted." Georgiana sighed. "I will not hold it against mama because you are right, it is the only thing she's ever known, inherited from

349

the generations before her. I have decided to try and think well of her and maybe one day she will think well of me."

"That is very mature of you, Georgiana," praised her brother. "Day by day it will get easier and the hurt of being abandoned will ease. Remind yourself of this declaration, so that on the tough days you will not become bitter."

Edward spent two days with his sister and aunt before returning to the regiment. It was a difficult parting, but Georgiana tried to keep her spirits up, reminding herself he would soon return.

Life quickly returned to normal and Georgiana settled into living life in a city. It was certainly busier than she was used to and as she gained more and more strength, enjoyed exploring it all with her aunt.

Lady Davenport finally wrote back, probably on Edward's bidding, explaining her relief that her daughter was well again and how she desired Georgiana to reside with her Aunt Lucy. Now the secret had been revealed, the best place for Georgiana was to be with her real mother. To many this would seem sincere, but Georgiana knew her mother, who was no doubt anxious that Lucy's possible return would become the talk of the town in all the wrong ways.

One evening, Georgiana decided to confide in Lucy and tell her about Kirkby. On her arrival in London she had written to Bessie, informing her friend of her removal to the capital. She sent several letters, but weeks later she could only assume postal communication had broken down and they had not arrived, after receiving no response. If Kirkby did really love her, he would seek her out, wouldn't he? Some nights as she spoke of him to Lucy, she shed tears of sadness and regret, on other nights she would be laughing, remembering the happy memories of spending time with him and his family. Finally, after weeks had turned into months, Georgiana came to the realisation she would not see him again. Love, for whatever reason, had been lost.

One of her habits, especially since grieving for Kirkby, was to go on solitary walks amongst the crowds, for she found the many distractions calmed her thoughts. On one of these walks, she was surprised to hear someone call her name. At first, she assumed it was for someone else, her name wasn't exactly rare. Then the voice called her specifically, "Miss Georgiana Davenport...Miss Davenport!" This stopped her and she scanned the crowd to find the man who was calling. At first, she thought it was Kirkby, even though it didn't sound like his voice. As the sound became louder, the small glimmer of hope was dashed - it wasn't him and she became cross with herself for believing it was. The gentleman who did appear, however, was still welcome all the same.

"It is you." The man grinned as he caught up with her. "Whatever are you doing in London, Georgiana? I never thought I'd see the day when your mother would let you out of her sight."

"It's a long story," Georgiana smiled. "What are you doing here, Samuel? I thought you were abroad."

"I've just returned home," Samuel Hastings said with a tanned face and healthy glowing skin.

"Annabelle didn't say you were coming home yet."

"That's because I didn't tell anyone. I'd seen all I wanted and viewed enough masters to last a lifetime. Pa will be cross I've returned early, but he'll get over it. I was ready to come home. Now tell me, why are you in London?"

They decided to enter a coffee shop and Samuel paid for them both to have a chocolate.

"When I heard Annabelle was marrying your Thomas, I couldn't believe it."

"Mama was extremely cross with me that evening, I'd never seen her so livid...apart from the night I refused Mr Southerly the elder, or the time I refused Mr Turner, and she was probably just as mad when my uncle wrote explaining I should accept the young Mr Southerly against her wishes."

"You've been busy." Samuel laughed. "Is there a proposal you haven't declined."

"There was one… but I was too late." Her voice trailed away and Samuel encouraged her to explain, sympathising as he listened carefully to every detail.

Following this reunion, the weeks raced by and each day Samuel turned up at Lucy's door.

"I thought you were returning home?" Georgiana asked him one day.

"I am…eventually. My family don't know I'm back yet, and I'm rather enjoying the company here, it would be a shame to leave it behind." He smiled at her, making her blush.

Samuel had always been Edward's good friend. In fact, Georgiana had seen a lot of him during their childhood, being close friends with his sister Annabelle too. He chatted with her amiably and danced with her at balls, but only ever as Edward's little sister. She admired him, but never allowed herself to dream of anything beyond friendship, knowing she was tied to Thomas Compton. When she was seventeen, Samuel had left to go on a grand tour of western Europe. At first his presence was missed, by herself and Edward, but quickly she forgot and rarely spent a moment thinking about him.

But now, something began to stir inside of her and she found herself missing him after he departed each evening, even though she knew he would return the following day. Every day they spent together saw her laughing and smiling, in a way she had thought unlikely to happen again, so distressed had she been over losing Kirkby.

"Samuel likes you," commented Lucy one evening as they were once again sitting by the fire.

"Really?" Georgiana blushed; she had thought this too.

"Why else do you think he keeps coming, he certainly isn't here for me." She laughed. "I expect he'll be asking for your hand within the week."

"Within the week!" Georgiana gasped. "I hope not."

"Whatever's the matter... I thought you liked him?"

"I do... I really do, but I can't help thinking of Kirkby. What if he comes back and I'm married?"

"My dear Gianna, he would have found you by now." She saw her daughter lower her head. "You cannot live thinking like this, otherwise you'll never be happy, never marry, never have a life of your own. You need to let him go."

Georgiana gripped Lucy's hand tightly and allowed a single tear to escape. "How do I do that?" she whispered.

"By taking a step of faith in the man who loves you now."

The proposal didn't come within the week as Lucy had predicted, nevertheless it did come. Samuel, knowing all about Kirkby, bided his time and waited patiently for Georgiana's heart to mend. When he felt like he had waited long enough, he asked her passionately to marry him and, without a doubt or a worry, Georgiana said yes.

35

Sophie

Sophie shut the boot of her car, her stomach turning over with nerves. "I'll see you at Easter, dad."

George gave her a humongous hug. "I'm going to miss you round here, pumpkin." He let her go. "Don't be so nervous, you'll be great."

"Do you think I'm doing the right thing?" It was the tenth time she'd asked that morning and they'd only been awake for a couple of hours.

"I have no doubt."

George Hastings waved as she drove down the drive. Lots of things had happened in Sophie's life within the last five months. After realising she had the ability to make her own decisions, things began to change dramatically. She announced to Elizabeth that she wasn't going to sign the contract because she had decided to apply for a master's degree in educational psychology - the one thing she'd always dreamed of doing. It wasn't too difficult to find a course that accepted new students after the Christmas break, and after an initial interview, was quickly welcomed onto the course.

As could be predicted, her mother was not best pleased - it was not part of her plan. After a lot of discussion, Sophie repeatedly reminded her mother that this was her life, which Elizabeth now accepted without too much offence. As a peace offering, Sophie had promised that her holidays would be spent at home, helping on the estate. "I guess that's better than nothing." Once Elizabeth had muttered these words, Sophie knew a blessing had been given.

In an attempt to continue mending bridges, Sophie made every effort to take an interest in her mother's life. It wasn't always easy, they often had fallings-out, leaving Sophie wondering why she had bothered, but their relationship was better than it had ever been before and she strove forward, knowing each tiny step brought her more freedom from the hurts that had built up over the years.

"You will tell me if you're struggling, won't you," Sophie demanded.

"You will be the first person I tell. Besides, I've been inspired to try harder with your mother, see things from a new perspective. Have I told you how proud I am of you?" He had – repeatedly.

Sophie hugged him one last time before climbing into her faithful car loaded with all her possessions.

Driving down the country lanes she smiled to herself, happy with the way she'd left things at home. This time, she might actually look forward to returning at the end of the semester. A little track came into view which had become very familiar to her since she'd arrived at the manor early that summer. Her wheels splashed into a pothole, covering the side of the car with a spray of mud. She had one final stop to make before leaving Middleton.

Rupert had been incredibly mature and civil after she'd given back her engagement ring, and never once had he tried to win her back. Deep down, Rupert knew Sophie never really loved him and he knew she was right, their marriage would have been more to please their families than to please each other. Still remaining her firm friend, he had burst into the manor one morning to announce he had been invited to play polo for the country and was about to travel abroad for a few international games. Sophie hugged him and showered Rupert with congratulations, wishing him all the best and making him promise to keep in touch.

Out of respect for Rupert, she had purposefully kept her relationship with Oliver purely one of friendship. Most of her free time was spent with the farmer's son who had changed her life completely. When she had chosen to leave, it was one of the hardest decisions she had ever had to make.

"You've come to see us off then, Miss Hastings," said Jack Morgan as he saw Sophie getting out of her car. "The estate won't be the same without you."

"I'll be back in the holidays, Mr Morgan."

"Make sure you come and call, I've enjoyed having a girl around for a change." He opened his arms to hug her goodbye. "I'll keep an eye on your dad for you."

"Thank you ever so much, I'll worry less if you're watching out for him."

Oliver came out of the farmhouse and her heart dipped; the moment had come to say goodbye. She was going to miss him dreadfully; the holidays couldn't come soon enough. She smiled across at him and caught sight of a large black bag hung over his back.

"Where are you going?" she asked as he came across the farmyard.

Jack smacked his son on the back. "You all ready son?"

"I most certainly am." Oliver grinned.

"Where are you going?" repeated Sophie again.

"Same place as you."

"What do you mean?"

"Call when you get there, Oliver," said Jack completely ignoring Sophie's puzzled face. "I've got to see to the cows," and he trundled off.

"See you dad," shouted Oliver after him.

Sophie tugged on her friend's jumper. "Where are you going again?"

"Same place as you." He began walking across to her car. "There's space in here, right?" He pointed to the boot and opened it up.

"Are you coming with me?" She really couldn't understand what he was talking about. "I wouldn't say no to a travelling buddy, but I can drive alone."

"I'm more than a travelling buddy, Sophie," he called as he walked back to the farmhouse.

She stood waiting for him to come back, wondering what he was doing. Before long he came back out again trundling a large suitcase behind him on wheels.

"Ready?" he asked, as he shoved it into the boot along with his black holdall.

Sophie stood there and watched him open the passenger door. "I'm sorry, am I missing something?"

"I'm coming with you Sophie." He grinned. "I've been accepted for a degree in education."

"At my university?"

"Yes." Oliver's grin turned into a wide, beaming smile, he was enjoying the effect his news was having on his friend.

"Why didn't you tell me?"

"It wouldn't have been a very good surprise if I had." He came across to her. "I started putting my life back together again at eighteen and I'm so proud of my accomplishments, but there's always been something missing – I haven't been truly happy... that was, until I bumped into you." He came closer and took her hands. "Sophie, you make me happy. When you told me you were leaving, I knew I had my own decision to make. I want to achieve my dreams and I can't think of anyone better to do it with than you. The question is, do I make you as happy as you make me?" He looked gently into her eyes waiting for an answer.

"I could not be happier with anyone else," she said without a hint of hesitation.

Drawing closer, Oliver lowered his head and kissed her. Then, with his hands wrapped round her waist, he smiled contentedly.

"I was hoping you'd say that," he said.

Epilogue

Fifteen years later, Georgiana sat watching her two youngest sons play on the grass behind the imposing Middleton Manor.

"Mama! Mama!" called her eldest son running out of the house and onto the lawn. He was so much like his father, in appearance and in temperament. Samuel Hastings had passed away early in the autumn and Georgiana missed him dearly: they had had a happy marriage together.

She turned towards William as he ran towards her. It was a big responsibility inheriting such a large estate at such a young age, but with Edward, now Lord of the Manor at Denholm Park, giving guidance to his nephew, she knew her son would be in good hands.

"Mama!" he called again, breathing heavily and trying to gain back his breath. "There is a gentleman to see you. He said to tell you he is newly widowed and wishes to have an audience with you."

"Did he tell you his name?"

"Yes," said her son. "His name is William Kirkby."

Thank you for buying
Mirror Image

If you enjoyed reading this book why not consider writing a review on Amazon so others can discover it too.

Check out Erika's website at…

www.erikacrosse.co.uk

Where you can read Erika's latest blog and sign up for her newsletter

You can also follow Erika on Facebook.

Or send her an email to…

erikacrosseinfo@gmail.com

Turn the page to read an extract from Erika's
book *A View from the Window...*

Chapter One

1798

'Name.'

'Emma Thornwell.'

'Place of birth.'

'Yorkshire.'

The man behind the desk looked down his nose and smirked. 'District?'

'Hull, sir,' Emma said proudly, sticking out her chin, though reddening slightly at the smug man's obvious belief in his southern superiority. He was the first Londoner she'd met and he wasn't giving her a good impression of the place.

His hand reached across the desk, causing Emma to stare down at the dirt-encrusted fingernails inches from her face. She looked up, her mouth half-open, uncertain of what the clerk expected from her.

'6d, miss,' he said to clarify the unspoken question.

Emma frowned. 'You want me to pay now?'

'That's the idea.' He waggled his fingers and nodded in the direction of her skirt, knowing this would be where her money bag was hidden.

'But I haven't finished my registration; you don't know what position I want, or what I'm capable of doing.'

'We always ask for the money in advance, saves people wasting our time.' He grinned, revealing a gap where a front tooth used to be.

Emma furrowed her forehead again as she found the slit in her skirt. 'Of course, I understand.' But she didn't, and she felt an uneasy sensation rising up inside. Once she'd found the slit, she discreetly pulled out a netted bag resting on top of her petticoat. A small sigh escaped her as she gave the clerk what she owed, taking careful measures not to touch his unclean hand.

She had no idea it would be this expensive.

With regret, Emma heard the coins drop into a rectangular tin on the desk and watched as the man pressed the lid firmly closed. He had taken every coin she possessed.

'Thank you kindly, miss.' The man smiled, but it wasn't a pleasant smile, his mouth being twisted at the corners so it looked almost sinister. Emma darted her eyes away.

'Type of work?' he continued.

'Pardon?'

'What work are you looking for?'

'Oh…' She wetted her dry lips with her tongue and looked down at the clean, cream-coloured paper underneath his grimy hand, poised and ready to continue the interview now her money was safely tucked away in the tin. 'Anything, I guess.' She knew it sounded desperate, but how was she to eat, where was she to sleep? She had nothing.

The man chuckled, flashing another smirk. 'Like that is it?'

'I need work, sir.' She lifted her chin. 'I can't afford to pick and choose.'

He scribbled something illegible before lifting his head. 'Reference.'

'I was told to only inform my new mistress of my previous employer.'

'Secrecy won't get you a job, miss.'

'I won't betray a trust, sir.' Emma ground her teeth tightly together, looking the clerk directly in the face. 'Maybe I'm wasting my time. I'll have my 6d back if you don't mind.' She held out her hand, though the shaking was impossible to hide.

The clerk slid his hand over the money tin. 'Whoa, slow down, miss. No need to do anything rash. I'll write *unobtainable* - will that do?'

'Yes, thank you, sir.' Emma retracted her quivering hand and calmed her nerves as best she could. 'Is there anything else you need to know?'

'Address.'

'Ah, well, I—'

'I need to be able to contact you, don't I.'

'The thing is, sir, I only arrived in London this morning and I have no lodgings at present.'

'Might make things a bit tricky, miss.'

'How about I call into the office daily to see if you've found anything?'

'All right, can't argue with that.' He slipped his hand away from the lid of the tin and scribbled something on the document. 'Thank you for your custom, miss.' He nodded his head and the threatening smile reappeared, spreading across his face.

Emma tried to smile nervously back, but a sudden waft of breath from the clerk's partly open mouth drifted into her nose, and with a jolt she stepped to the side, backing away from the desk with a simple nod of the head. 'Good day, sir.'

With trembling legs Emma made her way out of the registry office; she hadn't expected the visit to have been filled with such hostility. Gripping onto a handrail, she took a steadying breath of fresh air and looked up at the magnificent building which housed the offices. She snorted lightly through her nostrils: its elegance certainly didn't match the clerk inside. By the time she'd taken another breath, the shaking in her limbs had lessened considerably. All she had to do was return to the office and collect the name of a prospective employer, then she would never have to see that man again.

The fewer people you meet the better.

The warning sprang abruptly into her thoughts, catching her almost by surprise. Since stepping off the stagecoach that morning she had encountered only one person: the frightening man with the filth-encrusted fingernails. But work was vital, Emma argued to herself, how could she live without it? A sickening feeling suddenly crept into her stomach: she had given that man confidential details. Her eyes turned warily back to the double doors behind her and she swallowed hard. The registry office could be trusted, couldn't it? Employing people was their livelihood after all, without some kind of moral integrity, surely they'd cease to exist. This reasoning, however, only pacified Emma momentarily, for in her next breath the real question she should be asking flashed alarmingly through her mind: could she trust the clerk? Another feeling of nausea rose within her as she considered what she had told him in confidence. Should she go back inside to explain how important it was he didn't spread her details beyond any potential employer? She took a hesitant step forward and lifted a hand to her mouth, biting the knuckle of her thumb nervously as the fingers on her other hand wrapped around the cold brass door handle. But then suddenly, the memory of the sinister smile floated into her memory, causing her to stop and let go. There was nothing she could do.

Coming away from the door Emma began her descent down the smooth stone steps, taking care to avoid an awkwardly positioned puddle.

'Be careful, miss!'

Emma unexpectedly felt a warm hand touch her softly underneath the elbow and, with a puzzled expression, she looked round to see a young woman standing on the bottom step. Emma checked the floor and lifted a shoe: had she stepped in the puddle? Not that it mattered, she decided, setting her foot back onto the floor, her shoes were tatty anyway.

'No, miss, not the puddle,' said the young woman, seeing Emma had misunderstood her meaning. Then, with a nod towards the building, she released Emma's elbow from her touch. 'Be careful of the registry office.'

'Oh.' Emma glanced cautiously over her shoulder to the front door.

'You haven't been in, have you?'

'Well, yes, actually, I have… is there a problem?'

'You won't get your 6d back.'

'I-I haven't asked for it back,' Emma stammered as her uneasiness returned. 'I paid for the services. They will find me a position in return.'

'I'm sorry, miss, you won't.'

Emma moved down the final few steps to become level with the young woman, who, now that she was closer, looked as if she wasn't that much older than the eighteen years she was herself. 'W-what do you mean?'

'The owner's disreputable, miss.'

The bridge of Emma's nose crinkled. She hadn't been to school as a child; her mother had taught her to read and write. Girls with her upbringing didn't need an education, as long as you could use a needle, you'd be just fine.

Disreputable? The word didn't sound good, not good at all, and Emma felt her throat constrict and a panic begin to circulate around her body.

'A bad 'un,' translated the young woman.

'Oh.' Emma blinked rapidly, fighting back the threat of tears.

'I thought it best you knew.'

'Yes… thank you.' Emma looked uncomprehendingly up and down the busy street full of carriages and carts. What was she going to do now? She was all alone in London and not a soul knew where she was? She chewed her lower lip anxiously.

'You need help, miss?'

Emma blinked again and turned, a little surprised to see the young woman still standing next to her. 'I, erm…'

'Do you want me to show you Mr Jarvis' place?'

'W-who is Mr Jarvis?'

'He owns a registry office about a mile from here, there's no fee for the servant using his services. I use him all the time, he found me my current mistress.'

'Oh, are you in service?'

'General housemaid, nothing glamorous.'

Emma nodded.

'Would you like me to take you?' The young woman tilted her head gently and waited with patience for an answer.

'I wouldn't want to impose you must be busy.'

'Don't be silly, I'm on my day off. I've all the time in the world… I'm Lily, by the way.' She smiled warmly and tucked a hand into the crook of Emma's arm as if she'd known her all her life. 'You're new to London, I can tell. Keep close to me and you'll be just fine.

You can buy a copy of *A View from the Window* from Amazon

Printed in Great Britain
by Amazon

28336788R00209